CW00729511

Brothers and Lovers

Michael J. Davidson

AuthorHouse™ UK Ltd.
500 Avebury Boulevard
Central Milton Keynes, MK9 2BE
www.authorhouse.co.uk
Phone: 08001974150

This book is a work of fiction. People, places, events, and situations are the product of the author's imagination. Any resemblance to actual persons, living or dead, or historical events, is purely coincidental.

First published by AuthorHouse 9/9/2009

ISBN: 978-1-4490-0896-3 (sc)

This book is printed on acid-free paper.

Whatever you can do,

or dream you can,

begin it.

Boldness has genius,

power,

and magic in it.

Goethe

To the ladies without whose support this project would never have reached fruition. Siobhan Curham, tutor and editor-in-chief, whose advice, enthusiasm and encouragement kept me going, my lovely wife Julia and daughter Laoise, who read, edited and commented in their own inimitable way. Laoise's original design for the cover was invaluable.

A very large thank you.

Prologue

A Sunday in February 2006: 3.00 p.m.

United Synagogue Cemetery, Bushey, Hertfordshire,

United Kingdom

Heavy grey cloud blanketing the sky. Overhead power-lines droop between metallic pylons, interrupting horizons of greenery. The black-draped coffin is slowly lowered into a gaping rectangular cavity in the earth. Distant hum of an urban motorway provides tuneless accompaniment to the Rabbi's nasal intonations.

"*Al mekomo yavo beshalom*...may he come to his place in peace..."

Men thrust shovels into dark brown resistant mud. Hollow thuds echo, spade-loads clatter on the casket below. The line of mourners passes by solemnly, some tearful, others wearing tight-lipped frowns. The column winds its way along the aisles of memorials, pausing finally by washbasins for ritual cleansing the hands of the aura of death.

Assembling in the concrete chapel with high vaulted ceiling, men congregate on one side, women opposite. The words of the Rabbi resonate in the lofty dome.

"*...et nishmat..............asher ne-esaf el amo*.....the soul of.......... who has been gathered unto his people. A good man, loving husband, and father, he will be sadly missed after such a tragedy cut short his life in the earliest of golden twilight years. Those who knew him could never believe his age. He was always the epitomy of physical fitness. Throughout his life he never stinted on charitable works, was always available when a Minyan was required. A pillar of the community. A man of religion."

A slight, balding, thin-faced man reads the mourner's prayer, cheeks tear-stained. "*Yiskadal veyitkadash shmay rabah*.......May his great name be exalted and sanctified......."

A final 'Amen' from the hushed congregation.

The Rabbi clears his throat, hand caressing his pointed beard. "You are all cordially invited to no. 27 Albury Crescent, Radlett, Hertfordshire for refreshments. Prayers will be held at that address every evening at 8.00p.m. until Thursday."

*

Same day: 4.00 p.m.

Golders Green Crematorium, London

A tall, broad-shouldered man stands at the pulpit, hands clenching the sides of the podium. Wiry brown hair cut short, he speaks with the hint of an Israeli accent. "This is how my father-in-law wished to say farewell although he could not have imagined it would be at this sadly premature time. Nor could we, his family. This tragedy has taken from us our patriarch, a man of humour, an unquenchable spirit of adventure. Generous to absurd lengths, he was never happier than when surrounded by family and friends, skiing powder snow or diving beneath some exotic sea. And music, always music......"

The strains of 'A Whiter Shade of Pale' reverberate through the wood- panelled chapel as the coffin slides slowly through the curtained aperture. Some faces in the crowded rows of benches wear wry smiles, those who understand the song's significance. As the casket disappears the young man raises his eyes, his gaze passing over the aisles, meeting the swollen-eyed countenances of the widow and the daughters.

"He wanted no prayers, no entreaties to a supreme being in expectation of an afterlife. Just a wish that everyone present here today spend a few moments immersed in memories of good times spent together. No stone memorials, merely an acknowledgement that he helped bring fun, music and laughter into so many lives."

"When you leave here today, our family would be delighted to welcome you to no. 5 The Lane, St John's Wood, for as much food, drink and jazz as you can manage….."

Alone at the rear of the chapel, a veiled woman dressed in black stands watching. She is wearing dark glasses. Greying auburn curls peep out from beneath a dark scarf. She turns slowly and walks away.

Chapter One

Port Elizabeth, South Africa: Summer 1954

"Ag, no, kleinbaas, it's too, too warm!"

Four boys giggled uncontrollably, circling the dishevelled black man sitting cross-legged on the pavement. His ragged clothes and homemade sandals, pieces of motor car tyre tied to his feet with rope, identified him, one of many African beggars roaming the white residential streets. A semi-toothless grin creased the withered ebony face as he thrust the bottle back at the boys with a knowing look. It contained a misty yellow liquid. The label read 'Froodella', 'Nature's Passion Fruit Drink'.

Alec, eldest and tallest, self-styled leader of the little gang by virtue of bicep-size alone, grabbed the bottle then let out a yell. "Jeez, guys, the kaffir's right! Course it's too bluddy warm!"

He passed the bottle to Lesley, a chubby eleven-year-old, unfortunate bearer of quite substantial breasts as well as suffering an uncontrollable stammer. He juggled the bottle from hand to hand then gingerly placed it on the grass verge. "W-w-w-hat—'re w-w-w-e g-g-gonna d-d-o with it n-n-now, guys?" Coupled with his physique the speech impediment made him the frequent butt of cruel humour. Hence his nickname...... Lalla.

"Tell you what, boys," Alec grinned mischievously, "there's no hope of us being able to sell our Froodella to a kaff unless it's cool, hey?"

Nods all round. "Sooo......what we gotta dooo..." he looked round authoritatively, "is to get it into a fridge, right?"

More nods, with the African indicating agreement. "Yes, ja, kleinbasies, put him inna fridgidaire then you sell him to my friend Willem down there by the hospital. Heh! Heh! that Willem he drink any blerry thing! Heh! Heh!"

Alec looked around at the other three, eyebrows raised. "So, OK, then, whose house is nearest? Yours, Raymond, isn't it? Just round the corner, ja?"

Raymond, dark, curly-haired with deep-set green eyes, shook his head uncertainly. "I dunno, I mean, if my ma finds out we put a bottle of piss in her fridge she'll murder me."

The beggar burst out with a high-pitched cackle, spraying saliva through wide gaps between his few remaining teeth. "I knows it was piss! It was too bleddy warm, I told you!"

Alec turned to Raymond with a sneer. "Jeez, Raytjie boy, I never took youse for a mommy's boy!" He grabbed the bottle, thrusting it under the cowering boy's nose. "You a wuss or something?"

Raymond stamped his foot in anger. "Lissen, you know I'm not a bloody wuss, but I'd like to know if any of you guys would put the stuff in your mom's fridge, hey? Answer me that!"

The other three boys looked at each other uncertainly then Alec softened, placing a hand on his closest friend's shoulder. "Nah, we all knows you're OK, Ray, but hey man, we's only round the corner from your place. In any case it's only for an hour or two till the stuff gets cold. Your folks get home from the shop 'bout six, right?"

Raymond nodded reluctantly. "Ja. Well, OK then, so long as it's outta there by half past five the latest, you hear?"

They left the beggar chortling to himself and ran the short distance to Raymond's house, an imposing pebble-dash-covered double-story in a quiet suburban street.

Raymond looked at his watch. "Three o'clock, guys. That gives us two hours an' a bit. Out by half-past five latest, agreed?" Then, as an afterthought, "We gotta watch out for Euphemia. That maid'll split on us just as soon as spit. Make sure she don't see us."

The kitchen opened on to a back yard where the African maid and the garden 'boy', Joseph, a man of some forty years of age, had their accommodation, a 2-room brick outhouse. Their tiny bathroom and toilet was a lean-to built on to the side of the main house.

All was quiet, the servants in their rooms or out at neighbouring houses.

Raymond carefully placed the bottle with its noxious contents in the small freezer compartment above the ice trays. The others looked on smirking.

Lesley was first out the kitchen door. "Hey guys, how's about a b-b-bit of c-c-cricket in the g-g-garage t-t-t.till the stuff's c-c-old?" He boasted a thick ice-blonde head of hair which he grew long in front. Consequently he was constantly brushing the fringe out of his eyes except when plastered back with Brylcreem.

"Great idea, Lalla," Raymond yelled, tearing down the passage to the front of the house. "I'll get the bat and ball. Alec, you get the box wicket. But only till half-past five, you hear me?"

The game in the garage was played with the wicket at the back wall, the bowler bowling from the driveway, making a narrow pitch like a cricket net. Scoring shots were straight drives to the other side of the road. Smashing the neighbour's windows scored six and out!

*

As five o'clock approached Raymond eyed his watch anxiously. The game had proceeded as expected, he and Alec easily outscoring Mark and Lalla. "OK, guys that's it now. Let's go get that bottle. Lalla, you keep skei,(lookout) you got that?" Raymond rasped.

"Y—y-yes---yes-sir, m-m –mast—ster Ray," Lalla said grinning cheekily, "b-b-ut wh-wh-who m-must I-I watch out f-f-for?"

"Ach, stupido, anyone, Euphemia our maid, Joseph the garden boy, or even my little boet (brother) Larry."

Warily the three boys entered the kitchen, sidling up to the refrigerator door. Raymond opened the ice compartment and slowly withdrew the bottle of 'Froodella'.

Just then the door opened. Two small faces peered into the kitchen. "Wotcha got there, Ray, wotcha got? Can I have some? Please can me an' Lynette have some ....oooh its Froodella! Can we PLEEZ have some?"

"No, Larry, this is not for you..... this is for,.. er.... er... we're...er... gonna sell it...." Trying to hide his embarrassment Raymond turned to leave by the back door while Alec, Mark and Lalla were practically exploding with repressed laughter.

"If you don't give me 'n Lynette some Froodella I'm gonna tell! I'm gonna tell mom 'n dad!! I'm gonna tell!!" Little five-year-old Larry's face had turned bright-red, eyes brimming with ready tears.

Raymond looked at his three co-conspirators in desperation. All he received in return were amused shrugs of resignation. His brother was now screaming hysterically. He made his decision. Anything to stop the histrionics. "OK! OK! Larry, I'll let you have a small taste but none for Lynette, 'cos we wanna make lotsa money selling the Froodella. Just STOP CRYING, will you!"

With that he unscrewed the cap and poured a small amount of the golden liquid into one his mother's treasured blue-striped liqueur glasses.

Larry grabbed it eagerly, draining the contents in a single gulp. The change in his facial expression was one that would haunt and amuse Raymond for the rest of his life.

"Yeeeech! It's wee! It's wee!"

The cocktail glass smashed in fragments on the floor. Larry dashed to the sink and, using both hands, frantically slurped fresh water into his mouth, splashing and dribbling all over the kitchen floor.

Cousin Lynette could only stand and watch open-mouthed.

The four boys dashed for the back door as they heard the front door open.

"We're home, Larry, Lynette, Raymond, where are you?"

*

The aftermath of "The Froodella Episode" was predictably painful, although only for Raymond and Alec who lived nearby. Mark and Lalla escaped detection for Larry only knew Alec well enough to incriminate him. He and Raymond took their fathers' hidings stoically, bravely refusing to divulge the names of the other two donors.

There had been some satisfaction on Larry's face as the sound of the spanking with accompanying pained yelps echoed through the house. Their father Abraham had conferred with Alec's father Hymie who lived in the next road but one. An agreed punishment of twelve strokes with the paternal belt as well as confinement to the house for two weeks was agreed upon for both boys.

Needless to say, the "Froodella" Business venture suffered an irreversible liquidation.

*

The arrival of a new baby brother Martin for Raymond and Larry at this late stage in their parents' lives had a profound effect on the family. Especially on the relationship between Raymond, the eldest, the trail-blazer, and Larry, who at age five was totally unprepared for the Spartan disciplinarian of a nurse, and the loss of attention that he, now as a middle child, was experiencing. Subjected to the gang's merciless teasing he had tended to run to his parents for every real or imagined grievance. Now sympathetic hearings he was used to had been supplanted by impatience and being fobbed off with 'Agh, Larry, stop whining, go out and play.' This left him even more prone to tantrums and petulance.

*

1956 Pretoria Women march against Apartheid. 156 activists arrested accused of Treason including Nelson Mandela
1958 Last General Election (whites only) as Union of South Africa. Nationalists win large majority. Hendrik Verwoerd becomes Prime Minister

Summer 1959 5 years later

"There's no question about it, she's a dead cert!" Alec, aged 18, by now an authority on everything to do with the opposite sex, declared assertively. "I'm telling you guys no lies. Jimmy McEwan doesn't bullshit an' he says he's been all the way with her!"

The female alluded to was unconcernedly swimming countless graceful lengths of the green and white tiled pool at St George's Swimming Baths. Our foursome, Alec, Mark, Lalla and me, Ray, as I'm now known, got together for a swim every Tuesday and Friday afternoon after school. We called our gang the Swimmers.

We watched from the pavilion parapet, cherishing our individual fantasies, trying to hide the bulges in our skimpy bathing costumes.

"That's all very well, but Jimmy's nineteen, got a car an' everything, so it'd be a cakewalk for him," I mumbled, wrapping a towel round my neck.

Alec nodded "That's right, Ray, wheels is the answer. I bet she won't just meet one of us by bus, will she? An' in any case, even if she would, where would we take her?"

Alec and I went way back, through Primary school together. His dad, Hymie, was of east Mediterranean origins which accounted for Alec sometimes being shunted upstairs in the bus on account of his dark complexion. We didn't mind too much, there was always something going on upstairs. A drunken coloured lying in his own vomit, or a pass being demanded from a Bantu by a uniformed Gestapo-like South African Policeman. Usually not too gently either. Still that was the way we lived. We stuck together.

"So we might's well forget her, hey?"

"Agh Ray man, jus' shuddup!" Alec shook his head disdainfully. "My pa's always saying where there's a will there's a way so we'll work something out.... Jeez, will ya lookit that.....!"

He leaned so far over the parapet wall that Mark had to grab his legs to stop him dropping fifteen feet to the cement pool surround below. We all watched breathlessly as the girl climbed up the metal ladder, stalking lithely to the bench where her towel lay. None of us blinked as she shook her long auburn ringlets out from under the bathing cap and massaged herself dry. A groan in unison emanated from us as she dried her ample front, up and down. I caught myself wondering if the parapet wall would collapse under our four-ramrod pressure or if four little dents would appear in the wall-plaster after the not-inconsiderable erectile stimulation.

"H-h-holy m-m-mcreeloes, what a pair of kn-kn-knockers!" from Lalla, who, in the past few years had shed his puppy fat and flabby chest protruberances. These had often been a source of ridicule and jest from which our gang had always been quick to rescue him.

"O boy o boy o boy, that's what I want..." breathed Mark, "just like Esther Williams in 'Bathing Beauty'!"

If anyone required information on Hollywood films and female movie stars Mark always had the last word. His special favourite was Carmen Miranda of fruit-bowl headgear fame.

"That sure is one hell of a doll," I conceded, cautious as ever.

"L-l-lemme—at-at-at her !" from Lalla.

Poor ol' Lalla, maybe a bit on the slow side but girls think he's cute. For instance look what happened a few years ago, on his twelfth birthday outside the Willowtree Ice Cream Parlour, down one of the side streets off Main Street. For one and sixpence you could get a Knickerbocker Glory, strawberries, pineapple chunks, three scoops of ice cream and a mountain of whipped cream on top.

We were waiting for Lalla's folks to find parking when one of these skollies (street hoodlums) (we were from more respectable families) came up behind Lalla and pulled his pants down in front of a whole crowd of people, girls included. Right down, round his ankles! Well, poor Lalla went sort of scarlet and tripped arse over tit on to his face, tears streaming down his chubby cheeks. Naturally everyone round and about started laughing like mad but we didn't see it as funny, more an attack on our gang. So, led by Alec, we chased after these guys and proceeded to get the shit knocked out of us in no uncertain fashion. This was mainly due to the fact that they were bigger, stronger and more street-hardened. Like I said we were from respectable families. Still we managed to give a reasonable account of ourselves and dragged our limp bodies back to the Willowtree sporting collectively three blackened eyes, four missing teeth and one nose slightly out of alignment! So off to hospital and no Knickerbocker Glories that day!

*

Another pastime we Swimmers engaged in was 'skitting' (shoplifting) from Grahams, the magazine shop where the latest Superman, Batman and Captain Marvel comics were easy pickings. These we then swapped on Saturday mornings at the Grand Bioscope on Main Street. The cowboy movies provided us with fresh violent ideas on just how we Jewboys could get even with the Afrikaner skolllies. Our folks told us never to swap comics 'cos that's how you got polio. My ma knew a boy with one leg shorter than the other all because of comic-swapping. Needless to say we took no notice.

There at St Georges Baths that day however, far more important things were on our collective mind.

"Her name's Crystal Webber," Alec stated with authority. "Now lissen guys here's my idea......"

We crowded round, keeping half an eye on the curvy creature now undulating toward the changing rooms.

"OK, guys, this is it... first we draw straws to see who gets first bash at getting a date with her. Short straw wins, no chickening out. Everyone agree?"

Assent all round.

"So far so good, OK boys? Ray, how's about using your mom's car? You told us you could get a duplicate key for her Morris Minor...."

"Hey, wait a minute, Alec, I don't know if...."

"Lissen, you always said you could get it out from the garage up the road where you park it for her in the evening. You goin' back on your offer?"

"Well, no, but...."

Alec leaned across, so close I could smell the cigarettes on his breath. "Either you meant what you said or you're a bullshitter deluxe! What's it to be? Car or no car?"

I could feel the sweat collecting on my upper lip. "I'll get the car. Alec, don't worry, it'll be there but..."

"Forget the buts. That's settled then. Whoever wins gets to go to the Drive-in with Crystal Webber. That's my plan. Whatchu guys think?"

Unanimous approval. Alec beamed. "Fantastic! Let's go change an' draw lots over a Coke and one of Mrs. Fugard's sausage rolls!"

The rank overbearing smell of chlorine and semi-washed bodies pervaded the duck-boarded change rooms. We showered and dressed in the small metal cubicles, each of us lost in erotic fantasy, being entwined somehow in the back of my mom's Morris Minor with the exquisite Crystal. For myself, neatly attired in the gray trousers, black blazer, white shirt, and blue and red tie of "The School that crowns the Hill" as per the School song, I was relaxed. I never won bets on anything with anyone.

Well, would you believe it I drew the short straw! I stared at the measly segment I held in my hand to the raucous applause and somewhat relieved encouragement from my aquatic mates.

"You'll nail her good, Ray. God, do I envy you!!!"

"You lucky bastard!"

"You wanna sell the short straw?" from Alec.

I smiled nervously, shaking my head.

The discussion came to an abrupt end as Lalla gave a low whistle, pointing to the door of the café. Crystal and her friend, a short fluffy blonde thing, came through the entrance, giggling. I have to admit she was something, even in the unflattering green and black Convent Girls School uniform. I could not take my eyes off her and would probably have stayed there forever if Alec hadn't tugged at my sleeve.

"C'mon, Ray, let's go back to your place to finalise arrangements. We've got lots to discuss."

As we passed by the two females I tried my hardest to appear nonchalant. Not too successfully. Their tinkling laughter followed us right out past the payment kiosk and beyond. Did I imagine a momentary meeting of glances? I couldn't be sure.

*

We crowded into my bedroom, pulling the phone on its long cord under the locked door. God knows what my mother thought but she shrugged, smiled and said nothing when she saw us all together.

Jimmy McEwan had given Alec Crystal's number on a scrunched bit of paper. My right hand shook so violently as I dialled that I had to hold the phone with my left. Alec obliged by taking the hand-piece from me with a grin.

"You just do the talking, Ray. OK?"

All I could do was nod. Calmly he dialled the number then suddenly straightened up, passing me the receiver. Hand over the mouthpiece he murmured "All yours, Ray."

"Hullo." Her voice was tinkly clear.

"Hullo, is that er.... Crystal?" I mumbled timidly.

"Ja, that's me. Who's this?"

"Ah, you don't know me.....er....but..... I see you at St Georges Baths an', ah.......,"

"So who are you? What's your name?"

"My name's Raymond, ah I mean, Ray…"

"You got two names? Raymond who?"

"Ray Benjamin." The Swimmers have now stuffed hankies in their mouths.

"So wodju want, Raymond Ben-ja-min?"

I looked around at my mates, then took the plunge. "Well, I don't suppose you'd wanna go to a drive-in movie with me tomorrow night?"

"Hey man, you've got a bluddy cheek! Phoning me outta the blue like this, I dunno who the hell you are, do I? Howdja get my number anyways?"

From our vast experience of the movies I could do a passable Ray Milland in an emergency and this was fast becoming such an occasion. "Crystal, my dear girl, of course it's a cheek but then, every so often in one's life one feels the need to take a chance. I'm a gambler by nature. I've seen you so often in St. George's cafe where you and your friend Rita consume Mrs. Fugard's doughnuts and strawberry milkshakes. I'm the one who never takes his eyes off you not even for one second. I always leave my doughnut half-eaten because of you…"

The Swimmers are now all over the floor, holding heaving stomachs.

A short silence on the other end of the line. "Why're you talking funny?"

"Did you never see "Dial M for Murder", with Grace Kelly and Ray Milland?"

"Nah, I only likes Rock Hudson an' Doris Day."

"Oh well, never mind. That was me doing my Ray Milland." (return to normal dialect as the whole thing was a disaster now anyway).

"Oh."

"So you haven't noticed me staring at you all the time?"

"You the one with long curly black hair an' bandy legs? An stary eyes?"

My God she knew who I was! "Ja, that's me. My staring got to you, hey?"

"So..... why don't you ever come over an' say hullo then? You shy or what?"

Back to Ray Milland. Things were looking up slightly. "I suppose, it's because I feel so very special towards you from a distance that it might spoil it, you know, if I did that in front of your friends and mine. I value privacy, don't you?"

"Well, ja, maybe. I dunno. You got a car?"

"My dear Crystal, I would hardly ask you to the Drive-in without one, now would I???"

"Nah, I don't suppose. Hey, that was kinda silly of me, doncha think?" A delightful little giggle. "Anyway, what's showing?"

For this I was good and ready. "From Here to Eternity' with Frank Sinatra, Deborah Kerr and Burt Lancaster. It's a war movie but 'sposed to be helluvva sexy too."

"Can I bring my friend Rita too?"

For a few seconds I was speechless. "You mean like a double date?"

"Ja, she likes that other one in your gang, the one with the round face an' long blonde hair always hangs over his eyes. Rita thinks he's kinda cute."

OHMYGOD, it would have to be, could only be Lalla!!!!!

Chapter 2

Lalla was confused. The amount of advice he had received in the hours leading up to the rendezvous at the Donkin Memorial had left him pale, stuttering more than usual.

"W-w-wodju m-m-mean, m-m-make as if I'm t-t-tired, p-p-pretend to yawn H-how the h-hell d-do I d-do that?"

Alec bristled. "Lalla, man, don't be an idjit. You know how to yawn, you does it all the time. Then…you stretch out your arm and very casual, slowly sort of drop it like an accident on the back of her seat…"

Lalla's brow furrowed beneath the lank blonde fringe."B-b-but who says I w-w-want to y-y-yawn in the m-middle of the b-b-big p-p-picture? W-w-what if I don't feel tired?"

Alec slumped in disgust. "Lissen to me, you moron, and lissen bloody damn good. Movies you can see anytime. You'se going to a Drive-in with this chick, Rita who thinks you're cute, God knows why. So stupido, you'se halfway there already. Drive-ins're not for seeing the flamin' film. You got a chance to go all the way with a doll or at least further than you ever been before in your little life so shuddup an' lissen. You only PRETEND to yawn, like this, aaah! Just so you can get your arm round behind her then just move it slowly on to her shoulder. Then…."

Lalla's eyes widened. "Ja, then what?"

Our leader grinned lasciviously. "Then, my mate, it depends on how she reacts. Seems like you need all the advice you can get so OK, here's what you do….."

We all sat entranced awaiting the pearls of seductive wisdom about to drip from head Swimmer Alec's lips. Instead, he rose and sat next to Lalla, placing the reluctant would-be seducer's arm around his own neck and shoulder. Slowly he drew the hesitant arm down toward his breast."Now, ou maat, your hand's on her shoulder, moving down gently on to her tit. One of three things is gonna happen…" Alec looked round, enjoying the rapt attention. He looked hard at me then, with a broad wink, went on. "You too, Ray. Better lissen an' learn. I knows how far you've never got so this applies big time to both of youse."

I sat glowering, but said nothing. Truth hurts sometimes.

"OK, here we go. Number one, she rips your arm away an' slaps you in the kisser. Unlikely but if it happens it's overs-kadovers and youse can sit back an' enjoy the movie. Number two. Gently she pushes your hand away from her tit, that's if you got guts enough to get that far, but she leaves it on her shoulder. This is a better sign, she's telling you 'slow down' so what you do is caress her shoulder like this... (Alec demonstrates on Lalla who is sitting very still, eyes staring wildly into space). Do it gentle so she thinks you know what you're doing. Keep going a while then try for the nipple again. Number three…she does nothing or snuggles into you. This is whoopee! All systems go man! Your best bet is to go for broke. Nipple outside the sweater first then if you're able to sit still an' not have an accident yourself…maybe wear waterproof broekies hey? then try for under the bra. If there's still no resistance let nature take its course. She'll probably show youse what to do."

At this point all us Swimmers except Alec are sitting uncomfortably on our hands.

"OK, guys, that's all the advice I'm giving Lalla an' Ray Milland for now. Ray, you drew the short straw, better make sure your straw's not too short tonight, hey!" Really getting into his Oberleutenant mode now, was Alec. "So, now, let's go over the arrangements. Ray, you first."

"OK, don't worry about my side." I summoned up all the confidence I was not sure I had. "I'm all clued up. First I go get my duplicate key, tell my mom I'm parking the car then goin' to Alec's to listen to records. Then I drive the Morris down to the Greek's café for 7 o'clock sharp."

"Eerste klas, just right, my buddy," Alec clapped me on the shoulder. "Mark, what's your job?"

Mark's normally pale features shone crimson. "Agh, ja, I've got the pack of three Crepe de Chine in the back of my sock drawer. I'll get it an' meet you guys at the Greek's."

"W-w-where on earth d'ju g-g-g-get it?" from Lalla, wide-eyed.

"Had to get a torch one night from my dad's wardrobe an' there they was."

"Won't he miss 'em?"

"Nah, he had about five packets."

"Jeez!" Lalla breathed in disbelief. "H-h-how l-l-long have you h-h-had 'em?"

"Bout three years."

"Crikey, w-w-wodja d-d-do w-w-ith 'em?"

Mark stiffened. "None of your bloody business, cretin."

Alec interrupted immediately. "Take it easy, Mark. We don't really care much what you do with the FL's. Just as long as Lalla an' Ray 'ave 'em handy tonight, is all."

"J-j-just s-s-seemed f-f-funny th-th-thinkin about our m-moms an' d-d-d-ads usin' them th-th-th-ingies..." Lalla grinned weakly.

"I bet your folks must've used a tea strainer to produce a half-wit like you," Mark retorted cruelly.

Alec held up his hand. "Enough, enough, guys. We got a lot on our plate without fightin'. Anyways my job is to get a half-jack of my folks' brandy an' dilute it with Coke. That's what Jimmy says got Crystal goin', an' a shot or two won't do the pair of you any harm, neither."

Lalla and I were to shave whatever was visible, use my dad's after shave lotion and Mom's roll-on deodorant. (My dad thought men should smell like men. Alec knew better.)

*

Greek cafes in South Africa combine snack bar, fruit and vegetable, newsagent, tobacconist, sweetshop and usually several pinball machines.

They open early and close late and are often meeting places for dissolute youth like us.

That evening my mates were waiting for me and I had a story to tell. "What happened, Ray? You're sweatin' like a kaffir!" Alec never minced his words. Lalla and Mark just stared at me sitting glassy-eyed behind the wheel of the little Morris Minor. The windows were all steamed up.

I climbed out, gulping a deep breath. "You can't believe what a close shave I had, Ha ha! Getting out tonight, I mean. Cost me five bob though, most of my pocket money. Hope you guys got some cash for the movie tickets."

Alec nodded impatiently. "Don't worry, I got, but what the hell happened?"

"We'd just finished supper an' my mom says she wants me to babysit Larry an' Marty as they're going out. I forgot it was Euphemia's night off. I told mom we were going to your place but she didn't wanna know."

"So, what then?" from Mark.

"So, then I had a brainwave, had to think quickly, you know," I said beaming, milking the attention for all it was worth.

"G-g-go on, m-m-man," Lalla muttered impatiently.

"I says to my mom, is Euphemia out or is she in her room? And she says why an' I say it's a sorta special meeting of the Swimmers and very important that we're all there. I said we'd all club together and pay Euphemia if she'll babysit. Now you all know what a bloody cry-baby Larry can be so he starts performing and then my dad has to tell him to keep quiet. I go to the backyard an' Euphemia says she'll do it for five bob. So you guys each owe me one and thruppence, .OK?"

The Swimmers agreed without a murmur and paid over the ransom money. Without wheels we were dead and Crystal and Rita were safe as houses.

Alec clapped me on the back. "Bloody well done, Ray. An' gettin' the car, no problem?"

"Nah, that was a breeze. My ma's always tired inna evenings so it suits her well for me to park the car up the road. They can't see the other garage from our house. It's fulla petrol too."

Alec handed me the brandy and Mark bashfully placed the flat metal contraceptive carton in my hand. It did not look opened, just severely dented. With much back-slapping and lewd suggestions Lalla and I climbed back into the little Morris, reeking like a pair of hairdressers, or a bit like the obese ballroom dancing teacher with whom my aunt Fanny once insisted I take foxtrot and waltz lessons. My folks let me quit when I told them that Mr van Jaarsveld not only insisted on teaching all the young lads (there were two gorgeous female teachers I wouldn't have minded) but also pressed us very close to his big belly. And his cheap scent covering the sweat-stink ....UGH!!!

I drove carefully down Whites Road, a steep hill where I knew to engage second gear (I'd been driving illegally for four years, since my Bar Mitzvah!)

I could sense Lalla somewhat agitated in the passenger seat so offered him a swig of the brandy which he swallowed hungrily then spewed most of it back up, partly over my Caribbean floral shirt. Not a good start so I took a swig myself.

The pyramidal Donkin Memorial loomed into view above us. It commands a dimly lit open space overlooking the harbour and Main Street, Port Elizabeth's entire active centre. Apart from the beaches, that is.

There wasn't much moonlight, just heavy cloud. A good dark night for the drive-in. I managed a not too brilliant reverse parking with good view of the street side of the monument. Nobody was around.

"D-d-d-o you th-th-think th-th-they'll show ?" Lalla quavered

I took another sip from the half-jack. "Sure, any minute." With more confidence than I felt. I looked at my watch. Our dates were seven minutes late.

At this moment my thoughts were strewn with confusion. We were both aware of each other's limited experience with the opposite sex. Reality was, I suspected, that Crystal was probably a bit older and more sophisticated. Hence I had listened quite attentively to Alec's instructions. He for sure had gone further than the rest of us. So, truth to tell, I was probably even more apprehensive than Lalla. Well, maybe not quite.

A knock at the window caused me to jerk forward, both fists on the hooter, which obliged with a squawk. Lalla's mouth dropped open and stayed that way.

There they were, giggling like mad, two visions alongside, dressed alike in tightly bulging frizzy sweaters and even tighter jeans. I opened the window and a blast of sickeningly sweet perfume enveloped the interior of the Morris, thankfully drowning the odour of regurgitated alcohol and our aftershave. I did have a passing thought about how to explain to my mom when she next whiffed the insides of her car when it was supposed to be safely stowed in our neighbour's garage. But the concern passed quickly.

I managed, fumblingly, to open the door. "Hi Crystal, Rita. Nice of you to come. This is Lesley, nickname Lalla. I'm Ray."

They both smiled, blood-red lipstick straight from Lana Turner.

"Hi, Ray,"from Crystal. "Who are you today, Milland or Benjamin?" She had this nice way of looking you straight in the eye. Quite a package she was, all dark curls round a smiling oval face with a determined chin. I felt a melting inside. And chose Milland.

"I'll be whoever you want me to be, Madam, but perhaps you ladies ought to climb in, the movie starts in twenty minutes."

Lalla was standing speechless by the passenger door. The Morris Minor is a two door with the front seats folding forward to allow entrance into the back. I held my door open. Big mistake. Lalla had pushed his seat forward so both girls landed up in the back seat. Which left us no option but to occupy the front seats, unable to think up any excuse to separate them that did not have obvious carnal overtones.

They seemed quite happy with the arrangement. We arrived at the Drive-in just in time for the end of the newsreel. I racked my brain through the cartoons as to how to achieve the desired re-orientation. What would Alec and Mark say if this was as far as we got? The thought did not bear consideration.

My chance came at interval after hamburgers and milkshakes served on a tray attached to the passenger window.

"Ray, please can you let us out? Me an' Rita gotta go to the powder room." Tinkly giggle.

"Sure, no problem." I whipped open my door forgetting about the attached speaker. It catapulted into the car alongside causing some disquiet to the couple in the back seat. I couldn't see them because their windows were all misted from inside.

"HEY WHAT THE FUCK YOU DOING TO MY CAR?" came from within.

"Sorry, mate!" I called out, red-faced. "Just forgot about the speaker. Only a tiny scratch."

This must have appeased them for there was no further commotion from the frosted interior. Their car resumed a gentle rocking.

"Lalla, quick, get in the back seat," I hissed.

"W-w-what for? I-I-I c-c-can see fine from wh-wh-where I am."

No time to argue so I hopped in the back.

"Hullo, what's goin' on?" Rita's ash-blonde head poked through the open window. Lalla looked at me helplessly.

"Er, thought you might like to sit next to Lalla," I murmured. Behind Rita, I thought I could see Crystal smiling a little forlornly.

Rita wasn't having it. She'd probably realised by then that with Lalla, looks weren't everything.

"Nah, don't worry, me 'n Crystal used to holding each other's hands." This was said with hand held to mouth.

'From Here to Eternity' was a superb movie. I saw it several times after that. I'm sure the four of us enjoyed it. The only moment of embarrassment after I'd resigned myself to the seating arrangement came at the most passionate moment in the film. Burt Lancaster and Deborah Kerr rolling over each other in the surf. Never mind the girls in the back I was kind of involved all on my own behind the steering wheel.

"Ah, R-r-r-aym-m-mond …."

"Yes, Lalla….."

"Wh-wh-when am I s-s-supposed to yawn?"

Chapter 3

Crystal

It took forever for the mickey-taking over the Great Drive-in Fiasco as it inevitably became known to abate. Countless re-runs in my mind as to how it had all gone so wrong helped not one bit. Conclusion and moral of the catastrophic episode: never double date with a moron!

I did however suffer from the frustrating knowledge that Crystal had smiled at me in a way that did nothing to lessen my overwhelming desire. Which was to explore romantic possibilities that were now haunting my every waking hour, and I wasn't sleeping much anyway.

Decision: the gang approach wasn't the way to go.

Two weeks later, early evening, in between Maths and English homework I closeted myself with the phone behind my locked bedroom door.

"Hi, Crystal."

"That you, Ray?" that delicious giggle again.

"Ja, it's me. Lissen I'm phoning to say sorry…."

"Sorry, what the hell for? Me an' Rita had a wonderful time. But why's it taken so long for you to phone, hey?"

"No, well, I thought that night was such a cock-up, sorry, I mean mess-up, what with Lalla an' Rita an' all, that…"

"Ray, talk to me like that whatsizname film star, Ray Miller…"

Dumbfounded, I switched ears and accent simultaneously. "Milland's the name, actually my dear. Of course there was absolutely no need to apologise. I have been rather busy but believe me, you haven't been out of my mind for a second."

"More! More! It's so sexy when you'se talkin' like that."

Talk about sweaty palms, the phone nearly fell out of my hand just then. I kept up the persona, though only just. (Thank you, Mr. Milland!) "Obviously," I continued, "I realised the circumstances of that night were hardly conducive, 'specially on a first date, but…"

"Oooh! Such big words! You must be helluvva good in English, hey? But you see, a girl can't jus' go on a drive-in date with a guy she doesn't even know, first time, so I had to have Rita there for proteckshun, you know…. I mean, you could've been Jack the Ripper, then where would I have been?"

What would Jimmy McEwan's next move be? Never mind him, that pimply lout, what would Ray Milland's next ploy be?

"That's perfectly understandable, my dear. I should have known all along that it wasn't such a good idea but the thought of spending an evening with you, even with that numbskull Lalla and Rita, just was my top priority…."

Momentary silence. "God, you speak lovely, Ray…"

Changed ears again. Courage, Ray.

"Crystal?"

"Ja, Ray?"

"Can I see you again, sometime soon?"

"Sure. Whatchu wanna do?"

"Not bothered what we do, anything, anywhere, any time." (Oh! Hollywood Oscar, here I come!)

A short pause. "You wanna come over to my place Saturday afternoon. Got the house to myself. My folks are going boating on Zwartkops River."

(Almighty cruel Jesus Christ, Eastern Province playing rugby against Transvaal, and Alec offered me his only other ticket!)

"Ray, you still there?"

(Shit, Raymond or get off the pot!) "I'll be there, Crystal. What time?"

"They'll be gone by one or so…"

"See you Saturday." (Alec can bloody well take Lalla to the rugby!)

*

Saturday dawned bright, clear and windy. Great day for a rugby match but I hadn't lain awake worrying about the thrashing our home side E.P. were going to take at the hands of the bone-crushing Transvalers. My thoughts were sweat-inducing fantasies, translating Alec's seduction techniques into reality. Of teasing, round-faced smiles, bright eyes and tight jeans. And the rest.

I parked my bike 100 yards away from her house, a modest terraced cottage on Constitution Hill, chain-locking it to the iron railings. Between us the Swimmers had had six bikes stolen in as many months the previous year. No chance of recovery in South Africa then so we'd become security conscious of necessity. I waved a cheery goodbye to Alec and Lalla, who gave encouraging winks as they went on to the rugby. "Give 'er one for me, Raytjie, my boy," Alec yelled after me.

My watch read ten past one. 'Shit!' I cursed to myself, 'better have an excuse if her folks were still there!!'

The door opened. Crystal stood there, smiling shyly. Simple printed frock, not revealing but amply filled. Tiny waist, ribbon in her hair, no lipstick. Smelled nice though. Jimmy McEwan couldn't have done what he'd said he'd done. Not with this exquisite angelic creature.

"Hi Ray, come in. My folks just left few minutes ago. Your timing's spot on."

She held out her hand. I took it. Warm and dry. Not like my sweaty paw. She led the way into a comfy lounge and gestured for me to sit on the 3-seater couch. I did as I was instructed.

"Ray?"

"Ja?"

"You haven't even said hullo…."

I felt my forehead break out in prickly sweaty bands. "Sorry, Crystal, I guess I'm a little tongue-tied. Hullo, anyway," I managed sheepishly.

"Lissen here, before we go any further, please don't talk like one of your swimmers, talk like you did on the phone, like Ray Milson from Hollywood, OK? Makes me feel like we's in the movies."

I laughed nervously. "Oh, you mean Milland. OK I'll try, though it's a lot easier when you can hide behind the phone....my dear......"

"That's better. Let me get you a drink. Want some of the old man's brandy and coke?"

"Sure," I nodded. Amazing what an assumed identity and a liberal glass of South African Brandewyn will do to one's self-confidence. I eyed the radiogram. "What records have you got?"

"Lots. Take your pick from the cabinet." She was sitting on the arm of the couch, legs crossed demurely. Selection was easy. Glenn Miller followed by Ray Conniff then Sinatra. We sipped our drinks as three tracks went by without a word.

"You're a shy one, aren't you, Mr. Milland?" with a sly grin.

"I'm sorry, it's just that I guess you look so great, that dress suits you and, you're beautiful, you know that?"

This time it was her turn to blush. Still she kept looking at me with the direct gaze that took my breath away. "You like dancing, Ray?"

(Oh bless you, Aunt Fanny, for insisting on Ted van Jaarsveld's dancing classes!)

One never gets over the first major encounter with the opposite sex. Years later I would still recall each detail, how she drew the curtains hiding us from the world outside. How it felt as our bodies touched, hesitantly at first, then easily, naturally, moving together to the haunting big band sounds. Tuxedo Junction, String of Pearls, Moonlight Serenade. My universe contracted to an area about four feet square.

Uninhibitedly, her cheek nestled against mine. "They teach you to dance like this in Hollywood, Ray?"

"Actually, no. Ted van Jaarsveld's Dancing Emporium downtown by the Post Office."

I could feel her shaking, laughing in my ear. She moved her head away gently, facing me, smiling. The kiss happened without warning, delicious soft lips, minty with a touch of brandy. Nothing like Alec in his wildest dreams could ever have imagined.

Didn't seem as if time would ever move on. Sinatra told us to be 'Young at heart' then stopped. I gently disentangled myself from the clinch, lurching, slightly bowed, over to the record player. A quick turnover of the three long playing records and I was back in her arms, hoping she'd not noticed anything strange about my posture. She had, though and acknowledged it with a modest lip-nibbling grin.

"Ray....."

"Yes, Crystal?"

"Come sit down with me…"

Sinatra wanted us to 'Come fly with him'…it felt like we were well able to do just that. Things began to get heated. Alec's careful instructions to Lalla and me were rapidly being transcended. I had been right about her being older, wiser and certainly more experienced. Gently probing tongue, just occasional accidental brushing of highly sensitive areas. I discovered a gentleness in my hands. They seemed to elicit responses in Crystal that in turn escalated my familiar rising. Clothing got in the way and buttons and zippers were in the process of being undone when the front door slammed.

"Crystal!" A large voice from the corridor.

"Oh, crikey, my pa…. Quick, Ray…"

She made a desperate attempt to straighten her dress while I tangled my t-shirt round my neck. The door to the lounge swung open and a mountain man stood glimmering at us. The scene was a frozen tableau of accusation, anger and guilt.

"So who the hell is this twerp?"

A flash of recognition and understanding volted through my brain. Gerry Webber, of Webber's Gymnasium, Port Elizabeth's Premier weightlifter…OH DEAR GOD….!!!. Crystal's father!!!

"Pa! Why you home so early?" she gasped, still forlornly tugging her dress into approximate respectability.

The massive neck and blonde-gray crew-cut head swivelled to face me full on. "Never mind early, seems like I'm not a bluddy moment too soon…"

I could only stand timidly, mouth agape as he took two huge steps across our dance-floor and grabbed me, one-handed under my chin, lifting me clear off my feet.

"Pa, please don't hurt him, he……he's my new boyfriend, Ray."

"New boyfriend, my arse! Just forget about it, my girl. Look at the state of youse! Get your bloody clothes on straight and upstairs with you….NOW! I'll see you in just a minute."

"Mr. Webber, sir," I gurgled through the mutton-vice grip, "please sir, you're choking me…"

He looked at me with malevolent yellowed eyes. Beery breath washed over my face. "Crystal, do you know you've brought a bloody Jewboy into my house…."

"Agh, no pa," she looked at me questioningly.

"AGH YES, PA!" Gerry Webber roared, lifting me higher still. Spots danced across my line of vision. Sinatra was crooning 'Lady is a Tramp'. "Look at the curly black hair an' hooked nose. I know kikes when I see 'em!"

He tossed me backwards on to the floor like a rag doll. "An' what's more, haven't I told you a million times, all these Yids are after is a good time with Afrikaans girls 'cos they can't get it with their own kind? Didn't I warn you?"

Crystal was silent, staring at me, pity, fear and uncertainty on her face.

Webber bent down and grabbed me by the shoulders. His arm drew back and a fierce open-handed slap on the side of my head sent me flying across the room. I landed heavily against the radiogram which obliged with a shrill screech followed by Sinatra soothingly in the middle of 'I've got you under my skin'.

"Switch that fucking noise off and get up to your room, you little tramp. I'll see to this little crap-house and deal with you later. Now get!"

There was no arguing with him. Crystal did as commanded and at the door she turned, red-eyed, tears flowing.

"Agh, please pa, please don't hurt him, he's a nice gentle boy. Let him go, please...."

With a bellow, Webber charged at her, pushing her up the stairs. I had barely regained my senses but just sufficiently to realise that escape was the best and only option. I made a dash for the front door only to be caught by the neck of my t-shirt which ripped down the back. I had the front door open but just as I was wriggling out of Webber's iron grip I caught a huge hammy fist straight in my right eye. The lights all but went out. I was dimly aware of him screaming abuse as I staggered out the gate and somehow got to my bike where I collapsed in a bloody heap.

*

Misty countenances swam before my good eye. Familiar voices penetrated the dense fog swirling round my head.

"Ray, Ray, for Christ' sake wake up! What the hell happened to you, man?"

I was groggily aware of being shaken, of Alec's voice somewhere miles above me.

Then another familiar voice. "J-j-j-eez, R-r-ray, we woz just on our way back from the C-c-c-rusader ground. You-you-you m-m-missed a g-g-great g-game of r-r-r-rugby!"

God bless you, Lalla!

Chapter 4

I'd had some difficulty at home explaining my facial damage. Honesty was the last thing I'd considered as there had been some truth in what Crystal's father had screamed during his brutal tirade. My parents, to some extent, portrayed similar prejudices. Not strictly Orthodox, they were part-time Synagogue goers sharing common apprehension at the disappearance of Jewish heritage through inter-marriage. Frequently heard advice from my father and other Jewish fathers to sons….. "Treat Jewish girls with the respect you would show to your mother. Mit de andere (with the others) you can have fun….."

The best excuse I could come up with was a schoolyard brawl that had gotten out of hand. My feelings for Crystal though were pure respect mixed with overwhelming desire, the like of which I'd never encountered in my short life. So much so that I'd hardly shared any details of Saturday afternoon with the Swimmers. In fact, none at all although they'd pressed me pretty hard. Specially Alec, man to man.

"So, how far dju get, Ray my booitjie?"

"Not very, we were just dancing."

"Dancing? That's all? Wodja mean, just dancing? Was you close?"

"Ja, sort of…"

"Sort of, wodja mean, was you touching close, like cheek to cheek?"

"Well, ja…"

"And down there……. where the action is, thingy to thingy also?"

"I suppose," I felt my cheeks burn.

"Oh shit, Ray."

"What do you mean, oh shit?"

Alec shook his head sorrowfully.

"Come on, Alec, what you shaking your head for?"

"Lissen, Ray, you're my mate an' I don't wanna worry you none but...."

I grabbed him by the shirt. "But what?....what?"

"It's only that I was talkin' to Jimmy McEwan yesterday. He says that ..." he stared at me pale-facedly, "that a guy he knows got VD from dancin' close up like you done....."

"VD?" I stammered, "what the hell's that?"

"You mean you don't know? Christ, Ray, you know fuck-all about things. Hey, venereal disease, that's what, like infection an' stuff round your privates, can make you go crazy, like Syphilis and all that..."

"From close dancing, with clothes on? With a girl like Crystal? Agh pull the other one! You've gotta be jokin! Aren't you?"

"Jimmy McEwan didn't say it was Crystal, but he didn't say it wasn't either. He don't joke about things, ain't got no sense of humour...."

*

A sleepless week later I showed the angry red raised semicircular rashes on the inside of my thighs to my father.

"How long has that been there, Ray?" His lined face showed puzzlement, though not undue concern.

"Dunno, dad, about a week or so, I guess." Truth was, I'd only noticed it after my chat with Alec.

"Better let Dr. Goldberg have a look at it. Does it hurt?"

"No, just itches.........dad.....?"

"Yes, my boy?"

"What do you think it is?"

"I'm not sure, maybe a heat rash?"

(Heat rash, my arse. I've got Syphilis for sure, oh Christ! I'd been to the library three days running!)

*

"Dr. Goldberg, may I ask you a strictly personal question?" (My father was outside in the waiting room. The doctor was his first cousin)

I was lying trouserless on his couch, legs splayed, to give him full view of the offending area.

"Certainly, Raymond, go ahead."

"I.... I was....er... dancing, very....er...close, with a girl recently..."

"Yes...that's nice......" his hairless head gleamed, lit by the lamp trained between my legs.

I took a deep breath and burst. "Well, did I, did I, get the VD from her, from dancing cheek to cheek?"

Dr. Goldberg's magnifying headgear slid down over his nose. His hand shot up knocking the lamp off its stand with a crash. "VD!" he screeched. "VD???" His face had gone a deep crimson, and he threw his head back convulsively. I lay there totally vulnerable, my legs apart, worried about his heart condition and how long before I went crazy. Being a sort of uncle fairly far removed I still knew that there had been talk of early retirement on medical grounds.

"VD! OY Vay....,VD!" His shrill voice rose hysterically.

The door from the waiting room burst open. My father rushed in. "Joseph, Joseph, what's the matter? I heard a crash!"

Doctor Joseph Goldberg regained his composure slightly, his face wreathed in maniacal laughter. For my part I couldn't see what was so funny.

"Abie, Abie, you shouldn't be in here but lissen, Raychick is only seventeen so I can tell you, he thinks he's got VD!"

My father's face blanched."VD! Vot you talking? A heat rash, isn't it?"

Dr. Goldberg still had difficulty with his speech but just about managed a gasp. "No, not a heat rash, but VD, no definitely not VD!"

I sat up and grabbed my underpants, desperately trying to regain a shred of dignity. "So what is it then, uncle Joe?"

He collapsed in his padded leather chair, a broad smile across his jowelly features. "All it is, Ray, my boy, is a little fungal thing you rugby players get from not drying yourselves properly. Just like Athlete's Foot only it's in the groin. It's called Dobie's Itch and.....and, you most certainly didn't get it from cheek to cheek dancing!" The good doctor again quivered, somewhat unkindly I thought, into a paroxysm of giggles.

My father however was not so amused. "Cheek to cheek dancing? Ray, what's this all about? No, wait, don't tell me, wait till we get home. Your mother will want to hear all about this. VD and cheek to cheek dancing. Oy a broch!"

There was no hiding the truth after this. I didn't mention Crystal by name or her brute of a father's anti-Semitic tirade. The upshot of the visit to Dr. Joe was that my father put my eye injury, thighs and cheek to cheek dancing together and proceeded to give me a man-to-man lecture on Shiksas (a nasty and most derogatory term for Gentile females) and dishonesty. The good Doctor had painted my groin with bright red paint which burned like hell, stinging so badly that I could hardly walk. "No sport or swimming for two weeks. Paint on morning and evening and dry yourself properly down there in the future." was my uncle/doctor's parting shot whilst he and my father enjoyed a private joke. I think it was at my expense.

Brother Larry showed great and somewhat malicious interest watching the daily daubing of my groin. It was as if deep in his ten year old soul, there was a continual need for revenge for the 'Froodella' episode and other indignities which we as unthinking and callous youths had inflicted on him.

Nevertheless he seemed to want to emulate all my activities, marching up and down the garden with a walking stick to mimic my drum-major practice for the forthcoming School Centenary Parade. In the meantime my mother and Euphemia had to cope with a constant flow of red-stained underwear, scrubbed ferociously in the zinc tub outside in the back yard.

Chapter 5

At that time the question of violent retribution against Mr. Webber held little appeal for me. But the swimmers were having none of it.

"I say petrol bomb the bastard's VW KOMBI" gritted Mark, spectacles flashing in the bright sunlight. "You always see him cleaning and polishing the bloody thing outside their house. That'll get to him."

"What about filling his drains with quick-setting cement?" was my contribution, wanting as little confrontation as possible. I'd seen him too close up to want any more.

Alec sat ball-fisted on the bench overlooking the pool where only a few weeks before we'd ogled Crystal's front crawl. He waved his hands for silence."Lissen, guys, the Swimmers never ran away from a fight yet an' there's four of us and only one of him."

Mark disagreed. "Ja, but he's built like a brick shithouse an' can probly do judo an' karate an' all that Japanese stuff."

I fingered my still multi-coloured eye which had taken ten days to open and let the outside world in. "I think Mark's right, you know. He could most likely take us blindfold, left-handed, easy."

"Jeez you bunch of pansies, are you saying that you gonna let this bloody Nazi get away with callin' Ray a kike an' nearly blinding him in the bargain?" Alec eyeballed us with a ferocious glint and outthrust jaw. We all wilted in the face of our Leader's forthright challenge.

Lalla broke the deafening silence. "H-h-hey, g-g-guys, lissen, I've, I've g-got an i-i-i-dea."

"Oh boy, pay tenshun, you Swimmers," Alec sneered. "Genius Lalla's got an idea. So let's hear it already, you dummy."

"Wh-wh-who you you c-c-callin d-d-ummy?"

"Aw, let him be, Alec," I interposed. "Lalla, c'mon kid, let's hear your idea…"

Lalla flashed me a grateful look then swivelled his head round nervously. "OK w-w-well I th-thought one of us c-c-could go to the Gym, Gerry Webber's gym, an' you know, th- the powder th-they put on th-their hands, wh-when th-they l-l-lift the w-w-weights, you know?"

"Yes, yes," Alec stamped impatiently, "so what's with the powder?"

"W-well, d-do you re-remember l-last year we g-got itching p-powder from that sh-shop C-arnival Novelty d-downtown…put it d-d own Suzie L-lambert-s d-dress…"

After a few moments stunned silence the three of us looked at Lalla in amazement.

"Jesus, Lalla, what a bloody brilliant idea! Put it in the resin and the weightlifters will go bananas, itching and scratching all over the place." Mark clapped Lalla on the back so hard he practically choked.

Even Alec had to admit the scheme was delicious in concept. "Ja, an' the best thing is he'll never know who or why. What d'you think, Ray?"

I was grinning from ear to ear. "Fantastic! Lalla, you're a genius! Let's think about how we're gonna do this. Probably best to wait a week or two and then decide who goes to the gym, like who's most in need of building up a bit of muscle. Should be you, Lalla, it's your idea and you could do with a bit of bulk. You've lost so much flab you're like a stick insect!"

On that note of complete agreement we'd gone our separate ways, giggling at the prospect of the Swimmers' vengeance on beast Gerry Webber.

*

My main reason for suggesting a delay, which had elicited a suspicious glance from Alec, was that I had tried to phone Crystal three times during my enforced leisure but each time had to bang the receiver down as either her father or mother answered. I wanted to talk to her desperately before any Swimmers action took place against her father. Finally I struck lucky. "Crystal, it's me, Ray. OK to talk?" A tight whisper. (Milland from here on)

"Jeez, Ray, I've been so worried about you. Ja, it's OK, fine, no-one's home. Are you all right? How's the eye?"

I let a few moments go by, savouring the warmth and music of her voice.

"Ray?"

"I'm here, just getting pleasure hearing you talk again. I'm fine, the eye's just about back to normal. How're things with your dad?"

"Oh, him, he's drinking so much he's forgotten all about you. He still doesn't like Jews, though. You never said you were Jewish, Ray."

"Would that have made a difference to you?"

"Well, no, not really, but well, maybe, yes, maybe before I got to know you better. I never sort of knew any Jewish boys before, you know. But then, after that Saturday, I guess I liked you a lot. I realised that it was my pa's attitude that I'd somehow let get to me. D'you know what I'm trying to say?"

I swallowed deeply. "What your dad said about Jewish guys and Gentile girls, well, it's probably true for some of us, but what happened between you and me that day was the most sensational thing that has ever happened to me. I haven't been able to think straight about anything, just the moments in your lounge, dancing with you. For me that was so real…"

"Ray, I feel so much the same. I mean I've flirted with other guys before, even gone steady a couple of times but that day was special for me too."

"So what're we gonna do?"

"Wodja mean?"

"Are we gonna see each other? Can you get out, maybe in the evening?"

"Jeez, I dunno. It'll be difficult, you know, with my pa an' all, but, it all depends. I'll have to ask Rita if she'll say I was with her. Give me a few days. Better not phone me here. I'll phone you. Is that OK?"

My heart was flying moonwards. "Great. Number's 69161. If anyone else answers just say you're a friend from swimming class at St George's. Tuesday between six and seven's best."

"Ray?"

"Yes, Crystal?"

"Nothing.........speak to you on Tuesday."

*

It was decided. Alec and Lalla would go along to Gerry Webber's Gym, get membership application forms and spy out the place to see if they could find where the resin was kept. I would buy the itching powder. After school Mark would follow Webber when he left the gym to decide the best time to change the powders, preferably when the gym was attended by anyone other than The Beast, as he was now known to us.

In the meantime I spent days and nights dreaming up fantasies of secret meetings, tender nudgings and magical erotica far surpassing anything Alec or Jimmy McEwan could imagine in their wildest dreams.

Chapter 6

It had become a favourite ploy of Larry's to burst into my room, usually when I was in the middle of homework. "Ray...." in the nagging tone he'd developed.

"Yes, Larry, what is it? I'm in the middle of my Maths."

"Sorree, but you gotta come an' help me."

"What's the matter?"

"My radio won't work an' it's Superman on in a minute. Pleez you gotta come NOW.......!"

In the middle of rewiring the plug to Larry's radio the phone rang.

"Ray, can you talk?"

"Yeah, Crystal, yeah, it's OK. Jeez, it's good to hear your voice."

"RAYYYYY, Superman's on in a minute!!!!" screamed Larry.

I cradled the phone in my neck and finished the rewiring in a hurry. "OK, OK, Larry, there you are up, up, and away...I'm going to my room."

"YOU'RE TALKING TO YOUR GIRLFRIEND!!!!!"

I ignored him and dashed along the corridor.

"Can't talk long, Ray, my folks are out on the back stoep......may come in any minute. ....How's things with you?"

"Not bad. Larry's driving me mad. My little brother Marty's great though. Hang on, I'll just pull the phone cord under the door. My folks think I've gone mad..."

"Hah! That's a lot better than my pa. If he knew I was talkin' to you he'd grab the phone an' smash it over my head."

"Ja, I believe it."

"Shame, I feel awful about your poor eye. I'm really sorry, Ray."

"No, it's OK now. Just wanna say that I'm missin' you like mad...."

"Me too."

"So can you get out for a while, some evening?"

"Well, lissen, Rita's folks are away next Monday night. She asked me if I'd sleep over. So I asked my mom and she said OK. Haven't asked my dad yet. Still he knows Rita so it should be all right."

"And so....?"

"Rita said I could ask you over that evening...."

"Rita's suggestion?"

"Ja. She was mad as hell about what my dad did to you. Don't worry, she can keep a secret. I sort of liked the idea too, though."

I could feel the familiar excitement rising and barely managed a stuttered reply. "Ah, sounds pretty g-good to me, exciting, sort of."

"You think you can make it?"

"Should be fine. I can say I'm over at Mark or Alec."

"Ray, my dad's coming inside...better not talk anymore..."

"Right. I'll see you Monday night. Lookin' forward to it."

"Ray....?"

"Ja?"

That delicious giggle, "You don't know Rita's address...!"

The tension burst within me, laughing out loud. "I'm a bleddy idjit...where does she live?"

"39 Conyngham Street, Parsons Hill."

"That's easy, only a few blocks from our house. What time, round seven or so?"

"Ja, that'd be fine. Better go now, Ray."

"Maybe see you at St Georges Baths Friday. Buy you a strawberry milkshake."

"Great, see you then."

Just then there was a violent knocking on my bedroom door. "Raymond, you alive in there? Maybe you managed to electrocute yourself with the telephone cord?"

I opened the door and handed the telephone to my father. "Sorry dad, Larry was making such a racket with Superman on his radio....."

"Don't blame your little brother. What's so mysterious you have to talk behind closed doors?" He peered at me accusingly. "Not that little shicksele gave you the VD, yes?"

I was getting used to barefaced lying. "No, dad, just something at school..."

"OK, OK, Mr Mystery man." My father gave me a suspicious look. "That's a bit strange because, all your gangster friends are outside waiting for you. I told them you might be strangling yourself with the telephone cord..."

"Tell 'em I'll be down in a minute."

"All of a sudden I'm a messenger boy...tell 'em yourself!"

I took the stairs three at a time, mind racing ahead to Monday night. "Going out for a while. Won't be long," I yelled up the staircase.

"Done your homework?" my father's voice followed me out into the hall followed by "you dressed warm enough?" from my mother in the kitchen.

"Yes, yes, to all the questions. See you later."

"Later we'll be in bed. Take a key."

There they were, my three co-conspirators, Alec, Mark and Lalla, lounging by our garden gate in the gathering evening gloom.

"Hi, guys, howzit? What's doin', Alec?"

Alec shook his head in confusion. "Jeez, Ray, what were you doin' up there? Your dad thought you might be unconscious?"

"Nothing much. I was on the phone, if you must know."

"Can we guess? Crystal?" from Mark with a leer.

I nodded.

"Did you tell her what a miserable bastard her father is?" Alec demanded.

I shook my head. "No, not really. We couldn't talk much 'cos her folks were just outside on the stoep."

"S-s-so wh-wh-what's got you s-s-so excited your eyes are p-p-popping out of your h-h-head?" Lalla only just managed to blurt out, amidst a spray of saliva.

I reacted with suitable irritation. "Listen Lalla, you four-eyed twit, it's none of your damned business. If your eyes popped out any further they'd splat against those coke-bottle lenses of yours!"

I regretted the words soon after I'd let them out. Poor Lalla just stood open-mouthed and it was left to Alec and Mark to smooth the ruffled feathers.

"No need to talk to Lalla like that, Ray! We've always been open with each other, haven't we?" Alec patted Lalla on the shoulder.

"Yeah," Mark chimed in, "we's all part of the action jn this Crystal business, ain't we? We gotta right to know what's happening, that's so, yes, guys?"

There were murmurs of assent all round.

I took the criticism like a man. "Ja, I suppose you're right. Sorry Lalla. Guys, you were right. Crystal and I just talked. I'm, ah, gonna buy her a milkshake at the Baths on Friday."

"That's it?"Alec looked me straight in the eye.

"Oh, ja, she also misses her Ray Milland even though he's a bloody Jewboy!" What a bare-faced liar I was becoming! This remark was met by raucous laughter and jeers but I continued unabashed. "Come on guys, what have the rest of you got to report? Let's bike over to the Greek's cafe an' back and we can decide what the next steps are gonna be."

*

The Coca Cola floats at the Greeks' cafe were the best in town. A huge glass of Coke topped by two scoops of vanilla ice cream and a dollop of whipped cream on top.

"Lalla, so what happened at the gym?" I demanded.

"You all know where it is, opposite the W-W-Willowtree Milk B-B-Bar, down G-G-Grace Street. G-G-Gym's on the f-f-first floor. You walk in and there's a reception with this stunning d-d-doll at the desk. Unbelievable! T-T-Tits sittin' up an' lookin' at you...!" Lalla licked his fleshy lips at the image so well remembered.

"OK, OK, don't tell us your wet dreams," Alec said impatiently."What then?"

"She looks at me l-like I'd crawled outta a crack in the p-p-pavement and says, 'you sure need to develop that runty body you're walkin' around with!'" To his credit, Lalla joined in the laughter at his expense. "It's all very well for you-you g-guys. You know it's 'cos of my asthma th-th-that I c-c-can't play ru-rugger. Anyways, she g-gives me these forms an' then I asks her if sh-sh-she'll k-k-kinda sh-sh-show me around. She l-looks at me down this c-cute little n-nose an' says 'Show yerself around, Moonface!'"

The guys and me, we are practically on the floor now, eyes streaming.

"So, I s-s-says to her, 'now l-l-l-lissen here, that ain't no w-w-way to t-t-t-treat a new perspective c-c-client', turned my back on her and just walked off, just like th-th-that."

Alec clapped him on the back. "Lalla you are one big hero. Sounds to me like she fancied you big time."

"Nah, don't think I was her t–t-t-type. She obviously only goes for oversized apes. She'd p-p-probably go for you, Alec."

By this time we were helpless and Nick the owner must have thought we were smokin' dagga or something.

Once the laughter subsided, Alec was in thoughtful mode. "You know, I'm thinking..... if Lalla did a Charles Atlas course there he could get a bit of bulk on that weedy frame of his, bit of definition and he could also get to know his way around the gym."

"I already th-th-thought about that," Lalla interrupted," and I agree. I could do a course there" he suddenly had a funny look on his face, "an' you g-g-guys better watch out for Big Lalla then. Anyways, I did show myself around an' here's the problem we gotta solve..."

"Like fer instance"? we all queried in unison.

"Well, it's a huge p-p-place. The weightlifting's at the far end where these musclebound m-m-morons like Crystal's pa are gruntin' an' heavin'. What I did see was where they kept the powder. In little bowls next to each mat. A little kaffir named Samson comin' round with drinks an' towels an' stuff. It's all wide o-o-open."

I wanted to know if anyone would notice one of us trying to put our powder in the little bowls.

Lalla shook his head. "Nah, you need to get to the main drum an' I s-s-saw it. It's in the b-b-back where they make the c-c-c-coffee...."

Alec nodded appreciatively. "Lalla, you've done brilliantly. I reckon that it's possible, guys, wodja think?"

We all nodded affirmative.

"So what did you do then?" I asked.

Lalla was so inflated with pride that he leaned too far into his Coke float and got a dab of whipped cream on his nose. That didn't deter him for a minute. 'So never mind all your l–l-l-laughin', I went back to the s-s-snooty d-doll at reception....."

"Had another look at her bazumbas," from Alec.

"Ja, that's for sure, man," Lalla said with a twinkle behind the thick lenses, "an' th-th-en I do my J-J-James C-C-Cagney bit, y'know rolled my shoulders an' sorta leered at her...."

"What she do, blow you a kiss or sumfin'?" Mark chortled.

"No, actually, she was m-m-uch n-nicer second t-t-time around, sp-sp-specially when I r-r-registered....."

"YOU WHAT???????!!!!!" we all roared as one.

"You heard me. Take a good look at the Lalla you know now, guys, 'cos in a few weeks I'm gonna be transformed. Anyhow that's what the chick, her name's D-D-D-Donna, by the w-way, said. I'm doin' a six-week bodybuildin' course an' best of all, my folks are payin'!!!"

"Sensational work, Lalla." Alec smacked him on the back so heartily Lalla doubled over in a coughing fit. "You'll be our man on the inside and be able to get our itchin' powder into the big bin and then into the little bowls when the time comes."

"Talking about powder," I smiled triumphantly,"here's the stuff Mark and I got from the Novelty Shop on Westbourne Road. Six Packs of Dr. Scratch's Guaranteed Itch and Sneeze Powder. We tried it on the neighbour's little Daschund. Poor little bastard didn't stop chasing his tail for hours, sneezing like buggery an' scratchin' himself raw....serve 'im right for keepin' the whole street up all night with his yappin!"

"We had to water-cannon him with the garden hose to stop him bitin' his balls to smithereens," Mark grinned. "Anyway, next step is to try it on Nkomo, the garden boy two doors away. He needs a good lesson, that insolent Xhosa sod."

"I d-d-dunno if th-th-that's s-s-such a g-g-good idea," Lalla remarked.

Alec looked at him. "What's the problem?"

"W-well, I-I-I-I mean, he's just a poor ol' kaffir, can't we just make do with the d-d-dog?"

Alec nodded reluctantly. "Agh, Lalla, you'se such a bleddy pinko liberal, man. Anyways, we's democratic in the Swimmers, so let's us take a vote. On powdering ol' Nkomo ....let's see, Mark an me in favour, Lalla an' Ray against. Seems you guys are goin' a bit soft but becos it was Lalla's idea, the itchin powder, we gonna let him an' Ray have the decision. Just don't blame us if it works better on bleddy dachshunds! OK?"

"So what else did we find out?" I asked.

Alec tapped the spoon on the table. "We found out that that pig-shit Webber leaves the gym regular as clockwork, round six in the evening, spends an hour in the Carlton Hotel Bar then staggers home fairly pissed. The gym stays open till eight."

"That's great," said Mark. "If Lalla goes there from, say six to seven, he can dose the bin and bowls if possible an' it'll be dynamite the next morning."

Lalla held up his hand, but couldn't get his sentence started.

Alec laughed. "Lalla, this ain't school y'know. You don't have to hold up your hand when you wants to be excused. Guys, let our boy genius have as much time as he needs."

"G-gee th-thanks, Alec. What I just re-re-remembered. Behind the d-d-dizzy chick on the d-d-desk was a b-big poster advert for a W-W-Weightlifting competition. A group of thickoes d-d-d-demonstrating weightlifting and generally showing off their muscles. So, thinkin' about it, wouldn't it be amazing if we got our stuff in when it c-c-ould get to a whole l-l-lot of p-palookas at the same t-time?"

"Bloody brilliant! When's the Exhibition?" Alec and Mark shouted simultaneously.

"N-n-next Monday at seven-th-th-thirty...."

"Shit!" I bit my lip.

"What's up, Ray?"

"Ah, its just that....ah, well I s'pose I'd better come clean.... ah, Crystal's staying over at Rita's place that night an' I'm due to go over there. I was gonna ask you, Mark, if I could say I was coming over to sleep at your place..."

Mark nodded. "Sure, Ray, no problem..."

"What do you mean?" Alec demanded. "She's sleepin' over at Rita's place? All fuckin' night?"

"Ja, that's what she said. Rita's folks are away. Crystal already asked her ma and all."

Alec jumped up off his stool. "Swimmers, do you nincompoops know what this means?"

A confused babble of voices competed for attention. Even Nick behind the counter leaned over to hear what was coming next. But Alec leaned forward and whispered, so that only the three of us could hear. "It means that Ray Milland, also known as our old mate Raymond Benjamin of the Swimmers is almost certainly, no make that a definitely, after Monday night, gonna be a virgin no longer!!!"

"Aw, come off it Alec," I remonstrated. "You've just got a filthy mind. She's a really nice doll, believe me."

But he was having none of it. "Lissen, my boy, lissen to words of experience. Nice doll she may be, I'm sure you're right. But believe me, when a doll arranges to stay at a mate's house for the night, ALL NIGHT, AND her friend's folks are away AND she invites you over, she's plannin' all the way. She's got the hots for you, Ray, baby. Trust me and if not me, ask Jimmy McEwan. I'll put money on it!"

"J-j-jeez, Alec, you-you mean she-she's org-org-organizing it j-just like that, in- in-in c-c-old b-b-blood?"

Mark laughed out loud. "I'd hardly say cold blood, sounds pretty hot-blooded to me!"

"That's for sure," Alec agreed. "I reckon she fancies Ray big time. And becos' of her shitty father, she's gotta be careful for both their sakes so that's why all this sleepover is necessary. Guys, I reckon Monday Night could be huge for the Swimmers in TWO BIG WAYS. Ray, we don't need you at the gym. Better you're not there as Webber knows what you look like. Lalla can get the powder in and Mark an' me will go as spectators. You'll be representing us in a slightly different way, over at Rita's."

"But," I protested half-heartedly, "that means I'll miss all the fun at the gym."

"S-s-sounds l-like you'll b-be havin' quite a b-b-bit of f-f-fun wh-wh-where you're g-g-goin."

After the laughter had subsided, Mark turned to me with a serious look on his olive-skinned face. " Ray, it's probably best that you don't show your face anywhere near the gym. All hell's gonna break loose that night an' if Gerry Webber sees your face in the crowd, stupid as he is, he's gonna put two an' two together. Like in the movies, this way you'll have an unbreakable alibi...."

"Yeah yeah," I retorted, "an' I suppose Crystal and Rita will testify that I was there all night....how will Gerry Webber take that, I wonder?"

"OK , good point. I suppose we hope it won't come to that," Mark responded, sheepishly. "Anyway, Lalla, when do you start your course?"

"M-my f-f-first session's t-t-tomorrow evening s-so that' j-j-just s-s-six days t-to go."

"Cripes!"Alec grinned. "That receptionist dolly really got to you, hey?"

I got up from the table. "Guys, I better shoot off home. Got tons of homework and also gotta keep in my folks good books so's they don't make a fuss Monday night. See you at the baths, Friday."

Mark murmured softly. "Ray, you still got the Frenchies I lent you for the drive-in?"

"Oh God, yes. I'll give them back Friday."

"Don't bother. They may come in useful Monday night!!"

Chapter 7

St. George's Baths was filled to capacity with screeching children, it being one of South Africa's frequent Public Holidays, celebrating one or other victories in the interminable wars, white settlers against the black African Tribes.

We had congregated in Mrs. Fugard's cafe, animatedly discussing the forthcoming comeuppance of Mr. Gerry Webber, anti-semitic bully. Webber's attack on me personally had made us doubly eager for the plan to be put into action.

Alec took a huge bite from a jammy doughnut. "So, guys, we're all set for Monday night, hey? Can't believe it. Wonder if it'll make the headlines...can youse see it....'Gerry Webber Weightlifters Scratch 'n Sneeze Fiasco'...."

Mark sniffed loudly. "What about Sneeze'n'Scratch while you weight(lift)!"

"H-h-how's about 'Catch a Scratch at G-g-gerry's P-p-patch'" was Lalla's contribution.

"Maybe one of you should take a camera," I suggested. "I'd love to see that monster's face."

"I-i-i'll do it, R-ray, b-b-b-ut...."

"Yes, Lalla, "I said impatiently, then somewhat cruelly, "b-b-b-ut wh-wh-what?"

"H-h-how's about you t-takin' a picture of wh-wh-what you'll be d-d-doin?"

We all dissolved in hysterical laughter. Lalla had a wicked sense of humour, often enhanced by his speech difficulties.

Alec pointed. "Hey Ray, isn't that your little lady there just coming towards the cafe?"

Mark ogled, grinning. "Sure is, and she's lookin' real good outta school uniform. Hey Ray, you got enough spondoolicks to cover strawberry milkshakes for two?"

Red-faced, I muttered, half to myself. "Yeah, got a few bob on me. Better go across and see her. Lissen, guys, do me a favour. Get outta here an' don't stare in the window. Either go swim or piss off home, gimme a little break."

Alec nodded. "C'mon guys, he's right. Let's go do a few dives off the 20 ft board."

I watched Crystal come into the cafe alone. There was no doubting the effect on me just watching her as she looked around, then, the broad smile of recognition. I swear my heart rate doubled in that moment. She was wearing her usual tight fluffy sweater and orange jeans cut off just below the knees. The mass of auburn curls was still straight and damp from her swim and shower but if anything this accentuated the firm high cheekbones and strong yet feminine lines of her face. I couldn't take my eyes off her and knew what Lalla must feel like as my voice would not obey the commands coming down from my brain.

So I stammered "Hey, Cr-cr-cr-crystal, howzit?"

I was rewarded by that bright smile, perfect teeth, a little giggle, but did I imagine a little on the nervous side. Nervous of me?

"Hi Ray. I'm good, thanks. You OK?"

"Ja I'm fine too. Where's Rita?"

"Nah, she had to go to elocution lessons. Where're all your mates?"

"Swimming an' diving. I told them to get lost. You fancy a milkshake?"

"Wish I could but I gotta run. My dad's pickin' me up outside in a few minutes. Best if he doesn't see us together."

"Ja, I guess so." I said, disappointed.

She looked straight at me, eyebrows raised. "Still OK for Monday night?"

I gulped, trying not to show it. "Ja, what sorta time?"

"Agh, anytime after about seven'll be fine. I'm really looking forward to it, what about you?"

"That's for sure. Is Rita OK about it?"

"She's fine. Thinks its great, you and me." She looked anxiously through the window. "I better run, Ray. See you Monday night, hey...?"

And with a grin she was gone.

*

Monday Evening 6 p.m.

You know that when things start to go wrong, they go wrong spectacularly, especially in circumstances when an event is as eagerly anticipated as my sleepover date with Crystal was concerned.

I had completed my homework in record time and came down the stairs to join Larry for supper. Marty, being an ideal child was already fast asleep. As usual Larry was complaining about not being allowed Coca Cola with his eggs and sausages and our mother was patiently explaining about the damage Coke did to one's teeth.

"Look at your brother Raymond's teeth all full of fillings and always at the Dentist. Do you want to have to go and have the drill like Ray does? Tell him Ray, go on."

At that moment I was so concerned with getting out that I failed to notice that my mother was dressed, not in her normal housecoat which smelled continually of frying fish but in what she called her 'going out clothes'.

It was only after I had stuck my face close to Larry's and opened my jaw wide enough for him to see all the black amalgam adorning the rear of my mouth that I did notice her finery.

"You going out, Mom?" I inquired, stifling a choke.

"Yes, your father's taking me to an early show and then out to eat after so you'll be babysitting Larry and Marty tonight."

She couldn't help but notice my crestfallen expression. "Whatsamatter? You had plans tonight, on a school night?"

I hesitated "Well, yes, I had planned to go over to Mark's to do some Maths revising. He's weak on Algebra and his mom said for me to come over and maybe sleep over."

"No .That's impossible. Euphemia is off so she can't look after the kids."

My brother was looking at me with a look of malevolent satisfaction as if, impossibly, he knew at his tender age just what a momentous life-changing event in my existence was being screwed up on account of him. I made a mental note to take due revenge the next time no-one was looking. Problem was that my mind was already made up with decisions as follows:

First........no way was I going to miss out on this evening with Crystal.

Second........even if I had to forego the overnight, I'd keep that to myself till later.

Third........could I take Larry into my confidence? Answer no, so I had to get him into bed then slip out without him noticing.

My mother's voice intruded into my whirling scheming consciousness. "Right, Larry, if that's all you're eating, no Coke for you, brush your teeth and into bed. Ray, there's your cottage pie in the oven. I can hear your father revving the car outside. You know he hates to miss the newsreels so look after your little boeties and we'll see you later or tomorrow." With swift pecks and hugs for the two of us she grabbed her coat and raced out the front door.

I had decided on strategy three, risky though it was.

"Larry, I've got a huge amount of difficult Maths homework to do and I DON'T WANT TO BE DISTURBED. So, here's half a crown for your moneybox if you'll go straight to bed and go to sleep. Is that a deal?"

Larry looked at me suspiciously with those big spaniel eyes, trying to see an ulterior motive. "OK Ray," he said slowly, "but what if I wanna go to the toilet?"

"That's fine, you're ten years old, go by yourself but my door will be closed and I'm in my room concentrating so just go back to bed after. OK?"

He nodded solemnly, took the coin from my outstretched hand and marched off up the stairs to his bedroom. I breathed a sigh of relief and looked at my watch. It read 6.45. I doused my face with my father's aftershave, grabbed Mark's flattened tin of goodies and was just about to tiptoe quietly out the front door when a little voice echoed from the landing half-way up the stairs.

"Ray, Ray, where're you going?" Larry stood there in pyjamas, lower lip quivering, tears about to flow.

"Larry, lissen," I mumbled as persuasively as I could muster, "I've got to go over to Mark's to get some stuff for my Maths homework. I'll only be a little while so don't worry. Just go back to bed and switch off the light. I'll be back in just a few minutes."

Larry burst into tears. "I'm gonna tell! I'm gonna tell! Mom said you wasn't supposed to go out, you gotta look after me an' Marty."

I knew that in this mood there would be no placating him so I shrugged, made my retreat from the front door and gave him a reassuring hug.

"OK, boetie, shall I treat you like a little baby and read you a story?"

"I'm not a little baby!"

"I know you're not but if you wanna be big and grown up then surely you can get to bed and read one of your books by yourself without me having to be like your nanny? Marty'll be OK, he sleeps right through." The ploy seemed to work. I escorted Larry back to bed and started him off on one of the Enid Blyton Adventure books. I looked at my watch...7.10. I could still get to Rita's by 7.30. Closing Larry's bedroom door quietly, I had a brief look in at Marty who was sleeping peacefully and quickly retraced my steps downstairs and stepped outside, locking the door. The evening was cloudless and cool for October but the brilliant Milky Way shone brilliantly in the dark sky. I breathed a sigh and, shoving my guilt feelings as far down into my nether regions as was possible, set out on a trot for Parsons Hill.

*

In a side street off Port Elizabeth's Main Street, Alec and Mark sidled up to the entrance to Gerry Webber's Gym.

"C'mon Mark let's move it. We wanna get good seats close to the mats. You sure Lalla managed everything OK?"

"He was bluddy nervous but he knew what to do. After he did his weight training and a spell on the exercise bikes, he waited for the pint-sized kaff, called Samson, can you believe it, to finish going round refilling all the bowls with new resin. He then sprinkled all our stuff on top of the new powder so when the big boys grab handfuls this evening during the show it'll all be concentrated Dr. Scratch! That'll fix Gerry the beast an' his big boys!"

"Where's Lalla now?"

"We're meeting him inside."

"OK, fine, let's go, what you waiting for?"

"Alec, it's nothing, just, I'm sorta wondering how Ray's getting along?"

"Don't worry about our boy Ray. Got him to talk to Jimmy McEwan so he knows all the right moves. He got a few good tips. Crystal don't know what she's in for! Come on, let's go in."

The overwhelming smell and fug of liniment, sweat, wintergreen and cigarette smoke practically blinded them as they made their way past the Reception. A short appraising glance at Donna, the comely receptionist, and Lalla came bustling out of the interior.

"C-c-come on g-g-guys I've got places near the f-f-front!"

There was little time for discussion but Alec grabbed him by the shoulders and leaned over close, whispering. "You done great, buddy! Proud to be your good mate!"

Lalla's chest puffed out so far it was quite possible he might do some muscular damage. He led them to a bench right in front, with nothing between them and the mats on which the massive barbells stood. They sat, cowering down, endeavouring to be as un-noticeable as possible, just waiting for the entertainment to commence.

*

I ran up the garden steps of no 39 Conyngham Street, panting after trotting most of the way. Few lights were on and the street was dark. I paused at the front door to catch my breath then summoned up courage to ring the bell. The door opened and chubby little blonde Rita stood there, smiling.

"Hi Ray, welcome. Come in. Hey, why you panting?"

"Ja, I know. Ran all the way from Mount Road. Had a bit of a problem getting out, my little boet Larry causing trouble like usual."

"Wow, that's quite a run. Take a seat in the lounge. Crys won't be long, just had a shower. She'll be down in a minute. Can I get you a drink?"

"Love a beer, thanks."

I sat down in a large settee as Rita disappeared into the kitchen. The lounge was old-fashioned with a large fireplace and wooden-beamed ceiling. The huge radiogram occupied one entire wall with extra speakers.

"Rita said you'd like a beer, Ray. Here you go." Crystal had appeared silently from behind giving me quite a start.

"Wow, Crystal where'd you come from? I mean, I thought Rita said you were in the shower."

"Ja, I was. Had to get fresh after a hell of a day. Hey, you smell nice!"

"Dad's aftershave. Burns like hell. Sorry still catching my breath. Ran from Mount Road."

"So relax, take it easy....fancy some music?"

"Ja, anything you like..."

"Well how's about that Sinatra we were listening to when we were kinda rudely interrupted?????"

Strains of Sinatra being 'The Tender Trap' filled the room.

Chapter 8

"Ladeeez an' Gentlemen, youse all know me, Gerry Webber's my name!"

A green and gold one piece leotard, Springbok colours, bulgingly portrayed the Gym Proprietor's protruberances, mainly muscular. A Batman-type cape to match.

"Welcome one an' all to our Grand Weightlifting Exhibition. Great to see so many of you folks here to witness a really fantastic show. Taking part will be Mannie 'Muscles' Maritz from Pietermaritzburg, Natal.... take a bow, Mannie."

Ripples of applause as an overblown hairy monster of a man in a skimpy bright scarlet costume appeared from behind the screen. Tree-trunk neck, shoulders seemingly fused to wedge-shaped cauliflower ears protruding from a clean-shaven rugby ball head. He smiled. Black gaps where teeth ought to have been. Mannie took his place on the podium. On each of three mats stood dumbbell bars on bright metal wheels.

"Next,.....Sky High Liebenberg, from Pretoria, only man in South Africa who's lifted twice his own weight in kaffirs!"

More applause. A gigantic Neanderthal waving arms which at rest would have reached below his knees. He wore a tiny black bikini covering virtually nothing at all, with a black corset over one shoulder.

"Couldn't let these two buggers steal the show in my own gym so there's me, Port Elizabeth's very own Big Bruiser Gerry Webber!"

Deafening noise. Someone flicked the gym lights on and off repeatedly.

In the front row, five feet from the mats, Alec, Mark and Lalla sat open-mouthed at the gruesome spectacle.

"Oh my god," breathed Mark as the mountainous trio flexed torso's and struck poses, "we could be in very deep shit here, guys...."

"Shuddup, Mark!" Alec whispered out of the corner of his mouth. "We're supposed to be fans....smile, look impressed"

Lalla was shaking like a jelly, his well-developed waist flab quivering through a Gerry Webber Gym T-shirt. He blew his blonde fringe out of his eyes with a nervous gasp. "K-k-kill 'em, G-g-gerry," he managed in a soprano shriek. His shrill stammer brought a wave of laughter from the crowd, mostly oversized males but dotted about were several pneumatic peroxide blonde Amazons, huge shoulders and breasts to match. Leopardskin seemed to be the prevalent material. The packed gymnasium stank of sweat, perfume and beer.

Gerry stood on the centre mat, grinning at the audience. "Nou ja, folks, us three jus' gonna warm up a bit then we'll start. Bench presses, jerks, snatch an' lift. Then the Big Event...Sudden Death! Till two of us can't lift no more! Three tries and you're dead! Like High Jump, OK?"

He turned towards the screen. "Hey, Samson! SAMSON! Where the hell are you, you verdomde houtkop! (idiot woodenhead!)"

A smiling black face peered round the partition. "Ja, Baas Gerry?" Diminutive in a white Gerry's Gym tracksuit.

"Bring the bloody resin, you lazy black bastard. Quick-quick now hey! Don't keep the spectators waiting."

"Straightaway, Baas Gerry." Samson vanished then re-appeared carrying three large bowls of white powdered resin.

Alec gave Mark a sharp nudge. Lalla shut his eyes, disappearing behind his hairy fringe.

"Here we go guys," Alec breathed. "Revenge time. Get ready for a quick getaway...."

*

Rita stood up and stretched.

Sinatra was intoning to one and all 'Where or When.'

"Guess you two lovebirds don't want me around here so I'll just go up to my room. Got mountains of homework to catch up on. OK?"

I caught Crystal's glance and shook my head. "Hey, no Rita, lissen, it's your house an' all...."

She gave me her broadest grin, shook her head, blonde curls quivering. "Who're you kiddin', MR. RAY MILLAND? It's only in the movies when the friend sticks around when she's not wanted. Two's company, three's a crowd not so? I can read the signs, hey?"

She turned to Crystal who laughed, embarrassed, but didn't argue. Rita closed the lounge door behind her and I could hear her footsteps up the stairs. I took Crystal's hand and pressed it hard to my lips. A sudden image of Larry and Marty at home alone, my irate parents coming home and finding me gone flashed through my mind but the beer, Crystal's scent and nearness quickly extinguished any feeling of guilt.

I stood up. "May I have the pleasure of this dance?" In my very best Millandese. Like stretched elastic snapping back, we met in the middle of the Coetzee living room, eclipsing the hours, days and weeks since our last disastrous encounter which had ended so painfully in my face. Familiarity overcame inhibition. Dancing was intoxicating, we pressed together, swaying gently.

"I never danced with Ted van Jaarsveld like this, you know," I murmured in her ear, curls tickling my nose. "His stomach always got in the way.!!!!"

Explosive giggles from Crystal broke the romantic spell momentarily. Then she looked at me in the special way I recognised, nodded toward the large couch.

"That opens into a divan, Ray. See if you can work out how to do it. I'll get us another drink. Brandy an' coke do you?"

I nodded, embarrassed by changes in my nether profile. I managed partial camouflage by bending, concentrating on opening the sofa bed. Not without some inordinate fumbling.

Crystal appeared with two tumblers of ice and the dark staple drink of South Africa. We sipped, eyes locked.

"Wow, that's good," I gasped as the fiery liquid combusted my innards, adding to the already blissful state generated by the Castle Lager.

"Here's to my moviestar, my very own Ray Milland," Crystal grinned, switching off the main light. A small lamp barely illuminated the room which was now practically filled by the undone couch.

Sinatra was 'Flying us to the Moon'.

She patted the cushions, pulled me down alongside her. I shook my head.

"What's the matter, Ray?" She looked at me concernedly. "You look worried."

"Nothing, just, just thinking...no it doesn't matter..."

"No, it does matter. Come on, I need to know. You looked so far away...."

I leaned over and kissed the softest of lips. "I was actually....... remembering St. George's Baths that first day. You walking along, drying yourself, shaking your hair loose. Now...I can hardly believe this....us being here on our own. Can't think of anywhere I'd rather be, anyone I'd rather be with."

"Hell, man, you're one hell of a romantic guy, you know that? Mr. Milland, come here and turn off the lamp."

I did as I was told.

There in the darkened lounge of Rita Coetzee's parent's house I learned for the very first time the delights of sensuality, power and beauty generated by male and female. So unlike the ugliness of boys' banter, the drooling and slavering with which our juvenile imaginings in the school yard began and ended. Gently introduced by someone who knew more, so far in advance of me in this other world that all I could do was respond. Which I did, though to my great consternation, totally lacking in any semblance of control.

"You've never gone this far, have you, Ray?" Her voice in my ear in the darkness. With a hint of amusement. "Don't get upset. I also got too excited. Let's just relax for a while. OK?"

So we did. A mental note to thank Mark for raiding his dad's hidden supply....

*

"A-a-a-alec, d-d-doncha th-th-think we sh-sh-should m-m-move back a bit, s-s –ay nearer th-th-the e-e-exit?" spluttered Lalla as Samson placed the bowls containing the perfidious powder alongside the dumbbells.

"Not a bad idea," Mark mumbled, teeth chattering even though the temperature in the gym was steamy.

"OK guys, let's do it," Alec rasped, starting to push his way past irritated spectators.

The movement in the front row caught Gerry Webber's eye but he was already bending down, taking a full handful of resin, as were Maritz and Liebenberg. They rubbed their hands together energetically over the bowls and straightened up. Almost at once strange expressions crossed all three faces.

"What the bloody hell....Samson!!!" yelled Gerry, clapping his hands together.

"Shit,..... what's in this fucking resin?" from Mannie Muscles Maritz, rubbing his hands up and down on his jungled chest.

"AAAATCHOO!" Skyhigh Liebenberg let out a groin-squeezing sneeze after sniffing the deadly resin. Spinning dervish-like, he kicked his bowl over, scattering the powder all over the floor, creating clouds of dust spreading to the front rows.

"SAMSON!! JOU BLIKSEM!" screamed Gerry, trying desperately to rub the powder off his hands onto the mat. "TCHOOO!!! Samson, what the fuck did you put in the fucking resin? SAMSON!!!!!"

The spectators were now on their feet, standing open-mouthed. Worse still, breathing in as panic spread, everyone made for the exit at one and the same time. Volcanic sneezing and scratching universal as chaos reigned.

The boys reached the end of the row, making headway through the crowd to the exit when Gerry, through watering eyes, pointed towards them. "Those kids, daardie kinders, stop them! Get them! They must've, they....AYTCHOO! I'm sure ....they fucking doctored the resin! STOP THEM!"

A few hands were raised to intercept but by this time the gymnasium was in complete uproar. Everyone in the front rows was afflicted, with red gushing eyes, clutching swollen noses. Maritz and Liebenberg had dashed from the podium desperate to get to the showers. Gerry sprang into the crowd colliding full-on with Samson, who was crouching in terror, his eye- whites enormous in the ebony face.

"Get outta the way, you stupid kaffir!" Gerry yelled, lashing out blindly. The blow caught Samson on the side of the head, sending him reeling into the reception desk. Dazed, he crawled in amongst the feet of fleeing spectators, catching a few kicks as he tried to escape.

Totally blinded, Gerry Webber tripped over a dumbbell bar and fell heavily, his right leg twisted at a grotesque angle.

The melee allowed Alec and Mark to scamper through the exit and down the stairs into fresh air. One well-placed foot caught Lalla's ankle and he fell headlong, crashing heavily into Samson, lying against the reception desk.

Outside in the street Alec turned as Mark yelled out in consternation. "Where's Lalla?"

"Oh, hell, what happened? Didn't he get out?"

People were streaming out of the Gymnasium exit, handkerchiefs held to their noses and mouths, hands scratching frantically.

Mark ran back toward the entrance. Alec pulled him back. "Mark, it's no good, you'll never find him! Come on, before we all get nabbed."

"I'm not leaving Lalla in there." hissed Mark. "Gerry noticed us and he knows Lalla. He'll put two and two together and God knows what he'll do if he gets hold of him."

Just then a black face appeared amongst the all-white throng. "Hey, massa, you two, come here, got your little buddy, him with long yellow hair! Get him away from here before Baas Gerry finds him. He'll kill him for sure. He kill you all!!!" Samson appeared by a side alley dragging Lalla, a comatose shape, Gerry Webber t-shirt covering his face, the white belly shining in the darkened doorway. "I think the little massa knocked out," Samson muttered. "We take him down back street. I knows where."

Alec and Mark half-carried half-dragged Lalla's limp form from the side alley and thence back on to Main Street and relative safety.

"Dey mustn't see me wit you boys or I is all finished at de gym," Samson whispered. With a flashing white grin he disappeared back down the street to the gymnasium. The crowd was thinning, enabling Mark and Alec to escort Lalla back to the Main Street bus stop and safety of the way home.

*

I awoke with Crystal's soft breathing in the nape of my neck. The radiogram was still on, needle scratching the inner circle of the long-playing record, music having stopped long before. Sinatra had sung us to sleep, blissfully wrapped in each other. No lyrics would ever describe for me what we had shared with the immortal Francis Albert. There had been no second embarrassment, we had explored each other slowly, tenderly and patiently until finally, unable to stem the rising tide, just allowed the final moments to whirlpool us down or up, into sated oblivion.

Gently I tried to disengage my left arm from behind her head. She moved, mumbling in the depth of sleep. I looked at my watch.

"Oh... Jesus Christ!' I switched on the table lamp. Two thirty am.

Crystal was awake instantly. "What's up, what's the matter? Ray?"

"Shit, do you know what the time is?"

"What does it matter? Rita's folks are away till tomorrow. Go back to sleep, sweetheart." She turned over, away from me.

I shook her gently. "No, you don't understand, Crys. This evening, just as I was getting ready to leave, my folks informed me that they were going out. They insisted I had to babysit my brothers Larry and Marty. There was no way I could call you, didn't have Rita's number so..."

Crystal sat upright, wide awake now. "So what did you....how did you get out?"

"Well, I told Larry, he's ten, that I was just going to Mark's to get some homework stuff and I'd be back pretty soon. Marty was already fast asleep, he's easy, and Larry was tired. I'm sure he went off to sleep anyway but now...." I struggled to collect my clothes, scattered all over the room.

"Now you are in big trouble, it's the middle of the bloody night. Oh Jesus, your folks will be frantic... why didn't you tell me earlier?"

"I was afraid it would spoil things and ....you know, feeling the way I do and after what's just happened between us.....I feel really strong enough to go an' face the music, no matter how bad....."

She gave me one of her looks, deeply scything into my very soul. "Ray, I think you better go, run home like hell now. I do think you should've said earlier but just so's you know, I feel the same way about tonight. Just get going an' call me tomorrow..."

I tied my shoelaces in miniknots and scrambled to the front door. She wore only a towelling gown and clung to me, a long lingering exchange. "I'm mad about you, my moviestar. Go now..."

*

All the lights in the house were on. I'd covered the distance from Parsons Hill in record time. But there was no chance of slipping in unnoticed. I was sure the whole street could hear me panting. I slipped over the front wall and as quietly as humanly possible turned my key in the lock.

My mother stood in the hall, dressing gown, hair all curlered.

"Sorry I'm so late , mom....."

"Sorry? SORRY? LATE? WHERE ON EARTH HAVE YOU BEEN? WE'VE BEEN BESIDE OURSELVES WITH WORRY! LUCKY YOUR FATHER'S ULCERS HAVEN'T HAEMORRHAGED! OR ME A HEART ATTACK!! YOU LEAVE YOUR LITTLE BROTHERS ON THEIR OWN AND DISAPPEAR!!! FOR GOD'S SAKE, WHERE HAVE YOU BEEN??? IT'S NEARLY THREE IN THE MORNING!!!!!"

My breathing had returned to normal but my heart was pounding against my ribcage. I had decided during the sprint that only the truth would be good enough to counter my foolish irresponsibility. I took courage in both hands. "I've...er....been with the most wonderful girl, mom. Crystal Webber, her name is. I think that, no I'm pretty certain that we love each other. She's not Jewish but I'm sure you'll like her when you get to know her..."

My mother was staring at me, wide-eyed, mouth agape, red-cheeked. I began to be concerned for her health. "A SHICKSA NOG!!! OY VAY, THIS WILL KILL YOUR FATHER!! HOW, HOW CAN YOU STAND THERE AND SAY THIS???? DO YOU KNOW HALF OF PORT ELIZABETH WILL KNOW ABOUT THIS TOMORROW? WE PHONED YOUR FRIENDS, THE HOSPITAL, EVEN THE VERSHTUNKENE POLICE!!!! NOBODY KNEW WHERE YOU WERE!!!! YOUR FATHER'S TAKEN FOUR TRANQUILIZERS!!! HE'S GOTTA WORK TOMORROW!!!!"

I'd had enough. I turned to go up the stairs. "Mom, you and dad have got to understand. It's a new world. People mix, they fall in love. I'm seventeen years old and this is the first and probably the only girl I'll ever......"

I didn't see the slap coming. It felt as though the left side of my face had encountered one of Gerry Webber's best. I staggered on up the stairs, clutching my cheek. Crystal's parting words were still reverberating in my head. I sensed rather than saw my father appear at the head of the staircase. I took the stairs two at a time, brushed past him then turned, leaning out over the banister. "YOU'RE BOTH AS BAD AS HER NAZI FATHER! SOON AS WE CAN WE'LL MAKE OUR WAY TOGETHER IN THIS WORLD WITHOUT YOU AND YOUR CRAZY RELIGIONS!!! GOOD NIGHT!"

Chapter 9

"Rosie! Will ya take a look at this!" My father spread the newspaper out on the breakfast table.

I was in disgrace. Neither of them had so much as looked in my direction much less acknowledged my presence after the trauma of the previous evening. Brother Larry sat at the far end of the table wearing what I considered a sardonic smile of satisfaction at my exclusion and discomfiture.

"Oy vay, Abie , who would do such a thing?"

I craned my neck to get a glimpse of the Eastern Province Herald front page.

OUTRAGE AT GERRY'S GYM!

Police are investigating a practical joke that went disastrously wrong last evening at Gerry Webber's Gymnasium in Grace Street. A weightlifting exhibition was thrown into chaos when powdered resin was replaced with itching and sneezing powder. Bowls of the irritant were overturned, sending a noxious cloud into the auditorium. Spectators fled in panic into Main Street. Several people were treated for shock and asthma-like symptoms at Port Elizabeth's Provincial Hospital.

The Proprietor, Gerry Webber, was amongst those treated for acute respiratory distress as well as a fractured right tibia and fibula caused by slipping and crashing into a 200 pound dumbbell dropped by Mannie "Muscles" Maritz. Mr. Webber is at present recovering at his home on Constitution Hill, his right leg plastered up to the hip. Samson Ndebele, his Xhosa assistant has been sacked.

Mr. Webber believes that some youngsters are responsible for the vicious prank and swears that he will find them and 'donner them to pulp'.

Sergeant Rudolphus van Breda of the Port Elizabeth Crime Squad advised Mr. Webber to refrain from taking the law into his own hands and assured him that the culprits would soon be found and arrested.

*

"I don't like that Gerry Webber, Abie. Wasn't he in the grayshirts during the war? He's a verkakte anti-Semite." My mother pursed her lips self-righteously, moving plates and cutlery aimlessly round the table.

"Rosie, shush, what language! But yes, you're right, he's one of the OSB, real Nazis they were and still are."

"What's the OSB, Dad?" I leaned over the table to devour the report in full, which showed a picture of the gym, overturned benches and all.

My father cast a disdainful eye in my direction. "After your disgusting behaviour last night I should even speak to you? Your mother didn't sleep a wink. Nor did I. We suffered all night long. You should be ashamed leaving your brothers alone like that. What if God forbid there had been a fire? Or a burglar? In any case, what were you up to till three in the morning?"

Larry chose this moment to join in. "He said he was only going out for a few minutes and then he didn't, he didn't come back at all." A blocked nose reduced his mournful tones to a pained snuffle.

I did not think the time was appropriate to go into any more detail about Crystal at that particular moment in time. "I told mom last night, dad. I'm in love with a wonderful girl but I know you both disapprove so it's best I say nothing just now. But what's OSB?"

"Abie Benjamin, this is your son talking," my mother wailed. "He's been out all night *shtuppin'* some *shicksa* tart and," mimicking my injured tone, "it's best he says nothing. Nothing? I'll give him something!" She seemed to be casting round for a suitable weapon. "ABIE SAY SOMETHING!!!!!"

"Rosie, Rosie dearest, calm down. Remember the blood pressure, please, please, just sit down, let me talk to Raymond." My father mopped his sweating forehead with a checked handkerchief. "Raymond, Raymond, my boy, you just cannot imagine what damage you are doing to us, your mother and I. To say nothing of the shocking example you're setting for Larry there. I know that we're not the most observant of Jews but....just the thought of a son of ours..."

"Dad, mom, I'm really sorry about last night. Leaving Larry and Marty like that was irresponsible, unforgiveable, I know, but I did promise to help this girl with some maths and when you suddenly said you were going out I didn't know what to do. I didn't have a phone number where she was staying with a friend and so I thought I'd just nip over for a while.....but well, one thing led to another and.... you know I'm seventeen now and..."

My parents had listened to this sorry excuse in silence but my mother suddenly held her head in her hands, wailing, rocking back and forth. "OH MY GOD, MY GOD, seventeen years old and he knows all there is to know. About killing his parents, this he knows!"

My father stood up and placed a consoling hand on her shoulder. "Rosie, Rosie, take it easy, calm down. The boys'll be late for school. We'll discuss this tonight when everyone's a bit more composed. Raymond, get ready and Larry, wash your face and brush your teeth. I'll take you both in the car today."

I grabbed my bag and dashed for the door. My mother's voice followed me all the way to the front gate. "Calmer, Abie? The next time you see me calmer I'll be in a wooden box with both arms folded. Then I'll give you calmer....."

*

We crowded into the school latrine block. Alec locked the door, always calm in a crisis. He unfolded the front page of the EP Herald. "Well now Swimmers, my good buddies, this is where we find out just what us guys are made of."

Lalla's glasses had misted over completely. He brushed his fringe back, rubbed the lenses clean. "H-h-how d-d-did we-we-we know it w-was g-g-onna c-cause a riot, p-p-eople g-going t-to hospital?"

Mark nodded soberly. "I think we are in deep shit, guys."

"A-a-and B-bennie's l-leg in p-p-plaster," wailed Lalla.

"Personally, I'm more worried about the Police coming looking for us," I muttered. "Alec, d'you think Gerry will be able to identify any of you guys?"

Alec smiled his George Raft smile. "Hey you chickens, ain't you forgettin' the main item here?"

We looked at him perplexed. "Watcha mean, Alec?" Mark quavered.

He puffed up his cheeks. "We Swimmers decided that, as one of our members, Ray here, had been roughed up by that ape, Webber, we would take suitable revenge. Am I right?"

Silent assent. Alec motored on. "So, we voted unanimously to fix the resin, right? Lalla's brainwave, yeah?" He stuck his chin in our faces, then gave a broad smile as we all nodded. "An' didn't we screw the bastard real good, hey? Didn't we just? Broke his leg as well, that's a bonus, that'll teach him to meddle with a Swimmer never mind a Jewboy!!!" He held up the headlines.

At first we looked at each other uncertainly, then at Alec, our fearless leader. The dam broke. I grabbed Lalla and Mark round the shoulders. "Bloody hell, guys, Alec's right! It's a huge win for us Swimmers." With that we burst out into the playground, backslapping and cheering, causing not a little puzzlement amongst the other pupils enjoying their lunch break.

Alec turned to me. "Ray, my man, we came through for you. Now we gotta know how you made out...."

This was the moment I'd been dreading. Three pair of eyes fixed on me, four pairs if you included Lalla's milkbottles. I held the moment almost too long. "Guys," I mumbled, "Ray Milland's in love!"

The Swimmers, my three best mates in the world, looked at me open-mouthed.

"W-w-watcha m-m-m- mean, Ray?"Lalla blustered

I looked deep into each of the wide-eyed faces. Gave a knowing wink. "Fellas, last night I was invited to spend the evening with a real lady, who prefers me to be Ray Milland, the gentleman of Hollywood...."

"C'mon, Ray , get to the point! Didja or didn'tcha?" Alec glimmered.

I stood my ground. "Friends, all I can tell you is that a gentleman treats a lady with respect, good manners and ....and ....dis...dis...can't think of the right word...."

"D-d-d-discretion......." from Lalla.

I smiled gratefully. "Yeah, discretion, that's it. Thanks, Lalla."

Alec shook his head, gave me his most penetrating glare. "Not good enough, Raymondo. Not by a long chalk. We all played our part getting you to where you got last night so now give with the details."

I'd given this some thought on the way from my traumatic home situation to school. "All I'm prepared to tell you is....."

The three leaned forward, eyes glazing over.

"Is........I came home in the early hours of this morning, having left Larry and Marty, my brothers on their own, with me in deep shit with my folks, but ....left a big part of me back in Rita Coetzee's house in Parsons Hill."

"Watcha mean....a big part of you? Make some sense, man," Mark's face creased in bemusement.

Alec smiled. "What Ray's tellin' us guys, is that he went all the bloody way last night but the stupid *shmuck's* gone an' fallen for the chick! Am I right, Ray?"

I shook my head, then nodded. Out came Ray Milland with a vengeance. "Won't say you're right, and won't say you're wrong. Like I said, a gentleman has to protect a lady's reputation."

"He did it, the *bliksem*!" breathed Mark with ill-disguised envy plus admiration.

"You smooth b-b-b-bastard," Lalla shook his head incredulously.

"So Jimmy McEwan was right, hey, Ray?" gloated Alec.

That I was not prepared to take. "No, you're completely wrong there, Alec. I asked her about McEwan. All they did was some heavy 'smoochin'," I lied unashamedly. "So you can tell Jimmy he's full of bullshit!"

Just then the bell rang for the end of the lunch period and saved me from further grilling for the moment. I returned to my desk basking in the admiration and envy of my friends although my innards were still smarting from the anguish I'd left at home.

*

The phone rang. I yelled down the stairs. "FOR ME!" Pointlessly, as my mother was still unable to talk to me without screaming or crying or beating her hands on her chest. My father was not yet home from the shop. I pulled the cord under my bedroom door. I knew who it had to be.

"Ray, is it OK to talk?"

"Sure, Crys. Are you all right?"

"Then you know?"

"Well, it's all over the Herald."

"Ray, I can't talk for long... I'm in a phone box, outside the Greek's cafe. Everything's gone mad at home."

"Crystal, I wanted to ask you how your dad is but first, first of all I just wanted to say that every minute since I left you my thoughts have been about you and what I feel. Oh hell, I sound so bloody soppy. I'm sure Milland would be able to say something much more romantic..."

"You're quite romantic enough for me, mister. It's sort of *lekker* having my very own moviestar."

"Well, anyway, I'm really sorry I had to run off like that. You were right to be upset. I realised on my way home how it must have been for you..."

"No, don't worry yourself about that. Really don't. I understood very quickly after you explained. How was it when you got home? Awful, I bet."

"Ja, really heavy. My folks were awake. My mom just about closed the eye your dad didn't take care of..."

"She hit you? I don't believe it!"

"Sure did. She used to be quite a good tennis player when she was younger and this was a full force backhand drive!!!"

"Agh, no, don't be silly. She really didn't, did she?"

"I wish she hadn't. But you know, just like your dad, my folks are also pretty prejudiced, maybe even worse."

"So what did you tell them?"

I hesitated, then took the plunge. "I told them I'd met the most wonderful girl, that's you, and we were sort of going steady. Hope that's ok with you? Then I told them you weren't Jewish but they'd like you when they got to know you..."

"Ja, and then what?"

"Then SMACK!!!!!!!"

"Oh, shame, Ray, that's horrible. I'm so sorry. Why on earth can't our parents be a little more tolerant? Meantime, here my dad is in the worst rage I've ever seen. He keeps swearing that he's gonna kill whoever pulled that stunt at the Gym."

"Have they any idea who did it?" Hating myself asking the question.

"My pa is sure he saw some young guys in the front row move away just before the fun started. He thinks he recognised one of them but can't put a name to him yet. Thinks he might be a recent member."

I gave out an audible sigh of relief.

"Pardon, Ray?"

"No, I didn't say anything. I just took off my sweater." Lying was coming so easy now. "How is your dad? The paper said his leg was broken."

"Ja, he's in bad pain but he's also a real bloody pain in the arse, ordering us all over the place. That's why I got to this phone. I'm supposed to be getting him the Evening Post from Grahams. He's tough and fit though, so his breathing is much better already."

A voice from outside the door. "Raymond, you in there? Your mother and I want to talk to you."

"Crys, gotta go, can I call you?"

"No way. It's impossible at home right now. I can call you tomorrow evening round this time when I go to get the paper."

"Fine. Speak to you tomorrow night then. And Crystal, I'm really missing you like mad..."

"Me too, Ray. I just wanna see you again, soon as poss. Can't seem to worry too much about all our crazy folks right now. What do you think? Should we?"

"RAYMOND!!!"

"Crys, I've never used the word love before......maybe now's not a bad time.....love you..."

"Love you too, Mr. Milland. Speak to you tomorrow."

I descended the stairs slowly, preparing myself for the inferno. Still wanted to find out what OSB meant anyhow.

CHAPTER 10

My mother and father sat next to each other at the dining room table. Sweat beads were popping all over his shiny receding hairline. She wore her normal long-suffering expression, lines on her forehead creased as deeply as when she tried at great length and just about in vain to drum Algebra into my thick skull.

"What's OSB, Dad?" I queried tremulously. Might as well dodge the main event as long as possible.

It wasn't possible. My father glared at me through glinting spectacles. "Never mind the OSB. That we'll talk about another time."

"Ja, but I just...."

"No 'ja buts', mister smart guy. Just start talking. Your mother and I want to know everything about this little *shiksa curveh* of yours."

"Oy, Abie, don't use words like that in front of the boy," my mother pressed her hands together, prayer-like.

"What you talking about Rosie? That's what you been calling her the whole night long and fourteen times on the telephone to me at the shop today. And it was bloody busy the whole day, thank God."

My mother pursed her lips together but said nothing, her eyes betraying her anguish.

"Anyway, sounds like our little boychick's no longer a boy no more. Three o'clock in the morning means they weren't playing chinese checkers all night long!"

I wasn't entirely certain but there might have been an amused element buried deep down in my father's tone, maybe even a little paternal pride? The female of the house wasn't having any of that. I'm sure her antennae were as sensitive as my own.

She shook her head vehemently. "Abie, don't sound as though you're proud of what he's done. First of all leaving poor little Larry and Marty all by themselves? You know how nervous Larry gets at night, what kind of responsible boy does that, I ask you? Then he spends most of the night with a *shicksa*, who knows what he could pick up, a disease maybe, God forbid. Raymond, your father and I don't want to know who this little rubbish is. We don't want to know her name or anything." She sat back, arms folded. "All we want is a promise, first, you never leave your brothers alone in the house again and second, finish, an end to this business with the *shicksa*. Oy, when I think of the telephone calls, to the hospital, the police, your friends' parents, our friends, the whole town knows we got a son who stays out till 3.00 am on a school night and leaves his brothers, a ten-year-old and a five-year-old, if you don't mind, alone in the house. We're dying of embarrassment, I needn't tell you. Isn't that so, Abie?"

My father nodded energetically, wiping his brow clean of moisture. "Sure, Rosie. Absolutely right. Raymond, this is exactly what we want. We want your promise, right, right now, that you won't ever see this girl again. What do you say?"

I looked at the two people whom, until that moment I had loved unreservedly, who had showered me with unconditional affection and devotion all my life. For whom I had always tried my hardest to achieve, to earn their praise and respect. Who were now demanding of me that I turn my back on an emotional and primordial new life experience that up till now I had only dreamed about. Slowly I shook my head,

"What's this shaking of the head? Saying no to us, your parents?" My mother's voice had escalated several semitones.

I faced them both full on. "Dad, a few years ago, maybe not even that long ago, you gave me your 'sex lecture.' Remember that?"

He nodded, embarrassedly. "OK, OK... So what ?"

"Well, then, a few weeks ago after we went to Dr. Joe about the rash between my legs, remember? You told me to treat Jewish girls with respect but with '*de andere*' meaning Gentile girls, you said it was OK to have a bit of fun. Didn't you say that?"

Rosie turned to her husband. "You said this to our son?"

Reluctantly my father raised his hands in submission. "Yes, maybe. OK, *nu*, all right, we'd had a laugh, Joe and I about the rash and all, and I suppose I may have given Ray a little 'man of the world' chat, a little advice. You know it was so funny, that rash thing...." he tailed off weakly.

I interrupted him. "Dad, please dad, let me say what I want to say. I didn't think it was right, what you said. That one should treat some girls differently to others. In any case I think you were just talking about smooching, a bit of innocent fun. But dad, what's happened here is not fun, it'serious. You and mom have got to understand. She's different, Crystal is, and..."

"So that's her name, Crystal, is it?" my mother shrieked, losing control completely. "Abie, you've got to put your foot down, stop this right now, tonight, or he'll bring disgrace on our whole family!!!"

My father rose from the table, his face stern yet softening. "Raymond, you're only seventeen years old, much too young to be so serious. I'm going to say something now to you and your mother and I think we should all then have supper in peace and sleep on it. "He drew himself to his full height, wiped his forehead once more. "You know how much what you've done hurts us, but I think I'm prepared to try to understand this infatuation. No, don't argue. That's what it is. I was young once too, you know." He turned to face his irate wife. "Rosie, we've got to treat Ray like the young man he is now becoming. Maybe a little too fast for our liking but then these days everything's a little too fast for our generation. Know what I'm saying?" He stood there, hands clasping and unclasping.

My mother looked at him in astonishment. "That's all you got to say? That's it?"

"Yes, Rosie that's it! I'm still the Master in this house. Ray knows now exactly how we feel. He must make his choices. I hope he'll use his intelligence. Let's eat!"

She said nothing. Her expression did all the talking necessary. She shook a small bell alongside her on the table so violently it was a wonder the tinkle inside didn't break loose. "Euphemia!" she yelled. "Bring the supper! Immediately! Now!"

The door from the kitchen opened. Two huge eyes below an unruly mop of curly brown hair peered round the door. Larry crept into the dining room, propelled by Euphemia's firm hand on his rear end. His face portrayed his emotions, amazement, admiration, terror and perhaps a little respect. Euphemia wheeled in a heated trolley, wearing her starched uniform and glistening white thousand-tooth smile.

My father glared at Larry. "You been listening to our talk in here?"

His round little face registered complete innocence. "N-n-no, not a word, Dad."

"Fine, whatever you heard it'll be of interest when you're sixteen not now. At the moment, you eat your supper then off to do your homework." Face down my father then proceeded to do justice to an enormous plate of fried fish and chips flooded with tomato ketchup. As did brother Larry.

I think I loved my father more at that moment than any time before or since.

*

Next day at lunchbreak, Lalla was in trouble. His chubby face was wreathed in frowns, eyes behind the milk-bottle lenses even wider than usual. "G-g-guys, wh-what am I g-gonna d-d-o?"

We all crowded round. "What's up Lalla?" Mark wanted to know.

"J-jesus, f-fellas," he blubbered, "I'm supposed to go to Gerry's Gym after school for my next session. How the hell can I go there after what's happened? They'll recognise me for sure."

We looked at each other, searching for an answer. As usual, Alec came to the rescue. Smiling, he patted our not-so-flabby fellow Swimmer on the shoulder. "Lalla, my booitjie, I don't see there's a problem. First, Gerry's the one who might've noticed us getting up and moving and he's at home with a broken leg. Second, you joined a few days before the Great Sneezing Show at the Gym so they've no reason to suspect you anyway. But if you suddenly don't show up, then they may give youse a second look. You'll be givin' Gerry the clue he needs. They've got your name an' all on the books haven't they?"

"Oh, sh-sh-shit, man, I just d-unno if I can go b-back there," Lalla wailed.

Alec shook him into silence. "Course you can an' youse gonna be an even greater actor than our Ray Milland here (pointing to me). Call yourself a Swimmer? All you gotta do is play your innocent self.

Anyone asks you anything, sure you were there, but that's 'cos you doin' a course there. You wanna look like Charles Atlas, doncha?"

"Can't!" Lalla wept, glasses all misted over.

"Yes, you bloody well can and you must! You had to see Liebenberg, an' Maritz perform that night. They're your idols, ain't they? Yeah, an' you got your nose full of powder jus' like everyone else, dincha? Also, you had to run on account of your asthma, right?"

Mark placed a consoling arm round Lalla's shivering shoulders. "Alec's right, you know, Lalla. And you can do it easy, we all got confidence in you. Look how brilliantly youse handled the powder an all!"

I joined in and we formed a tight little bunch around him. Lalla swept his long lank of blonde hair out of his face and a small smile appeared.

"See," Alec grinned, "you got your mates around you an' what's more we'll come downtown with you. We'll be just down the street if there's any trouble. Be right there with you..." he muttered with more confidence than I'm sure he felt.

"Oh yeah?" Lalla wiped the tears and snot from his face. "Wh-what can you g-g-guys do against all those tough b-b-bastards, that's what I'd like to know?"

"Just don't worry, go in there and do your routines just like normal, like there's no tomorrow and say nothing to no-one." Alec held out a large fist and we all grasped each other's hands in a Swimmers handshake. "Agreed"?

"AGREED" in unison.

*

Neither Lalla nor we Swimmers need have worried. We accompanied him to within a hundred yards of the Gym. He went in shaking like a leaf but came out an hour later, beaming. "S-smooth as s-silk, g-guys. Gerry's at home in plaster and everyone's still in shock so no-one took any n-notice of l-little ol' m-me. An' just look at these biceps!" He rolled up the sleeves of his schoolshirt to reveal the small bumps on his upper arms. "Just wait a few w-weeks, you'll see. Donna says we g-g-gonna start on my ab-ab-abdominal m-muscles on M-m-Monday!"

We propelled our brave warrior to the Willowtree Milk Bar for a celebratory milkshake.

*

I got home just in time to answer the telephone. Ignoring the black look from my mother I rushed up the stairs and closeted myself in the privacy of my bedroom. "Crys, I knew it was you. Thought about you all day..."

"Didja Ray? That's helluvva nice .Thought about you too."

"How's your pa today?"

"Agh, terrible. Sits around swearing and drinking all day. Orders us all around like bleddy kaffirs.....oh sorry, Ray, you don't like that word, do you?"

"No, you're right. I don't. It's like your dad calling me a kike, and my folks callin' you names. Also I know the natives don't like it at all."

"You're really a deep sorta guy, aintcha Ray? I really like it when you talk serious. I close my eyes an' pretend we're in the movies. I'll never think of you as anyone but Ray Milland. Promise you'll always talk to me that way. Makes me feel all warm inside. Like I felt the other night."

I could almost see the smile, hearing the giggle. I took a deep breath. "Of course I will, Crystal my dear heart, you have my word as a gentleman."

Her infectious laughter sounded like a xylophone through the black receiver I held in my sweaty hand. "What happened with your folks, Ray? Are they still mad at you?"

I lay back on my bed, the telephone cord stretching taut under the door. "My mom is but my dad, well he seems to be a bit more tolerant. You know he says he understands, he was young once too, etc etc, but he calls it an infatuation."

"What do you call it, Mr. Milland?"

I closed my eyes. Uncontrollable stirrings were affecting my stage voice. "Ummm, let me see, I think you're the best thing that's happened to me in my short little life."

"Agh, you're such a flatterer"!!

I sat up, familiar feelings becoming more insistent. "Crys, when can I see you again?"

She heard the urgency loud and clear. "Ray, what's the matter? You sound different, like you were choking all of a sudden!"

I smiled. "Use your imagination, young lady, I'm lying here on my bed, talking to the most delicious female in the whole wide world... what do you think is happening?"

"Jeez, Ray, that's not fair. I'm standing here in a bloody phonebox!"

"Don't tell me something was happening your side as well?"

"Course it was, you idiot. After the other night you should know what effect you have on me..."

This had gone far enough. I could hear footsteps in the passage on their way to my bedroom. Sure enough, the call came loud and clear. "Raymond, your father is sitting down for dinner. I'm pulling the cord out of the extension in one minute. Enough already!"

I stood up, cupping my hands over the mouthpiece. "Can I see you at St Georges tomorrow after swimming? Maybe I can arrange to scale the car one evening. I'll take you for a drive. Round the Marine Drive, down by the beach. How does that sound?"

"Wonderful! Great! I'll see you at the Baths, round four o'clock, by the diving boards."

At that moment I had no idea what excuse I was going to invent, or how I was going to 'borrow' my mother's Morris Minor again. I only knew I was going to make it happen. "Crystal, I'll see you tomorrow at the diving boards. Four o'clock. Can't wait. I'll be there!"

A rattling of my door handle. "RAYMOND!"

"Even I heard that, Ray. You better go. See you tomorrow. Love ya."

The phone went dead in my hand. I whispered to the inanimate black plastic instrument "Ja an' I love ya too!"

"RAYMOND!!!!"

"COMING! KEEP YOUR SHIRT ON!!!!"

Chapter 11

The fountains of St. Georges Baths were working at maximum pressure, creating spray rainbows across the lush lawns. I sat on a bench overlooking the pool, waiting impatiently. Looking at my watch every few seconds. Suddenly hands came from behind, covering my eyes.

"Guess who, Mr. Milland?" Crystal's talcum, faintly mixed with chlorine plus her essential freshness rendered me speechless. For a short while.

"Jeez, Crys, I thought you weren't gonna show," I gasped, holding her hands tightly against my face. I opened my eyes and turned to look at her. Taking in the green and white school uniform which failed completely to hide the feminine shape beneath. Damp hair severely pulled back into a ponytail, emphasizing her prominent cheekbones. Glowing complexion, hazel eyes dancing in amusement.

"Oh, is that so? What gives, you don't trust me?"

Milland reasserted himself. I stood up, drawing myself to my full height, just about three inches taller than Crystal in her sensible brown school shoes. "Of course I trust you, my dear. It's just that every moment away from you is such exquisite torture..." with a smile and a wink.

"Agh, man, you're so full of bullshit, but don't stop, I kinda like it."

I dragged her down on the bench beside me. "OK, now listen, this is what I can arrange. Next Monday evening I can skit (steal) my mom's car... she always asks me to park it in the garage up the road for her an' I know they are gonna be in 'cos they got a poker evening at home. So

I can say I gotta go to Alec's house to swot and we can go for the drive. How's that for you?"

She nibbled her lower lip. "Monday, ja, I think that's OK. I'll arrange with Rita to go to her place. Can you pick me up from there?"

"For sure. My only problem..." I looked at her with a slightly perturbed frown.

"So, what? What's the problem?"

"That's nearly a week away. I'm not sure I can last till then!"

Crystal laughed, shoving me playfully. "That's all? Too bleddy tough, man. You just gonna have to manage. Take lots of cold showers!" She looked at her watch. "Hey, I better go. I gotta pick up some stuff for my dad. He's still creating merry hell at home."

"Any idea who pulled that stunt?"(hating myself for asking)

She shook her head. "Nah, Police haven't got a clue. They had poor Samson, he's the kaff- sorry, native boy who cleans at the gym down at the Mount Road Police Station an' grilled him for hours but he doesn't know a thing. Shame, though, my pa sacked him on the spot. Not right is it?"

I gulped, guiltily. Crystal stared at me, eyebrows raised. "I don't suppose you or your mates'd know anything about it, do you?"

"Me? How on earth could I know anything? Don't you remember where I was that night? Where we both were? What we were doing?" with as much assurance as I could muster. The lie hurt though. But what could I do?

She smiled tenderly. "Ja, of course I remember. But hey, lissen, I gotta go. Sorry. I'll see you Monday night. What time?"

A quiver of anticipation sparked through me."Bout seven. I'll hoot outside Rita's."

She planted a moist kiss right on my lips and was off, her school satchel and kitbag swinging wildly as she ran.

*

Getting the car was a breeze. My parents were keen poker players and the monthly Monday night game was a highlight, four couples smoking, chatting and drinking.

It had been a blur of a week, school, rugby and swimming occupying daytime, homework and listening to favourite radio programmes in the evening, PC 49, Much Binding in the Marsh and Round the Horn were special although a lot of the topical British humour went over my head. Throughout, the prospect of Monday night dominated most if not all my quieter moments. Even my parents had been relatively uncritical when I proposed swotting with Alec that evening. They seemed to prefer to regard my apparent enthusiasm for schoolwork and sport, in fact anything unrelated to Crystal as an indication that maybe, thank God, I could be coming to my senses. .

I would park her car, I told Mom, and then walk over to Alec's. Be home round eleven.

The Swimmers had even cut down on meeting for fear that anyone investigating the Great Itching Powder Mystery at Gerry's Gym would have suspicions about a group of lads, which included Lalla, going round as a tightly knit gang.

The feeling of elation, of semi-incoherent euphoria engulfed me as I drove the Morris Minor past the intended neighbour's garage and round the corner towards Parsons Hill.

*

I hooted twice. The door to Rita's house opened and Crystal ran down the garden path, waving. I swallowed deeply. God, was she only a vision!

"Hi Ray, you goin' my way?"

My tongue returned from halfway down my gullet. "For sure, Miss Webber. Wow, don't you look absolutely adorable!"

The waft of her perfume nearly sent my tongue back from where it had only recently emerged. Low cut blouse and loose skirt, a change from the usual uniform of sweater and tight jeans. A silver crucifix dangled on a chain nestling in her cleavage. She snuggled down in the passenger seat, leaned over, hand on my thigh and brushed my lips with her scarlet mouth. I hadn't turned off the engine and my foot accidentally stamped on the accelerator. The Morris jumped forward violently in protest and stalled.

"Hey, where did you learn to drive, pal?"

"Young lady, just hold on to your seats. Here we go!"

Years later, I would always remember the sheer exhilaration as we set off that night, just the two of us, away from the disapproving world. I chose as many back roads as possible, so as to avoid any possible recognition. Past St George's, past the Crusader Ground where Rugby and Cricket Tests were played, down the steep hill of Brickmakers Kloof. This led to Baakens River Valley and South End, a deprived area housing Port Elizabeth's Coloured and Malay population. Then on to King's Beach where the British Royal Family had swum in front of cheering crowds in 1947. By 1948 we had a Nationalist Government, anti-British and pro-apartheid party in power. The hated word only emerged some time later.

At Humewood Beach intersection I stopped at the robots (traffic lights) and reached over to the back seat. "Here Crys, think you can open these two bottles of Castle Lager?" These I'd 'borrowed' from my father's locked liquor cabinet. I knew where my mother kept the keys, on a big bunch she hid from Euphemia and the garden boy. ("The *schwartzes* (blacks) they'll steal anything not locked up!" was her phrase)

"Sure. Got an opener?"

I handed it over. With a snap and a fizz we each held the bottles to our mouths. I wiped foam away with my sleeve, reaching in my pocket. "Want some Wrigleys Juicy Fruit?"

Crystal giggled. "Mind if I finish my beer first?"

"Absolutely." Smiling I gunned the little car forward, past the promenades where hordes of locals strolled together with the thousands of holiday makers in the season. It was important to get through this area as quickly as possible, Port Elizabeth being a relatively small town, recognition of my mother's car could occur all too easily. Past the Summerstrand Hotel and we were out on the darkened Marine Drive. Emboldened by the alcohol, I threw my arm around her shoulders, gently pulling her toward me. There was no resistance and the next thing her head was resting on my shoulder. A hand was considerably higher on my thigh. Unmentionable Things began to happen.

"How far we gonna go, Ray?"

"Er, I think maybe we'll stop at Shelly Beach..."

Her scream of laughter in my ear was so loud that my hand on the wheel slipped, nearly landing us and the Morris in the *fynbos* by the side of the road.

"W-what the hell you laughing at???......oh....OH...I get it ..."

I managed to get the car back on the road, but her hand was pressing deeper into my upper thigh. Desperately I peered into the blackness of the road ahead, pierced only by the dimmed headlights. An unmarked turning appeared almost immediately, a sandy road leading towards a picnic clearing overhung by trees. I swerved into the gap, past a signpost that neither of us bothered to read. The Morris trundled along over jarring bumps. I brought the vehicle to a standstill under the trees. Turned off the lights. A full moon struggled to make its presence felt through the dense branches.

The sudden silence only emphasized the rushing sound of heavy surf on rocks, which could only be a few yards distant, hidden by dense foliage. Turning towards her, the meeting of beery mouths was as violent as it was sweet, well, beery anyway. Pent-up tensions of the days and weeks since our first encounter drained away as limbs, hands lips, tongues searched, rediscovered.

After what seemed an eternity we came up for air, gasping. The Morris windows were all misted over.

"Ray....."

"Crys.......?"

"Think maybe we should have some Wrigleys now?"

"Sure, wait a minute..." I struggled to find the packet in my trouser pocket which was no longer in its normal position then desperately fumbled getting the little white tablets out. We chewed momentarily.

"Ray, you got a blanket?"

"There's one on the back seat."

"Let's go down that little path to the beach....."

"Great idea."

The moonlit beach was a tiny sandy cove between jagged rocks. White-foamed breakers roared and crashed, exploding in giant sparkling jets. Crystal spread the blanket on the sand and lay back, head and neck extended. "Come here to me, my handsome movie star...."

I did as I was told. The night was warm and balmy. Clouds drifted across the face of the moon, from time to time blackening our private little enclave. Clothing ended up in a small pile alongside us. Vainly we tried to stem the rising sap which was threatening to engulf us.

"Wait a minute," I wheezed, "gotta get something else from my pants..."

I saw her smiling, white teeth glimmering. "Isn't this just like that film we saw at the Drive-in, with Burt Lancaster and Deborah Kerr, Ray? From Here to Eternity?"

"Ja, I remember," I mumbled, rummaging amongst the discarded garments. "Got it!" I crawled back triumphantly to my by now impatient lover.

The gentleness with which we had become lovers at Rita Coetzee's house just a few weeks earlier was now overtaken by an urgency, a bestial animal-like coupling, a final commitment that could only be recognised as total belonging.

We lay back exhausted. Full cloud cover had now darkened the sky and all we knew was the roaring surf and our slowly recovering breathing.

Torchlights shattered our perfect paradise. We blinked as beams were shone directly into our eyes. Crystal screamed as she grabbed the edge of the blanket to cover our nakedness.

Two dark uniformed figures loomed up above us as we cowered, shivering now uncontrollably.

A deep rasping growl came from behind the blinding lights. "OK you two little lovebirds....let's have a good look at you!!!!" .

Chapter 12

"Hey, Dirkie, come over here, man. Look at this....two little totty lovebirds having a bleddy good time. Looks like we got here not a minute too soon..."

The torches traversed the length of our cowering figures. I held Crystal tightly to me with one arm, the other hand clutching the blanket. "Please Officer, we're not doing anything wrong," summoning up all the dignity I could muster. I could feel Crystal shaking against me.

Lightbeams found our faces once again. A chubby pimply face leered right up close. Brandy fumes wafted over us. "No Piet, it's OK. They's both white. Jes' let 'em be."

The other giant shape stood over us, staring, shaking his head. "Maybe they's white but what the hell are they doing fucking here on a Coloureds only beach, hey? Tell me that, Dirkie."

Crystal's face was suddenly spotlighted. "Hell, Piet, she's very pretty. So, okay little girl, how old are youse?"

Crystal lifted her chin above the blanket. "Ag, sir, please, I am already eighteen."

"An' what's your name?"

"Crystal, sir. Please let us go. We are very sorry we're on the wrong beach. We didn't see a sign."

The light shone on me. "An you, boy, how old are you?"

I took the lead from Crystal. My Afrikaans was nowhere near as fluent so it came out a bit jumbled. "I'm also eighteen, sir." Mr.

Milland would have been disgusted with my performance. My whole body seemed to be shaking along with Crystal's.

"This chappie is not Afrikaans, Dirkie. What's your name, hey?"

"R-r-raymond, Off-off-officer." I sounded a bit like Lalla on one of his bad days.

Both men laughed raucously. "Raymond? Raaaymond? That's a sissy name. You a sissy, Rayyymond?"

Crystal sat upright. "No, Officer, he is most definitely NOT a sissy. We call him Ray and I wouldn't be here with a sissy anyways...."

The policemen squatted on their haunches, malignant smiles on their faces. "OK, so he's not a sissy, but he's got two names and the two of youse is here stark bleddy naked on a Coloureds only beach in the pitch dark...."

The officer named Dirkie stood up and stretched. "Piet, lissen, I think maybe we've given these kids both a hellovva fright. It's enough, now. Let 'em get dressed and outta here."

But Piet was not in such a lenient mood. "Are you mad, Dirkie? First, I don't think they's eighteen, an' what about the car parked down there by the kaffir picnic spot?" He looked at me accusingly. "You got a driving licence, boy?"

I looked at Crystal questioningly but said nothing. She gave a hardly noticeable shake of her head. There was no way out of this. On a Coloureds only beach, no licence, driving under age, no insurance, someone else's car. What would my parents say? AND OHMIGOD what about Gerry Webber, Crystal's Nazi father?

While I sat numb and silent, Crystal stretched for her bra and blouse, giving the constables an eyeful of her uptilted breasts. She slowly pulled the blouse over her head then dragged her panties and skirt under the blanket, keeping her eyes fixed on the two gawking males. Piet had momentarily forgotten his questions and was standing, swaying slightly, gaze riveted on Crystal's reverse striptease. She stood up, moved closer to him. I saw her swallowing, then, hands on hips, faced the man square on.

"My name is Crystal Webber. My father is Gerry Webber. He owns Gerry's Gymnasium."

Both the uniformed men's mouths dropped open, speechless. "Didja hear that, Piet? Gerry Webber's daughter! Oh hell, man, Gerry bleddy Webber!"

"I heard, Dirkie. So what? What difference does it make?"

My beloved stripper took the initiative. "Please officer, we know we are in trouble but if my father finds out, he'll kill us both!"

I still sat under the blanket, eyes popping from Crystal's humble sweet pleading face to the officers as they tried to digest the situation. There was no question they had consumed copious amounts of Cape Brandy. The smell even over-rode the fresh sea breeze.

Crystal sidled even closer to the younger one. "Dirkie.....can I call you Dirkie? My father has many friends on the PE police force. If he finds out that you put us in jail he will make big trouble. For us, sure, but also for you. We can tell that you guys have drunk an awful lot of brandy tonight."

I could hardly believe what she was attempting. A combination of seduction, threats and blackmail! On two South African Policemen!

Piet, the taller and more threatening of the two regained his former aggressive stance. "You trying to threaten us, you little trollop?"

Crystal gave him her friendliest smile. "Absolutely not, Constable. It's just...., it would be so easy for you to let us off with a warning. We've had a hell of a fright, as Dirkie said. All we wanna do is get dressed and go home. Honestly, my pa would murder us both..."

Piet gestured to his partner. "Dirkie, come let's talk. Over to those rocks."

They wandered away to the edge of the surf. This gave me the chance to grab my clothes and regain some semblance of dignity, almost ending up with my right sandshoe on my left foot. Crystal grabbed my hand as we stood waiting and shivering, in bright moonlight as clouds drifted away.

After some moments of animated argument the officers returned. They grabbed us by the shoulders and marched us off the beach. "Come, you two, let's have a look at this car of yours. Whose car did you say it was?"

I gulped nervously. "Er, my ma's actually. She lets me drive it sometimes. But er ....just to park it in our neighbour's garage up the road. I'm er, getting my learner's licence soon...."

"Oh, so you admit you haven't gotta licence hey?"

I could have kicked myself but they would have found out soon enough anyway. Crystal wasn't too happy with me, though. I could feel her glare right through me. We reached the Morris, parked just beyond a notice which read Coloureds only, "Slegs vir Kleurlinge." We stared at the notice glumly.

Piet jerked me by the collar of my shirt. "Sooo, my little sissy-boy, you can read, can't you? Raaaaymond, what's your surname, hey? And don't mess with me, you hear?"

"Raymond Benjamin, sir. Ray's my nickname for short."

Dirkie chuckled. "I think I'd stick with Ray, wouldn't you, Piet?"

Piet smirked. "Benjamin hey, a little Jewboy. What's a Yid like you doin' with Gerry Webber's daughter? He hates Jews."

Crystal and I looked at each other, then at the two policemen, then down at our feet.

"You two are really in deep shit now, aren't you?" Piet licked his fleshy lips, savouring the irony of the situation. There was little doubt his attitudes were identical to those of Crystal's father.

Suddenly Dirkie piped up. "Benjamin, that your surname, boy?"

I nodded.

"Who's your father?"

"Abie Benjamin, sir."

"Of Benjamin's Men's Outfitters, down there by North End?"

"Yes sir. That's my dad's shop. I work there sometimes."

Piet turned to Dirkie inquiringly. "So his dad's shop is Benjamin's. What's the big deal?"

Dirkie smiled broadly. "No, Piet, man, that's the shop our family have been buying our clothes from for the last twenty years. Old Abie Benjamin, he's one of the really good Yids. Gives us plenty time to pay, always hands out lekker presents every Christmas. My folks got all my clothes there when I was a kid an' I still goes there. No kidding, he's one of the really okay Jews..."

This speech seemed to stop Piet in his tracks. We held our breath to see which way the wind would blow next.

He took out his notebook, apparently deep in intense thought. Took a pen from his pocket, opened the notebook, held the pen there for a moment, looked at the Morris, then at us. Then put the pen and notebook back in his pocket. Dirkie stared at his partner, obviously his superior, a smile still on his face.

"What you smiling that stupid smile for, Dirkie? You look like a moron, grinning like a baboon. These kids have committed a whole string of offences here, apart from the danger of lying here *kaalgat*, buck-naked on a Coloureds only beach. They haven't seen half of what we've seen, what drunk kaffirs and coloureds get up to, specially if they find a nice pretty Afrikaans girl all naked. You kids are mad, you know?"

We stood there, nodding sheepishly.

Then he smiled, exposing black gaps in his front teeth. "Now, you two, lissen to me now and lissen bleddy good." He looked directly at Crystal's chest which was rising and falling rapidly, her crucifix glinting in the moonlight. "Youse are right, Dirkie an' me, we's had a few brandy an' cokes tonight, more than we should. But because of that we's in a good mood. An' 'cos we's in a good mood, an' also 'cos on account of who your fathers are, we's gonna forget we saw you here tonight."

Crystal and I could barely restrain ourselves from hugging them both and each other, but somehow we managed, keeping almost straight faces.

Piet wasn't finished. "For your own good, both of youse, an' I'm talkin' good sense here now, you gotta stop this bullshit between a bleddy Jood and a nice Afrikaans girl. It just won't work, not here in South Africa. An' I bet you're right, your parents would half- kill the pair of youse." He gestured toward the Morris. "Now we's gonna follow you kids back to town an' you better drive bleddy carefully, Mr. Sissy Jewboy Rayyyymond Benjamin, cos we gonna be on your tail all the way. You hear me?"

I nodded energetically and rushed round to open the passenger door for Crystal. To my astonishment she sidled up to Piet and planted a kiss on his semi-shaven cheek. Then did the same to Dirkie. "Thank you very much. We are very happy. Maybe I can get you some complimentary tickets to Gerry's Gym, hey?"

The constables nodded enthusiastically. "That would be great," Dirkie grinned. "Just leave them at the desk of the Mount Road Police Station for Dirkie Smit and Piet van der Walt."

I started the engine. Just as I was about to put the car in gear, Piet knocked at the window. I wound it down. The brandy fumes all but paralysed me. "You, Benjamin, make sure you never touch this or any other car till you gets your full licence. If I hear that you have been driving before that you will go inside, father or no father. Clear?"

"Very clear, Officer van der Walt. And thank you once again. Baie baie dankie."

With an enormous whoosh of relief I reversed the Morris back down the sandy road then on to the Marine drive, heading back to town. The lights of the Police car kept a constant vigil just fifty yards or so behind us until we reached the Humewood robots. With a flashing of their headlights they turned off towards the airport while we kept on towards Parson's Hill and Rita's house.

We had driven the entire journey in total silence. I stopped the car at the end of Rita's road, looked at my watch then at Crystal who still sat silently looking straight ahead, an indecipherably glum expression on her face. Gently I took her hand which she just let lie limply in mine.

"Crys, it's only quarter to nine. Would milady like to go to the Drive-in?" in my best Hollywood accent.

She just shook her head. Tears were staining her cheeks. I hadn't noticed. "Hey, Crys, what's the matter? I know we've both had a hell of a shock but thanks to you, they let us off. You were totally unbelievable. Terrific. First getting them to ogle you with your little striptease and all then coming out with your dad's name, cool as you like. You had them drooling..."

"Ray, I know, I know all that." She wiped her cheeks with a tissue. "We were lucky also that the one knew your father...but....."

"But what"?

"It's what that arse Piet said about us, you know, you being Jewish and me Afrikaans, that it would never work..."

"And that's all he is, Crystal, an arse. Don't tell me that what he said made a difference to you. It certainly didn't to me. You know, about us, I mean."

"Didn't it say anything to you, Ray? Didn't it show you how difficult it's gonna be for us? Not that we didn't already see it in both our folks attitudes..."

I pondered this for a while. Then shook my head vigorously. "No, no, it's all of them who are wrong. They've lived their lives in this hateful system, black and white hating each other, Jew and Christian so suspicious that they think apartheid is the answer. It just isn't. It's up to us, the young ones who should be breaking down all this bullshit, people like you and me..."

Crystal said nothing, just turned her tear-stained face towards me, a little smile forming at the corner of her delicious mouth. "My, oh my, Mr. Milland, you're a real smooth talker when you wanna be, hey?" She pulled me toward her. I tasted the salty smoothness of her cheeks as our lips and mouths met. The gearshift lever of the Morris played an insignificant role as we stayed locked together for what seemed like an eternity.

"Ray?"

"Ja... I. mean....yes, Crystal....?"

"D'you wanna get in the back seat?"

"You mean, by myself?"

The merry sound of her giggle filled the Morris' interior. "Don't be stupid, man, this gear knob's getting in the way..." With the street light barely illuminating the scene, Crystal at first failed to notice my broad grin. "Uh-oh, my movie star's makin' jokes now, hey?"

"Took you a while to catch on, though, didn't it?" I gently disentangled myself, switched the ignition on. "Lissen, its best we don't stay here near Rita's. Tell you what, the Old Grey Rugby ground's not far, just up the road. Less chance of anyone lookin' in on us, let alone Dirkie and Piet. I think we've had enough surprises for one night."

"Ja, you're bleddy right." Giggling she squeezed my gearlever hand tightly. "Let's go, doll!"

Minutes later we bumped down a dirt road into trees overlooking the playing fields. The night was now almost totally black, moon and stars engulfed by clouds. The new neon lights on Cape Road in the distance cast a ghostly orange glow. We stood leaning against the front bonnet. She moved around to face me, arms around my neck. No doubt where pressure was being applied. And being responded to.

"How's about us getting in the back seat, Ray?" she murmured, throatily. "Or are we waiting for a rugger match to start?"

I opened the door. "After you, Miss Webber."

"Push the front seats forward. Gives us a bit more leg room....."

I did as I was told. Until that moment I had found many things in life challenging. Like swimming the 25 yard length of St George's Baths underwater, tackling Alec Goldfarb running full-tilt towards the tryline or facing Mark Sher's bodyline fast bowling. But very high on that list would be achieving more than frustrated passionate wrestling in the back of my mom's Morris Minor that night. Especially after the unbridled loving down on the beach earlier. It was as if we needed to expunge the memory of the encounter with the two policemen, so devastating the afterglow of our lovemaking. But the back seat just wasn't designed with Crystal and me in mind.

"Ray" came her disembodied voice in the blackness.

"What?" I gasped, coming up for air.

"Give me your hand."

Gently she guided me, instructed me. Leaned back until, astute pupil that I had become, her breathing accelerated rapidly, body arching with a series of shrill yelps.Then subsided, relaxed, bending her legs up to her chest. My poor hand embedded somewhere there in paradise.

"Jesus, Ray! You're brilliant, you know that?" Her eyes glowed in the orange gloom. Smiling she pushed me back into the corner. "Now, it's your turn, Mr. Sexy. Just lie back."

I felt my belt undone, trousers unzipped. Closed my eyes, not sure what to expect. The touch of her hands I was familiar with. But what followed drove me into sheer tumultuous ecstasy. It did not last long. She sat back, looking at me with a curiously triumphant smile. "So, Mr. Milland, you OK?"

I could only nod, eyes burning with sweat. "You're really something, Miss Webber" was all I could manage.

She moved across, nestling her head into my shoulder. "Almost as good as doing it properly, doncha think?"

In the dark I could just about make out the glint of contented amusement in her eyes. Couldn't think of a response.

What seemed like an eternity passed in silence. We may both have dozed off.

Finally, I forced myself regretfully to look at my watch. "Oh crikey, half past eleven! Better get the car back fast." Only then did I realise that we'd been sitting in the misted-over Morris for over two hours!

Clambering into the front seat I hurriedly drove back to Rita Coetzee's house. Crystal leaned toward me, brushing my mouth with her lips. Seemingly in no hurry to break the mood. The thought of my parents starting to phone Alec, Hospitals and Police in that order galvanised me into action. I held her face gently for a moment, then opened my door to the outside world. Walked round, opened her door like a proper Hollywood gent, like she was some kind of princess.

"Hey, what a gentleman!"

I walked her to the gate. After another breathless clinch she turned, blowing a farewell kiss then started walking up the garden path towards the house. "I'll phone you tomorrow, OK, Ray? Same time?"

I nodded, stood for a moment straightening my clothing then with a deep inhalation, plunged back into the car and trundled off into the night. Looked at my watch. Past midnight I cursed aloud as I approached the corner of our road.

Outside our house stood a police car, blue lights flashing. All our front room lights were blazing.

"Bloody Hell!" I sat motionless, hands glued to the steering wheel. I switched off the headlamps. Panic started deep in my stomach ending with tightness in my throat. Beads started to roll down my forehead. Hammering deep in my chest. What could possibly have happened? Why were the police at our house this late at night? Surely my parents couldn't have, wouldn't have panicked that much? Had they looked in the neighbours' garage? Even so, why the Police? They knew I'd driven the car. Would they suspect me of using the car without a licence?

Too many possibilities for my fevered imagination to cope with. Dirkie and Piet, had they changed their minds, reported us after all? After accepting Crystal's offer of tickets to Gerry's Gym? Was that them at the house? Surely not!

What else could it be? But in any case what to do? In a semi-hypnotic state I found myself reversing the car back round the corner, heading to Alec's house. Alec would know what to do. Maybe come up with some way out.

Halfway there I realised going to Alec's wasn't logical. All he would have said was that he didn't know where I was and no, we weren't studying together.

"Get a hold, calm down, man," I whispered out loud. If it was Dirkie and Piet there was nothing for it but to go and face them. If my parents had reported me and the car missing then maybe that was why the police were there, but surely they wouldn't have, not with all their poker friends there? For the life of me I couldn't think of a simple explanation.

I stopped, turned the car around. Sat for what seemed like an eternity. Only one thing to do. Go back, face the music. Slowly I pulled my scrambled senses together. My parents would be livid about the car and about Crystal. The entire Port Elizabeth Jewish Community would know about it by lunchtime tomorrow, but well, so what? Was that so bad?

"Shit! Shit! Shit!" I slammed the gear lever into first and headed back home. This was shaping up to be the worst night of my life after being far and away the best. Tried vainly to picture Crystal's face as she'd blown that kiss. Some night!

I cut the engine, free-wheeled down the incline towards the brilliantly lit house. No point parking the car up the road. Stopped behind the Police car. Climbed out, locking the Morris carefully. Slowly walked the marathon up to our front door.

Key in the lock, Pushed the door open. My parents in their dressing gowns. Expressions on their faces was indescribable, rage, hurt, anxiety..... a full house, their poker friends would have said.

"So here you are at last, you bloody little tstotsi," my mother screamed. My father said nothing, just gestured for me to follow him into the living room. At the dining table sat a stern-faced sergeant of the South African Police. Not Dirkie and Piet, I was momentarily relieved to notice. But that didn't last long. I tried in vain to gain some idea of how much shit had hit the fan.

The policeman broke the silence. "So this is your young troublemaker, is it?"

No-one said a word, all waiting and staring in broiling anger. My father seemed fixated on my groin.

I looked down, saw the undone zipper. "C-c-can I please go to the toilet?" I didn't wait for permission, just rushed out of the room. Not sure whether anyone else had noticed. Or the stain around my crotch.

"Jesus!" I swore at myself in the mirror, did up the zipper. With tightly gritted teeth strode back to face the Inquisition, hands clasped in front of the tell-tale area.

"Mom and dad, I'm sorry about taking the car. I haven't any excuses."

My parents looked at each other, shaking their heads despairingly. "We wish it was only the car, Raymond. That's bad enough but....."

I looked at the policeman in complete bemusement. "Then what..?."

The Policeman opened his notebook. "I am Detective Sergeant Rudolphus van Breda from Mount Road Police Station. We have been making enquiries about the criminal act at Gerry Webber's Gymnasium on September 14th last month. Tonight we interviewed Alec Goldfarb, Mark Sher, and Lesley Jackson. It seems from what they tell us that you four all conspired to cause chaos at the Gym by putting itching and sneezing powder in the weightlifter's resin. No, we know you weren't there, your friends were loyal and stuck up for you, but it appears that this was a revenge act on Mr. Webber because he assaulted you when he found you with his daughter, Crystal. Is that correct, so far?"

I nodded, miserably.

"Mr. Webber, who was seriously injured, remembers the young blond lad, Lesley Jackson, who recently became a member of the Gym and clearly states that he and the other two were in the front row that night, then left quickly as the powder exploded in everyone's faces. We also interviewed the native boy cleaner, Samson Ndebele a second time and he says he helped your three friends escape into the street."

The sergeant folded his notebook away and stared accusingly at me. "I needn't tell you that Mr. Webber is a highly respected member of the Port Elizabeth Community. If what your friends say is true, there may have been a case of assault against him for his attack on you but as that was not reported at the time, there is not much we can do now at this late stage. However, we cannot allow the action of your friends with your connivance to go unpunished. As you are all juveniles, you will be required to appear at the Juvenile Court in due course. Now, of course, this evening I come here and what do I find? Your parents do not know where you are, your mother's car is missing and you come home bold as brass, and apologise to them! Well, young man, I have to warn you and your parents, that driving without a license and insurance is a criminal act." He turned to face my parents. "What's more, allowing a minor to drive, even such a minimal distance as between your house and the garage up the road makes you as guilty as your son. Obviously I can't take action against you, boy, for stealing a car belonging to your mother, but I can tell you that your name is down in our Police file, you hear me? From now on you had better be squeaky clean, Master Benjamin and take your driving test pretty smartish. Also, when you do you had better know your stuff inside out because you are a marked man as far as we are concerned."

My father, pale-faced, stood up and cleared his throat. "Sergeant, you can take my word that this will not happen again. Until Raymond gets his license he will not touch the car again." He looked sideways at my mother. "And Rosie, that means no more letting him park the car. That's partly what caused all this mess! But Raymond, if our begging you last week not to continue with this Webber girl wasn't enough, then I'm sure that this fiasco will bring that episode to an end, both from our side and from Mr. Webber's point of view."

In the circumstances, faced by the Sergeant and my outraged parents, there was little or nothing for me to say. I merely nodded, head down and mumbled. "Yes, dad, of course. You're right. It won't happen again. I'm very sorry, Sergeant for all the trouble."

The Policeman stood, picked up his hat and marched to the door. "I'm sure your parents will take very stern action with you so you won't ever think of pulling stunts like this again. I know what I would do if you was my kid. You wouldn't sit for a month. Now is all of this absolutely clear?"

Crestfallen nods all round.

"OK then. I will see you and your three friends at the Juvenile Court in due course and I will overlook the extremely serious waste of Police time. I bid you all good night."

With that he stalked to the front door leaving me to face the combined wrath of father and mother. Strange though it may seem, the only thought in my head at that moment was that I would never, never give Crystal up, no matter what.

Chapter 13

The forbidding colossus that constituted the North End Law Courts had been sufficient to instil an almighty fear in all our hearts. A fortress-like redbrick building surrounded by an open concrete square, it overlooked Port Elizabeth's busy main shopping artery, a street that came in from Johannesburg in the far north. The name changed several times, Princes Street to Queens Street then Main Street leading to the majestic Victorian edifice of City Hall and Market Square.

I had not spoken to or seen Crystal since the newspapers published our four names as the perpetrators of the Gerry's Gym Sneezing Outrage. She had not been to St Georges Baths and all my attempts to contact her either direct or through Rita had failed dismally. Three weeks had gone by and the fact that I had lied to her about my knowledge of the Swimmers revenge, as we liked to call it, preyed heavily on my mind.

In the meantime, my parents had consulted lawyers on my behalf and were assured that at worst we would get a severe reprimand, a fine and quite possibly strokes of a cane. The fact that Gerry had previously assaulted me led our family lawyer, Sam Leibowitz, to believe that there might be some grounds for leniency.

So there we stood, the Swimmers, shoulder to shoulder in the dock of the Juvenile court. Two days of argument had passed during which the prosecutor and our lawyer had tried to convince Judge Sharwood, a stern yet avuncular-looking man, on the one hand that we were good-for-nothing hooligans who deserved pretty harsh treatment, and on the other that it was a practical joke, a mild revenge for the beating Gerry Webber had inflicted on me which had gone spectacularly wrong.

We were very aware of Gerry's brooding presence in the public enclosure, especially as he was being wheeled in and out in a wheelchair. Our parents too sat in the public gallery well away from the Webber tribe, but by this time knowledge of the initial violence towards me had softened their response to our wrongdoing. My parents had listened with some sympathy as I described the beating I had sustained. Mercifully Crystal had not been called nor had she been anywhere near the court

But now the talking was over. The Judge had listened to our apologetic statements, had heard Gerry Webber's hate-filled tirade, and statements from some of the customers who had suffered the worst had been read out to the court.. He was now about to proclaim his decision.

"All Please Stand.......*Almal Asseblief Opstaan*!"

Judge Sharwood drew his black robe over his shoulders and stared sternly down at us as we stood solemnly awaiting our fate.

"You boys have been playing with fire and quite a few people have been burnt. Several people were hospitalised and Mr. Webber is on crutches and restricted to a wheelchair for ten weeks because of your stupid practical joke. I should revise that. This was not a joke, this was a serious misdemeanour, intended to cause havoc in a crowded auditorium. I think you four can count yourselves fortunate that in the panic, no-one was trampled to death. That could certainly have been the case and you would have been up before a much higher court and on much more serious charges."

Silence pervaded the courtroom as the Judge continued. "Although the motivation for this attack was described by you, Raymond Benjamin, as revenge for Mr. Webber's assault on you weeks earlier, may I remind you all that, firstly, two wrongs do not make a right, and secondly, in the absence of testimony by Mr. Webber's daughter, Crystal, it was merely your word against his. Your friends, Alec Goldfarb and Lesley Jackson testified to finding you semi-conscious after the attack. Having listened to Mr. Webber's account, I am inclined to believe that you indeed suffered at the hands of a man who, because of his size and profession, should never employ his superior strength to inflict injury on anyone let alone someone much smaller and less able to defend himself as you undoubtedly were that day. In these circumstances, and bearing in mind Mr. Webber's very obvious anti-semitic bias, I am inclined to be somewhat lenient in the punishment I feel is justified in this case."

A strangled cough and grunt came from somewhere in the public gallery, almost certainly in the vicinity of Gerry Webber and his wife.

The Judge continued unabashed. "Because of your age, I will not saddle you four with criminal records. You will each pay compensation of £50 to Mr. Webber, you will meet the costs of the court and you are hereby restricted from entering or being within 100 yards of Gerry Webber's Gymnasium for a period of three years. This applies equally to Mr. Webber's family home and especially to you, Raymond Benjamin. You are hereby prohibited from having any contact with Mr. Webber OR his entire family, and that includes his daughter Crystal, for the same period. Do I make myself clear?"

Four heads nodded in unison, a deep gulp from me.

The Judge turned his head towards the public gallery. "I realise that this case has exposed deep hatred and prejudice amongst the white community which saddens me. Our country suffers sufficient international opprobrium because of our apartheid laws which we regard as necessary for the present due to the unique mixture of races in South Africa. But amongst the whites in our town, I find it deplorable that such animosity exists." He stared pointedly at Gerry Webber. "So I also request, although I cannot order, that Gerry Webber, his family and associates shall not seek out or attack these four lads or their families. I hereby instruct our Police to maintain vigilance with regard to the relationships between these families and to report any infringement which I assure you all, will be dealt with harshly to the full extent of the Law. Case dismissed."

With a flurry of the black gown, he was gone.

*

The scene at our house later was hardly that of wild celebration. I maintained a cold silence, answering questions with nods or shakes of the head. My parents seemed to convey a sense of relief, whether because of the relatively benign outcome or the ban placed on any contact between Crystal and me, I couldn't be sure. Probably both. In any event I was totally uncommunicative to everyone and breathed a grateful sigh when all the other parents and my partners in crime had gone home and I could hide myself away in my room.

Larry as usual was at his most irritating. "Ray, Ray, Ray's in trouble, ha ha!" He made a face and ran up the stairs ahead of me.

"Get lost, you little shit."

"RAYMOND SWORE..... MUM! RAYMOND USED THE S-WORD.......MUM!!!" He stood defiantly at the top of the stairs. With possibly too much force I pushed him bodily out of the way and he staggered against the opposite wall letting out a piercing yell.

Seconds later my parents came tearing up the stairs. "What happened? Larry, what's the matter? Stop screaming and tell me." My mother grabbed my by now hysterical brother and tried to placate him.

"What happened with Larry?" my father wanted to know. "We haven't got enough *tsorris* on our heads already, the two of you have got to fight like an animals?"

"Dad, I didn't need him jeering and laughing. He knows that there's trouble and just wanted to get right under my skin like he always does with his whining. I didn't hurt him, honestly."

"YOU DID, YOU PUSHED ME HARD AGAINST THE WALL! YOU'RE A BIG BULLY!"

As I moved toward my room, Larry tore out of my mother's grip and launched himself at me. "YOU BULLY! YOU LIAR! I WISH YOU HAD GONE TO JAIL!"

"I've had all I can take from you, you miserable little pipsqueak." I merely slammed the door in his face and lay on my bed. After a few minutes during which Larry's tantrum subsided outside my room, there was a knock at my door. Enter my father. He seated himself on the chair next to my desk, "Raymond, can we talk?"

"Don't feel much like talking at the moment, dad. I really didn't hurt Larry. He really is a spoiled brat and a nasty one too."

"I don't want to talk about Larry. He's only ten years old and will grow out of these tantrums."

"He just seems to hate me, always having a moan about me to you and mom."

"Look, Ray, let's leave Larry for the moment. I want to talk about this whole business..."

"Dad, I really don't feel like discussing anything right now..."

"Well, I'm your father so I'm going to say my little bit and then leave you in peace or misery whatever. All I want to say is that I watched you through this court case and I came to realise something. I realised that you couldn't care less about the penalty or the judge or the outcome. All you were thinking about was this girl. Am I right?"

I turned on my side and looked at this kindly man, whose main aim in life was to give his family a secure and trouble-free life. Who was having great difficulty coping with the events of the past few weeks and months. My heart went out to him. I nodded "Yes, dad, you're quite right. All I could think about was Crystal. Sorry if the truth hurts you but you mentioned it first."

"Look, Raymond, all we said about *shikses*, well, it's how we are, where we've come from, and the prejudice runs deep, almost as deep as in your friend Mr. Webber. But watching you, I realised how deep this attachment had grown and I want to apologise for our harsh behaviour. Your mother gets a little hysterical and over the top sometimes but as we've said before, in this society mixed relationships are the exception and very seldom work out. You know all the examples we've thrown at you but..."

"Dad..." I wiped damp tears from my eyes, "that doesn't mean it will always be that way. It doesn't mean that just because things are difficult here in South Africa, that elsewhere in the world things might not be a lot more tolerant."

"So, you'd look elsewhere in the world, would you? Maybe so. Things here in South Africa aren't so kosher, I know, what with all these people who supported the Nazis, and one day the *schwartzes* will take over. Maybe the future here isn't so rosy but all I want to say to you now, I know you're hurting and I recognise that not seeing Crystal again is a huge blow. But listen to me, son, you've got things to accomplish...... Matric to pass, it's September now, only two months to go before your exams and to get into Dental School like you were planning. You know you need a first class pass. All these things are very important right now. So try to get your mind on to these goals. I won't say there's lots of other fish in the sea because at the moment you certainly don't want to hear that. Let a few weeks pass and maybe things will start to look different. Just remember that we love you and want the best for you. And that's the end of the lecture."

I could see the moisture in the corners of his eyes behind the spectacles and reached out to him. He came and sat beside me on the bed. I sat up and threw my arms around him. After a while he stood up and gave me the saddest smile I'd ever seen from him. Without a further word he turned and walked out the door. I got up and went to sit at my desk. I could see the sea in the distance, Algoa Bay, with ships out at anchor. I let my mind drift, closed my eyes and tried to summon up visions of the future, but all that appeared were blurred visions of Crystal, her smile, her mouth, her eyes crinkling with laughter, and sometimes that passionate look she gave me which.... "OH bloody hell.... I don't even have a single picture of her!"

My head in my hands, I let it all out and cried.

Chapter 14

December 1959

A huge crowd had gathered outside the E.P. Herald newspaper offices. The Eastern Cape Province Matriculation results were due to be made public at noon so literally hundreds of our contemporaries were pressing against each other trying to get as close as possible to the large board on which the lists would be posted. My fellow swimmers were all there, Alec, Mark and Lalla. Being during the Christmas holidays and because we were all now school-leavers, no school uniforms were visible. Only t-shirts, shorts, sandals and worried expressions.

We hung back at the periphery. Alec, Mark and I were confident of good results whilst Lalla was hoping for a University Pass which would enable him to get to Rhodes University to study Pharmacy. Alec and Mark had both been accepted at Cape Town University to do Medicine, whilst I had been offered a place at Wits University in Johannesburg for Dentistry. It all of course depended on the results which were going up any minute.

"Hi, guys!" Rita Coetzee appeared suddenly in her usual uniform of tight jeans and bulging t-shirt. She hugged each one of us in turn, saving a deep meaningful glance for me. "How're you all feeling? Confident?"

We nodded nervously. "N-n-n-not r-r-really..." Lalla stammered. "Hope I scrape a Varsity p-p-pass..."

Rita giggled, tossing her wild blonde curls. "Sure you will, Lalla. You're a brainbox. Me, I'll be lucky if I just get an ordinary pass, but no matter, I'm gonna be a hairdresser, so all I need is my hands and my good looks!"

I had seen Rita several times at the Baths since the Court Case, repeatedly asking her to arrange some kind of contact with Crystal. "Not possible" had been Crystal's response. I had all but given up. Crystal was forbidden to go to the Baths and was working part-time at the Gym so that Gerry could keep tabs on her.

Rita pulled me to one side. "Ray, can I have a quick word?"

"Sure. What's up?"

"Lissen, Ray, I know you've been on at me all the time to get Crys to meet you. Believe me I've tried but she is so scared of her old man that she just kept on saying it was out of the question. For both your sakes."

"Yes, I realise that. And so?" My heart was beginning to beat like a little drum in my chest.

"Look, Ray, I've seen you two together. I knows you're both hurting, not seeing each other so I suggested to Crys that today maybe you guys could get together here amongst the crowd."

I could hardly breathe. "Where? Where is she?"

"She's at the gym till the results come out then she told Gerry that she's gonna come down to the EP Herald and meet me. So the two of you can sort of disappear for a while, maybe celebrate your results together." She gave me this wicked all-knowing wink.

Just then the crowd started to press forward. Cries of jubilation rose from some, tears from others. A large notice had been pinned to the board and bodies jammed forward in attempts to get close. The four of us and Rita waited until the crowd started to thin then made our way to the Notice.

It is quite extraordinary how one's name explodes off a notice board as if it was a neon sign. There it was, Benjamin, Raymond..... First Class Matriculation Exemption. I let out a yelp of delight, "MADE IT!!!!!" to everyone and no-one.

The five of us grabbed hold of each other and kissed and hugged. We'd all got the results we were hoping for. My first thought was to telephone the shop to tell my folks. Then suddenly there she was, right in front of me. I couldn't believe my eyes. "Crystal, hey, er what a surprise...." I was totally tongue-tied. She looked exquisite, smiling with the sultry look in her eyes that I had grown to know so well, totally focussed, just staring at me.

"Hi Ray, it's been a long time..." She reached out and touched my hand. "Congratulations! First Class Pass, hey? But I never doubted you'd get it."

"And you too, Crys. I saw your name at exactly the same time as mine. I guess I even looked for yours first!"

We just stood there amongst the heaving crowd, looking at each other. Then, suddenly a violent carefree impulse convulsed me. I threw my arms round her and kissed her full on the lips. All the pent-up longing that had built in me during the two month separation exploded to the surface and, as I felt her responding, my arms gripped even tighter. In amongst the general celebrations, we were like the eye of the storm, with gales lashing around us. We would probably still have been there hours later had Rita not tugged at us. "Come on you two lovebirds, let's go down to the Clifton Hotel and have a beer to celebrate.....!"

*

The Clifton Hotel, known to all as the Cliff, is a seedy run-down hotel down one of the side alleys off Main Street. Used mainly by commercial travellers and sailors from ships in port, the off-street bar or *kroeg* is patronised mostly by heavy drinkers. The lounge bar though is reserved for residents and females are allowed. The barman was a friend of Rita's so we were allowed to have our beer shandies in relative comfort.

Alec stood up and raised his glass. "So folks, here's to the Swimmers and our two lovely ladies. Here's to all of our futures..."

We all sipped at the frothy brew. I was aware that Crystal was distinctly uncomfortable, looking over her shoulder every few seconds. "What's the matter, Crys? You look worried..."

She leaned over, whispering softly. "It's just that I'm very nervous. You know my dad knows everyone in this town an' here I am sitting drinking with the guys who caused him such grief."

I saw her point. "You're right. For sure you shouldn't be doing this here in public and especially," I gave a knowing wink, "not with us juvenile delinquents!" I took hold of her hand and squeezed. "Just the same, it's so good to see you again. You can't imagine how much I've missed you...."

She returned the pressure. "Ja, me too, Ray. I dunno how we managed to swot for the exams after all the hullabaloo but I 'spose in a funny way, it was better. We were sort of forced to sit an' concentrate on the exams."

"I was sure you were never gonna forgive me for lying, knowing the plan for the gym thing but what could I have done? That night was so special for me and if I'd admitted what I knew you would have ....it would have changed things so much, I just couldn't....."

Crystal leaned over, her lips brushing my cheek. "Mr. Milland, in this movie the hero is allowed one white lie an' that's all. I realised afterwards when the shit hit the fan why you hadn't said you knew about the itching powder. I admit I was a bit mad for a while. Hell, after my pa beat you up, he really deserved what he got. But if you ever lie to me again, it's over, you hear me?" She turned to Rita. "Lissen, Rita, I gotta get back to the Gym. My dad will be tearing his plaster cast off if I'm not back soon."

Rita stood up, gave Alec a broad smile and kissed Crystal on the cheek. "OK, Crys, if you don't mind I'll stay on here with the boys for a while an' celebrate. Talk to you later."

"I'll walk you to the entrance," I said, keeping hold of her hand as if it was part of me.

As we neared the main door she turned, eyes glistening."What're we gonna do, Ray?"

"Wish I knew, Crys. I only know that life's been hell not being able to see you or look forward to meeting with you. You got any ideas?"

She looked anxiously up and down the side street. "Tell you what. My dad's coming out of plaster this weekend and then we're going off to the Kirkwood farm for Christmas. When we come back I'll be getting ready to go to Stellenbosch University. So if we are gonna see each other it's gotta be early next week. I think dad feels that he's put an end to us now so he can relax about it a bit. But it'll have to be during the day, he's wise to my sleeping over at Rita's!"

I had a sudden brainwave. "OK, here's what we can do. My folks are both busy at the shop this time of year and Larry's earning some pocket money doing chores for them down in North End. Also they take Marty with them to the shop on a Monday as its maid's afternoon off. So what about you coming over to my place, say this Monday afternoon?"

She bit her lip. "That's very dangerous, Ray. What if someone, say, like your neighbours, see me? Everyone knows about us, what then?"

"You wear a disguise, baseball cap, dark glasses, ride your bike fast, straight into our garage and then same way out."

Crystal pondered for a few seconds then gave me one of her looks that said it all. "OK, Mr. Milland, you're on. I can make an excuse for the afternoon somehow."

The old excitement jetted through me. "You know where I live?"

She laughed uproariously. "Course I do, idjit. I've often ridden past your house wondering what it's like inside your big mansion." She clapped her hands together. "And now I'm gonna find out how you rich Jewish people live......." Her hand shot to her mouth, face reddening in embarrassment. "Oh, Ray, sorry, man, I didn't mean anything ..."

I slapped her on the backside. "Crystal, that's what I mean, you should be able to say that to me, and I should be able to tease you because of your *verkrampte* racist old man. It's gotta be easy between us so's we can say whatever we like to each other." I pecked her gently on the cheek. "Now you better get going before someone sees us together. See you Monday, you gorgeous creature(in my best Millandese)."

She hugged me close, nuzzled my ear then a full deep kiss smack on the lips.

"Bout two o'clock, loverboy?"

"The garage door will be open... just ride straight in." I watched her walk up towards Main Street, her undulating strides filling me with delightful imaginings.

*

The garage door was wide open. I sat in the entrance hall, watching anxiously through the window. The conditions were favourable, house empty, street deserted. The weekend had dragged by infuriatingly slowly. My parents had celebrated my First Class pass with continuing drinks, vastly over-catered food amidst joyous family gatherings. I felt some sympathy for brother Larry, who now was being assailed with remarks like 'there's something for you to aim for, young Larry. What an example you've got to live up to' and so on from various aunts, uncles and indeed both our parents. To which Larry gave his usual petulant frown and made some excuse to be elsewhere. Marty didn't help either being the apple of my parents' eyes. Larry's attitude towards me was so resentful that I simply ignored him. In the midst of all the festivities my poor middle brother adopted an almost invisible position.

I tried my best to sound enthusiastic and, to tell the truth, the prospect of going up to the Golden City of Johannesburg did fill me with excitement and not a little apprehension, leaving the warm cosseted family nest. But over-riding it all was that auburn-curly-head and provocative smile, the openly inviting eyes that had dominated my consciousness for the last six months. The thought of being separated for our University courses was still vaguely in the future, to be dealt with as and when. For now, just the sight of a masked figure on a bicycle was the centre of my universe.

Suddenly there she was. With a slight wobble she steered her bike up the slope of our cricket-pitch-driveway and into the garage. I leapt through the small door that led from the hall, tugged the sliding door closed and helped Crystal stow the bike in the corner next to the collapsed table tennis table. She was wearing a full length raincoat, a sunhat and dark glasses which completely hid her identity from the world. I did not allow her even a second to divest herself of the disguise but we were in each other's arms right there in the darkened garage.

After a breathless clinch which could have lasted for ever as far as I was concerned, we came up for air. The scent she was wearing, mixed with the feminine aroma of her body after the strenuous cycle ride was intoxicating, to say the least. I led her through to the hall and, noticing her wide-eyed survey of the surroundings, made a sweeping bow. "Welcome, Miss Webber, to the Benjamin residence. Wouldst Mademoiselle like a conducted tour?"

With a mock curtsey Crystal took my arm. "Yes please sir, but only a shortened version, if that's OK?"

Very aware that she was comparing each room to her own home, I made facetious comments as we progressed through lounge, dining room, kitchen and breakfast rooms. Then coyly ushered her up the banistered staircase. "That's my folks' bedroom, Larry's room, Marty's room and uh, this is my room."

She walked in and over to the window. "Wow, you can even see the sea from here."

I nodded, proudly. "Ja. I love watching the ships out in Algoa Bay, they often anchor out there.. One day it's gonna be me on one of those ships." I looked deep into those almond shaped eyes, "maybe with you on my arm, who knows?"

Crystal laughed, perhaps a little too gaily. "Nice idea, Ray but there's a lot of stuff in the way. We gotta qualify and then there's your folks and mine....."

"Don't think I don't know all that but you know something, before I met you all I could think of was going up to Varsity, getting my degree then travelling to Europe having a good time, skiing, listening to Jazz, all that stuff. Now, I guess, what seems more important right at this moment, and don't think I'm nuts or anything..... I just don't wanna do any of that alone."

She didn't say anything then, looked at me with a sad little smile, then pulled the curtains across, throwing the room into an eerie half-light. Sat down on the bed and reached out for my arm, pulled me gently to her. The tenderness soon gave way to an urgency, as clothes were scattered, all the tensions and frustrations of the past months dissolved in moments, the mutual knowledge that this was right, no matter who or what tried to obstruct us, somehow we would find a way.

We lay side by side, hands entwined, staring at the patterned shadows on the ceiling.

"I like the sound of your dream, my movie star. I'd like to share it with you but...."

"No buts, Crys, we'll manage. We've survived two months now. Being in different towns will be difficult but with a goal like that to keep us going....Think you can get through the in between times?"

Crystal leaned over, kissed me gently on the lips. "If you can, lover boy, I sure as hell am gonna try." Looked at her watch. "Now before the dream ends in early catastrophe I'd better get outta here before your folks, Larry, whoever, gets back. Where's Marty, by the way?"

"You've forgotten. I told you before. Its maid's day off. My folks take him down to the shop, showing him off to all the customers. He's a really cute little guy."

"And where are you supposed to be?"

I hesitated. "I told them that I was bringing you back to the house so I couldn't help them at the business today...."

A pillow came flying across the bed, catching me full in the face. "You are such a bullshitter, MISTER MILLAND, and I hate you. Now what's the truth?"

I grinned, slowly pulling on my shirt. "Actually I agreed to share the shop duties with Larry. Neither of us is much good in the selling department and the customers always ask for my dad anyway. Both of us there together just get in each other's way."

Smiling, she busied herself tidying the bed. "You're getting nearly as good as Rita and me at arranging things, aintcha?" Looked at her watch. "Oh Crikey, it's half past four, get me outta here... Lissen, like I told you, we's off to the farm in Kirkwood on Friday so I just dunno if....."

I grabbed her by the shoulders, looked deep into her eyes. "Crystal Webber, I love you. They are not gonna take you away from me, that's for definite."

She nodded. "Yes, I believe you, Ray. And I feel exactly the same about you, so there!"She stuck out her tongue suggestively then laughed." I will try phone you before we go on Friday. Can you be by the phone so your folks don't pick up?"

"Say, Thursday at about five. They'll still be at the shop."

"OK. I'll make an excuse to go down to the Greek's. I better get going."

We took the stairs two at a time then into the garage through the small side door. Her full disguise in place I slid the garage door open just enough for her to squeeze the bike through. She looked back through her sunglasses, gave a little wave, a small smile and trundled uncertainly down the driveway. I opened the garage door fully for my parents return then retreated to my room and lay on the bed, breathing deeply of the scent of her, the blissful memory of our lovemaking.

I must have fallen into a deep sleep, only waking at the sound of the front door slamming.

My father's voice. "Raymond, we're home."

Footsteps on the stairs. Larry poked his head through the partly open door to my room. "Hi Ray, what's up?"

"Nothing much, you just woke me up, that's all."

"Oh, sorry." Larry sniffed, head twisting from side to side. "Say, what's that funny smell?"

I blanched. "No, nothing, that's a new aftershave I got, a passing Matric present...."

Larry looked around suspiciously. "Nah, don't believe you, that's a girl's smell, like the maid uses when she goes out."

"Larry, you don't know what you're talking about. What do you know 'bout girls' smells? Get out and leave me alone."

But my brother wasn't buying. He wandered across the room with an accusing look in his eyes. "I think...... I think your girlfriend was here, that's what I think!"

I sat up, stared hard at the defiance shining out from the face of my young brother. Weighing up the options I decided that taking Larry into my confidence, man to man, was the best route open. I smiled conspiratorially "Larry, you're just miles too clever for me. You're right. I can't argue with you. But lissen, hell, you're my brother and in 18 months you'll have your Barmitzvah. You know what that means, don't you?"

Larry smiled smugly, ignoring my question. "She was here, wasn't she?"

I sighed resignedly. "Yes, Crystal was here, but what I was saying about your Barmitzvah was that you'll be a man then and men learn to trust each other with secrets. You know mom and dad would be very unhappy about Crystal being here, ja? And you don't want them to be unhappy, do you?"

He hesitated for a few moments then nodded uncertainly. "Yes, but..."

"No buts. I'm asking you as almost, nearly, a man, to keep a secret, keep this to yourself so as not to upset our parents. Can you do that?"

"OK, Ray but ....can I have your two wheeler bike when you go to University?"

It was difficult not to laugh with amusement and relief. I had intended for him to have the bike anyway. "Sure, Larry, that's a deal. Can we shake on it?" I clasped his small pudgy damp hand in mine and looked hard into his eyes. "This is a man's shake. This means we keep this secret, no matter what. OK?"

Just then a bell rang from downstairs and my mother's voice echoing up the stairs. "Dinner's on the table, you two. NOW!"

*

It was just as dessert of canned gooseberries and ice cream was being served by Euphemia that my father turned to me and smiled. "So what has my brilliant First-class Matric son been doing this afternoon while we've been slaving away down at the shop?"

I caught Larry's eye as I stammered. "Ah, I was looking up all the books I'm gonna need for First Year, you know Botany, Zoology Chemistry and Physics. Another guy in our class, Tony Lazarow is also doing Dentistry and gave me a list....."

My mother, always more alert in the evenings than my hardworking and exhausted father, butted in. "What's going on between you two? What's the look you're giving Larry?"

I shook my head. "Nothing, ma, you're imagining it."

"Imagining, never! I saw you look at him. What is it? Larry, look at me, WHAT'S GOING ON HERE?"

I saw Larry's lower lip quivering. He was not yet man enough to withstand a full interrogation from our mother. I made a snap decision.

"Mom, dad, I had a guest over this afternoon. I swore Larry to secrecy and," I nodded approvingly at my younger brother, "I think he would have honoured that promise if you hadn't started on him."

"What do you mean, a guest? OH NO! Not that *shikse*! ARE YOU MESHUGGAH!" My mother sat heavily, splashing gooseberry juice on the tablecloth. "Abie, this rubbish of a son of yours, he had that '*cureveh*' here in this house! For all we know he maybe even *shtupped* her in his bed! Or God Forbid, in our bed! Abie, Abie, SAY SOMETHING!"

Before my father could gather his senses I stood up, swallowed and in as dignified a voice as I could muster, addressed the table. "Yes, Crystal was here. She is most definitely not a whore, or *cureveh*, as you so tastefully described her, but a delightful, bright, kind and wonderful person, in spite of the father she has. And yes, we will continue our bond, even though we are going to be in two different towns. Thank you, Larry. I know you would've kept the secret. Mom, I'm sorry you feel this way about Crystal. You're not unlike her father, drowning in hatred and fear and suspicion. But in a few weeks I'm off to University, always assuming you are still prepared to support me. I know it's gonna cost a lot of money but if you do I promise that I'll repay every penny when I start work as a Dentist. If not, then I'll look for jobs to earn enough to pay my own way. But I am now old enough to expect that you, my parents, should respect my choices and accept that I'm aware of the problems in the route Crystal and I have chosen. Dad, we had a talk after the Court Case and you said things might be clearer after a few weeks. Well, they are. We still love each other and we're gonna do our best to keep this going while we are apart." I sat down again and hungrily tucked into the gooseberries, my very favourite dessert.

The silence round the table was palpable, broken only by sobbing sounds from my mother. I ate noisily then, finishing, placed fork and spoon neatly on the plate, excused myself and retired to my room. I was aware of heated voices from the dining room and then silence. I half expected another visit from my father but after half an hour when it didn't happen, I undressed, got into bed and consoled myself with delicious memories of the afternoon in that precise location.

*

Next morning at breakfast the icy atmosphere was finally broken by my father. "Raymond, your mother and I talked deep into the night. What you said was the speech of a mensch, although it was not what we wanted to hear. However, we have agreed to carry on and support you at University as we planned and let time solve whatever the future holds. But, and its a big but, we must warn you that the Court instructed you to have no contact with the Webber family so by bringing her here you endangered not only yourself but us as well. So if you insist on taking such risks in future we ask you to consider our position in this town and especially with a bully like that Gerry Webber. For heaven's sake, don't do anything so foolish again...."

"Dad, look, Crystal is going off to their farm in Kirkwood for Christmas and New Year and then she will be off to Stellenbosch early in the New Year. This was goodbye for us for a while and that's why we took the risk of her coming here. It won't happen again, I promise you. Mom, is all this OK with you?"

My mother shook her head, wiping her eyes but saying nothing.

My father waved a gnarled finger at me. "Your mother is too upset to talk, but yes, we are agreed even though it is not something we would ever have wished on our worst enemy. But enough." A small twinkle behind the spectacles. "We are still a family and what's most important is that we go to the shop and earn a living. So Raymond, it's your turn to help today. You coming?"

*

Thursday 5.00 pm.

The phone rang. I was ready.""Hi Crys. You OK?"

"Not too bad. Gonna be bored outta my mind on the farm. Nothing to do but pick an eat apples 'n oranges. An' you?"

"Helping at the shop. Busy as hell over week before Christmas. Getting along better with my folks. Had to tell 'em you were here, though."

"You told them. Why?"

"Doesn't matter. Mom guessed an' we had it all out. They're not happy but agreed that they would still support me at Varsity and time would tell. I told them we were gonna keep it going long distance and they sort of accepted."

"God, my pa would have killed me if he knew."

"Well, I s'pose he's a bit more extreme. My folks are just scared of the unknown while your dad is kind of virulent."

"Yeah, that's right. Lissen, I better go now. How do I contact you?"

"OK you got a pencil? Yeah? So you write to me at Dalrymple House, Men's Residence, University of the Witwatersrand, Milner Park, Johannesburg. Got that?"

"Yes. I'll write soon's I'm settled. Ray....."

"I know what you gonna say, and I love you right back..."

"Gonna miss you like mad, my movie star..."

In my best Millandese, "Dear Crystal, dear heart, promise you'll think of me each night before you go to sleep then again when you wake."

"And in my dreams too. Love you, Ray, bye....."

I kissed the black plastic mouthpiece. "Bye."

Chapter 15

Marais Huis
Stellenbosch University
25th January 1960

Dearest Ray,

Firstly I'm lousy at letter writing. Please don't be mad at me for the time lag but we were in Kirkwood picking and eating apples and oranges till we nearly burst. In that little dorp everyone knows everything about everybody so I couldn't post a letter without pa knowing. We got back to PE and Rita said you'd already left for Joburg. I only had a few days to get sorted for Stellenbosch and since then it's been a mad rush.

Our residence is fine, I share a tiny room with a nice girl from Aliwal North, Marie Bezuidenhout. She hardly speaks English! We're both doing BAs so we've been busy getting books and stuff. There are lots of events in our first few weeks here, Initiation and lectures, lectures, lectures! I fall asleep then dream about you and wake up all hot and bothered, with everyone, including the lecturers, looking at me and laughing. What have you done to me, my movie star?

Guess that's all my news for the moment. Got to start reading, big time, But I'd much rather be sitting in the dark at the Old Grey

Cricket field all tangled up in the back seat of someone's Morris Minor!

Much Love,
Crystal XXXXX

Dalrymple House, Mens Residence
University of the Witwatersrand,
15th February 1960

Dearest Crystal,

You have no idea how I longed to get that first letter from you, but when it came the guys in the common room thought I'd gone berserk. I gave a yell, ran off to my pokey little room and lay on the bed with a big hollow in the centre as if that huge weightlifter Manie Maritz had slept in it. Still, I read your letter over seems like a million times especially that last bit. How I'm going to get through the next few months I just don't know. I guess Freshers' activities and initiations will get me involved. I'm sharing a room with a guy from a small farming village in the Orange Free State, Bennie Goldblatt. Believe it or not, he's Jewish! Because there were no Jewish girls in his village, Marquard, it's called, his parents wouldn't let him go out with or associate with any of the Afrikaans girls. So the guy is 18 years old and has never danced with or had a date with a girl! He's also doing Dentistry. One thing I don't have is a picture of you. Maybe you could send me one to keep me warm at night?

We've got a fierce Initiation ceremony here soon called 'Meeting Phineas,' the University Mascot. This, we're told, involves being led, pillowcases over our heads in the middle of the night, down a disused sewer beneath Empire Road. There we have to swear an oath of allegiance. This is set for next week, I'll keep you posted. We have a Freshers Concert with first year girls from Sunnyside Women's Residence (don't worry, not one a patch on you!) and on top of all this the lectures have started in earnest.

It sounds like you're settling in nicely. Stellenbosch is a beautiful town, all the quaint old Cape Dutch houses and picturesque wine country. I remember driving through when we visited family in Cape Town one year. So I imagine you walking in the vineyards and up the hillsides. Wish I could be there with you. Joburg's busy, and hot as hell. I want to get to play rugger and squash just to stop getting a big belly.

At Varsity there's a lot of talk about unrest in the black townships, After the Brit Prime Minister's 'Wind of Change' speech I'm not surprised, but there are very active anti-apartheid student organisations here at Wits. I've been to one or two of the lunchtime meetings.

Anyway, my little one, without getting all Ray-Milland sloppy, just know that I think of you all the time, I close my eyes and can see you , every inch of you and.... oh well, better stop this, it's getting unhealthy!

I miss you more than words,
Be well, all my love
Ray XXX

Marais Huis,
Stellenbosch University
12th March 1960

Hi Ray,

Many thanks for your lovely letter. I'm dousing this letter in perfume so you don't forget me! Especially rehearsing with all the Sunnyside Freshettes! Hope you like the picture. Taken at Humewood beach just before we went away at Christmas. Do you think I look a bit too thin? How did the Initiation go? It sounds frightening. Did it smell vile down there under Empire Road?

Here we are getting heavily into studying now but I won't bore you. Although Stellenbosch is supposed to be enlightened compared to the Northern Transvalers at Pretoria University, Tukkies, what a nickname! they are still heavily in favour of apartheid. I don't dare give the other side of the argument that I learned from you, my liberal boyfriend! It would just make enemies for me. I'm just concentrating on the studies. I agree with you about Macmillan's speech. What does he want to poke his nose in here for? It'll cause nothing but trouble amongst the blacks. I'm worried about you going to those meetings. There'll be Special Branch guys there looking out for troublemakers. Don't want my movie star in jail, that's for sure!

There've been a few socials with boeremusiek and volkspele but I don't go in for that kind of stuff as you know. Boys here are immature and rough, so you've no need to worry. I think with all the pretty Joburg lassies I should be more worried. When you play rugger, be careful, I don't want my boyfriend's nose or ears squashed by the hairyback Transvalers!

I'm missing you like mad, write soon,

Love as always,
Crystal XXX

Dalrymple House, Mens residence
University of the Witwatersrand.
2nd April 1960

Dearest Crystal,

Wow, the combination of the perfume and the picture really knocked me for a loop...brought back all the memories. No, you're definitely not too thin. I have it in a frame on my table. The guys are all jealous. Don't worry about the girls up here. I've fought them off bravely (only joking....really!)

The Initiation Ceremony was quite scary. Meeting Phineas is supposed to be a secret but I'll trust you...he's a five foot high clay Scots statue in kilt, sporran and all. We had to bow down and scrape our noses on the floor of this old sewer and mumble this oath of allegiance. Ugh!

Yes I am going to play rugger, there are some amazing players here at Wits, Wilf Rosenberg and Joe Kaminer, Springbok potential, two

Jewboys just like me! But I'll be playing for the under nineteens so it's not as rough as the open rugby.

This Sharpeville Massacre has really stirred things up here in Joburg. Those poor kids shot down in cold blood. And now Luthuli and Sobukwe arrested, all their organisations banned. This isn't the way to go. They should be talking to the black leaders not throwing them in jail. They can't keep 25 million Africans under forever. Here at varsity there's a protest march about Apartheid with the Black Sash, a Women's organisation. I may join the march if our schedule of lectures allows. It's all we can do to grab a half-hour lunch break and it takes ages to get the smell of the dogfish off me! I want to be a Dentist, not a fishmonger!

The Freshers' Concert went off well, except we forgot a lot of the words and had to be prompted! Still, that's show business!!! Rag Week is set for May and we have a large Residence float to join the procession through Joburg. Apparently there's a lot of boozing involved. (remember your old man's brandy and coke?)

I sniff your envelope every night before I go to sleep. The dreams I dream of you would be censored!

Be good, work hard and don't get involved with those Matie hairybacks!

Love as always,
Ray XXX

Marais House
Stellenbosch University
4th May, 1960

Dearest Ray,

Thanks for your newsy letter. Can't say I agree with you about the black leaders, they are talking revolution and war. It's not the ordinary black folks, they're simple lovely people and all they want is food, housing and jobs. These ANC activists are troublemakers and the Government is absolutely right to keep them locked up. Obviously the police thought there was going to be a major riot in Sharpeville and they panicked. So would you if you saw a horde of blacks running towards you with stones and stuff. I'm worried about you going on these marches. Please be careful. Stick with your studies.

Nothing much happening here other than work, work, work! Never knew there was so much to know about the History of Art. South African History's great, though. We have a Rag Day as well but it'll be mainly around the University. I was asked if I wanted to try for Rag Queen or Princess but I'm too shy!

My pa came down to see me. I don't understand how he seems to know that we are still in touch, but he asked me all kinds of questions, like are we corresponding. I had to lie but think he still suspects even though we're a thousand miles apart!

Anyway, don't worry, I'm still mad about my movie star!

Love and big kisses (and the rest!)

Yours
Crystal.

Dalrymple House,
Mens Residence,
University of the Witwatersrand.
21st May 1960.

Dearest Crys,

I got a bit worried as your last letter took longer than usual. Also your dad's visit reminded me of the whole situation back in PE. But, well, I just keep reminding myself of all the times we were together and after a deep sniff of your envelope, I feel my optimism coming back. Rag week was amazing. We built the float in one night and were ordered to go to this window in the front of Res. where we had to drink whatever they shoved at us in one gulp. I wasn't sick but had a massive headache the whole day. Still, it was a major parade through Joburg and crowds lined the streets. Really something to remember. Our float was a Sputnik-like satellite. Not brilliant but we had a good time - if it wasn't for the hangover!

I'm struggling with all the studying, Botany especially. We've got mid-year exams at the end of May, so frivolities have ended. Hard slog till June. When are your mid-year holidays? I know it'll be difficult to see each other in PE but it would be nice to have something to look forward to. Ours are from 19th June till 5th July. I'm proud they asked you to try for Rag Queen but, as I'm sure you would have been elected, you would have had all these big Seniors flocking round you. Am I getting jealous or what? My folks have promised me a moped if I get through this year. Will you trust me enough to come for a ride?

You and I will have to try and resolve our political differences. I think Macmillan was right. South Africa will have to become multiracial. Those kids at Sharpeville were only the first. They don't want to be second class citizens where us whites live like kings. Verwoerd being shot, although not by a black, is what's going to happen more and more. Look out Miss Webber, come the June holidays I'm going to have to re-educate you, make you a more liberal person!

Don't worry too much about writing long letters. Receiving the scented envelope with your handwriting would just about be enough. A few words would be nice.

Work hard and be good,
Love as always,
Ray XXXXX

Marais Huis,
Stellenbosch University.
6th June,1960

Hi Ray,

I guess this will be the last letter before we start our vacation. I'll be back in PE on the 24th. Somehow we'll have to try and get together. Seems like years, doesn't it? Do you think Varsity has changed you much? I feel liberated, away from pressure at home, able to come and go as I please (within the Res rules of course!) but not having to think up excuses for where I'm going. I hope my folks will treat me like an adult. I'm not optimistic about pa. He was against me going to Varsity even though it's Afrikaans medium. He thinks girls should just be housewives. You know what he's like.

I don't agree with you about giving votes to the blacks. Look at the rest of Africa. They're children, they need European expertise to teach them skills but it'll take years. You can't just wave a wand, making them into sophisticated human beings overnight. Pa says they will never be equal to us but you know what he thinks, he'd shoot the lot of them! Anyway, you and I aren't gonna solve the problems. Leave it to the politicians.

I have to cut short this letter as I've still got a mountain of reading to do. Good luck with your exams. I'm sure you'll get your usual A's!

Love you like always,
Crystal

PS Phone Rita when you get back and we'll try and arrange a get together. Can't wait!

Chapter 16

Port Elizabeth. Last week of June 1960

I had hardly knocked on the front door of Rita Coetzee's house when it was flung open. Crystal stood there, eyes shining, a broad smile showing her even white teeth. She was barefooted, dressed in a loose fitting tent dress, yet hiding little of her lissom form beneath.

"I watched you walk up the path, Ray. You look different somehow, sort of grown-up."

She held out her arms and we melted into each other. "You too, Crys," I mumbled into her neck, "I like the hairstyle. Suits you."

The embrace went on endlessly, leading to a long-awaited passionate kiss. Crystal then pulled away slightly from me, gasping. "Hey, boy, something tells me we're glad to see each other!" With a seductive smile she looked down between us where my excitement had become obvious. "I'm so pleased......you like the hairstyle, I mean" She gave that giggle I so adored. "I was worried you might not approve but the hairdresser in Stellenbosch said it was the in thing and that having it shorter framed my face."

I cupped her elfin face between my hands. "I missed you, Crys. Just lived for your letters. Perfuming them was brilliant. Drove me mad."

We were still standing in the entrance hall. Crystal led me into the lounge and pointed toward the settee. "Let me get you a drink, Ray. What'll you have? I'm having a beer, OK?" I nodded. She padded off toward the kitchen, still talking. "I'm so glad Rita organised for us to meet here at her place this afternoon. What with my dad still very suspicious I didn't dare be seen with you in public. He knows lots of people and has spoken to God knows how many of his mates to keep a look out for his precious daughter in case she's still seeing that... that... no, I can't say it ......you do know what he calls you, don't you?"

I followed her into the kitchen, folded my arms round her from behind. "No, but I can guess. Come on, what does he call me?"

She wriggled sensually against me. "Oh no, I can't possibly repeat it."

I tightened my grip round her waist, my growing erection pushing harder into her firm rear. "OK, you know what?" my voice taking on a slightly coarser sound.

She turned to face me and now there was no holding back. "No, what, Ray?"

"This 'vervloekte jood'(accursed Jew) can't wait any longer to make up for six long months. Can we use the settee?"

"Better than that. Rita said we can use her bedroom. Her bed's a bit narrow, though."

*

The bed was just fine. All the pent-up frustrations of the six-month separation exploded in a fiery bout of lovemaking that was as intense as it was brief. We lay dozing for what must have been an hour then, after a second far more languorous session, showered and dressed to await Rita, our generous hostess.

"So, Raymond, how were the exams?" Crystal said, sitting down next to me on the sofa.

I couldn't help bursting with laughter "Well, not entirely great, I failed Botany."

"You what? I don't believe you. Why're you laughing?"

"I was laughing at the way you suddenly came out with this matter of fact question, just after we'd been upstairs making violent passionate love for hours. It just seemed funny, that's all." I put on a more serious expression "Anyway, like I said, I failed Botany. I hate the bloody subject. Never was keen on flowers anyway, but, well, just missed, got 47%. And you?"

"Not too bad, got through all three subjects, average 60%."

"That's great, Crys. Well done......Your folks must be pleased?"

"Ja they were, but, well, my pa's still on about you, you know. He says every time he takes a step on his left ankle, which is still sore, it reminds him of you and what he'd like to do to you...he's also become a member of the OSB."

I sat up, mouth open in shock. "You're kidding...the Ossewabrandwag?" I stood up, pacing the floor. "I found out all about them. Do you know who they are? They're the most reactionary secret fascist organisation, allied to the Broederbond. For God's sake, they supported the Nazis in the last war!"

Crystal bit her lip, anxiously watching my anger slowly building. "Ja, he says the government isn't tough enough and even Verwoerd he reckons is worrying too much about the United Nations and Britain. The OSB wants to keep South Africa isolated from Africa and the rest of the world."

I shook my head in frustration. "That can't be allowed to happen, Crys. We've got to start talking across the colour line."

"You say that, Ray, but when I see Africans walking down Main Street or worse, in North End, I just wanna steer clear of them. They look at you with hate and arrogance in their eyes. I just want to be far away from them and their smell, you know...."

"But they're human beings, Crys." I could feel the frustration mounting as I said the words.

She was getting more animated too. "Ja, but they're hundreds of years behind us, it'll take generations to bring them up to our standards."

I sat down then stood up again, pounding one hand against the other. "You know, it's not so long ago when us so-called civilised whites were chopping people's heads off, to say nothing of Hitler gassing six million Jews in his concentration camps just twenty years ago. You call those civilised standards?"

Crystal rose from the settee, placed her hands on my shoulders, looking deep into my eyes. "My dear Ray, don't get all annoyed. We're all entitled to our opinions and as I said before it's up to the government to help the blacks improve."

In spite of her nearness, and the intoxicating perfume that I recognised from all the letters, I just couldn't help myself. I shook my head vigorously. "But that's just it, Crys, this Government and the people your wonderful dad supports, want, through virtually no education at all, to keep blacks permanently as an underclass, to do the dirty work. They don't ever want to share power with people who are five times more numerous. In the same way as Hitler, they regard the blacks as sub-humans, just as the Germans regarded us Jews. Those children at Sharpeville burnt their books and the classrooms because they knew or were told, correctly, that the education they were getting was aimed at making them a permanent servant class." I could feel my face reddening and beads of sweat trickling down my neck.

Crystal stepped back, the dimmed lounge lighting reflecting in the moisture welling in her eyes. "Ray, my pa may be extreme, but he's lived all his life amongst the blacks, here in PE and on the farm. It's the only way of life he's ever known. He's certain that Apartheid is the only way to deal with them and reckons white liberals, communists he calls them, know nothing about dealing with kaffirs....oh, sorry, that word again."

I walked over to the window, turned and looked at this girl, this love of my young life, a person whose inner thoughts I was only now tuning into. And what I was hearing I wasn't sure I could live with. "And you, my lovely Crystal, how do you really feel? The same as your dad? What did they say at Stellenbosch? The supposedly liberal thinking Afrikaans University? I bet they aren't far off you and your father."

She stamped her foot angrily, not meeting my gaze. "That's not fair, Ray, and you know it. To bracket me with my pa, especially after we have just been upstairs together like we'd never been apart. That hurt a lot."

I was immediately contrite. "Ag, Crys, I'm so sorry. I know you and your dad are poles apart. But I guess six months at Wits has opened my eyes to what's been happening in this country and......"

Suddenly the phone rang. Crystal answered, listened briefly then turned to me, eyes wide open in alarm. "It's Rita, Ray. My pa's on his way over here. Quickly, out the back door. Shit, I can hear his car outside. Dunno how he knows we're here, must've forced it from Rita. You'd better get outta here fast. Over the back wall and through the neighbour's house to the next street. Quick!"

Through the front window I caught a glimpse of the balding Gerry Webber striding up the path. Part of me wanted to stay and confront the gigantic weightlifter but memories of our first encounter, logical discretion and Crystal's arm propelled me through the kitchen door and out to safety. As I climbed over the back wall I heard the sound of Rita's front door slam and raised voices.

By the time I reached home my jumbled thoughts were slowly becoming lucid. I lay upstairs on my bed and let the events slide by me, extreme pleasurable ones coupled with angry frustration at the clear political chasm that had formed between Crystal and me, then the final panicky retreat.

I had barely dozed off when the phone rang.

"Ray.....are you OK? It's Rita. Lissen, I'm so sorry for what happened but old man Webber came to the salon and created a hellovva scene. He said he knew you were back and suspected me of arranging a get-together. It was more than my job was worth to let him rant and rave in the salon so I told him, then thank God I got you out of there in time."

"And Crystal? How was she? Did he hurt her?"

"Ja, well, he walloped her across the face. He didn't believe she'd been there on her own so she had to admit you'd been together. He started to threaten all kinds of hell, even gonna speak to her Residence Warden at Stellenbosch Varsity stopping all mail to her from you. Apparently the judgement against you allows him to do that."

I felt the pent-up anger rising within me, clutching the black telephone handpiece so tightly, my knuckles cracked. "God, the man's a monster. Is Crystal badly hurt?"

"Well she'll have a nasty black eye but I guess she's all heated up inside and gave as good as she got. Told him there was no way he could stop you guys being together eventually. In the end he forced her to promise that she wouldn't contact you or anything until she was her own boss and he was no longer supporting her. I think she agreed to that because he threatened to come over to your folks' house and taking you and your folks apart. She was thinking of you, Ray."

I wiped the moisture from my forehead that was threatening to drip down my cheeks. "Ja, I realise that. Thanks, Rita, for phoning. And for arranging for us to be at your house. Seems like that may have been a sort of temporary permanent farewell?"

"Yeah, I guess you guys better cool it for the time being. "

I lay down on my bed, thoughts racing wildly round my mind. I tried to picture what must have occurred between Crystal and her father and it only made the fury inside me worse. Gradually I managed to accept the fact that she had taken the punishment, compromising herself to protect me and that I had little alternative but to adjust to this new reality. I must then have dozed off, as the next thing I knew I was being woken by a gentle knock on my bedroom door.

Larry's face peered round the door. "Hi Ray. Sorry, did I wake you?"

"No, it's OK. Come in. Where've you been?"

"Riding my bike, I mean, your old bike. Took Marty on the pillion. He loved it. Its great. The three speed gears are crazy, man. Thanks a lot."

I looked at my brother searchingly as he sat on the edge of the bed. Now nearly twelve years old, he had lost a lot of his puppy fat and was starting the puberty growth spurt. His round face still had that babyish quality but the whining habit had gone. We both adored our young brother Martin so brotherly affection had replaced the antagonism that had coloured our earlier years.

Larry stared at me through the new spectacles he had begun to wear for short-sightedness. "What's up, Ray? You look like you've seen a ghost."

I lay back on the pillow and waved my hands nonchalantly. "Nothing much. Just a bit fagged out after all the swotting and exam tensions."

Larry shook his head. "Don't believe you....I heard you on the phone about Crystal. Are you in trouble with her old man?"

I was just about to reply when my father walked in the room, white-faced.

"Raymond, I've just had a horrible phone call from that beast Webber. He says if you so much as phone or write or make any approach to his daughter, he will immediately report you to the police and have you arrested in breach of the court order."

I sat up, rigid. "Can he do that, dad?"

He nodded. "Yes, son, I'm afraid he can. I checked the legalities with our lawyer Sam Leibowitz. Webber has every right to bar you from any contact. Also he is well in with the local Police as you might have guessed."

I fought the tears that threatened to flood my face. "We'll find some way, Crystal and I.......you don't know what she means to me, and somehow, we won't allow him to ruin our lives."

My father moved across from the door and sat alongside me, Larry remaining wide-eyed at the foot of the bed. He put his arms around my neck and hugged me hard. "Raymond, my dear son... I have tried to advise you on this before, but now you simply must accept the hard truth. If you see her again, Webber will have you arrested. And if you are found guilty of ignoring a court order, you may get a criminal record which will stop your career in its tracks. So now, I'm begging you, swallow this bitterest of pills and just get your mind round what is of major importance; succeeding in your studies and getting a profession. Who knows, time has a funny way of solving problems. At the moment you have no choice but to get her out of your mind. And failing that, then make sure that you do nothing that will cause Webber to go to the Police. Is that OK with you, Ray?"

I nodded, too overcome with the finality of it all to speak. My father leaned over and kissed me on the forehead and as he made his way out, Larry stood up, came over and hugged me. "Sorry, Ray, I'm really sorry."

The tears came easily then. "Thank you, Larry." I looked tenderly at my young brother then took a deep breath. "Listen boetie, I just want to say that I know I haven't always been a good brother to you. I've always wanted to apologise to you over the Froodella thing but wanted to do that when you were old enough to understand. I think you're already enough of a man to forgive me for that. It was a terrible thing to do and I've regretted it ever since."

Larry's eyes were now watering as well. "Don't worry, Ray. You gave me your two-wheeler. That's enough of an apology. But I think dad's right. You really want to steer clear of that monster. I saw his picture in the paper. He looks real mean."

"I know, Larry. Perhaps we can just write letters through Rita or something. But I don't think I can ever give her up. "

Little did I know that four long years would pass before I saw Crystal Webber again.

Chapter 17

The telephone rang a day before my return to Johannesburg for the final term of the year. "Hi Raymond. This is Rita. Listen, can you pop in to the salon before you go back. I've got a note from Crystal for you."

I gunned the Morris frantically, ignoring its protests. The envelope reeked of her perfume. I inhaled so deeply giddiness just about rendered me incapable of reading the familiar neat handwriting.

My dearest Raymond,

I have hardly stopped crying since I watched you disappearing over the back wall of Rita's house. Please accept my apology for my father. I realise now that for us to try to continue seeing each other in PE would place you and your family in danger. Probably me as well. He is a ruthless beast. I hate saying that about my own pa but there's no point trying to argue with him. He hates you and all Jews and will not hear any discussion about you without flying into the most awful rages.

So, my love, and you are really the most fantastic person I have ever known, I have agreed not to see you again or write to you until I am independent. I fear that even then my father will be trying to prevent anything happening between us but maybe at that time we can make a plan to be out of his clutches. In the meanwhile, dear Raymond, go back to Wits, get stuck into your studies, socialize, yes, I mean that, go out with other girls and just for the next few years, forget about me. No, I dcn't really mean that last bit, maybe just think of me every so often. I know you will. But don't write to Stellenbosch at all. The court order has given my pa the power to tell our Residence to prevent any letters from you getting to me. Rita has promised to phone me so you can drop her a line, but for the moment it's probably best if we both concentrate on our studies.

I will never forget you,
Crystal. XXXX

I folded the note neatly, placed it in the inside pocket of my windbreaker nearest my heart and drove slowly homewards through the quiet streets. Although deep down I had been expecting this, the actual spelling out left me totally empty, gulping with a mixture of sadness and anger, especially at the mindless intolerance and hatred that was the driving force behind Crystal's father's actions. Reaching home I avoided any contact with anyone, just tip-toed up the stairs to my room where, blinking away tears, I started my packing.

*

1961 South Africa leaves the British Commonwealth and becomes a Republic. The ANC declares armed struggle against Apartheid. The Treason Trial defendants are found not guilty after a five year trial.

1962 Nelson Mandela is arrested. Helen Joseph, a white Jewish Liberal is also arrested. United Nations' sanctions resolution against South Africa passed. Robben Island maximum security prison is completed.

Israel declares an arms embargo against South Africa.

1964 Nelson Mandela is sentenced to Life Imprisonment for treason. A bomb explodes in Johannesburg Station. One woman killed, many injured.

*

June 1964

Dalrymple House,
University of Witwatersrand, Johannesburg

I had been awaiting Larry's visit with great enthusiasm. I now merited a single room as a fourth year student and he was coming to spend a week of his June vacation in his final Matric year at School with his big brother. Our Dental School timetable decreed that our mid-year holiday was short as we were now working in the clinic at Milner Park. This meant I remained in Johannesburg instead of driving down to Port Elizabeth as I had done during past vacations, a seven hundred mile trip in the ageing Morris Minor I'd inherited from my mother. This was the same car that had seen some frantic action in its history, the Drive-in with Lalla, Rita and Crystal, leading to the climactic trysts at Shelley Beach and the Old Grey Cricket ground. If that olive green Morris Minor could talk!

I met Larry at the Johannesburg railway station, the scene of the recent bomb outrage. We made our way back to University Residence. He was now as tall as I was, lean and fit through becoming an ardent squash player, but still wore his thick-lensed spectacles.

He unpacked and sat down on the borrowed camp bed. "So Ray, what's it like looking after real patients?" he said grinning.

"Hard work," I replied with a grimace. "A bit like concentration camp with staff looking over our shoulders every minute. Interesting, though. We're doing simple fillings and extractions and stuff like that."

Larry looked at me admiringly. "You mean you give injections as well, already?"

"Sure," I replied, with a little hint of pride. "The first time was a bit nerve-wracking but they trained us pretty well. We had a laugh yesterday. One of the guys, Tony Franks, who's a bit ham-fisted, stuck the needle through the patient's cheek, spraying local anaesthetic all over my trousers. I was at the chair next to his. Seems every year someone has the same thing happen."

Larry laughed. "So what happened then?"

"Well, the staff member took Franks outside and made him read up the anatomy of the jaws. He has to have staff supervise him giving injections for the next two weeks."

"And the patient?" Larry queried, giggling.

I was still laughing out loud. "Well, he wanted to know if the hole in his cheek would heal up OK or was he gonna leak saliva forever!" After a while I got serious. "How are things in PE?" I asked.

He thought for a moment. "Well, School's fine. They're all amused that I'm taking over your role as Drum Major of the Cadet band. Did OK in the June exams and I'm playing no 2 in the School Squash team."

I clapped him on the shoulder. "Hey man, that's really great, well done. How are mom and dad?"

"Fine. Dad's still working hard at the shop although his two partners are taking some of the workload off him. Mom's still smoking, you can hear her cough from way up the street. Won't give up, though. And Marty's just too cute for words."

After a few moments silence Larry looked at me with a grin. "You want to know about Crystal, don't you?"

I nodded. "Yes, I do. Did you get to speak to Rita?"

"Yes. I went to the salon like you asked me. She was busy but took a few minutes off and we managed a coffee next door."

I waited impatiently but my brother shook his head solemnly. "You won't be too happy about this, Ray but....."

"But what?"

"Well, she's.... Crystal that is....she's now back in PE having got her BA. Got a teaching job at the new PE University."

"I know that," I rasped. "So, hey, that's good. Why the long face?"

Larry gave that rueful grin once more. "Well, Rita told me that Crystal's now going around with Jimmy McEwan again. She says it looks quite serious."

I felt like a dagger had pierced my chest. "Not that big oaf, surely?"

Larry nodded. "Ja, that's what Rita says.. Apparently Jimmy is a favourite at Gerry Webber's Gym so he's very well in with her bastard father."

I was silent for a while, contemplating the news then, with a shrug, forced a smile. "I guess that's all for the best. We couldn't hope to go on for years like there was gonna be some magic get-together after all this time." I paused for a moment, partly to catch my breath which the sudden pain in my chest had produced. "I have to tell you that I've been going out with a nice Jewish doll here for a while. Nothing serious as yet but her parents welcomed me into their house like I was a prospective son-in-law. I suppose now that Crystal's fixed up I can relax and maybe take this thing a bit further."

Larry shook his head. "Doesn't sound as though you're 100% keen to me though."

I shook my head. "I'm not sure. My head has been filled with thoughts of Crystal for four long years. You'll find out when you have your first real girlfriend. You just cannot get it out of your head. Or your dreams. It keeps coming back like a familiar taste." I breathed out heavily. "But Jimmy McEwan, hey, who would have believed it?" I shook my head violently. "No, this girl, Arlene her name is, is ideal, Jewish, from a well off family here in Joburg. Mom and dad would be thrilled to bits but..." I stood up, grabbed my coat and gestured to Larry to follow me. "Come on I'll show you around the campus."

*

The week with Larry sped by. I showed him the inside of Dental School, the lecture theatres, the Conservation Surgeries where forty students worked on patients in a massive green-tiled hall. The Laboratories where we made dentures amused him, with the fetid smell of melting wax and Bunsen burners polluting the atmosphere. What I found most impressive was his maturity, his achievements in his final year at school seemed to have increased his self-confidence. The visit to the Anatomy Dissection Hall at Medical school had helped him make up his mind about a future career. "Definitely not doing anything like that," he stated firmly. "I think it will be Cape Town Varsity and Accountancy for me."

We were invited to Arlene's house for Friday night dinner. Larry's reaction to Arlene was predictable. "Mom and dad will love her. She's what they would have liked in a daughter. Probably instead of me..." He bit his lip, a small sign of the old insecure whining Larry of his younger days. But the moment passed. The evening spent at the Yudelman's house was as warm and homely as I knew my parents could have wished for.

On the way to the Railway station Larry seemed subdued. I asked him what was wrong. He merely shook his head. "No, nothing much."

"I don't believe you," I replied. "Come on, out with it. I can see there's lots on your mind."

He nodded. "I guess..... that..... seeing you here at Dental School, so far advanced in your course, in just another two years you'll be a qualified Dentist, sort of makes me feel a bit queasy. I've got such a long way to go. I've got this decision to make which will affect the rest of my life. It's kind of nerve wracking, you know what I mean?"

I patted him on the shoulder. "Listen, Larry, don't think you're alone. Everyone goes through this phase of uncertainty. Think hard before making a final career decision. Grandpa gave me sugar cubes on his way to and from work so I got to spend many hours at the dentist. He died when you were a baby and by then we knew how bad sugar was for the teeth. I had lots of experience with the drill. Also I was good with my hands, remember my Meccano set?" He nodded, smiling. "So the decision for me was easy. You've always been good at Maths and figures. Keeping statistics about cricket scores etc. I think Accountancy is absolutely right for you. Don't forget uncle Max and uncle Bernie are accountants. Go see them. Find out what it's like. Then make up your mind."

We had arrived at the station and I walked him to the platform. We found his compartment and he loaded his case on to the rack. It was not a moment too soon as the train whistle blew. He looked at me, eyes moist, and gave me a hug. "Thanks Ray. It's been a great week and I guess your little talk now helped me a lot."

I returned the hug. "Love to mom and dad and Marty. And......if you see Rita you can tell her about Arlene." I hesitated slightly. Another whistle blew and a cry of 'All Aboard'. "If you do see Crystal, well, tell her I still think about her a lot BUT.... I think she can do better than Jimmy Bloody McEwan!"

The train began to move. I ran down the corridor and leapt out on to the platform. Larry was leaning out of the window, waving. I waved back, a lump in my throat. For all his new found confidence, he was still a frightened little lad, a fear that I understood all too well.

I sat in the Morris for a long while. The week with my brother had brought back memories with a vengeance. The latest news had me burning with frustration and, yes, jealousy too. I tried desperately to blink away the images of Crystal. Now they were intruded upon by that big lout McEwan and the anguish grew relentlessly.

As it was a Saturday I was not on duty at the Dental Hospital. I drove slowly back to Residence and using the illegal 'long tickey', a piece of electric wire which one used to short-circuit the public telephone , I dialled Arlene's number.

Chapter 18

1965 Adam Faith cancels his South African Tour because of Apartheid. F.J.Harris, a white South African, is convicted and hanged for exploding the bomb in Johannesburg Railway Station.

1966 Robert Kennedy visits South Africa. Hendrik Verwoerd, the Prime Minister is assassinated. B.J. Vorster, reputedly more extreme than Verwoerd, becomes Prime Minister.

JULY 1966, Port Elizabeth

The celebrations were over. I was now Dr Raymond Benjamin, a fully qualified B.D.S. Rand, Dental Surgeon. My parents and brothers had journeyed up to Johannesburg for the ceremony, their elation partly tempered by the fact that, after nearly two years, Arlene and I had ended our relationship months before. Amidst some acrimony, she had become engaged to a thirty-year-old businessman. Ironically I had been invited to the party, which I attended for a very short time. Embarrassingly, most of her family had been so used to my being around, several of them came up to congratulate me!

Port Elizabeth had changed little in the years I had been in Johannesburg. Mostly I missed my three friends, Alec, Mark and Lalla. They had all obtained their degrees. Alec and Mark, now qualified doctors, were doing their internships at Groote Schuur Hospital in Cape Town, while Lalla, now a Pharmacist, was working in Hillbrow, Johannesburg. Although he and I had tried to keep contact in the Golden City, our paths had crossed less and less frequently.

Now back in the familiar surroundings of my hometown, I had decided to seek locum employment in Port Elizabeth before joining two fellow graduates who were leaving to work in London, UK. The plan was to travel by sea, aboard an Italian Liner, the 'SS Africa', up the east coast of Africa. We would be stopping at various countries *en route*, ending in Trieste in Italy after passing through the Suez Canal. From there we would take a train across to Calais, then a ferry to Dover and on to London. We all had letters of introduction to Dental Practices in London so were confident that jobs would be easily available in the British National Health Service.

My parents were naturally saddened at the thought of my leaving although I tried to console them with a promise that it would probably only be a year or two. My father had made approaches to his local Dentist to tempt me with a permanent position but my determination and ambition to travel, experience the jazz clubs and theatre in London and above all, to go to the Alps to learn to ski, overcame all opposition.

For the time being, it was back to the family home, my old bedroom with its magnificent sea view and the family discussions that inevitably became entreaties. Rita had telephoned early on a Sunday morning with a cryptic suggestion that I meet with her and Crystal later for a hamburger. My mind was whirling with unanswerable questions.

Firstly though, it was necessary to survive a Benjamin breakfast.

My mother was distraught. "Why, why, why couldn't you have married Arlene, Ray? She was such a lovely girl. And what's more, her father said he was so keen for you to open up a surgery in his shopping centre in Houghton. You would have been set for life!"

For the umpteenth time I tried to explain. "Mom, you have got to understand. Firstly, the romance had already broken up several times. I knew that we weren't right for each other. Second, her father was much too dominating. It was as if he wanted to own me. I just couldn't imagine settling down at the age of twenty-two without seeing a bit of the world first. Please try to see my point of view."

My father was more conciliatory. "Ray, I know you've got to get this out of your system. You've done us proud. I haven't told your Mom this yet but as a reward for all your hard work, I'm prepared to pay half of your boat cost and also give you some pocket money for when you arrive in London."

"Abraham Benjamin, are you crazy?" My mother waved her hands in the air in anguish. "You're actually encouraging this meshuggeneh (crazy) trip? You know he'll never come back, don't you!"

"I know nothing of the sort, Rosie. We did discuss that we should give Raymond a generous present for qualifying, not failing a year, and saving us paying all those extra fees. Some other boys took eight years to qualify. We agreed he deserved a big reward. Well, what I'm offering is good and generous. I'm sure that after a year or two he'll long for our sunshine and our beaches and the South African way of life. And you know what also? The way this verkakte government is going, with that Nazi Vorster Prime Minister, maybe being out of South Africa for a year or two is not such a bad idea."

My mother was silent, her bloodshot eyes mirroring her disapproval. I tried to pour oil on the obviously unhappy waters. "Look, mom and dad, this is something all the Dental graduates are doing. We can earn far better in England than in SA at the moment and, yes, dad's right, who knows what's around the corner here? With B. J. Vorster in power, the ANC talking armed struggle, apartheid is not going to last forever. When the end comes it could be nasty."

My father followed me up to my bedroom and together we stood at the window, looking out over Algoa Bay in the distance. "Dad, many thanks for the offer. I'll treat it as a loan not a gift. I'll have some locum fees coming in as well next month so I should be more than OK. And I promise I'll pay you back."

"It's a gift, a reward," he retorted. "I don't want no paying back. You've earned it with your hard work and dedication."

I put my arm round his shoulders. "Thank you so much, dad. It's really appreciated." I took a deep breath. "But you know, although it's winter, it's a bright sunny day and I haven't had a smell of the sea since December so if you guys don't mind, I'm gonna take the Morris and take a drive, see some friends and maybe just cruise round the Marine Drive. OK?"

I didn't wait for a response. I'd agreed to meet the girls at the Pollok Beach drive-in hamburger joint. I had no idea what the situation was but the excitement in Rita's voice told me something momentous had happened. So, treating the old Morris like a racing Ferrari, I gunned the groaning engine for all it was worth and made the journey from Mount Road to the beach in record time. My heart was pounding in time to the Rolling Stones 'Satisfaction' on the car radio. The thought of seeing Crystal again after years of separation took its toll on the gears and clutch of the faithful little car.

I saw Crystal before she saw me. She was sitting on a bench overlooking the crashing surf. Being winter, the beach was practically deserted. The sun was shining but a cold wind was whipping off the wild ocean. I parked behind the bench. She turned and her face lit up.

"RAYMOND!!!" she yelled and flung open the door of the Morris. We were in each other's arms, gear lever notwithstanding. It was as though no time had passed. The sensations were the same, no, they were far more, far, far more than I could have dreamed. We sat speechless, clinging to each other, not daring to let go.

Eventually, we did separate and just looked at each other, both swallowing in great gulps. She was smiling that same smile, the auburn curls were shorter, more groomed, but her youthful exuberance was still there, coloured by the cold sea breeze but also the obvious joy she was feeling at our reunion. I'm not sure what she was seeing on my face. I knew my mouth was open in amazement that, after six long years, here we were, actually touching, hugging and revelling in being close together again.

Finally I found my voice."Crystal,,...I.. I... I don't know what to say ..."

She touched my lips with her fingers. "You don't have to say anything, my dearest Ray. Your face always said it all anyway, and your wide open mouth!"

We both started to laugh. Then she grew serious. "You must have wondered what was going on this morning. I asked Rita to phone you because I wanted this to be a surprise. She really has been a wonderful friend to both of us."

"I thought the two of you......er....so where is she?" I managed to whisper.

"She dropped me here a few minutes ago. She knew we'd want to be alone and said she'd come back in an hour or so and you could buy us each a hamburger and a milkshake."

I had regained a little of what remained of my composure, so reverted to the old Ray Milland routine. "That will be my absolute pleasure, my lady, but first don't you think we have some recent history to cover?"

She squealed with delight. "You've absolutely no idea how much I've missed both of you, my new dentist and my movie star!!"

We sat holding hands, eyes locked, oblivious to the surroundings, ignoring the thunder of the waves, the occasional car driving by.

Crystal settled herself comfortably in the bucket seat. "Firstly, I know you knew that I was going steady with Jimmy McEwan. After I came back to PE it was really lonely and I was miserable. I'd always been friendly with him and the thing was, he was really easy with my dad, doing regular stints at the gym. Your boetie, Larry, told Rita, must be two years ago now, that you were involved with a nice Jewish doll in Joburg so I guess Jimmy and I drifted into a sort of comfortable thing, you know, going to movies, dances and all that stuff. I couldn't get you out of my mind though, and so, when after a while Jimmy started getting itchy, what I mean is he wanted a full blown sex affair, I just couldn't, you know, after what we'd had." She was silent for a moment then shrugged. "But then he asked me to marry him..."

I shifted uncomfortably in my seat, looking out of the window which was pointless as it had completely misted over. "When was this, how long ago?"

"About three months ago. He bought me an engagement ring and everything. My folks were happy as anything but I just couldn't. I mean, I said yes, we could be engaged but I wasn't gonna go to bed with him till we were married. He asked when that would be and I suppose, at the back of my mind I knew you would be back around this time so I kept putting him off. Rita heard from Larry when he was back from Cape Town a few months ago that your romance was going sour so I just thought, if I can hold on till you came back, and I could maybe get to meet you again and see what my feelings were..."

"McEwan couldn't have been happy about all that" I said, as a little memory bubble popped in my head ('Jimmy McEwan says he's been all the way with her').

Crystal nodded, somewhat sheepishly. "You're so right. He became very nasty. Accused me of keeping him on a string while I was waiting for you to come back. Got quite heavy, he did."

"And when did all this happen?"

"Well, it's kind of recent. Just last week. We had a flaming row and I gave him his ring back."

"Bloody Hell!" I sat back in my seat, squeezing her hand mercilessly.

"Ow! That hurts!"

I released the pressure immediately. "Gee, Crys, I'm so sorry. Can I kiss it better?"

A smile returned to her face. "You can do better than that, Mr Milland. You can give me a proper kiss to make up for it."

The kiss was long and slow, refreshingly minty. I'd forgotten just how soft her lips were and how sensual her tongue. No, correction, I hadn't forgotten, but the delicious renewal was all the more delightful for the long separation. After an eternity we both sat back breathless.

Crystal looked at me intently. "So what now, Ray? Where do we go from here?"

"I really don't know, honestly. This has really stunned me, seeing you again and meeting like this. One thing I know for certain...."

"And that is?"

I grabbed her hands. "For me now, I want us to be together always. Just that one little kiss, that's all it took. There's no doubt in my mind, Gerry Webber or no Gerry Webber."

She leaned across and nuzzled into my neck. "You know, I feel exactly the same. So what do you suggest?"

"Well, first tell me, you're working at PE University. Are you living at home with your folks still?"

A little frown crossed her face. "Yes, I'm not earning enough to get a place of my own. So I've still got my pa looking over my shoulder. I've saved quite a bit of money though. And you, what are your plans?"

"Well, I've got a locum here in PE, at Dubrovsky's Practice in North End for two months. My dad goes there and he fixed it up for me, and then..." I hesitated, unsure whether to break the news.

"Then what?" Crystal queried, uneasily.

"Then I'm booked on the Lloyd Triestino ship, 'SS Africa', to sail up East Coast through Suez to Trieste in Italy and on to London by train to work for maybe a year or two. I'm so sorry," I added hastily, "but this was planned with two of my classmates months ago. My dad helped me with the cost of the ticket. How could I have known that we'd meet again like this?"

Crystal was silent, too silent for my liking. She drew away from me and pursed her lips. "So you're here in PE for two months, then vanishing for a year or two?"

I nodded bleakly. "I guess I could cancel the trip but I couldn't face living in PE, getting bogged down in a Practice in North End. I really want to see a bit of the world before settling down somewhere, who knows where?"

"Not even with me?" she pouted, with a ghost of a smile.

"Crys, you know there's just no way we could be together as a couple here in PE. Between your dad and my folks, they'd tear us apart in no time." I noticed her start to smile. "Why the smile? What's there to smile about?"

"Because I've just had a tiny idea. Maybe a little crazy, but here goes. I gave back my engagement ring because I wanted to see what my feelings for you were when you came back. Even this tiny get-together has made me realise that I was right. But now, well, as I was listening to you, I remembered....... my room-mate at Stellenbosch, Marie and I were talking about going overseas touring when we'd saved up enough money. Soooo..." her grin widened.

I was now all ears. "Yes, come on, what's in that scheming little head of yours?"

"OK, listen. You're here for two months. We'll have to be very careful not to give a hint that we are seeing each other during that time, but if I act all upset about my broken engagement, need to get away etc., and start talking about Marie, and a possible trip, maybe, just maybe I can get on that boat too!"

I sprang forward in my seat, banging the hooter as I grabbed Crystal's shoulders. "Are you serious? Do you think you could get that past your dad?"

"Look, Ray, I'm 22 years old, a qualified teacher, earning my own money. I'm entitled to be independent now and, yes, I think this can work. Look, there's Rita, in her car, let's go and have that hamburger. I'm starved!"

*

Over three cheeseburgers and double thick chocolate malted milkshakes the plot was all set out. It was hard to know which of the three of us was the most excited, and Rita wasn't even going! It was very simple, really. A 'very depressed' Crystal would decide that she needed to get out of PE after the disappointment of her broken engagement. She would use some of her savings for a boat trip to Europe and a few weeks touring then home again. She would name Marie Bezuidenhout as her travelling companion who would supposedly join the boat in Durban. In the meantime Crystal and I would meet secretly at a friend of Rita's flat near the beach once or twice on selected afternoons a week so that no suspicions were aroused. Then on 10th September, at different times, we would separately board the 'Africa' at PE Harbour and keep far away from each other while we said our goodbyes. Then as the ship left port.......well, we didn't dare think about that!

Arriving in London in late Summer, we would both get work, live and earn for a while, go to theatre and jazz clubs, and then, when we'd saved up enough, learn to ski in Austria or Switzerland, whichever was the cheapest.

It all sounded too good to be true. As we parted, the taste of chocolate milkshake was delicious in a lingering goodbye kiss. Crystal and Rita climbed into Rita's Volkswagen Beetle and slowly drove away, waving and blowing kiss after kiss. I drove home in the little green Morris, humming to myself, smiling insanely at the astounding way things had turned out. Or were promising to turn out. I was realistic enough to know that with the malignant Gerry Webber around, Crystal would have a harder job to keep her side of the arrangement. I licked my lips, still tasting her, pulse still racing, the way it always had in her company.

The clouds had rolled away the sunshine. I switched the windscreen wipers on full as the rain pelted down. I was simply not prepared to regard the change in the weather as an omen. Ah, well, time would tell!

CHAPTER 19

The morning of Sunday 10th September dawned bright and clear. The usual Port Elizabeth wind, from which it got its nickname, 'The Windy City', was nowhere in evidence and the sky was a vivid cloudless blue. Sleep had not come easy the previous evening. My mind was bubbling with the gut-wrenching uncertainty of whether our elaborate yet simple deception would work out in practice later that afternoon.

The previous two months had flown by. While doing my first locum as a qualified Dentist I had learned that merely obtaining a degree did not automatically confer expertise necessary to provide patients with competence one would gain with months, if not years of experience. However my employer, Isaac Dubrovsky, was extremely patient and tolerant, helping me iron out the gaps in my dealing with real live paying customers, the elements missing in the supervised and protected environment of Dental School.

Fortunately, mishaps were few. I found that patients were mostly prepared to accept my uncertainties with humour. For my part, I kept proposed treatments well within my capabilities.

On Wednesday and Friday afternoons my surgery was used by a Dental Hygienist. Crystal was able to arrange her lecturing sessions at the University accordingly. We were thus able to spend magical hours together in Rita's boyfriend's luxurious apartment at the back of the Summerstrand Hotel, with lounge and patio opening straight on to a deserted strip of beach. Every meeting felt like a first, as though each few days between had been a separation of years. We made love until exhausted, then crawled out on to the sand and plunged into icy waves. The world beyond ceased to exist for us. Time and again we found ourselves berating the bigoted society that existed in Port Elizabeth and in fact, South Africa generally, that so frowned on a loving relationship like ours, a bond which was growing stronger with each meeting.

On the final get-together, two days before the 'Africa' was due to sail, we lay together on a blanket on the sand, warmly clothed against a biting sea-breeze, gazing up at the sky. Crystal leaned over on one elbow, a concerned look on her face. "Ray, my love, does it ever cross your mind that we may never again be like this, here in our own home town, able to be an ordinary couple and look everyone straight in the eye?" Tears were forming, glistening in the bright sunshine.

"Much, much too often, Crys" I replied. "I just wish I knew the answers. Our different backgrounds firstly. No chance we could be treated as an ordinary couple. Who knows, maybe South Africa will change but, I guess, for people like us, not soon enough. Hatred and mistrust are still much too strong. That's why our only choice is escaping." I leaned across and gently licked away the salty tear-drops.

"Yes, I know, but do you think it will be different in England?" she asked, smiling uncertainly, but at the same time snuggling into my shoulder.

I nodded emphatically. "That's for sure. Letters I've had from friends in London tell me how free it is there, all races getting to know one another, having relationships. Sure, there's prejudice too but by and large, no-one interferes in your lives, you don't have to belong to any specific community, you're just a Londoner."

Crystal wriggled closer. "Hey, lover boy, what's happening to you down below?" She giggled, pointing lasciviously. "Don't we have to be out of here by five o'clock?"

We had reached a level of familiarity that required no second urging. I stood up, bent over to reduce my obvious disturbance, and pulled the blanket out from under her, rolling her over in the sand. "Hey", she yelped, "that's not funny, I'll get my hair full of sand!"

"Never mind," I laughed. "That's what that great shower afterwards is for. Come on, before you-know-who loses interest!"

Afterwards, we locked the door, sadly pushing our key through the letterbox. We both knew it was the last time we would be needing it. Arm-in-arm we strolled out to the car park.

"So, Mr. Milland, the next time we meet will be on board the 'SS Africa'," Crystal murmured, a nervous smile flickering round that full-lipped mouth.

"I guess so, Miss Webber. Be sure to bring your sailor suit! And remember, whatever happens, don't come aboard until well after three o'clock. I'm going to be in my cabin just before two hopefully and I'll try and get my family off before three. We've just got to keep well out of each other's way after that. The ship sails at five, then we're home free." I couldn't resist a cinematic farewell. "In the words of Humphrey Bogart, 'Here's lookin' at you, kid'....."

I watched with some trepidation as Crystal drove away in Rita Coetzee's little Volkswagen then waited a short while before hopping into the Morris and making my way home for our last Sabbath dinner.

It was a sombre meal. Even Euphemia's ivory smile in her usually cheerful ebony countenance was subdued. My father said the Sabbath prayers before the dinner and my mother wore her perpetual long-suffering anguish. Only Larry and Martin attempted to lighten the heavy atmosphere with questions about what life in London would be like.

"Boy, do I envy you, Ray, going to see all those great Jazz musicians, Oscar Petersen, Dave Brubeck, Art Blakey, Ella Fitzgerald. Wow!" This was Martin's contribution, having been introduced to Jazz through my collection of LP's. He was actually becoming quite a talented pianist in spite of his tender years, although playing everything by ear and not taking too much notice of the several piano teachers who had tried to force him into classics.

"Not only that, though, he'll be able to go to Lords and Twickenham to the Rugby and Cricket internationals," said Larry, wistfully. "And Wimbledon too! Will you get us some autographs, Ray?"

"Ja, I'll do my best, guys, But first I'll have to earn a bit of money. Going to all these shows and games costs dough, you know."

My mother rang the bell she kept by her place on the table. "Euphemia!" she called out to the kitchen, "you can bring the coffee now and take off, you hear!"

After a few moments Euphemia waddled into the dining room carrying a tray with coffee and chocolates. She then began to clear the dishes. The tone my mother used when she ordered our rotund maid round had always made me wince but they had this love-hate relationship, with fairly good-natured slanging matches that frequently had Euphemia responding in kind. Both women seemed to understand each other so I never commented, just had this inner feeling that two human beings ought to develop a far more even-handed respect toward each other. I wondered whether life in London would confirm my judgement.

Euphemia stopped clearing momentarily and beamed at me. "Massah Raymond, you gonna get cookin' like this in Eng–a-land, huh? I bet youse not gonna taste chicken like ah does nowhere in London, that's fer sure....!"

I stood up, laughing. "I'm pretty sure no-one cooks like you do in Eng-a-land," I said mocking her pronunciation, then pointedly, with a look at my mother, I said, "Here, let me help you carry the dishes to the kitchen."

There was a stunned silence round the table. I picked up some plates and to my delight, Larry and Martin did the same. My parents were left staring open-mouthed as I led the procession out to the kitchen.

When we returned my father was smiling. "I guess you're trying to train your parents in the ways of the new South Africa, are you?"

I went over and hugged him and did the same for my mother who was still in shock. "What will be will be, mom and dad, but whatever happens, you two are still the best parents a guy could wish for."

The rest of the evening passed like a traditionally warm Jewish Friday night dinner with one difference. This was a family about to see their eldest son depart for an unpredictable future. I found myself wondering later as I drifted off to sleep, what kind of Friday night dinner was happening in the Webber household.

*

The 'Africa' was a beautiful ship, streamlined, gleaming white. The interior had luxurious wood-panelling throughout and it boasted a small swimming pool on the top deck which we were impatient to inspect. The crew were immaculately outfitted in spotless white uniforms, welcoming boarding passengers and visitors with frenetic Italian enthusiasm. My parents, Larry, Martin and I were shown to my cabin, which I was to have to myself for the two day voyage to Durban when my two friends Alvin and David and one other would join the ship, having travelled from Johannesburg. The accommodation was somewhat cramped, with a small shower, toilet and basin. Four bunks, two up, two down.

I unpacked my two cases into the tiny cupboard, every now and then casting an anxious glance at my watch. It was two thirty. My father noticed and shook his head. "You anxious to get rid of us, boychick?"

"No, not at all, dad," I replied guiltily. "Course not....I am pretty excited though."

My mother meanwhile ran her fingers over the bunk I'd chosen and shelves above, looking for dust. "Clean enough for our boy, Rosie?" my father said with a grin. She nodded then proceeded to give the tiny shower-room and toilet the once-over. Satisfied, she turned to go out into the passageway.

"Where are you off to, mom?" I yelled after her.

"Ain't you gonna show us the rest of your boat, Raymond?" she shouted back.

We all scurried along after her retreating figure. It was complicated, finding our way through the companionways, halls, and various decks. Finally we came out on the top deck with lifeboats, deck-quoit court and pool. We wandered the full circuit in spite of the wind which had grown in ferocity during the hour that had passed. I sneaked another look at my watch. Three thirty. I crossed my fingers, hoping that Crystal would be safely on board by now.

An announcement came over the ship's PA system. "Will all visitors please leave the ship immediately. The 'SS Africa' sails at five o'clock." I began to guide my family gently but firmly toward the level at which the gangplank allowed passengers and visitors access and exit. Beads of sweat were popping out on my forehead despite the howling wind which was bringing temperatures down rapidly. We were nearing the main entrance. I grabbed my father by the shoulders, and hugged him close. "Dad, believe me, this is the most difficult thing I've ever had to do so please, let's just not have a big tearful scene. It's only for a year or so and I'm going to be back here, you know that, but I've got to spread my wings a bit. You understand, don't you?"

He nodded but in his eyes was the saddest expression I'd ever seen. "Go well, Raymond, my boy, Have a wonderful trip. Oy! Whole east coast of Africa, the Suez Canal......mind you, things are getting hot there between Israel and the Arabs. Don't go anywhere without people from the boat, you hear me? It's a dangerous time."

"Shush, dad," I protested. "You'll have mom in a panic. She's upset enough already!"

He nodded. "You're right, Ray, but just remember what I said, willya? Still you're in for a great time and you deserve it. All the sights of Europe, marvellous! I really envy you. Wish I'd had the same opportunities when I was your age. Everything of the very best and write often, you promise!"

He turned to my mother. "Rosie, don't make a scene. He's a grown man and he's going off to see the world. Just give the boychick a big hug and kiss and for heaven's sake don't let the floodgates open!"

My mother clasped me fiercely, her wet cheeks rubbing moisture onto my face. "Travel well, Raymond. Do well, eat well, look after yourself and come back soon. I know I've been harsh on you sometimes but it was always for your own good. Give your mother a kiss and we'll go down and watch the boat leave from the jetty."

I did as I was told.

My brothers grabbed hold of me, both at the same time, I nuzzled them affectionately and then, with a last wave, my family trudged down the gangplank to the jetty below. I turned hurriedly, intending to rush up to the top deck where not only would I be out of the way, able to see them waving, but also to have a wonderful view of my hometown, the town in which I'd spent most of my twenty-two years. My innermost feelings were a mixture of love and tenderness for my ageing parents and brothers, coupled with not a little guilt at hurrying away from them to avoid a confrontation with Crystal and her parents. The feverish excitement at the successful conclusion of our deception, weeks on board with the girl of my dreams for so long brought me out in a cold sweat in case any last minute hitch should occur.

The hall and staircase were crowded so I decided to take the lift. I pressed the button. A red light came on and a bell rang. The double doors opened and I came face to face with the biggest nightmare of my life. Gerry Webber stood in front of me, his mammoth frame practically filling the entire lift opening. I was not too sure who had received the greater shock, him or me.

"W-WWHAT THE FUCK!!!!!" he spat at me. "YOU! WHAT THE HELL ARE YOU......." A look of realisation crossed his beefy features. "OH, HOLY SHIT! NOW I GET THE PICTURE!" he roared. With a huge fist he pushed me backwards then turned. I could see Crystal and her mother cowering behind him, eyes wide in alarm. Webber reached into the lift and grabbed Crystal by her shoulders, practically throwing her bodily against me. We lost our balance and crashed into a huge urn which toppled over and splintered into pieces. Crystal lay on top of me with Webber standing over the two of us. At this stage I was vaguely aware of white uniformed crew members standing open-mouthed, as well as dozens of passengers and visitors who were lining up to leave the ship or say their goodbyes It was clear that no-one wished to interfere with the colossal heavyweight who looked as though he was about to commit murder.

Someone yelled out, "Get the Captain!"

Gerry turned a malevolent eye to the voice in the crowd. "YEAH, YEAH, YOU BETTER GET THE CAPTAIN. DOUBLE QUICK TOO BECAUSE I TELL YOU, THIS BLOODY SHIP IS NOT MOVING ONE INCH WITH MY DAUGHTER AND HER FUCKIN' JEWBOY PAL TOGETHER. NO BLOODY WAY!!!!!!!"

By this time I was just about able to stand, crunching pieces of porcelain underfoot. Crystal managed to rise slowly alongside me and stared defiantly at her father. "Pa, you are making a spectacle of yourself. I'm old enough to do what I want, you've always said so. Well, now you know. Ray and I are going on this trip, I've paid for it with my own money and there's nothing you can do about it!"

This was not the first occasion I had seen Crystal in this pugilistic mood. The last time she had won over two gullible police officers. But this was not going to be so easy. In panic I wondered whether I ought to confront Webber in her support.

The next thing I knew I was standing in front of my lover, hands on hips, and looking her crimson-faced father straight in the eye. "Mr. Webber, Crystal and I are over twenty one and are entitled to go where and when we please. You have no right whatso........."

CRACK!

I have no clear recollection of what happened next. I was aware that I had been smashed full force on the side of my head, and had careered across into the crowd of onlookers. I was vaguely aware of a collective sound.....the united gasp of the dumb-struck spectators. I heard Crystal scream and her mother remonstrating with her dervish–like saliva-foaming husband. I saw through one eye the spectre of Webber as he bodily picked Crystal up and strode down the gangplank, her legs waving wildly in the air, hands tearing at his moon-like face. I heard him yell at his wife to get Crystal's luggage. Groggily I staggered across the entrance to the edge of the gangplank and was just in time to see Gerry Webber pass my parents whom he shoved roughly out of the way. I tried desperately to follow down the gangplank but my legs gave way under me and my world suddenly went black.

*

I found myself being stared at by blurred faces. I was lying on a settee in an adjoining lounge. Someone thrust a strong-smelling bottle under my nose and I sat up, groaning. "What's happened? Crystal, where is she?"

A kind-looking face with a clerical collar appeared in the mist above me. "Shush now, my boy, you've had a nasty blow, been unconscious for nearly an hour." He wiped a cool cloth across my forehead.

The realisation then hit me full force. I sat up, pushing the priest aside. "An hour!!! Crystal, where is she? What did that beast do with her?"

"Calm down, my boy. I'm afraid that brute force has triumphed here today."

I could see other faces peering at me from behind the cleric. Then the crowd parted to let a gray-haired man in a white uniform through.

"Is the boy conscious now?" I heard him say to my white-collared benefactor.

"Yes" came the reply. "But he's had a major blow to the head and is still semi-delirious."

I sat up then. "I am NOT delirious! I want to know what has happened! Are you the Captain??" I shouted at the white uniform.

"Yes, I am, Captain Luigi Vestanza. Are you feeling better, my son?"

"I would be if someone would kindly tell me what happened to Crystal Webber. She was supposed to be travelling with me and that monster of a father of hers attacked me. The last I saw he was carrying her off the ship....." I let out a moan as a sharp pain shot across my face. "How can that have happened? How can your crew allow a man to attack someone on your ship and kidnap, yes, kidnap one of your passengers?"

There were murmurs of support for me in the crowd of people surrounding us. Shouts of "Shame", "Disgraceful" and "Outrageous" came from several sections.

The Captain leaned over close to me and whispered, "I think it would be better if we talked in my office, Mr.er, er...."

I sat up, attempting some dignity. "My name is Raymond Benjamin. Dr. Raymond Benjamin!"

The Captain looked startled. "You are a Doctor, sir?" he asked nervously.

"No. I am a newly qualified Dental Surgeon. And I want to know what happened to ....my....my.....fiancee, Crystal Webber!"

With marginally more decorum, the Captain helped me stand, escorting me slowly past the gawking onlookers. After limping what seemed like the entire length of the ship we reached his palatial office where a white-robed nurse gave me some tablets and a glass of water. I sat in a large armchair while the Captain spoke on the phone. It was clear he was in some kind of argument.

"No, that's impossible. We have a sailing schedule. I cannot delay the ship. We were due to leave twenty minutes ago."

There was silence while he listened to whoever it was on the other end of the line. Then he looked at me and smiled sheepishly. "I am sorry. I have the Port Elizabeth Port Authority on the line. They wanted to delay our departure on the grounds that an assault and possible kidnap has taken place on board. We closed the gangplank soon after the father of your...er.... fiancée carried her off as it was close to sailing time. However, your parents were told what had happened and they were also assaulted by this man. They reported the incident to the Port Authority who in turn reported the matter to the Port Elizabeth Police."

I shook my head, suddenly terrifiedly aware. "My parents.... assaulted? Where? Are they all right? And what on earth happened to Crystal? We'd planned this trip together! WON'T SOMEBODY PLEASE TELL ME WHAT'S GOING ON!!!!"

Captain Vestanza nodded sympathetically. "Try to relax, my son. I understand your feelings. Firstly your parents are all right. They were just pushed out of the way by this gigantic man. They are not hurt but extremely upset. Sadly, however, the father of the girl has influential friends in the Police. They told the Port Authority that it was a domestic argument, no-one was seriously injured and that in any case there was a court order restricting you from being in contact with the girl."

I stood up, shaking with anger. "Yes, but that order was taken out five years ago and expired two years ago. He had no right to take her off the ship!"

"Please Dr. Benjamin, understand our position. We cannot enter into what may well be a protracted legal argument with the Police. We have a schedule to sail out of Port Elizabeth at five this afternoon. It is now five thirty. Our Head Office has told us that we will be penalised extra Harbour duties if we do not sail by six o'clock. I am afraid that there is very little else we can do."

I hung my head, totally defeated. All the planning, the euphoric anticipation of a romantic sea voyage and a life together with Crystal far from the tyranny of Gerry Webber had evaporated in a matter of a few hours. I rose from the chair and turned to leave, my legs still shaking.

"If there is anything I can do to help you, Doctor, please let me know," the Captain called after me.

I turned to face him. "Did you say that my parents were assaulted? Can I speak to them? They must be beside themselves with worry. Will they still be in the Port Authority Office?"

He nodded. "They were still there when I spoke with the Port Captain. Sit down, I will try the number."

My father's voice was quivering with rage. "Ray, my boy, that frightful crazy man, that monster! Are you all right?"

"Yes, dad, just a few bruises. They said he assaulted you and mom. Are you both OK?"

"We're fine. He just pushed us aside like we were cardboard. Look, I'm sorry we couldn't do much this side. Webber has friends high up in PE's Police and they've washed their hands of it all. The ship cannot be held in port. I understand they are preparing to leave right now."

"Dad, I'm so sorry about all this. I wish that it had all gone according to plan. We only started going together again two months ago and, well, I'm really sorry if you thought I was deceiving you but I knew how you felt about Crystal and so......"

"Raymond, my lovely son, we realised what a strong bond there was between you and this girl. In fact you seemed so happy and contented we guessed you were seeing her secretly but said nothing. Believe me, if it had meant us getting to know and even to love her as the choice you made, we would have done so. But you tried to fight a man who would stop at nothing to prevent you and Crystal making a life together. Well, as we say in Yiddish, I guess it's 'passhert' or in other words, fated, not meant to be. I can imagine how you are aching right now, but maybe when you meet your friends in Durban and have a good fascinating trip, time will help heal the agony. Just go now, boychick, maybe have a good stiff whisky tonight and... may God bless you always. Your mother is too upset to talk but she sends you the same blessing."

The tears were falling hard and fast now, unashamedly dripping on to the Captain's desk. The nurse leaned forward with tissues which I accepted gratefully.

The Captain strode round to my side of the desk and placed a hand on my shoulder. "Dr. Benjamin, I would like to offer my sympathy for what has occurred. Unfortunately it all happened so quickly that no-one was able to prevent it and indeed knowing the stature and strength of this man, it is possible that many could have been hurt trying to stop him." He smiled wanly. "We Italians understand the affairs of the heart probably better than most other people. You will recover, my boy, believe me, and in time there will be other loves in your life, especially for an attractive young man like you with a good profession." He hesitated momentarily. "There is one other course open to you, of course......."

"What's that?" I asked.

"You could choose to leave the ship and try to sort out the situation in Port Elizabeth. Naturally I could not guarantee that you would not lose what you have paid for the voyage. Sadly, I cannot give you much time to consider as we have a schedule to sail within half an hour."

I tried desperately to collect my equilibrium and think logically. Leave the ship, lose the fare money, and attempt to fight a battle against impossible odds with a monster like Webber, secure in his contacts with all the powers that be in Port Elizabeth, or admit defeat and leave behind the most important person in my young life? With the gaping hollow in my stomach and the throbbing in my head I stared at the Captain and the genuinely sympathetic expression on his face. This was a war I could not hope to win.

After a few moments I smiled brokenly and shook his hand. "Thank you Captain. I think I'll go to my cabin now."

He nodded. "Yes, it is best you take some rest now and, may I cordially invite you to dine with me and my guests this evening. There are not many for the first section to East London and I think maybe you will enjoy the company, but only if you feel up to it."

"Thank you, Captain. That's very kind. I would like to very much."A thought suddenly struck me and I turned back, with a wry grin. "I was wondering, what happened to Crystal's luggage?"

The Captain smiled thinly. "Yes, we had to repack her belongings which were already neatly laid out in the cupboard and shelves in her cabin. I had her luggage delivered to the Port Authority Offices."

With a great lump in my throat I went up by lift to the top deck still very unsure of my balance. I could feel the engines vibrating and wanted more than anything else to catch a last glimpse of my beloved home town, Port Elizabeth, before it faded into the distance. I was leaving behind my family and now, suddenly, also the one person with whom I had hoped to spend the rest of my life. I knew with certainty that hatred, fear and intolerance had defeated us, and that I would most probably never see Crystal Webber again.

*

The 'SS Africa' cleared the breakwater and on the distant jetty I thought I could make out the tiny figures of my parents and my brothers waving frantically. I waved back, cheeks wet with tears. I was aware of my friend, the priest and two women alongside, also watching the receding harbour. We stood there until Port Elizabeth was a distant smudge on the horizon. The cleric introduced me to his wife and the other woman, whose name was Elise. We were all apparently guests on the Captain's table that evening. I excused myself and made my way back to my lonely cabin, to reflect on what might have been.

Chapter 20

Elise

I must have slept for an hour, waking suddenly when the constant thrum of the engines ceased and was replaced by a quiet electric humming. I wriggled over to the porthole and, to my amazement, I could still see the distant outline of Port Elizabeth, with the lights beginning to twinkle in the hazy evening horizon. Puzzled, I looked at my watch. Only seven thirty. I was due at the Captain's table for dinner at eight. The enormity of the disaster that had overtaken Crystal and me returned like a bad taste. After a few moments I decided that a shower and shave might take my mind off events.

*

There were six other privileged passengers seated at the Captain's table. An Italian band played softly in one corner of the Dining Hall. Not many tables were occupied and those that were only had a few people eating. On one side of me was the Pastor with his wife, originally from Germany, having spent fifteen years in South Africa. They were now returning to Wiesbaden, to a small parish where they would spend their retirement. I thanked him for his kindness that afternoon but noting my mournful demeanour, they sensitively avoided discussion of the calamitous happenings in the ship's Entrance Hall.

On my other side sat Elise, to whom I had been introduced as the 'SS Africa' left port. She was elegantly dressed, quietly spoken, and attractive in a somewhat underplayed fashion. Teaching High School in Pietersburg, Northern Transvaal, she was due to meet her long-time fiancée in Durban for an overseas trip. She looked to be in her mid-thirties and spoke with hardly a trace of an accent.

The Captain was in jovial mood and at his insistence the wine flowed copiously. Having introduced us he raised his glass. "May you all enjoy with me what I assure you will be a most memorable journey. My dear friends, our itinerary takes us past many differing countries, different cultures and religions and we will have time every few days to go ashore and sample those fascinating places." He looked at me directly. "For our newly qualified Dental Surgeon, Raymond, I offer a special welcome. He had a particularly nasty experience in the Departure Hall this afternoon so may I take this opportunity to wish him especially, a most enjoyable voyage. Let us drink to him and to all of us!"

Highly embarrassed, I acknowledged the toast and drank thirstily. "Thank you, Captain. As you can imagine I am having some difficulty coming to terms with what happened so I think, for me, the best thing would be just to try and enjoy your hospitality, and especially the company, the food and wine and the lovely music!"

A chorus of Hear! Hear! and clinking of glasses reverberated round the table. The Pastor turned to me and shook my hand firmly. "Well said, young man. Are you feeling any better now?"

"Yes, thanks." I nodded. "I had a good sleep but I woke when the engines stopped. And we are still in sight of Port Elizabeth. Do you know why?"

Captain Vestanza answered immediately. "Yes, Raymond. The reason is that we have less than a day's sailing to the next port of East London. That means that we have to pay more Harbour duties if we dock there too early. So we anchor out here in Algoa Bay until much later then sail at dawn. It's all about saving money these days, you know!" A ripple of laughter spread round the table.

Years later, my mother would recall, before they went to bed that night, how she and my father stood in my bedroom and saw the lights of the 'SS Africa', anchored way out in the bay. She remembered saying that she knew then with certainty that I would never return to live in Port Elizabeth.

As the wine flowed, the conversation grew more relaxed. The others at the table were an Italian couple returning home to Italy and an elderly former Colonel in the British Army who was going to visit family in England after retiring to South Africa.

After eating her meal practically in silence, Elise turned to me with a sympathetic look. "I'm sure you don't want anyone prying into what happened but I do feel very sorry for you. I did see most of it so if you want to talk about it...." She left the sentence unfinished.

I think that, what with the large amount of wine I'd consumed, I was grateful for the interest and warmth in her voice. "Yes, I guess it was quite a spectacle, wasn't it? We'd planned this trip together in spite of huge animosity between her father and my family. We managed to keep it a secret until this afternoon."

Before I knew it, I had related the whole six-year saga. Elise was a good listener, just nodding and smiling and even at times seeming close to tears. Dessert and coffee came and went, and still, at the Captain's urging, the wine waiters kept refilling our glasses. "And that's it, I'm afraid, end of story," I said, draining yet another glass. By this time I must confess my head was spinning and the throbbing on the side of my face had become bearable, numb, almost.

"You poor thing," Elise murmured, placing a consoling hand on my arm. "You have got to believe this, but I am so much more sympathetic hearing your story because..... .....oh, hell no, I'm sure you aren't interested in my sorry tale....."

Her touch was like an electric shock. I didn't know whether to move my arm away, or not. In the end I just let it rest there. She seemed in no hurry to remove it.

"No," I said, "Fair's fair. You've listened to all my problems. I'd be happy, in fact, honoured, to hear yours."

She hesitated, but just for a moment, then, her cheek muscles tightening visibly, she began. "Well, OK, then. You see, it's not all that dissimilar to your experience. I come from Pietersburg in the Northern Transvaal, a small little town where everyone knows everyone's business. I'm thirty-five, by the way and for the last ten years I've been engaged to a Jewish farmer. The whole town knows that Mendel and I have been sort of engaged except his mother who just point-blank refuses to accept me."

"You're not Jewish, are you?" I asked then immediately cursed my stupidity. 'Blame it on the wine' a little voice told me. "Sorry," I mumbled. "Silly question!"

She smiled a little ruefully. She had beautifully even white teeth, my professional instincts reacted approvingly. Deep-set almond shaped grey eyes and dark brown hair cut short with a fringe framing an oval elfin face. "No. Anglican, actually. But I was prepared to convert if that would satisfy his mother."

"And that wouldn't do the trick?"

Elise shook her head. "No chance. She didn't want to know. The old lady said she would kill herself if Mendel married out, not me especially, just anybody who wasn't Jewish. But as all the other eligible females in Pietersburg were Afrikaners and a lot younger, I don't think I had much competition." The bitterness in Elise's voice was increasing and I listened avidly, my own situation and its similarities evoking a common bond of empathy with her.

"So where does that leave you guys now?"

She pursed her lips. "Well, I guess I read Mendel the riot act this year. I said I wasn't prepared to wait for his mother to die before we got married, nor was I going to be the cause of her killing herself. So I gave him an ultimatum. He has to decide by the end of this year."

"So what was his reaction?"

"This trip was his reaction," she smiled grimly. "He said that we could go overseas on this wonderful ship, spend a few weeks touring Europe and then see how we both felt. His treat!"

By this time we were both so absorbed in each other's stories, neither of us had noticed that our fellow diners had left, with only the Captain and the Pastor remaining, also deep in conversation. We had had large snifters of Brandy thrust at us and not wishing to snub the Captain's effusive generosity, had sipped the fiery liquid very tentatively. The combination of various alcoholic beverages was having its effect on both my new confidant and me. Our speech was becoming indistinct and garbled, as was our reaction to the irony of the situation.

"So, Elise, you mean he's taking you on this trip to convince himself that he should defy his mother and marry you?" I mumbled, semi-articulately. "I don't think that's very gentlemanly at all, if you want my opinion."

"He won't defy his mother ever," she said. "If she knew we were going on this trip together it would kill her, he told me." I could see her eyes filling with tears.

The band was playing something lilting, slow and romantic. The trumpeter laid down his instrument and sang in Italian. I stood up unsteadily and bowed. "Would you like to dance?" I slurred.

Elise looked up at me and smiled. She actually was very pretty in a prim sort of way, I realised. "Yes, why not?" she said laughing, half-rising out of her chair. "You're sure you can keep upright?"

I bent forward and took her hand. "I may need a little support but yes, after University drinking, I think I'll just be able to manage. Maybe after all our confessions we could do with a little relaxing dance, don't you?"

"Definitely," she murmured as she came into my arms. Behind her, the Captain caught my eye and gave a broad wink. I winked in return and whirled my partner round the floor. She was an excellent dancer, and not for the first time in my life I blessed Ted van Jaarsveld's dancing classes of my youth.

The song came to an end and we stood in the middle of the floor, still close together.

"I love that tune," Elise said. "Let's ask them what it's called. Maybe they'll play it again for us."

It was an Italian song called in English "A Grain of Sand" and they played it not once but several times for the next hour. We were by now the only couple on the floor and, as the lights dimmed, our dancing became more intimate, bodies pressed tightly together. I could feel, even in spite of the events of the recent months and the afternoon past, that I was reacting to the closeness and warmth of this gracious woman I'd only just met. There seemed to be no reluctance on her part either, so that when the band finally stopped for the evening, we walked out on deck, arm in arm. The wind had died and it was a brilliant star-speckled night. In the distance the lights of Port Elizabeth twinkled tantalizingly as if mocking the fickleness of humanity.

"You're an extremely good dancer, Ray," she murmured, resting her head on my shoulder. "Glorious night, isn't it?"

"Sure is. You're not such a bad dancer yourself, Elise. I feel as though we've known each other for years. Strange isn't it?"

"How are you feeling, deep down, I mean?"

I hesitated. "You mean about Crystal, and her father?"

"You don't have to say if you don't want to."

"I know. But it's OK. I want to... I guess I'm extremely angry. I'm still unable to believe it but I guess it's good to let one's feelings out and just plain amazing that I found someone like you, almost in the same boat..." I gave a small laugh. "Sorry about the pun!"

We both started to laugh then, and, as if magnetised, came together face to face. The kiss was deep and tender, and lasted forever, bodies tightly-knit. The hours of dancing close had familiarised us with each other so that, coupled with the alcoholic loosening of inhibitions, there was an inevitability as to how the night was going to end.

"I have another woman in my cabin," Elise gasped, looking at me questioningly.

"I don't.........," I smiled, ".......have another woman.... in my cabin, that is."

She smiled, staring at me archly. "Is that an invitation, young man?"

I said nothing, merely tightened my grip around her pert waist and somehow, we managed to navigate the tortuous passages, finally landing up looking at each other in the confines of my tiny four-bunked cabin.

*

The sudden vibrations as the engines of the 'SS Africa' started up intruded on my consciousness, together with a king-sized headache. I managed to open one eye which I closed quickly, the glare of sunrise through the porthole practically blinding me. I turned away from the light and tried again, opening both eyes slowly. Elise was looking at me, smiling, up on one elbow, on the wall side of the narrow bunk. I blinked, felt an urgent need to pinch myself which I resisted. "Am I dreaming, or is this real?" I muttered.

"Very real, Raymond. I would say almost beyond real." Elise stretched languorously. "My, my, you are quite a lover boy, aren't you?"

The rumpled bedclothes lay in a heap on the floor of the cabin. We were lying naked, the narrowness of the bunk ensuring that our bodies were only inches apart. I was unable to stop myself gazing at her full breasts, voluptuous hips and flat stomach. For her part, Elise ran her hand over the hair on my chest. In spite of the throbbing in my head and face, I could feel excitement rising uncontrollably.

"My, my," Elise murmured again, noticing. "I would have thought the past few hours would have left you exhausted......" she drew me to her, allowing my erection to nuzzle her dark triangle.... "but obviously not that exhausted."

*

In retrospect, I must say I felt no guilt, no remorse. Although images of Crystal kept flashing through my mind, I rationalised that we were two lonely souls, each with our own brand of sadness and regret, reaching out for warmth, sympathy, and understanding. Upon finding it in such romantic and wine-laden circumstances, the passion that had enveloped us was not difficult to understand.

I have a somewhat blurred memory of our first moments in the cabin the previous night. Increasing urgency of our embraces, frenzied removal of clothing in the cramped space between the bunks and drunken clumsiness as we clambered up on to the upper bunk fizzed around in my brain. We must both have realised simultaneously, as two strangers, no-one to disturb us, no-one to object or interfere, our own consciences thoroughly assuaged by the alcohol, that on this night, in this place we were hurting no other human beings.

Our coupling at first was slow and tentative, a voyage of mutual discovery, as I had heard it described. Then, darkness covering our inhibitions, we allowed ourselves to give free rein to whatever titillations and innovations we were capable of. What became clear quite soon was that this was a first for both of us with a new partner.

"She must have been quite something, this Crystal of yours," Elise said afterwards, wiping damp hair from her forehead. "Were you thinking of her during, ... you know what I mean?" In the dark I could just make out the veiled amusement in her eyes.

"No, I wasn't," I at least half-honestly replied firmly. "And you, was I being a Mendel substitute for you?"

Elise laughed aloud, her breath still sweet, with just a tinge of brandy. "You must be joking. After ten years we were like an old married couple!"

*

I lost count of the number of times we made love that night and early morning. It was like a kind of spiritual cleansing, leaving no guilty feelings, only a warm satisfaction that we were each able to give comfort and solace to the other, our needs and sadness practically identical.

We managed to shower together in the tiny cubicle, which nearly led to another confrontation on the much-abused upper bunk. But bravely we resisted, the call of breakfast, or rather missing breakfast and consequential raised eyebrows proving the deciding factors. Elise returned to her cabin for a change of clothes and we met in the dining room which, since breakfast was practically over, was deserted. Nevertheless, we ate contentedly, ignoring any inquisitive looks from the waiters.

"You slept well, I trust, Senorina Elise, and Doctor Raymondo?" Captain Vestanza suddenly appeared with his broad smile, a Latin accent, and not a trace of irony.

We nodded emphatically, "Yes, very well indeed, Captain." Elise gave him her most fetching look. "And thank you for a wonderful dinner and dance. Everything was superb."

I bobbed my head in agreement, wiping toast crumbs from the side of my mouth. "Yes, Captain Vestanza, it was just what the doctor ordered, especially after yesterday."

He beamed, fingering his black moustache. "I am so pleased. Now, we are landing in East London in an hour and you young people have the day to explore this lovely little seaside town. Like yesterday, the ship sails at five so make sure you are back by then." And with a bow, and not a whiff of a knowing look, he was gone.

We looked at each other and burst into a gale of laughter. I tried to mimic the twirling of a phantom moustache and that sent Elise into a giggling fit that nearly had her choking over her coffee.

*

We hired a taxi to take us to Nahoon Beach and barefooted, carrying shoes and socks, walked the length of the spectacular beach with the massive waves crashing into rocks. We were treated to the spectacle of a school of porpoises parading across the bay. Being the end of the South African winter, there were no bathers braving the cold ocean, just a few warmly clad walkers all of whom smiled and said, "Good Morning."

Lunch was at a small seafood restaurant overlooking the cliffs which bordered the beach. A bottle of white wine and delicious prawns was more than enough after the huge feast the night before and the plentiful breakfast.

"What are you thinking, Doctor Raymondo?" Elise wanted to know. We were sitting outside on a terrace, the wind was light, just ruffling her hair, and giving her cheeks a rosy glow.

"I guess I'm just thinking how incredible life is, with its ups and downs. Here we are, you and I, yet twenty four hours ago we were strangers. Now it's as if we have no secrets from each other. All in one night and morning."

"Yes, and what a night and morning," she reminded me, her cheeks blushing even rosier. "It's extraordinary. I had been undecided about coming on this trip for months, you know. My instincts told me that Mendel and I were going nowhere and that a vacation like this could well be a disaster...."

"So what made you finally decide?"

"I don't really know. I suppose deep down I recognised that after ten years, even if we did marry, it would be fraught with difficulties in a small community like Pietersburg. In fact I had sent some applications to a College in Boston USA for a teaching post there. So I thought, what the hell, the trip sounded amazing. What could I lose?" She reached out and took my hand. "And I guess the last twenty-four hours with you have made me realise that there's such a lot more to life than trying to placate a nasty old woman in the back of beyond like the Northern Transvaal."

I stared at her in surprise."You mean, you might not come back to SA at all?"

Elise squeezed my hand harder. "I thought before I left that I didn't have much going for me where I was anyway. I'm due substantial holiday time which I could use in lieu of notice. My parents died several years ago. My social life consisted of Mendel, in secret a lot of the time, and going out with other married couples as the odd couple, pretending to be just friends for appearances' sake. But everyone knew and I suppose it just became a habit until a few months back, I just woke up one morning and said to myself, that's it, and gave Mendel the choice."

"And now?"

"Well, young man, now....I don't want to make you swollen-headed, but you....you've made me feel like a woman again. I was beginning to forget."

A light patter of rain had begun, the clouds rolling in from the sea. I escorted Elise inside, and paid the bill. We stood uncertainly at the restaurant entrance, watching the shower turn into a cascade.

"We've got till five o'clock," I shouted above the clatter of the storm. "I thought we might have time for a movie but...."

She linked my arm in hers. "I've got a better idea," she looked up at me provocatively. "Why don't we get a taxi back to the good old 'Africa' and, well," she raised her eyebrows, "we could watch the storm from the lounge or ..."

I smiled, feeling a rising warmth within. "Or we could watch it through a very small porthole!"

*

The next hours passed swiftly. We both knew instinctively that by the following afternoon, when the ship took on the full complement of passengers, our present intimacy would become much more difficult if not well-nigh impossible. So, inevitably, most of the time was spent in my cabin. To say that I found Elise insatiable would be an understatement. It was as though, with me, she was trying to make up for all the frustrations of her severely restricted relationship, with a man several years her senior. That evening we dined late, danced for an hour then returned to our love-nest to spend the night wrapped in each other's arms, dreading the coming day.

*

Apart from a brief walk round Durban beachfront we spent the morning in the cabin. An hour before the commencement of new passenger boarding we tidied up the bunk and made our way to the top deck. From that vantage point we watched the crowds coming aboard. When in the distance I spied Alvin and David approaching, we hurried down to the Entrance Hall to greet them. I noticed the Cabin allocation listed the fourth occupant of our cabin was to be a Mr. M. Schwartz.

Alvin Woolf was as tall and gangly as David Hirsch was short and thickset. Alvin sported a loud sports jacket and a huge grin, his wiry brown hair cut short, almost a crew cut. David was dark-skinned with pitch black hair grown fashionably long. He and I had always had a much closer friendship than with Alvin, a fact that in the past, had surfaced in little barbed, rather jealous remarks. However, for now the greeting was friendly and I took the opportunity to introduce them to Elise, who was standing to one side. I knew from their reaction to her that they instantly suspected something more than a recent acquaintance but shrugged it off nonchalantly.

Just behind them came a rotund middle-aged man whom they seemed to know. Before I could be introduced, Elise came bounding forward and enveloped him in a bear-hug. "Mendel, welcome on board! You're gonna love this ship. It's marvellous!"

I stood dumbfounded. So this was Mendel, her fiancée! Alvin and David watched them as they walked arm in arm to the notice-board. I noticed my friends watching me a little less accusingly but the expression on my face must have given them some doubts.

After perusing the Cabin allocations Mendel turned to my two friends with a delighted smile. "Hey guys, we're sharing a cabin! With someone called Raymond Benjamin!"

I had great difficulty avoiding Elise's glance. So this was 'M.Schwartz'. For the next three weeks I was to share our tiny accommodation with the fiancée of the woman with whom I had just spent two nights in the most passionate fashion possible.

"Er, that's me." I mumbled. "I bet you didn't expect to be sharing with three newly qualified dentists," was the best I could come up with. There was a delighted cackle of laughter from David and Alvin.

We shook hands. He had a jovial open face, with what one could describe as typically Jewish features. Florid face, thickish lips and large nose. But there was no mistaking his amiable grin. "No, I guess not, but I suppose any tooth problems I have can be dealt with right in the cabin!"

For her part Elise retained her serene and welcoming facade. "Come Mendel, let the boys show you to your cabin and I'll see you in the lounge when you've unpacked." She smiled at the three of us gaily. "Look after him, fellows, he's not been on a ship before!" And with a whirl, and just the most cursory eye contact with me she vanished down the hall towards the outer deck.

I led the three men to the cabin then left them to their unpacking, my excuse being the acute lack of room for all four of us at once.

I found her on the seaward deck looking out at the famous Durban Bluff and the swirling ocean beyond. "I don't know how this is going to work," I said, bitterly, keeping my distance.

"Nor do I." I could see she had been crying.

"I thought you managed brilliantly down there. My friends were really suspicious at first but after you gave him that big welcome...."

"I could see that, so I laid it on a bit thick. Mendel must have been a bit surprised." She gave a wry smile.

"I think he was delighted, he was grinning ear to ear." Then the thought surfaced. "But, bloody hell, we're sharing a cabin! I've come to think of it as our cabin. Not fair is it?" I bit my lip savagely.

"Ray, listen to me," she pleaded. "We knew it was going to be awkward but because the ship has these rules, only married couples having cabins, there's going to be little or no opportunity to ....well, not even for me and Mendel, so we are just going to have to be good shipmates. Our truly wonderful time together will have to remain...... as our delicious little secret, until......"

"Yes, until when?" I retorted roughly.

"I really don't know," she replied forlornly. She looked past me and a look of panic crossed her face. "I think they must be finished unpacking by now. Let's go to the lounge separately." A determined look crossed her face. "This is an opportunity for you, Raymondo, to show that you're not only a good dancer, a sensational lover, but also an actor par excellence!" She flung her arms round me, kissed me full on the lips for a moment then turned and was gone.

I remained staring at the sea, completely stunned. The catastrophic and anguished memory of being torn away from an ecstatic voyage and future life with Crystal, anaesthetised to an extent for two days and two nights of passion with Elise, came crashing down on me. I held my head in my hands for quite a while, anger and remorse whirlpooling inside me, before turning resignedly to commence what looked likely to become the most frustrating period of my life.

Chapter 21

We were now a quintet. Elise and her four men had become inseparable. The 'SS Africa' cruised seamlessly through the calm Indian Ocean, nearly always in sight of land. We had a day in port in Lourenco Marques, where a magnificent lunch was provided at the splendid Polana Hotel, a monument to colonial Portuguese architecture. Beira we found poverty stricken and decaying. The voyage was now entering tropical waters so the daytime heat was stifling. Under shades at the pool became our favourite if somewhat crowded meeting place.

Our group frequently became a quartet as Mendel was struck down by violent seasickness in spite of the tranquillity of the sea, spending many hours in the confines of our cabin. For me this had two beneficial results. First, I was able to enjoy secretive communication, verbal and tactile, with Elise when my buddies weren't looking, and second, because the cabin now exuded the ever-present sour smell of vomit, I had an excuse to spend my nights sleeping on a sun-lounger on the top deck. Staring at the brilliance of the tropical night sky, my mind whirled with images of Crystal, screaming, hands outstretched as her brute of a father carried her down the walkway and out of my life. Vivid recollections of our days by the beachside apartment, the physical encounters which were never enough, flooded my mind with guilt. What else could I have done? Should we have planned better? Could we not have foreseen the likelihood of Webber seeing us before the 'Africa's departure, realising what our foolhardy plans were? The answers came back affirmative.

Somehow, there was a fated inevitability that, one way or another, her father would always prevent us being together.

So I lay there alone, gazing at infinitesimal beauty, terrified of closing my eyes in case the images of Crystal would fade and leave me sodden with guilt over the ease with which I had fallen into the embraces of another woman.

We spent memorable days ashore in Dar-es-salaam, Tanganyika (to become Tanzania) and Mombasa, Kenya, visiting Fort Jesus amongst other fascinating places, What struck us most were the dramatic changes of culture from white / Western dominated South Africa, Portuguese influence in Lourenco Marques and Beira, followed by the Arabic essence of Dar-es-salaam. Kenya, however we found overwhelmingly African in every aspect.

After returning to the ship laden with curios from Mombasa I decided to bring matters concerning Mendel to a head with Elise. I cornered her on deck while the others were in our cabin. "Why don't you just tell him?" I demanded roughly. "You said yourself that it was going nowhere. Put him out of his misery."

"I can't," she whispered. "He's paid for my trip and everything. Just think what the rest of the journey would be like."

"So what are you going to do when you get off the ship in Italy?"

She grimaced. "Well, before we left we agreed that this would be make or break for us. The way things are now, I'm not sure we'll be even talking to each other by that time. You've seen for yourself how, what with being seasick, he's become a real pain."

I felt a momentary stab of remorse, even sympathy for my stricken cabin-mate. Yet as I looked at Elise there in the gathering dusk, the physical attraction remained uppermost. I even found my eyesight beginning to play tricks in the fading light as her face seemed to metamorphose into Crystal's and with a start I had to shake my head to clear the confusing and upsetting images.

"What happened, there, Ray?" She stared open-mouthed. "You were somewhere else for a moment. I could see you blank me out."

"No....nothing, just my eyes....think I was blinded, looking straight at the sunset, that was all."

She looked all round the deserted corner of the deck where we were standing and, certain there were no onlookers, took my face in her hands and kissed me hard on the mouth. "You know, Ray, there's another side to this equation. What about you?"

"What do you mean?"

"Well, listen, we got together in really unusual circumstances. You had your bust-up with Crystal and her father in Port Elizabeth, I was having doubts about my feelings for Mendel. What happened between us most people would call a holiday fling or shipboard romance on the rebound. Wouldn't they?"

I just nodded my agreement, waiting for the axe to fall.

Elise was caressing my cheeks but her head was shaking side to side. "You say tell Mendel, but if I did and you and I went on together, what would be in store for us? I'm a lot older than you. You're just starting on your big adventure. Would you really want to be involved with a nearly middle-aged woman who wants children soon and hasn't many years left to do that? Do you want to be a father in the next couple of years, Ray?"

As we stood there leaning against the railings I could feel the engines start and the ship began moving away from the quay. I found myself looking hard at her, seeing her face, the small smile lines round her eyes and the corners of her full-lipped mouth and realised that she was absolutely right. Yet, I did not want to let go, nor was I prepared to admit that I agreed with her.

"Elise, that's nonsense. We make each other come alive, you said that over and over and it's true. We can't just let it disappear." I could see moisture from her eyes rolling down her cheeks. I wiped the tears away with my fingers and put my arms around her, holding her close.

We must have stood there like statues for quite a while as the 'SS Africa' cleared the harbour and ploughed her way regally out to sea.

"Hey, what's going on here?" David had appeared from nowhere, standing in front of us, hands on hips, a sardonic smile on his face. "Don't tell me, Ray Benjamin, that you're up to your old tricks?"

Startled, we drew apart quickly, the fading light fortunately hiding our reddened faces. I walked over to my friend and rested my hands on his shoulders. "The lady was upset, Dave, something said between her and Mendel during the tour today. I'm just a convenient shoulder to cry on, OK?" I whispered confidentially.

David didn't answer, just kept looking from Elise to me and back again, not entirely satisfied.

"OK?" I said louder.

This time he gave a half-hearted grin and nodded. "By the way, Mendel won't be joining us for dinner. He's still being sick, started not five minutes after the boat started to move. Jesus, does the cabin reek!"

"Does he need anything?" Elise said. "I can give him some more of those tablets he said were helping."

"Don't think so," David replied with a little laugh. "He can't even keep a glass of water down. I said he'd be better in the fresh air but he's so nervous of being unable to stop himself vomiting, that he just wants to be near the toilet. He's not having a nice time."

Elise turned to me and gave a small smile. "Thanks, Ray, for being so understanding. Sorry I had to pour out my troubles like that but, well, thanks a lot. I think I'll go and see him anyway." She turned so that David could not see the sly wink she gave me and, wafting her scent behind her, she was gone.

David gave me a knowing look. "So what's with you and her, man? What's going on?"

I punched him lightly on the shoulder. "Not what you're thinking, with your one-track mind. We spent two days on this ship with virtually only our own company. I know more about her and Mendel than you, and I do feel for her. She's a real lady, a hell of a lady and she's got problems. I had problems. We got to know each other and became good friends."

"Just friends?" David raised a sceptical eyebrow.

I punched his other shoulder, slightly harder this time. "Just friends. Got it?"

He smiled. "OK by me, mate. Let's go have a drink before dinner."

*

Dinner was a fairly sombre affair. The tour of Mombasa had left everyone pretty exhausted and the next day, Captain Vestanza promised, would be hectic. "Tomorrow we cross the equator and there will be the traditional celebration about King Neptune and the waves. We will all be in fancy dress costumes and there will be a mystery ceremony. So get some good sleep, yes?"

As the band would be involved in the next day's activities, there was no dancing. Elise excused herself early, leaving Alvin, David and me to prop up the bar. I fended off further interrogation about Elise from my friends as stoically and dishonestly as I could manage. Finally they gave up in disgust and we parted for the night, the two of them to face the still-sour atmosphere of the cabin and me to my coterie on the top deck.

I was awakened by a gentle nudge, and the familiar scent. "Ray, it's me. I couldn't sleep. I guess I just wanted to, er, well, to be with you tonight for a little while anyway."

I sat up, half-conscious. "Elise, hi! No problem, I was dreaming about you in any case. What time is it?"

In the darkness I could see the whiteness of her smile. "It's just past three o'clock. You sure you don't mind?"

I wriggled over, making room for her on the lounger. "No, what a question!. Here, come snuggle under the blanket." As she did so I could feel her warmth and closeness having an almost immediate effect. So could she.

"Ray, please, let's just lie here and cuddle for a while. Nothing more, is that OK with you?"

I nodded and held her close. "Fine by me. Think we can get some sleep like this?"

"Yes, loverboy, just for a while. These few days have been as difficult for me as they have for you, but right now, just being like this is wonderful. Are you sure you can restrain our friend down there?"

I laughed softly, kissing her ear. "I'll make sure he's on his best behaviour."

We lay in each other's arms just listening to our breathing which gradually became regular. The gentle motion of the 'Africa' ploughing through calm tropical waters lulled us both into a deep yet not entirely untroubled sleep.

*

The brilliant sunrise woke me, together with the sounds of the ship's activities welcoming a new day. I was alone, Elise having disappeared sometime during the night. It had been in some ways, an even more erotic experience than those we had shared in the cabin. I was aware that this might well form a pattern for the rest of the voyage. I gathered my blanket and wandered down to the cabin to shower and change for the momentous crossing of the equator.

*

We were shown a map which indicated that the equator passed through Uganda, northern Kenya and the southern tip of Somalia. The ceremony consisted of crew members taking over command from Captain Vestanza and his officers. They were dressed in ancient maritime costumes, long white beards and carrying fierce-looking three-pronged harpoons. The band played rousing Italian military music and some officers were cross-dressed in tarty outfits, symbolising the prostitutes welcoming sailors after long voyages. The festivities ended with the entire cast being hosed down with fire hoses, climaxing with Captain Vestanza and his officers being unceremoniously dumped in the pool. Champagne corks fizzed and passengers were liberally sprayed with and encouraged to drink copious amounts.

We all stood on a small platform above the pool and had a bird's eye view of the proceedings without being doused with champagne. Mendel emerged looking pale and drained.

David clapped him on the back. "Mendel, good to see you, mate. Have some champagne!"

"No, thanks, Dave, not on top of my raw insides."

"How're you feeling now, Mendel?" I asked him, shouting above the raucous yelling from the deck below.

"Pretty weak," was his reply.

Perhaps I was imagining a faint element of dislike in the look he gave me but decided to ignore it. "I think you should get some food down you. You look like you haven't eaten in a week."

"I haven't," he said with a wan smile. "I'll try something at lunch, maybe something light."

Elise put her arms round his shoulders. "Have the tablets helped, Mendel?"

"Not sure, doll. Don't like to think what it would have been like without them, though."

"Well," I murmured, "speaking as a newly qualified Dental professional," this got hisses from Alvin and David, "maybe you should try increasing the amount you're taking, especially as our next stop is

Aden, about four days at sea. We round the Horn of Africa and into the Red Sea."

"They make me bloody sleepy, those tablets," Mendel complained. "I'm missing half the trip."

On the deck below a massive tidy-up operation was in progress. "Looks like the ceremony's over, folks," said Alvin. "Why don't we try some lunch? Come on Mendel, cheer up, it can only come back up again!" Never one to unduly sympathise with anyone was Alvin.

*

That lunchtime seemed to be a turning point for Mendel as he seemed to recover and become more a full member of the quintet. This in turn meant that there were no opportunities for Elise and me to spend any time together. The next five days at sea were spent in communal relaxation, reading and playing deck games. In the evenings the band played 'A Grain of Sand' several times, dancing to which was the only close contact I was to have with my 'older woman'.

*

Aden, Republic of South Yemen

Due to the existing security problems in this trouble-torn province, soon to be independent of Britain, we were restricted to the modern harbour and an adjoining market. Aden sits on a peninsula which has the ancient natural harbour in the crater of an extinct volcano on one side and the modern harbour on the other.

As a group we were shepherded aboard a motor launch and came ashore under the sharp scrutiny of two officers of the Aden Harbour police.

"You are please not to be proceeding further than harbour boundary," said one, a hawk-like countenance with no humour whatsoever. Where we were allowed to wander was a heaving Arab market, sparsely patrolled by British and Aden officers.

Alvin was in his element. "Watch me bargain, fellas. I want a slide projector. Bet I can get one dirt cheap here!"

He entered one bazaar selling photographic goods and started to haggle. The rest of us strolled along the concrete jetty, lined by oriental shops with stalls outside selling everything from watches, jewellery and electronic goods to clothing, leather and spices.

Alvin caught up with us, breathless. "The bugger wanted £25 sterling but I beat him down to £15 then I said I'd come back and take it off him."

I looked back to see the shopkeeper standing outside his stall, waving and jabbering. I felt a slight unease but said nothing.

When we reached the harbour boundary and could go no further, we had a cup of unbelievably strong sweet Turkish coffee while we waited for Alvin to emerge from his umpteenth foray into the shops.

"David," I murmured quietly, "is Alvin going to buy anything or is he just having fun?"

"Search me," David replied. "Al likes to throw his weight around a bit. Why do you ask?"

I shrugged. "No skin off my nose, but I've been watching the shopkeepers he's been baiting. We've got to pass all of them on the way back."

"I thought that too," Elise said, worriedly. "Our police escorts have vanished and......"

Suddenly a triumphant Alvin emerged from the shop closest to us with his prize, a slide projector wrapped in tissue paper. "Got it! Guess what I paid ? All those other bastards were trying to rob me!"

"So, nu what did you get it for?" Mendel took another sip of the thick dark drink. "Wait let me guess.....£12?"

Alvin shook his head, smiling broadly. "Just £7, boys and girls. You want to buy anything here just let me handle it."

"What about all the others that you bargained with?" I inquired. "We've got to walk by all their stores on the way back."

"Don't worry about them, they're all really friendly."

But they weren't. No sooner had we finished our coffees than we were surrounded by a crowd of angry stallholders and bearded shopkeepers, yelling at us in Arabic, gesticulating wildly, particularly threatening towards Alvin. We formed a tight group and tried to force our way through the throng. Progress was slow and we found ourselves in the middle of a mini-riot.

"Where are our bloody police escorts?" Alvin yelled, a small Arab boy hanging on to his shorts, nearly pulling them down around his knees. He strove to keep them up, hold his purchase and swat the terrier-like little chap away with his elbow.

"Can't see them!" Mendel bellowed. "This is getting ugly, folks. I think we've got to run for it!"

Somehow we tore ourselves loose from the virulent mass of vendors and ran towards the end of the pier where our launch would take us back to the safety of the 'Africa'. Mendel and I each took hold of one of Elise's hands and semi-dragged her along. Gone were thoughts of any souvenirs. As the barrier came into view there must have been at least fifty local inhabitants united in fury at us infidels.

Fortunately the two policemen finally showed up and remonstrated with the mob, enabling us to pass through the barrier and on to the launch. Four pairs of angry eyes focussed on Alvin. Gasping for breath Mendel blurted. "Big bargain hunter, hey! You nearly got us killed!"

"You're an arsehole, Alvin. I tried to warn you about getting back," I said. "Do us all a favour in future, go shopping and bargaining on your own, OK?"

David said nothing, just shook his head. Alvin looked suitably apologetic and, clasping his purchase tightly, sulked at the far side of the launch.

All our group had to show for our visit to the Jewel of Yemen was a £7 slide projector!

CHAPTER 22

In 1870, the Suez Canal's first year of operation, 486 transits were made, or 2 per day. By 1966 there were 58 per day, due to the enormous growth in oil shipments from the Persian Gulf. The original transit time was 40 hours. In 1966 it was 15 hours. During the period 1957-1966, President Nasser nationalized British and French assets. There was considerable Egyptian military build up on both sides of the Suez Canal in the latter part of 1966.

The Captain had been especially effusive during dinner the night before our arrival at Port Suez, on the southern end of the Canal. Addressing the buzzing Dining Hall he explained the security arrangements.

"We have arranged a full day tour for all passengers who wish to join. At six am tomorrow a launch will take you ashore. There you will board a bus which will take you sightseeing through the city of Cairo, the Pyramids and the Sphinx. The bus will return you to Port Said where you will rejoin the ship tomorrow evening. There will be opportunities to leave the bus at various points but I must warn you that conditions in Egypt are very fragile at present. You will see military activity, for the situation in this part of the world is like a powder keg waiting for a match. May I remind you that you will be under the control and protection of the Italian Consulate. This means that although some of you may have South African passports which are unacceptable in Egypt, as long as.....," here he paused for dramatic effect, "you behave responsibly, you will be safe and made welcome."

There was an upsurge of excited conversation. We knew of rising tensions in the Middle East from news bulletins so there had been doubts as to whether we, as South Africans, because of Apartheid, would be able to leave the ship.

"Wow!" Mendel shouted, smiling at Elise, "Cairo, the Pyramids and Sphinx....what a win, hey?"

"Are you sure it'll be safe?" Elise frowned apprehensively.

"You heard what the Captain said," Mendel replied. "We'll just have to make sure our three upstart Dentists don't cause an international incident!"

"Yeah, like upsetting half the shopkeepers in Cairo, baiting them down to nothing, hey, Alvin?" I asked sweetly.

This brought a laugh all round our table. Alvin took it in good humour, though slightly red-cheeked. "Part of the tour takes us to the oldest Christian church in Cairo, which is next to the Ben Ezra Synagogue. Wonder if they'll let us in there?" he mused.

"Probably not," David said. "Anyway, be sure to have plenty of film for your cameras, people. Who knows when we'll ever come to Egypt again."

"Never, if President Nasser gets his way. He wants all Arab Nations to unite....under his leadership, of course. Not good for Israel, I guess." I looked round, daring anyone to challenge my statement, but no-one did.

Elise stood up and stretched. "Guys, if you expect me to be ready tomorrow at six then I'm gonna get a good night's sleep." She pecked Mendel on the forehead, blew kisses to her other three escorts and, with a smiling nod to the Captain, she was off.

After brandies and a long look at the unbelievable night sky, with the Milky Way at it's very brightest against the darkness of space, we decided that Elise had the right idea and went our separate ways to bed

*

The next day dawned, a clear blue sky with distant haze on both horizons where lay the sandy wastelands of the Sinai desert to the east and mainland Egypt to the west.

The days and nights since our Aden adventure had melded into blurred memory of heat, suntan oil and, for me, increasing frustration.

Mendel had now fully recovered and was with Elise virtually every minute. There were times when I had to severely restrain myself from blurting out my feelings but Elise seemed to have a sixth sense about this and nearly always caught my eye with a smile or a shake of the head. So my acting role continued and I began to think of eventually trying out in London's West End theatres!

As the ship drew in to Port Suez, we gathered on the deck as an armada of small Arab *dhows* converged on the 'Africa', laden with every variety of tourist souvenir imaginable. The hawkers hung from the sides of their fragile craft, thrusting their wares at us with long bony arms. Anyone on deck who showed an interest in anything was immediately assailed by feverish broken English encouraging them to buy.

I took a fancy to a leather bound photograph album with pictures of pyramids and Sphinx embossed on the covers. Alvin tried to discourage me but as the price asked was only a couple of Egyptian pounds (less than forty British pence) I took the chance. The item was brought up a rope ladder by a young swarthy-looking lad in a filthy flowing, white robe. His smile was punctuated by two large gaps in his front teeth and he was clearly only interested in the coins I was holding out.

"Why don't you give him some dental advice?" Mendel chortled. "Maybe you can do a trade!"

"He needs a lot more than advice," I said, recoiling from the boy's breath and BO. I held out the coins, which were grabbed by a bony fist emerging from the garment sleeve. My album was wrapped in cellophane. With a bound the boy was over the side.

Alvin took the album. "Do you mind if I open this?" he asked, mischievously.

"Go ahead." He undid the cellophane wrapper. "Hey, what're you doing?"

"Have a look, smartarse," he held out the album with a grin.

I saw immediately. Instead of containing the black pages one would expect, the pages were just ordinary grey cardboard, the sort you'd get unwrapping a new shirt. To disguise the deception, the edges were painted black and in some places the black paint had run on to the pages and smudged. I looked over the railings to see if I could catch a glimpse of the boy but he and the dhow were nowhere to be seen.

Amidst laughter, especially from Alvin, I recovered quickly. "Oh well, I guess that should be the worst con-trick I fall for in my life, isn't that so, folks?"

*

The bus ride to Cairo was unpleasant, hot and sweaty, no air conditioning and a bumpy road. Our discomfort vanished when we caught our first glimpse of the Pyramids and Sphinx.

"Takes your breath away," gasped Elise, as we climbed up the multitude of stairs to the King Cheops' burial chamber and Sarcophagus. We were all pretty puffed out, but in absolute awe of the magnitude and precision of these almost four thousand year old monuments.

A short ride on camels was obligatory, with David's and my animals so fond of each other they kept rubbing against themselves which left no room at all for our legs. Elise declined this golden opportunity.

Cairo itself was overwhelmingly oppressive, the great River Nile a brown flowing cesspool of unmentionable flotsam. Traffic noise and milling crowds were unbearable and our group were delighted to escape for the visit to the religious sector. Our olive-skinned guide, Mustapha, raven-haired with aquiline features and penetrating black eyes, ushered us off the bus into Old Cairo's tranquillity.

His English was hesitant but passable. "Here is Coptic Christian Church of St. Sergius, oldest church in Egypt, sometime building round 4th century AD. Very beautiful, you think?"

We all nodded politely. Alvin had drifted off to one side, then pointed toward a side alley. "I see a sign there for Ben Ezra Synagogue. Can we go have a look?"

The change in Mustapha's demeanour was astonishing. His friendly smile disappeared, pointing a bony finger at Alvin then waved at all of us. "You Jew? You Jew?"

We nodded nervously. "Yes, we're Jewish," I said, as assertively as I could manage, realising all eyes were suddenly on me. "It would be very interesting for us to see the oldest synagogue in Egypt."

"YOU CANNOT GO THERE! IT IS FORBIDDEN! IT IS INFIDEL PLACE! CLOSED!" Specks of spittle flew from the guide's mouth as he ranted.

Mendel tried to placate him. "OK, OK, Mustapha, take it easy. We meant no disrespect but ...."

Mustapha shook his head violently. "I no guide you no more. You get on bus now!" Then he pointed a clenched fist at Alvin and me. "YOU JEW! WE GONNA KILL YOU ALL!!!!!!"

We needed no second urging. Mendel pulled Elise up the stairs of the bus as the rest of the group stood aghast, then, pushing and shoving, followed suit. We informed our driver that we were returning early to the ship at Port Said and that the tour was over. The driver nodded and the last we saw of Mustapha was his fierce bearded face wreathed in hatred, wildly gesticulating as we drove away. The group breathed a sigh of relief as Cairo receded into the distance.

*

After a long desert drive, it was late afternoon when the bus driver announced that we would be arriving shortly at the Port Said docks.

"My God," shouted David. "Look at that!"

"Oh wow!" I breathed, "Its a ship sailing in the desert!"

"Don't be stupid," Alvin rasped. "It's the Suez Canal, you bonehead!"

"He knows that," Elise laughed at him. "It's his sense of humour, silly!"

Nevertheless, to be surrounded by a sea of sand with suddenly the upper part of a ship appearing and no water or sea visible, was a strange experience. We also noticed military vehicles, tanks and troop carriers everywhere.

After the harrowing end to the tour we all collapsed in the air-conditioned lounge and ordered Mario the barman's longest and most thirst-quenching concoctions.

"Well, Ray, did you get good shots?" David inquired.

"Sure did," I nodded. "My old Minolta may be a bit out of date but it takes great photos. And you?"

"Yes. Especially the Sphinx and Pyramids. Also managed to get one of the sign to the Ben Ezra Synagogue."

"Can we have a copy of that please?" Mendel and Elise asked simultaneously and we all broke up laughing.

I knew at that precise moment that Elise's and my romance had been exactly what she had said it was, two lonely heart-sore people thrown together on the ocean, finding joy, solace and yes, extremely satisfying physical comfort in each other. She and Mendel planned to split from us after Trieste and she would make her decision regarding her future with him without any further loving encounters with me.

I had developed immense respect for her and even some for Mendel, so the last part of the voyage was spent in dreamy wishful thinking that if things did not work out between the two of them, she might always be able to find me in London. At the same time I developed a lump in my throat thinking about Crystal, how she was coping, and whether I would ever see her again.

But first there was Venice!

*

The 'SS Africa' had sailed from Port Said across the Mediterranean, through the exquisite Greek Islands to Brindisi in Southern Italy where we docked for some hours before moving on up the coast to magical Venice. What a city! And what an approach, past magnificent churches, canals with vaporettas and gondolas vying for space with countless larger vessels. Piazza San Marco just took our breath away.

This time there was no conducted tour. We were free to wander the enchanting city at our leisure. To our delight, the Captain had given us all complimentary tickets to a performance of Othello in the open air auditorium of the Doge's Palace that evening. We took in the Bridge of Sighs and more churches and galleries than we could handle but kept coming back to the glorious St. Mark's Square with the amazing clock tower.

Elise looked at the brochure she'd been given by Captain Vestanza whom I noticed had a definite lecherous look in his eyes each time he saw her. "Guys, we're all a bit footsore now. I know I am. What do you say we have a coffee here then take a Vaporetta tour down the Grand Canal?"

She got no arguments from the rest of us, so we boarded the large, open-sided vessel and found seats near the front.

"Damn!" I swore, as I tried to take a shot of a particularly spectacular church.

"What's the matter?" Elise looked concerned.

"No, nothing, just finished my last film. Should have got some more at that kiosk on the square."

"Here," Alvin said. "You can have one of mine. Replace it when we get to another shop."

"Thanks, mate." I grinned and caught the small box he threw at me. "Oy, be careful, I nearly dropped that!" I busied myself unwrapping the film then opened the camera. Suddenly a slight swell caused by a passing boat caused the vessel to lurch and we were all momentarily thrown off balance. My Minolta, which I'd been holding open on my lap started to slide and as I caught it, the exposed film popped out, landed on the deck and with a splash, disappeared into the Grand Canal.

"SHIT!" I yelled, and everyone turned to see what had happened. "My bloody pictures, Egypt, the Pyramids, Sphinx, all just went into the bloody water!"

Our group rallied round sympathetically after an initial burst of shocked laughter. "Don't worry, Ray," Alvin said, "We'll have taken many of the same shots. I'll make copies for you."

"That's such a shame, Ray," Elise patted me on the shoulder. "Never mind, we'll also give you some of ours."

"Damn! Damn!,Damn!" I cursed. "How could I have been so careless?"

"The boat hit a sudden swell, Ray," David said. "We all nearly fell off our seats. Take it easy, man. It's only a film."

Still, the loss threw a pall of depression over me for the rest of the day, only partly mitigated by the grandeur of the open air auditorium at the Palace, and the magnificent voices in the production of Othello. Naturally, being in Italian, we could not understand a word but as South Africans, the irony of it being about a black man was not lost on us. Also, four hours is a long time to be sitting on stone seats, even with the meagre cushions we hired.

We returned to the ship well after midnight, ravenous. The dining hall was closed and so we managed to scrape up some snacks from the bar and after a nightcap, said our goodnights. I was still maintaining my nocturnal presence on the deck, even though the nights were not as steamy as in the tropics. I just preferred the solitude.

I had just about closed my eyes when a familiar perfume and my name softly whispered invaded my semi-consciousness. "Ray, are you awake?"

This had not happened since the night before the Equator. I looked at my watch. 3.30. I raised the blanket with a bleary smile. "Come on in, the water's fine!"

I could tell as she got in beside me that she was wearing only a bathrobe. Her warmth enveloped me. "I felt so sorry for you today, Ray, losing the film," she whispered. "You were like a little boy who'd lost his favourite toy."

I could feel familiar responses in both of us. "I'm feeling much better already," I murmured in her ear. Our hands were already beginning an exploration of what had been familiar territory during the early part of the voyage.

"Ray, Ray, d'you think it's .....it's safe? It's been so long, and tomorrow's the end......I just wanted to tell you......that........oh, yes, that's very nice...oh...yes, don't stop........."

*

Love on a sun lounger can be many things. But uninhibited is not one of them. Nevertheless, when emerging from a drought one tends to drink greedily. In our case we were able to reach mutual satisfaction as quietly as was humanly possible, even though at that late hour, it was unlikely we would disturb anyone. However, after dozing in each other's arms for what seemed an eternity, Elise shook me awake and, with a deep and soulful kiss, sat up, disentangling herself from the blanket and me.

"I guess this was like a farewell, Ray, my love. I'd better get back now, for appearances sake before the sun comes up. The boat leaves for Trieste at six. But I just want you to know that you've given me something I thought I'd lost, the ability to love, and give, and enthuse, and be happy. You helped me with that in a difficult time in my life, Ray, and I'll never forget you." She blinked away tears. "But never mind, whatever happens between Mendel and me, I'll be passing through London and maybe get to see you again. Even though I know how difficult it was, you made this trip more than bearable for me and helped me make decisions which...."

"ELISE!" She was interrupted by a strangled cry from the doorway leading on to the deck. Mendel stood there in his pyjamas, wide-eyed. "Oh, Jesus, what's going on here? Who's that with you? Raymond...., you bastard!"

Elise ran to him, clutching her robe tightly together. "Mendel, it's not....it's nothing..... nothing.... I promise. I .....I ....just couldn't sleep and took a walk. Ray and I were just talking".....she ended lamely.

He pushed her roughly aside. "You know what? I don't think I believe you. I saw what was going on. I'm not the idiot you seem to take me for. I've seen the looks and winks and the way you dance together. I had my suspicions early on but then nothing really happened I could be sure about. But I had the feeling things were different. Now I know why. How could you do this to me?"

It was then that I saw Elise lose her cool for the first time. "Do this to you?" she spat angrily. "TO YOU? When for the last ten years I've had to hide and behave like your backroom whore to save your precious mother from having a heart attack?"

"Don't bring my mother into this!" Mendel fired back.

Elise slapped him squarely in the face. "Your mother has always been in this!" she yelled. "She was always there, with us in the bed in your room, in the car when we screwed in the bush, it was always your mother, your bloody mother we had to think of rather than ourselves. All my friends told me I should get out rather than hang on in the hope that ......oh what's the use? This was inevitable and I'm glad it happened now. It's over. From tomorrow we'll go our separate ways. Right now I'm going back to bed...."

Mendel clutched his cheek. Then he turned to me with a look of pure hatred on his face. "You little shit, you were laughing at me the whole trip while shtupping my girlfriend. I'd like to break your neck ..." He advanced threateningly towards me but was pulled away by Elise.

"Don't you dare touch him! I'm sure, though, he could beat you senseless anyhow." Elise was now speaking in a low but furious voice. "Ray was there when I needed him and he needed someone just as much. I mean, it was at your insistence I boarded the ship in Port Elizabeth in case someone from your family might see us together in Durban and tell your beloved mother. This was about you and me, Mendel, you putting your mother first and me believing and hoping you would one day change, or she might die. But you know what? It's my fault. I should have left Pietersburg years ago." She drew a deep breath. "Well, this trip has taught me that I can be independent and that my time with you was wasted. So just go back to bed and tomorrow we'll discuss how much I owe you for the trip. After that we go our separate ways." She blew me a kiss. "Ray, see you in the morning." Without looking at Mendel she turned and stalked away through the doorway.

Mendel and I looked at each other for a while, saying nothing. Then with a shake of his head he turned, leaving me alone with my thoughts. I felt no guilt for what had just happened but felt some sympathy for him, having taken it for granted that Elise would forever be satisfied with second place to his intolerant mother. A similar reaction, I realised, to that of my parents regarding Crystal, except that in the end they might well have come to accept and maybe even to love her. That thought produced an exquisite agony of longing for my curly-headed, giggling, sparkling-eyed, first and thus far only real love of my life.

I was woken by a steward shaking me at the same time as the engines started. "Senor, please, it is necessary to go back to your cabin as we arrive in Trieste in two hours. You must prepare to disembark."

I rubbed the sleep from my eyes, grabbed the blanket and made my way to the cabin where an icy atmosphere reigned. Mendel had already packed, his case in the hallway while David and Alvin were practically ready to go.

"Morning guys," I said brightly. "Beautiful day in Trieste. All set for the next stage in our adventure?"

Alvin shook his head disgustedly. "Jesus, Benjamin, couldn't you keep your hands off her? What's the matter with you?"

I looked him squarely in the face. "Listen here, Alvin, my mate. What happened or didn't happen between Elise and me is none of your business. What Mendel chooses to believe is up to him. But we're going off to London and they will sort things out between them. As far as you and I are concerned, the less said the better. Now, if you guys are finished packing let me have a bit of space, OK?"

*

A fond farewell on the Trieste wharf it was not. We had a train to catch which would take us via Milan, Paris and Calais then on to the ferry to Dover. Elise and Mendel were supposed to be touring Italy then driving through France and ending their trip in London, from where they had planned to fly back to South Africa. Obviously in the aftermath of the previous night I had had no opportunity to speak with Elise so had no idea if their plans had changed.

It was sad to take our last look at the 'Africa', our home for the past three weeks, and to say goodbye to Captain Vestanza and the crew members with whom we had become extremely friendly. I offered to shake Mendel's hand but was rejected. I managed to smuggle a telephone number of my aunt Estelle in London into Elise's hand as we hugged and kissed in spite of the situation. From the cab I looked back and waved at her standing forlornly by the kerb. The thought crossed my mind that in the space of three weeks I had been torn at harbourside from two women who had had a major impact on my young life. There and then I decided to try and get in contact with Crystal as soon as I was settled in London .Whatever it took, through Rita or maybe with Larry's help, I was determined to reach her.

David was talking to me but Alvin was smarting from my response in the cabin. I decided to play it cheerful. "Well, guys, now it's just the three of us on our way, how's about drawing a line under all this bullshit? I know a lot more about their situation than you do, and in any case it's up to them to find a solution."

David nodded. "Yes, I agree. Let's not fight Mendel's battle for him between us. Is that OK with you, Al?"

Alvin nodded, not very agreeably. But for now, that would have to do.

*

Milan Railway Station

It was hot and steamy, a late European summer. The compartment was cramped and crowded so we decided to try and find an empty one.

Alvin had recovered his sense of humour. "Guys, listen, let's take off our shoes and socks and maybe that'll deter any garlicky Italian peasants coming into our compartment."

We laughed and removed our footwear. I stood up. "I'm hungry. Think I'll go get us some sandwiches and drinks in the meantime. There's a kiosk down the platform. Got any lira?"

I was halfway down the platform, bare foot, when, to my horror, the train started to move. There was nothing I could do but gaze helplessly as the carriages disappeared from view. There I was, no shoes or socks, in shorts, no passport and only a few coins in my pocket. I rushed to the kiosk for assistance. No good, no spikka da Inglish. I ran out through the gate, spotting a desk with an Information sign above but there was no-one manning the desk. I was sweating profusely now and looking about wildly, totally panic-stricken.

"C'e qualche cosa,che non va bene,giovanotto?"

I turned and came face to face with a kindly-faced, white-haired gentleman. I shook my head. "Sorry, but do you speak English?"

The man laughed. "I should! I'm English, myself. What I said was, 'is something the matter, young man?' You're not English, are you?"

"No I'm South African, and I don't know what's happened. Our train just arrived and I got off to get sandwiches and the next thing I see is the train pulling out!"

"Course you don't know. But let me put your mind at rest. That happens here in Italian railway stations. The trains come in, drop a carriage or two then go out and come in on another platform. You're crossing to Calais, are you?"

I nodded, breathing a sigh of relief. "Yes, and thank you so much, Mr. er ...?"

"John Edwards. Pleasure, dear boy. As it happens, I'm on that train too, so go get your sandwiches and come back here. I'll see what platform it comes back on."

I was never so ecstatic to see my two barefooted chums again. The foot ruse didn't work though because our compartment filled up with a noisy Italian family, chewing garlic sausages and taking absolutely no notice of any aromas that were rising from our suntanned feet!

I only saw my saviour Mr. Edwards briefly before the train finally departed as he was in a first class carriage but made it quite clear to him that he had saved my life.

His reply was short and to the point. "Well, Ray, perhaps you can persuade your Springbok rugby and cricket teams to let our English boys get a few points against you for a change. That'll make me feel a lot better!"

*

The train journey through the Swiss Alps was unforgettable, our first view of snow-capped peaks. The train stopped in Paris but we had no time to do any sightseeing. Zipping through the flat northern

French countryside we realised that our long journey was coming to an end, an uneasy feeling that freewheeling was over and soon we would be faced with earning a living for ourselves. The ferry crossing was rough from Calais to Dover, but by now we were all seasoned sailors with no Mendel to cause any reflex heaving!

As the famous White Cliffs came into view we had a beer to celebrate and leaning over the rails, relished the pitching and heaving of the squat vessel, dreaming that the gold-paved London pavements were just waiting for three young dentists to make our appearance.

We had been told that the Overseas Visitors' Club in Earl's Court was the best place to find initial accommodation and that was where we ended up on our first night in England. The accommodation was sparse, but after the long travel we slept the sleep of the dead, wondering what the future held for us here in the land of the Queen, Harold Wilson and Big Ben!

Chapter 23

1967 June. Israel demolishes Egyptian forces in the Six Day war, occupies entire Sinai Peninsula, retakes Jerusalem and West Bank from Jordan and Golan Heights from Syria. 1967 Christian Barnard performs first heart transplant at Groote Schuur Hospital in Cape Town. ANC and ZANU-PF declare war on white governments in SA and Rhodesia 1970 United Kingdom General Election and Edward Heath's Conservative Party defeats Labour's Harold Wilson. In South Africa the whites only General Election elects B J Vorster as Prime Minister. Helen Suzman is the only Progressive party MP. Vorster has talks with Ian Smith in Rhodesia.

*

After working for four years as an associate dentist for two South Africans in Potters Bar, a suburb on the northern outskirts of London, Raymond has decided to buy his own practice. He has spent his time fulfilling dreams, learning to ski in the French Alps, seeing his idols from the Jazz world at Ronnie Scott's and enjoying London Theatre and the social whirl centring round the Overseas Visitors Club in Earl's Court. His dental colleagues and former shipmates, Alvin and David left England after two years, to return to South Africa. Mendel and Elise went their separate ways after Trieste.

*

"Selborne",
Mutton Lane,
Potters Bar, Middlesex.
14th June1970. .

Dearest Mom and Dad,

Hope you guys are all well. Great news! I have made an offer which has been accepted for a fabulous property and practice in Chelsea, just off Kings Road, one of the best areas in London. This is the in-place in town, Swinging Sixties London personified! You should see the clubs and restaurants....and the mini-skirted dolly-birds! Woweeee!

The owner is an ex-South African and is retiring due to a bad back. The house is on four floors, the basement is a mess, full of junk, the ground floor has a surgery, waiting room and office and then there is a three bedroom flat above. The practice has been going for twenty-two years but is neglected at present due to the owner's disability. This means that there is a huge amount of dentistry to be done and a massive patient list so am sure I can build it up into a three-man practice in no time. I've had a valuation and am sure that the price of £19,500, split £4,500 for the Practice and £15,000 for the property is very fair. Two problems, however. First I need to refurbish the basement to provide a waiting room, surgery and kitchen/laboratory and the ground floor into two more modern surgeries. This will cost around £4,000, and take about two months. Second, I can get a mortgage for £13,500 on the property and with a bank overdraft of about £5,000, plus my savings of £4,000 I reckon I'm about £6,000 short if I want to get the refurbishing done immediately.

Any possibility of a loan????? I'll pay it back with interest!!!!! Thing is, I'll be living above the surgery so will not have any rent to pay and no travelling to work which is a major consideration in London. Let me know soonest by phone at the surgery in Potters Bar where I will continue living and working until the purchase is completed. Thing is, I could do the refurbishing slowly over six or nine months and pay for it out of income but I'd like to get the place modernised quickly so that I can get associates coming in early, rather than be working in and around builders for up to a year. Does that make sense?

How are things with Larry and Marty? Is Larry enjoying Cape Town Varsity? Here I've got many South African friends, dentists mostly. I see aunt Estelle and uncle Harold quite often. The English are not so easy to meet. Have been across to Paris a couple of times and met a Jewish girl, would you believe, Betty Partouche, who showed me round. Don't get excited, no involvement OR wedding bells there but Paris is a wonderful city. Looking forward to the winter, when a group of us are going skiing to a place called Courchevel in the French Alps. Playing quite a bit of squash so am keeping fit.

That's all for now,

Love as always,
Raymond

*

"Dr. Benjamin, there's a call for you from South Africa. Your father. On the phone in reception."

Fortunately I was only in the middle of a patient examination. Hurriedly excusing myself, I dashed to the office.

"Dad, how are you guys?"

"Your mother and I are fine," came the warm voice I knew so well. "Got your letter last week. It sounds very good, this property. Near your uncle and aunt, isn't it?"

"Yes, dad. I discussed it with them and they're very excited for me, but maybe also because they'll be able to get free dental treatment on their doorstep! Chelsea is a very well-to-do area, you know."

"Well, Raymond, I spoke to my bank manager and have instructed him to send £10,000 to your account. May take a few weeks as the authorities are a bit sticky this end but should go through."

"Why £10,000, dad? I only asked for six!"

"Raymond, listen to me. I looked at your sums and I realised that you would be on quite a tight margin so we, your mother and I, decided that a little extra would give you a cushion in this your first big venture. Also, don't mention interest to me. How would I take interest from a son? You'll all three get it when we're six foot under anyway! So let me know when the money arrives, OK?"

I gripped the receiver tightly, a large lump forming in my throat. Looking around, I grabbed a tissue from a box on the desk and wiped my eyes. "Dad, I don't know how to thank you both. I know you're sad about me living here but I really feel that I'm going to do better here in the near future than I might back home. Also, things happening in South Africa look potentially dangerous. Here we now have a Conservative Government, it's a good time to invest so if you two and the boys ever have to run, you'll have a place to stay."

"OK OK, enough already," my father interrupted. "Now I have some other news. Your brother Larry has had a bit of trouble in Cape Town. He's been very active politically and was picked up by the police for an illegal demonstration against Apartheid, Group Areas Act and all that."

My jaw dropped wide in astonishment. "Larry arrested? Is he all right? Have you spoken to him?"

"Yes, he's OK. He was bailed by his girlfriend Serena's father, who's a prominent Cape Town lawyer, and then the charges were dropped. He spent a very uncomfortable night in jail though. He's violently opposed to the government and is so argumentative that we think he'll be in trouble again soon as they will now be keeping an eagle eye on him. Please God he gets his degree then maybe he will join you. Things are pretty close with him and Serena, so who knows?"

I nodded, a tingle of guilt rushing through me. "I'll drop him a line. We haven't corresponded for a while. Have you met Serena?"

"Yes, very nice, very intelligent girl. She came down for a weekend with Larry. Comes from a very nice family too. And what about you, boychick? Any prospects? What about this girl in France?"

I smiled into the phone. "No, nobody serious as yet. You'll be the first to know, I promise." I had a sudden overwhelming urge to ask him if there was any news about Crystal but fought it down bravely. "How's Mart?"

"Yes, Ray, that was the other thing. We're a bit worried. He seems to have developed *petit mal* epilepsy. He gets minor little blank periods. They've done tests but everything is normal, his reflexes and all that. So they've put him on barbiturate tablets which make him a bit sleepy. Your mother's beside herself. You know how she always looks on the black side...."

I felt a sudden stab of concern, momentarily lost for words as I swallowed nervously. "You've taken him to a Neurologist?"

"Yes, he examined Martin and told your mother not to be a hysterical Jewish mother. I could have killed him."

I frowned and shook my head. "That's not very sympathetic, not to mention pretty unprofessional."

"Yes, but he did give him a very thorough examination. Couldn't find a thing wrong so it's just something we have to get used to, I suppose. Anyway, Ray, that's all our news. This call is costing so much I might have to reduce that ten thousand! Good luck with the new venture. Your mother sends her best love, you know she hates talking on the phone. All the mazel in the world my boy."

"Dad, I won't forget this. Thank you so much. Look after yourselves, the pair of you, and give Marty and Larry my best love. Tell them to write soon. Bye now."

I put down the phone, taking care to hide my tear-filled eyes from our inquisitive receptionist. Elated and concerned at the same time, I trundled back into the surgery to placate my, by now somewhat impatient, patient.

*

Driekoppen Men's Residence,
University of Cape Town
Milner Park, Cape Town.
20th July 1970.

Hi Ray,

Thanks for your letter and best of luck with the new property and practice. You really have done well there in London and your life sounds pretty good what with all the skiing and jazz, to say nothing about the girls, which you only hint at but I can read between the lines!

So dad told you about my arrest. The bloody South African police are worse than the Nazis. We had staged a demo against Job Reservation and the Group Areas Act and were marching down Adderley Street when we were confronted by at least 100 armed and shielded S.A.Police. They said it was an illegal march and we must disperse immediately. Then, after barely a few minutes, and without further warning, they charged us. We went a bit mad I guess, throwing ourselves at them and getting a bit beat up. The next thing I knew we were bundled into a Black Maria and off to the Police Station, thrown in a cell with a bunch of drunks and left without any discussion overnight, just some soup and bread and a bucket for a toilet. Not funny I can tell you.

Anyway, luckily for me, my girlfriend Serena's father is a top Cape Town lawyer. She got him to come and bail me out. Somehow he got the charges dropped against me and that was the end of that. I have had some dire warnings though to steer clear of political activities for a while. But the situation here in South Africa is getting worse all the time.

I'm also worried about Marty. He gets these blank periods, just a few seconds when he's just not there, but the docs say there's nothing to do but take these tablets. Happens to him often on the squash court and the drugs are making his concentration on schoolwork very hazy.

I guess that's all for now. I've got three years to go and I'll be an accountant. Wow! Looks like Serena and I are headed for the matrimonial Chupah, but not till I qualify. After that who knows? I'll need to work and save for a while then maybe we'll come and join you. Not too sure her parents will approve, though.

All the best,
Larry.

PS I heard that Crystal got married to an Afrikaans farmer and is living on a farm north of Cape Town. Hope that doesn't upset you, but perhaps it's for the best!

*

I read Larry's letter with a pounding heart. The news about Marty's problem filled me with a foreboding that I could not suppress. Although I had missed so much of his growing up there had always been an instantaneous rapport between us, an understanding, and mutual affection together with our love of music and appreciation of zany humour. The news of Crystal's marriage also caused me some anguish, even after four years and in spite of the dalliance with Elise. It was as though I had been unable during those years in London to develop any meaningful feelings for any member of the opposite sex, always fighting shy of allowing emotional attachment to develop, preferring one night stands with no strings, to any kind of relationship.

I immersed myself in the planning, financing and refurbishing of the new Surgery venture and on the 30th September 1970, packed my few belongings into my little white Mini and headed into London to begin an exciting new era as a property-owning, self-employed dental surgeon in the fashionable Chelsea surrounds of SW3.

*

January 1972 Bloody Sunday massacre British Army kills 13 civil rights marchers in Northern Ireland

February 1972 Miners Strike in UK. Prime Minister Edward Heath declares State of Emergency.

March 1972 North Vietnamese artmy invades South Vietnam

September 1972 11 Israeli athletes murdered by Black September Arab terrorist group at Munich Olympics

October 1973 Yom Kippur War in Middle East. Egypt and Syria attack Israel but are defeated. America imposes ceasefire.

*

October 1973

Three years had flown by as if on wings. I was overjoyed as were my parents with the news that Larry was now a qualified Accountant and was taking a job in Cape Town. I reckoned that it wouldn't be long before he would pip me to the wedding finishing post. In fact my parents had hinted that their engagement was imminent.

Living and working in the swinging surroundings of Kings Road, Chelsea was as far removed from the countrified suburbia of Potters Bar, Hertfordshire as it was possible to get. For one thing, there were virtually no mums with small children, the essence of the Practice consisting of young often glamorous working people, some city gents, retired dowager ladies and colonels and a smattering of television and radio personalities. I had had no difficulty in expanding the surgery to accommodate two other dentists and although we concentrated on treating patients privately, we did cater for youngsters with wisdom tooth problems on the National Health Service and also provided Intravenous Anaesthesia for highly nervous customers.

My apartment above the surgery was fairly spartan. I'd only furnished the lounge diner and one bedroom as the refurbishing the practice had had first claim on the finances. A power shower had always been an absolute necessity in my life so I'd splurged on a proper Aqualisa cubicle and electric shower in the otherwise simple bathroom.

Socially there had been several girls for one or two dates but always the comparison with Crystal seemed to intrude and I realised that I was in danger of permanent bachelorhood or becoming a long-term one night stand expert. Having a fairly luxurious but practically empty pad in which to 'entertain' was a huge plus when trying to impress the opposite sex. The emptiness of the mornings after when I longed to be on my own as quickly as possible was a major concern, influencing decisions whether to invite someone in for a nightcap, even when the sap was running high.

*

I had just returned from a week's surfing in San Sebastian on Spain's Bay of Biscay coast with two friends to find a huge pile of mail on my coffee table where Katherine, my plump Irish cleaning lady had neatly placed it. The engraved invitation from South Africa was right on top.

Melvin and Lucille Levy
and
Abraham and Rose Benjamin
are proud to announce the Marriage of their children
Serena and Larry
To be solemnized at
The Gardens Synagogue ,Cape Town
on
Sunday 17th March 1974 at 3.00 pm.
Reception and Dinner Dance at
The Mount Nelson Hotel.
Music provided by the Hilton Ross orchestra.
Dress :Lounge suits

I sat and stared at the invitation with mixed feelings of elation and perhaps a tinge of envy. My young brother a married man! A qualified professional taking on the responsibilities of a husband at the comparatively young age of 25, whilst I, his older brother was still single and unattached, seven years his senior. Of course I had known of the plans for some time but seeing the engraved invitation somehow solidified the situation into reality. From what I had gathered his bride-to-be came from a pretty wealthy family and so Larry would have a pretty easy entry into married and professional life. A tiny splinter of resentment crept beneath my genuine pleasure at the news, thinking of the hard slog I had endured during the past seven years and the tough initial period in the new Practice. Also, I'd needed the help from my father. But I soon suppressed that unjust emotion and made the decision to be with my family at the celebration.

My flights to and from South Africa were swiftly booked. After just over two years, the practice was running smoothly, two Australian dental associates providing ample support for me to take the three weeks off. I was looking forward immensely to returning to my native country for the first time in seven years. The plan was to visit Port Elizabeth, and look up my old mates. Then, with our parents in tow, Marty and I would drive along the Garden Route, do some surfing at my favourite beach on earth in Plettenberg Bay on our way to Cape Town.

From what I had learned of Serena, she was highly intelligent and a very able young lady, a qualified Optician and, like Larry, very concerned and involved in South African politics. Pictures that I had seen of her showed her to be an attractive brunette, with an engaging smile. Her father was highly respected in Legal circles in Cape Town and her mother a gracious and popular hostess, very active in many charitable committees.

The letters I had received from my parents fairly bubbled with excitement, coupled with many snide suggestions that I was letting my brother get a head start in providing them with grandchildren and when was I going to get busy and give them some *nachas* (pleasure) as well?

The only aspect of the forthcoming celebrations that caused me and my parents concern was that Martin was still suffering these mild attacks, although the medication seemed to be controlling their intensity. My intention was to have a detailed discussion with the neurologist who was treating him to see if there were any new developments in the treatment of mild Epilepsy.

*

12th March 1974   Plettenberg Bay South Africa

"Come on, Marty, last surf with your big brother!" I yelled across the sand of Lookout Beach. The waves were breaking at an ideal distance some 200 yards off-shore. The evening sunshine cast long shadows over the mile-long white crystalline expanse. Only a few bathers were still in the water, although the air and water temperatures were balmy and idyllic.

"Coming, Ray. Just getting my flippers!"

"Don't be too long, boys. We still got to have dinner and pack. Don't forget we're leaving early tomorrow," my father called out from his canvas beach chair. He and my mother watched anxiously as Marty and I swam out through the foamy breakers, with our fins giving us the propulsion needed to counter the incoming surge.

*

The week had rushed by. My arrival at Port Elizabeth after eight years of absence filled me with poignancy and feelings of regret. My parents were showing their age, being now in their late sixties. The town itself exhibited no great difference, apart from a few new buildings and some motorways. Martin seemed his normal irrepressible and jovial self. We spent the week driving round seeing my old friends, Alec, Mark, both practising Doctors and Lalla who, after working as a pharmacist in Johannesburg had now returned to Port Elizabeth and was running a very successful Pharmacy of his own in Newton Park, just on the bustling Cape Road. They were all married with young families and heavily involved in their professional and domestic lives. Our teenage escapades seemed generations ago. We met a couple of times for lunch and I was very aware of the vast chasm which had developed between my life in London and theirs in good ol' PE.

I was reminded of the Jeremy Taylor quip, mocking a South African Airways stewardess, complete with broad accent...."We are landing at Jan Smuts Airport, Johannesburg, South Africa. Please turn your watches back twenty-five years!"

*

One stop I made on my own. Rita was now the owner/manageress of the hair salon and was very much the competent business woman. When she saw me through the glass frontage her hand flew to her mouth and she came running out to meet me.

"Ray Benjamin, Jesus, what are you doing here?" I was immersed in a heavily perfumed bear hug. Her formerly frizzy golden curls were gone, replaced by a chic Marianne Faithful-type straightened and highlighted blonde arrangement. The chubby cheeks and rounded features were still there though. I was dragged into the salon, much to my embarrassment and the amusement of the clients under beehive type driers.

"So Ray, what's the occasion? What's it been now, eight years, since you left?"

"That's right," I nodded. "Eight years exactly in August, since that day, remember? Oh no, you weren't at the harbour were you?"

"Crikey, no and I'm glad I wasn't. What a pig that man was - and still is." She handed me a cup of coffee. "I guess you'll want to know the latest about my poor friend, hey?"

I frowned. "What do you mean, your poor friend? What's happened with Crystal? I knew she got married. Is there something new?"

Rita smiled sadly. "You bet, Ray. I guess she never really got over you and her, know what I mean? After all that kerfuffle on the harbour that day she went into a deep slide, drinking and messing with one guy after another. Moved out of her folks' house, wouldn't have anything to do with them. Nothing anyone could say, we hardly saw each other for quite a while. Then all of a sudden she meets this farmer from the western Cape, and the next thing they's married and she's living on the farm in the back of nowhere, about 200 miles north of Cape Town."

I clasped my hands together over my face. My head was spinning, partly due to the overheated temperature of the salon and more especially the dramatic news of Crystal and her changed circumstances. I sipped the oversweet coffee. "I knew from Larry about her marriage but nothing about the drinking and stuff. So what's happened now?"

"She phones me out of the blue about six months ago, says she's divorcing Andre, that's this farmer, and isn't coming back to PE, but what do you think, she's going to America!"

"America!" I put my cup down, none too gently.

"Ja, Philadelphia. She's got into Pennsylvania University to do a Law degree."

"Wow!" was all I could say. I could feel the old vibrations starting all over again, images of our magical time together flooding my brain.

"Are you OK, Ray?" Rita looked concerned. "You looked like you've seen a ghost or something."

"No, I'm fine, it's just, well, I had wondered what happened to her and I guess at the very least I'm pleased she's out of her monster of a father's clutches."

She nodded with a suggestive wink. "That's for sure. So, anything I can do for you while you're in PE?"

"No, thanks all the same, but I'm only here for a few days then down to Plett for a week then on to Cape Town for my brother Larry's wedding."

"Larry, your little boet, getting married? Man do I feel old!"

I smiled. "Well you certainly don't look old, you're looking good, you really are. Are you married?"

Rita laughed. "Me, hell no, I'm having much too good a time. Running the salon, more than enough money, lotsa holidays and just playing the field." She paused, looking serious. "Listen, Ray, do you want me to let you know Crystal's address when she's settled?"

"Better than that. Give her my London address. Here it is." I scribbled the Chelsea surgery address down on a scrap of paper. "It would be great to hear from her again."

"You still on your own, Ray?" She favoured me with another lascivious smirk.

"Yep, just like you, Rita. Playing the field!" I said with a wry smile. "I'd better be going. Thanks for the coffee. Really nice to see you again." We shared a warm hug and kisses on both cheeks.

As I left I watched her busying herself with her various clients, stopping briefly to give me a cheerful thumbs up. I sat in Marty's mini for quite a while, lost in thought, before starting the engine and driving home.

*

"Last one, Marty, let's wait for a big one!" I yelled above the roar of the surf. We were treading water about 250 yards off the beach, the water was clear and comfortably warm. The sun was dipping over the distant hills, lending a reddish glow to the trees and brush bordering the sand. We had spent the best part of an hour body-surfing the waves, having sensational 100 yard rides then paddling our way back to the deep. Few swimmers were still in the water and none as deep as we were.

"Hey, Ray, look back at the beach. LOOK!" Marty shouted.

I looked back alarmed. "What's up?"

"Everyone's standing up watching something out here!!!"

I looked around in a panic. My immediate concern was sharks, as there had been a few attacks in recent years. But what I saw made me scream in delight. As the swell behind us gained height I could distinguish several grey shapes rising with the uplifting wave. Unmistakeable. "DOLPHINS!!!" I screamed."TAKE THE WAVE!"

We both finned like mad to equal the speed of the breaker and as it began to curl we were right on the top. Ten or twelve feet below us I could see the dolphins sharing our water. The exhilaration I felt, and Marty must have felt it too, was one I would never forget. The wave began its majestic break and together side by side Marty and I zoomed down at dizzying speed. I caught his eye momentarily and saw his broad ecstatic smile. There was a glimpse of grey presences alongside and below, then we were immersed in white fury as the final break burst around us, leaving us cruising ahead into the shallows. The wave took us right on to the sand where we lay breathless, euphoric as a succession of wavelets broke over us. We took off our fins and looked at each other.

"That was something I will never forget, buddy," I smiled as I shook his hand.

"Me neither, What a way to end. Fan-bloody-tastic!"

It was only as we walked up the beach to where our parents had been sitting that we realised that dozens of people were standing and applauding. Like we were returning heroes or something. My father ran forward with towels. "Oyvay, boychicks, you gave your mother and me heart failure! Those dolphins, how did you know they weren't sharks?"

I looked at Marty and grinned. "We didn't. We just reckoned we could out-surf them!"

My father looked at his wife who just stood there shaking her head, trying hard but in vain to hide the smallest of smiles. "Nu, come, enough surfing already," she muttered. "Dry yourselves and get changed."

'Once a Jewish Mother, always a Jewish Mother' I thought to myself.

As we left the beach onlookers crowded round to shake our hands. Apparently not only the dolphins but also the gigantic size of the wave we had caught had won their admiration. Mounting the wooden walkway, I looked back at this place which more than any other place, in South Africa or elsewhere in my travels, I adored unreservedly and wondered just when I might ever come back.

The Beacon Isle Hotel, set on a rocky promontory between the three main beaches, was the scene for our final dinner before we were due to set out for Cape Town early the next morning. After our parents had gone to their room, Martin and I took a stroll on the floodlit rocks and watched in awe as the huge breakers came crashing down against the foundations of the hotel.

"What a place, hey, Marty!" I put my hand on his shoulder.

He didn't answer for quite a few moments, then, as if emerging from a deep sleep, he said, "Sorry, Ray, did you say something?"

The day which had contained such blissful excitement for us, suddenly turned sour for me, my concerns for my brother surging with the angry tides. I tightened my grip on his shoulder, saying nothing, but the look on his face told me that he was aware, not only of my concern, but also that there was something not right, over which he had little or no control.

Chapter 24

We arrived at the President Hotel in Cape Town, weary after a six hour journey passing through the magnificence of South Africa's famed Garden route. Picturesque Knysna with its massive lagoon opening on to the Indian Ocean. Huge rocky promontories, the awesome Heads, guard and overlook the isthmus leading in to the lagoon from the mountainous seas.

Just before we reached the Knysna outskirts we had been doubled up with laughter. A barren hillside was dotted as far as the eye could see with lines of newly built toilet huts, reminiscent of and as regular as a bald man's hair implants. Obviously these had been built in anticipation of a future new native location but as yet the toilets were all that were there. And the name of the estate.....Flushing Meadow!

"Only in South Africa!" was my comment, tears running down my cheeks.

"Never you mind, Raymond, the Government is doing a lot for the blacks," my father said defensively, but even he could not hide a smile. Apparently the original plan had been to move the inhabitants of the shanty town a little further along the road, to this new estate, but they had refused to move. Result...... hilarious stalemate.

Our journey continued on to the Wilderness, with its seemingly unending white beaches and rolling surf, lakes and forested hillsides forming an almost theatrical backdrop. My father bubbled with excitement. "Look boys, that's where your mother and I had our honeymoon, the Wilderness Hotel. Hells bells, Rosie, that's 37 years ago! Do you remember.....it took us two days to get here from Port Elizabeth in our little Ford, dirt roads and detours. And we went rowing on Fairy Knowe Lake, so romantic it was."

My mother, sitting next to him in the back, nodded, a wistful look crossing her lined face. "Very different now, isn't it, Abie, all these holiday homes and hotels. It was so peaceful back in 1937."

Martin and I exchanged grins, rolling our eyes back playfully. "Ah, yes, we remember it well," Marty crooned, aping Maurice Chevalier's French accent.

The road wound inland after Mossel Bay with mountain ranges overlooking the coastal strip. I drove, with my father relieving me for an hour here and there. Because of the barbiturates he was taking Martin had been advised not to drive long distances. I had seen no recurrence of the sudden loss of awareness evident the night before and it seemed to be a topic to be avoided, with no-one wanting to dull the joyous anticipation of the forthcoming festivities.

The magic of the approach to Cape Town, with Table Mountain and its satellites, Lions Head and Devils Peak, was somewhat tarnished by the shanty town 'locations', hundreds of tin shacks with corrugated rooftops lining the National Road. We passed the Airport, a vast industrial area and on to the freeway system which took us past the harbour to Sea Point and the President Hotel. After London, the sight of humble African domestic servants, energetic employees at the petrol stations and now baggage handlers at the hotel was a reminder of the social differences between Africa and Britain. The sheer subservience was something I found hard to accept, having intensified my already liberal outlook in London.

After checking in, there was tea for the old folks on the terrace and a swim in the pool and Castle lagers for Marty and I. True to forecasts, the late afternoon March sun was blazing down with a gentle breeze off the sea making an ideal combination.

"Hi guys, welcome to Cape Town!"

Simultaneously, Marty and I raised our heads from comatose position on our sun loungers. We jumped up to see our parents in a hugging clinch with Larry. By his side, looking on smiling, stood an attractive brunette, slightly taller than him, wearing tortoise shell glasses, whom I instantly recognised from the photos as my brother's bride-to-be, Serena. After they both embraced Marty, Larry turned to me. "Ray, you're the only member of the family whom Serena hasn't met. Serena, meet my big brother Raymond."

A cool, appraising look followed by a dry, warm handshake and pecks on both cheeks. "It's lovely to meet you at last, Raymond. Larry has told me all about you."

I smiled. "I hope he's left out all the embarrassing bits."

Serena shook her head and grinned. "No actually, those were the bits he went into the greatest detail about."

There was something in the direct way she looked at me that gave me a slightly uncomfortable feeling. 'What the hell had Larry told her about me?' I thought. I returned the look, resisting temptation to make a clever retort, instead giving her the broadest of smiles. "A big Mazeltov to you both, I 'm sure you'll be very happy. You've certainly made the old folks ecstatic. Also it kind of takes the pressure off me, for which I'm extremely grateful." I turned and grabbed Larry in a ferocious hug. "Great to see you, mate.....I can't tell you how happy I am for the both of you. Lots and lots of luck. We in for a big party, are we?"

Larry nodded. "For the next couple of days you guys are at leisure, see the sights, get a bit of a tan. You're pretty pale for a South African, you know. Thursday evening we've booked La Perla restaurant in Sea Point for all the family, Friday after Shul (Synagogue) dinner at Serena's parents in Constantia." He leaned over and whispered "Wait till you see their home, a bloody mansion, pool and tennis court, the works."

"So far so good. Then what?" I asked. "When does the drinking start?" I thought I detected a small frown on my brother's fiancee's face but ignored it.

Larry went on undeterred. "Saturday morning I'm afraid there's more shul, followed by a luncheon at Serena's Aunt Phyllis' place and then........the bachelor party Saturday night! Some of my Varsity mates have mapped out a pub and jazz night-club crawl. God knows where they're going to take us."

"As long as you don't turn up at three o'clock on Sunday afternoon, staggering and reeking of cigars and stale beer, I don't mind," Serena said firmly, chin jutting. "But God help you if, well, you know what I mean. Ray, can I rely on you to keep him in one piece and deliver him on time?" This time a piercingly sweet smile.

"Absolutely, sister-in-law-to be. Marty and I will make sure he arrives at the Gardens Shul in good condition and on time. You agree, Mart?"

With a broad wink Martin shook his head apologetically. "I don't know about that, Ray. You haven't seen Larry after a few drinks. He gets kinda wild, sorta uncontrollable, you know?"

Larry intervened, laughing. "Serena, doll, don't take any notice of our kid brother. You know what a joker he is. Probably I'll have to take care of the pair of them." He turned to our parents. "Mom and dad, how's the room? OK? Shall we all go up and have a look? We asked them especially for large, sea-facing."

I guess the main thing I remember about my first meeting with Serena was how her cool, almost aloof demeanour towards me and indeed my parents as well, seemed to indicate a fairly condescending and dominant personality. I reckoned that my brother would have his work cut out to be master of their house.......

*

Cape Town is a truly wondrous city. Majestic Table Mountain flanked by Devils Peak and Lions Head dwarfs the urban sprawl. Further round from Sea Point, the road cuts into cliffs, blocks of apartments precariously wedged into the mountains with spectacular views over the four Clifton Beaches, leading to Bantry Bay and Camps Bay. Here the equally splendid Twelve Apostle peaks reign supreme over the dramatic and unspoiled rocky coastline. Even at the height of summer however, the sea bathing is only for the stoic, being the icy cold Atlantic Ocean. For warmer bathing one must travel round the Peninsula via Hout Bay and the breathtaking Chapmans Peak drive through to the warm Indian Ocean waters of Muizenberg,

Needless to say we did all the tourist things. The Cable car up the Mountain, a visit to the Castle, a relic of the original British and Dutch rule, the Kirstenbosch Botanical Gardens, and wine-tasting in Stellenbosch.

Understandably Larry and Serena were tied up most of the time during the week so the next time we saw them was at La Perla, a large fashionable restaurant on the beachfront in Sea Point. Serena's parents were extremely friendly and hospitable but in a crowd of more than sixty people there was little or no opportunity for more than a few words. Her father Melvin, was a sleek, well-groomed man with a full head of iron gray hair and strong angular features. His wife Lucille was as different from our mother Rosie as it was possible to be. Elegant, bouffant hairdo, slim to the point of being gaunt, she carried herself with grace and hauteur. Easily identifiable as Serena's mother apart from her glossy blonde hair colour, she moved around making introductions and generally playing the hostess to perfection.

My father did take Melvin Levy aside momentarily and I was close enough to overhear him. "Melvin, I just want to thank you again for what you did for Larry. We were very grateful that you were able to get him out of that awkward situation."

Our genial host laughed, clapped my father on the shoulder. "Please Abie, no more thank-yous. It wasn't a big problem and in any case I could hardly let my beloved daughter's intended languish in jail, now could I?"

I couldn't help getting involved. "Mr. Levy, my brother is up to his neck in anti-apartheid activities. What are the chances that he will need to be very careful in the future?"

"Ah....you're the big brother from London...... Raymond, isn't it?"

I shook his hand. "Yes, and can I please add my thanks for helping Larry. We were all very relieved. The publicity the anti-apartheid movement is getting in London is pretty extensive, and drastic Government actions against them here in SA makes me quite worried for my brother."

"Yes," he replied, frowning. "I have had long chats with Larry and my hot-headed daughter, who is equally up in arms. I have warned them that because our Government here is paranoid about opposition to their policies, they're employing quite draconian but I have to say, necessary tactics to quell demos and suchlike." He waved his hands, pointing to the clatter of food and wine being served. "But hey, listen, this is not the time for such serious discussions. This is a *simcha*, a celebration! What do you say we forget all about these political problems and rejoice with the happy couple. Come on, the champagne is being served!"

The meal was excellent and seeing family whom I hadn't seen for years passed the time most enjoyably. Questions were asked about my life in London and how I managed the miserable weather but it seemed as though an undercurrent of unease ran through attitudes of people unable to consider leaving the country. Most agreed, however that the troubles and urban violence would increase and demands for full one man one vote would alter their comfortable existence permanently.

*

The Levy residence in Constantia, was palatial. Approached by a circular gravel driveway the mock Tudor home stood in grounds of at least three acres, with tennis court and pool, ornamental ponds and manicured lawns, a Hollywood-like scenario. Although we arrived in the early evening after the Friday night Service, the grounds were floodlit, glinting glassware on tables set on the extensive terrace.

I could see by the stunned expressions on my parents' faces that this was far more luxurious than they had been led to believe.

"Wow!" breathed Martin. "Where are the film stars?"

"I can't believe this," my father said, shaking his head. "Larry said that Serena came from a comfortable home, but this....this is multi-millionaire's stuff."

"That's for sure," I muttered as I brought our car to a stop on the spacious parking area outside the imposing mansion. "Looks like our little Larry's landed with his bum right in the butter, hey, mom?"

My mother looked like the proverbial rabbit caught in the headlights. "Abie", she whispered, "I feel so underdressed. I mean, Larry should have warned us he's marrying into royalty!"

"Come on, mom," laughing, I helped her out of the car. "You look fabulous. You can handle the competition anytime."

She gave me a grateful smile. "I hope you boys will remember your table manners, don't disgrace us, promise?"

"We promise," Marty and I said in unison, and with a little light-hearted humour easing the tension, we escorted our dumbstruck parents to the large double oaken doors and rang the bell.

The doors were opened by a uniformed, coloured maid with Larry standing smiling right behind her. "Welcome to Chateau Levy, family! Shabbat Shalom!" He pointed. "Serena'll be down in a minute."

Down a winding staircase, Serena came bounding gracefully, looking stunning in a flowing white dress with a bright pink sash round her middle. She was wearing her hair brushed tightly back, tied in a ponytail, framing her somewhat narrow features. She was sporting a different pair of glasses with thin gold frames, which I for one thought suited her better than the previous tortoise shell ones.

"Hi everyone! Shabbat Shalom to you all!" She gave each of us her routine double pecks, grabbed Larry by the arm and waved us towards a large portal. "Follow us. Come through to the lounge and have a drink."

We entered a massive, oak-panelled room with French windows to the terrace beyond. The maid now offered us drinks from a tray and we made our way outside to where the rest of the Levy clan were standing together with a few of our relatives. Serena's parents immediately came over and started to introduce us to those we hadn't met the previous evening.

"You have a most beautiful home, Lucille," my mother said. "Larry's description didn't do it justice."

"Why, thank you, Rosie," she replied gaily. "I must admit we do love it here, especially now in the summer. It's so ideal for entertaining."

"The Levy's have really made me feel right at home here, mom, dad," Larry said. "They welcomed a starving student from University and overfed and spoiled me completely."

"Yes," laughed Melvin. "And all he had to do was cope with our headstrong daughter!"

"Dad!" Serena punched him playfully on the shoulder. "Don't give Larry's folks the wrong idea!"

"Why not? I'm sure Larry knows who's boss in this house and it sure ain't Lucille or me!"

Serena made a face then laughed. "Come on, you guys, Ray, Marty, Larry, bring your folks. Let's show them the pool and tennis court."

We followed her down a stone staircase from the terrace across sculpted lawns to an enclosure which housed a large, floodlit pool complete with sun loungers adjacent to which was an all-weather, artificial turf tennis court. We could only stand open-mouthed at the sheer luxury of it all. I found myself wondering why Larry hadn't fully divulged the extent of the wealth he was marrying into. Perhaps a little embarrassed when compared to our far less salubrious background, as well as the poverty amongst the vast majority of South Africa's population?

A bell sounded from the direction of the house. "Come on folks, tour's over," Serena said, "that's the call to dinner. Dad'll be making Kiddish any minute now."

All the men were provided with skull caps as Serena's father recited the ancient blessings followed by sweet red wine and '*kitka*' or '*challa*', the traditional plaited bread. We were all seated at two long tables with exquisite silverware and crockery, served by three uniformed waitresses. The balmy evening meant that we all discarded our jackets and ties and the informality generated animated conversations as the two families grew better acquainted.

Later, after a sumptuous four course dinner, Marty, Larry and I managed to escape the crowd for a quiet smoke at the rear of the house.

I punched Larry playfully on the shoulder. "Well, mate, you certainly landed in one hell of a situation. What a place, what a family, and I gotta say, Serena is quite a chick!"

He nodded, smiling bashfully. "Yeah, couldn't believe my luck when I first met her. She was in big demand with all the sports guys and heroes, you know. But when we both got involved with the National Union of South African Students, and she and I started talking, it seemed like she was more interested in politics, anti-apartheid and stuff. We hit it off from then on."

"Her folks seem really friendly, especially her dad," Marty said.

Larry hesitated. "Well, yes, he is, but he is a really strong character. I wouldn't like to be on the wrong side of him. You should see him in court. He's amazing."

I smiled. "I think Serena has a bit of that toughness too. You'll have to be on your best behaviour!"

A slight frown crossed Larry's face. "You know, the only problem I can foresee is that Serena and I both feel that our future is outside South Africa. Like you, Ray. At least until a democratic majority, a black government takes over here."

Surprised by his sudden seriousness, I shook my head. "Yes, so what's the problem?"

He drew hard on his cigarette, blowing out a cloud of smoke. "Basically, her parents are dead against us leaving. She's an only child and they feel that with their wealth they can insulate us and themselves from anything that could go wrong in South Africa."

"You've talked about it with them, then?" I asked.

Larry nodded. "Yeah, and met with absolute refusal to consider it, but Serena and I feel so strongly........"

Martin's eyes opened wide. "You mean she'd go against her parents?"

"Well, we're only getting married on Sunday and it'll take time for us to get on our feet financially but if things here get any worse then yes, I think we might have to go against them."

"LARRY!" Serena's voice echoed from behind the side wall of the house, followed by her in person. "What're you guys doing? Of course, I might have known. Quick fag out of sight, hey? Listen, Larry, people are starting to leave. You're needed."

Marty and I were left to finish our cigarettes on our own. We looked at each other with raised eyebrows, our concern at what Larry had just told us casting a new light on our brother's situation. The evening ended with gracious farewells amidst fevered excitement for the eventful weekend ahead.

Later that night, back in our room at the hotel, as we lay in the darkness, unable to sleep, Martin's disembodied voice called out to me. "Ray..."

"Yeah?"

"Wodja think of what Larry told us?"

I was silent for a few moments before answering. "I think that the two of them will have to be very strong to go against her parents. Staying here in SA would give them an unbelievable life of luxury. Leaving, well, who knows how much help her dad would give them if they ignored his wishes."

"Ja, I agree. Well, time will tell. Me, well, when I listen to you describing all the stuff you are doing in London and all over, I can't wait to get into Dental School, qualify and come and join you."

The darkness hid my broad smile. "Well first you've got to get through Matric. How're the studies going?"

"Not too bad. These tablets make me a bit sleepy, though. Makes it bloody difficult to concentrate. Talking of sleep, we better try and get some. Early start tomorrow with shul all morning."

"Oh, shit, I'd almost forgotten. The Saturday Service is so long and drawn out."

"You still very anti-religion, Ray?"

"Yes, since forever. The only big argument I ever had with dad, apart from the rows over Crystal, was always about religion. You must remember, you were there for most of them."

"Yeah, I feel much the same way," Martin answered. "But somehow mom and dad don't fight with me so much. I'm still their baby and get to do pretty much as I please."

"Aren't you lucky," I laughed and rolled over, hugging my pillow "Time to sleep, buddy. See you in the morning".

"Nice spending time with you, big brother. G'night."

*

We survived the Saturday Morning service which lasted over four hours and consisted of the Reading of the Law and involved many family members being given the honour of being called up to read portions. Marty and I were given the job of holding and 'dressing' the 'Torah' - the precious scrolls that have been the foundation of the Jewish religion and code of ethics for thousands of years. Both my father and Melvin were called up, as was Larry, the Chossen, (bridegroom-to-be). Up above in the women's gallery I could spy my mother brimming with maternal pride alongside Serena and Lucille all dressed in utmost finery and wearing the most elegant hats. The young bearded Israeli Rabbi gave a humorous and eloquent sermon which ended as usual with a warning against the folly of intermarriage and moving away from Orthodoxy. My thoughts drifted as the speech rambled on, images of Crystal flashing before my eyes, which were temporarily closed, wondering how life was treating her in America. I was rudely disturbed by a jab in the ribs from Martin, who drew my attention to several people vastly amused at my contented repose.

At the conclusion of the Service there were drinks and snacks followed by an exodus to the spacious Green Point apartment of Serena's widowed aunt Phyllis, in a very exclusive building, two buildings actually, known as Twin Towers. There followed yet another gargantuan feast, after which we gratefully returned to the President Hotel for a swim and a rest before Larry's long-awaited Bachelor night.

His Best Man, Aaron, who was his room-mate at Driekoppen Mens Residence, had hired a chauffeured limo for the evening so that none of us would be driving. Martin and I were picked up at the President Hotel after strenuous warnings from both parents to limit the drinking and frivolity and to take care of Larry at all costs.

"Raymond, you're the eldest. Your mother and I are relying on you to be responsible. Don't let Marty or Larry get in trouble, you hear me?" My father had come out to issue final warnings as we boarded the luxurious vehicle.

"Don't worry, dad, we're just going to a Jazz Club and have a steak later. We'll be fine." I waved cheerily out the window, his slightly bent frame making me realise how frail he had become. The evening breeze had strengthened into a typically strong Cape westerly wind and as the limo moved away, he turned and with a last gesture of caution, limped slowly back into the hotel foyer.

*

There were eight of us in the limo. Aaron produced a bottle of Scotch and glasses from the liquor cabinet. A bucket of ice and a few bottles of soda and the evening had begun. First stop was an Irish pub off Adderley Street, in the centre of downtown Cape Town. Great jugs of frothy Guinness were the required intake and, after two rounds in half an hour, Aaron led us back to the limo, which, driven by an amiable Cape coloured man named Carlo, who had no front teeth, was parked nearby.

"Come on guys, long way to go!" yelled Aaron. "Carlo, we wanna go to the Hout Bay Hotel. OK?"

"Yes, baas Aaron," came the reply. Over Kloof Nek, isn't it?"

"That's right. Come, you lazy Kaypie, get a bloody move on!!" A second bottle of scotch covered the drive up towards the foot of Table Mountain, past the cable car station and over the wooded area forming the rear of Lion's Head. The Hout Bay Hotel bar was heaving and we left after one round of Castle Lagers, mainly because it had taken nearly twenty minutes to get served. By this time the conversation was becoming pretty raucous, with Aaron and the other Driekoppen residence inmates giving a rendition of the Cape Town University song as Carlo drove us back to Central Cape Town.

Virgins of Varsity,
win our admiration,
to hell with masturbation,
Let's add to infancy
with yet another pregnancy!

Needless to say I was keeping a fairly sharp eye on Marty, as alcohol and barbiturates can be a fairly toxic mixture, but he was showing creditable restraint and limiting his intake as was I. Not so the main personage of the evening, our brother Larry, who already at this early stage of the evening was slurring and staggering.

The next stop was the Navigators Den, a seedy bar by the harbour. Here, females of various dusky shades of colour were lounging around the tables near the jukebox. Larry, having chosen some music, was inviting one of the ladies to dance and was being none too subtly rejected. I grabbed him by the collar and pulled him away. "Larry, listen buddy, these girls are in it for money," I whispered in his ear. "They're prostitutes, are you with me?"

He pulled away, protesting. "Just wanna dance, have I gotta pay her to dance?"

Several burly men by the bar were eyeing us watchfully. I decided to try and get our group to make a dignified exit but Larry was now approaching a second girl, tunelessly rendering a drunken version of "I'm getting married in the morning."

Martin, Aaron and I closed in on him and gently but forcibly steered him towards the exit, an archway hung with fishing nets and rusty anchors. Outside, in the cooler, less smoky atmosphere he staggered towards the limo. "Jesus, can't a guy have a little fun, that girl was mad for me, she wanted me to take her outside!"

"You better save your energies for Serena tomorrow night," Aaron laughed as we shoved him into the back seat. "Hey Carlo, let's go listen to some jazz, how's about Naaz or the Catacombs in Woodstock? You know where they are?"

"Sure do, baas Aaron. You better tell master Larry back there, these girls, they poison. Probly got VD." He gave a shrill cackle as we left docklands behind.

Larry was sitting, chin in hands, mumbling incoherently. "My last night of freedom an' my friends an' my brothers won't let me even dance with a woman!"

"Aaron," I shouted above the babble of conversation, "don't you think we'd better get something to eat to soak up all the alcohol? Otherwise there's gonna be a hell of a mess in this lovely limo."

"Yeah, good thinking," he yelled back. "Carlo! Take us to Nelson's Eye Steakhouse, up there in Gardens, you know it?"

"Sure do, baas Aaron," came the reply. "An' maybe you'se can bring me out a steak sandwich. Us poor coloureds can't eat inside with you white folks."

I had a hollow feeling in the pit of my stomach as I climbed out of the vehicle. The craziness of the apartheid system was sharply focussed in my mind by that one little innocent request. I felt a surge of sympathy for all those people denigrated to second class status by this horrendous, state-imposed racism.

Nelson's Eye Steakhouse was packed and we wedged ourselves into a corner booth, nursing beers while we waited for our mammoth steaks to arrive. Larry had calmed down somewhat and there was not much point in conversation as no-one could hear anything above the hubbub.

"Let me take Carlo's steak sandwich out to him," I yelled, when the huge order arrived. "I feel shitty about him sitting out there."

"Ja," Marty nodded. "That's just about sums up everything that's wrong here in SA."

Kenny, one of Larry's friends, wasn't so sure. "You know, the problem with the Africans and coloureds is that they're way behind in development. It'll need a few generations before they're ready to have equality here."

This could have developed into a major political argument in spite of the deafening noise around us but our gigantic steaks arrived, exquisitely barbecued on an open fire.Solutions to the South African dilemma were put on hold and, as it turned out, were not raised again the rest of the evening. The steaks were followed by Dom Pedro's, a delicious concoction of liquidised ice cream, cream and liqueur of your choice.

The night had turned cooler when we got back to the limo to find Carlo fast asleep, slumped over the wheel. He woke with a start when Aaron tapped on the window. "Come on, stand up, you lazy KP!" he yelled. I had come to understand that this manner of speaking was in effect a demonstration of affection rather than an overbearing emblem of superiority and Carlo seemed to enjoy the banter as much as anyone.

"OK, rightaway, master. Wheres to now?"

I looked at my watch. Eleven thirty. Larry was gently snoring, his head resting on Marty's shoulder. "Hey, Aaron, looks like Larry's just about had it. What do all you guys think?"

Aaron protested. "I promised Larry a Jazz Club so let's see who's on at NAAZ in Woodstock. Not a nice area but usually great music. Dollar Brand sometimes plays there."

Everyone was happy to make that the last stop so Carlo put his foot down and we zoomed across town to a mixed race area where the poverty some of South Africa's citizens endured was all too obvious. Quite a comparison with the Levy's palace in Constantia, I thought to myself, but said nothing.

We never got into the Jazz Club. The limo cruised to a stop outside. We noticed several youths loitering nearby who immediately took an interest, surrounding our grand vehicle. As we attempted to get out they leaned toward us trying to get a look inside. The odour of cheap brandy was in our faces. Larry and Marty emerged from the other side to be accosted by two large hulks.

"Hey, kerels, look at the rich boys come slumming in their big fancy limo!" one shouted in Afrikaans.

Martin attempted to explain. "Listen, fellas, it's my brother's bachelor party tonight, he's getting married tomorrow. We don't want any trouble."

I came round to their side of the limo. "Come on guys, let's go inside. We're just here to listen to the music."

The largest one, a barrel-chested thug with a blonde crew cut moved towards Larry and grabbed him by the lapels of his jacket. Larry looked up bleary-eyed at his assailant. "Whatchyore problem, big boy?" he slurred. "Leave me alone, I'm getting married tomorrow. y'know."

"Oh, izzatso?" barrel chest smirked. "OK here's a wedding present for you, smartass." With that he punched Larry straight in the mouth, blood splattering everywhere instantaneously.

Without hesitation, Martin launched himself at the large lout, only to be felled by an equally heavy blow to the side of his head. He toppled over and lay slumped against the side of the limo.

By this time people were coming out of the club amongst whom were two heavyweight doormen. Barrel chest considered the odds, they were only four and heavily outnumbered. He gestured to his mates to retreat. "Komaan, kerels, we taught these Jewboys a lesson...let's go!" They wandered off down the street, laughing and jeering.

Larry was sober now, wiping his bloody mouth with a handkerchief. But Marty was still lying against the side of the car. Suddenly his back arched, he collapsed on to the street, his body shuddering in a series of violent spasms. His face contorted into a hideous rictus, with his neck bent back at an impossible angle.

I knew immediately what it was. "Oh, Christ, he's having a grand mal! Somebody get to a phone, call an ambulance. QUICK!" I cradled Marty's head on my lap and tried to quell the convulsions. All to no avail. I had read enough about this form of epilepsy to know that the main first aid was to prevent the person swallowing or biting their tongue. "Can anyone get a fork or a spoon....something to get his jaw open.!!!! Please HURRY!""

It seemed like an eternity before Aaron came running out of the club with a spoon. "Here you are. Try this," he said, from somewhere up above us. "We've got hold of an ambulance. They should be here in a few minutes. Lucky we're close to Groote Schuur Hospital."

It took some force to jam the back of the spoon between Marty's teeth. Eventually I managed to prise his jaws apart. The spasms were slightly less now, with his arched back slowly relaxing. Everyone was crowding round us, offering bits of advice. I knew that the main thing was to get him to a hospital and have him seen by a Neurologist. This attack was certainly not a typical petit mal seizure. Deep down inside me a terrifying suspicion arose that my baby brother's life was in some danger.

Larry leaned over me, wide-eyed. "What's happening, Ray?"

Marty was quiet now, eyes closed. "He's had a grand mal attack. He needs to see a Neurologist, as quickly as possible."

The blue lights of the approaching ambulance lit the dark street with revolving shadows. The two paramedics hopped out and prepared a stretcher.

I turned to the rest of our group. "Aaron, let Carlo take you guys back now. Larry and I'll go in the ambulance with Marty"..... I looked at the ambulance men.... "if that's OK with the medics." They nodded back. "Better not go back to the President Hotel and probably not a good idea to say anything till we've seen a doctor at the hospital. So off you go, guys. Real pity such a good night ended this way...."

"We're ready to go now, sir," said one of the medics. Larry and I clambered into the back of the ambulance alongside our sleeping brother. We looked at each other in shock. Neither of us could say a word, just stared at Marty lying there, wondering what catastrophic consequences this sudden, unprovoked altercation would have for Marty and indeed for the entire family, or families - as we were now becoming.

CHAPTER 25

The paramedics transferred Martin swiftly from the ambulance into a cubicle in the Accidents and Emergency department of the imposing Groote Schuur Hospital. I explained briefly to a white-coated Registrar what had happened. By showing him my card with qualifications, I confirmed that I was a Dental Surgeon and knew that my brother suffered from Petit Mal Epilepsy. "But the punch on the side of the head must certainly have produced the attack he had tonight. It was much more extreme, definitely a Grand Mal seizure," I said, trying to stay calm. "I really think he needs a Neurologist."

Martin now appeared to be in a peaceful sleep. The Doctor did a brief examination then nodded. "Ja, I agree. From what you say, he'll need a brain scan. Trouble is, there's no Neuro on duty now and the scan department will only be available on Monday."

Larry and I looked at each other helplessly. "So what on earth do we do now?" I asked irritably. "It's a real problem for us. We're here for his wedding" I pointed to Larry, "tomorrow afternoon, or rather," I looked at my watch which read 12.30, "later today."

The Registrar shrugged. "Well, I could have him admitted now and he could sleep it off here overnight. He seems to be OK at the moment though so you could take him home when he wakes up. His vital signs are all fine." He thought for a moment. "You being a dentist, can you give intramuscular valium?"

I nodded. "Yes, I give it regularly intravenously in my practice in London."

The Doctor turned to a cupboard and handed me a packet of syringes and a small box of Valium ampoules. "Look, if and when he has another of these major attacks give him a 2 milligram shot in his backside or thigh. That's what is used now routinely to lessen the violence of a Grand Mal episode. Otherwise, you did exactly right getting his mouth open, but here, use one of these instead of a spoon." He handed me a few wooden tongue depressors. "You can let him sleep it off here and see how he is when he wakes. He'll remember nothing, I'm pretty sure."

As if on cue, Marty opened his eyes. "Hey, guys, where am I? What the hell happened?" He looked around wildly. "Larry, Ray, what's going on? I just remember........ getting out of the limo......... then a big guy smashing Larry," he hesitated, shook his head as if to clear the muzziness, "then nothing!"

The Doctor patted Marty on the arm reassuringly. "Ja, you had a big blow on the side of the head, then had, like a fit, but more intense than the ones you've been taking the tablets for."

Martin sat up, wide-eyed. "You mean I had a Grand Mal attack?"

The Doctor nodded. "Yes, that's the term for it. But how are you feeling now?"

"A bit dazed, one hell of a headache here," he pointed to his left temple."That's where I got hit, was it?"

Larry and I both nodded. "That's not surprising, but you look OK to me now," I said. "The Doc has given me an injection to give you if it happens again, but hopefully nobody's gonna bash you on the head at the wedding!"

The Registrar interrupted. "Now you're awake I just want to do a few more tests and then you can go and have a good night's rest. I'll give you some tablets for the headache." He checked Marty's various reflexes then straightened up. "All OK," he said smiling and turned to me. "So what you should do is speak to a GP and get a Neurologist appointment as soon as possible. Stress that you'd like a brain scan, OK?"

We helped Marty get unsteadily to his feet. "Can we get a taxi from here back to our hotel?"

The Doctor pointed. "There's a taxi rank just outside the main block. All the best, and good luck for the wedding!"

*

The taxi ride back to the hotel took just ten minutes. The three of us were silent, lost in our own thoughts. As we arrived, after helping Marty out of the shabby old Chevrolet, Larry tapped me on the shoulder. "Ray, I'm gonna drive back to Residence now. All my stuff for the wedding is there. Can you manage OK from here?"

I nodded. "Yeah, not a problem. Are you sure you're all right to drive?"

"I'm fine. Really stone cold sober after all this." He rubbed the side of his mouth "Any marks you can see, Ray? Won't do for me to have a big bruised mouth on my wedding day."

I looked closely. "No, just a little redness. It'll be OK, don't worry."

He nodded, relieved. "That's fine. I'll be back at the Hotel at about one this afternoon as we're all leaving in the posh hired limos from here. But ....I'm not sure what to do."

"What do you mean?"

He hesitated, making sure Martin was already inside the foyer, out of earshot. "What do we say about what happened with Marty? I mean, if we say anything everyone's gonna be really upset, especially mom and dad."

I thought for a moment then nodded. "You're right. No point in spoiling the day for them and there's not much we can do on a Sunday anyway. But what I might do is have a quiet word with Doctor Joe. He may know a Neurologist here in Cape Town. I'm sure that he'll do everything possible first thing Monday morning. Hopefully he'll be able to arrange a scan for Marty quickly. By then you and Serena will be on your way, won't you?"

"Ja, our plane for Mauritius leaves at eight in the morning so it'll be easier to break the news after we've gone. I must say I'm not happy about running off in these circumstances but......"

"Don't be silly, mate, this is the biggest day of your lives. Not to worry, I'll make sure we get this sorted out quickly."

Larry grabbed me and gave me a bear hug. "Thanks. You were really solid tonight. See you later." I could see the tears in his eyes as he turned and made his way to the car park.

Marty was sitting on a circular settee in the hotel foyer waiting for me. The look of concern on his face was enough to cause a knot of anxiety in my chest, but I tried to adopt as cheerful an approach as possible. "How's the head now, boetie?"

"Bit better, now. Those tablets are pretty good. What a night, hey, Ray?"

I helped him stand up. "That's for sure. Come on now, buddy, bedtime. You're gonna sleep the sleep of the righteous tonight!"

I knew that there were many questions he wanted to ask but I pre-empted them with a steadfast look straight in his eyes. "We agreed there's no point in telling anyone about this little adventure tonight, especially not mom and dad. You know what they're like. Let them have a great day tomorrow........." I peered at my watch, "Christ it's nearly 2.30 am! It's today already.....Larry's wedding day! Don't worry, we'll get the medical people on your case tomorrow first thing. OK?"

Marty nodded unhappily but followed me back to the room where we undressed and got into bed with minimum fuss. The time was 2.45 and after switching off the light I lay awake for what seemed like hours, terrified at what next week would bring for Marty and our family.

*

I always had trouble being less than honest with my mother. So when Marty and I surfaced for breakfast, a typically huge buffet of grilled sausages, bacon, massive array of fruit, etc, she fixed me with those ageing but perceptive eyes and wanted to know how the bachelor evening had gone.

"It was brilliant," I smiled brightly, determined to carry off the deception. "We had this great chauffeur, Carlo, and had a ball, saw some great pubs, a bit of jazz at Naaz and the best steak I've ever had at a place called Nelson's Eye."

"And," she said, unconvinced, "not too much to drink, I hope? What about Larry? Those friends from Residence, I think they're a bad influence on him."

Marty came to my rescue. "Mom, Raymond was a very responsible big brother. He kept a strict eye on Larry and I and at times we were even a little fed up he was watching every drop we drank."

My father interrupted. "Rosie, Rosie, for heavens sake, they're grown-ups. You can see they're in one piece. They told you they had a good time. So nu, leave off already!"

Our uncle, Doctor Joe was nowhere in sight so, almost relieved, I decided to delay any discussion till much later, after the celebrations.

My mother looked at her watch. "It's nearly twelve. Time to get ready. Go on boychicks, go make yourselves beautiful. Is Larry here yet? Oy! My son's gonna be a groom, a husband, I can't believe it! And he's getting there before you too, Raymond. You'd better hurry up, you don't want to be an uncle before you're a father do you?" With that and a little smile, she waddled off to the elevator.

Marty and I breathed a sigh of relief, smiled at each other and went off to 'make ourselves beautiful'. As we entered the lift, Larry arrived, looking splendid in his dark lounge suit complete with white carnation. A quizzical look from him, directed at our mother was answered by an affirmative but hidden thumbs-up from Marty and I. Aaron, the best man, handed out carnations and we all crowded into our room for a little raid on the minibar to build up our strength.

An hour later the convoy of glossy black Rolls Royces moved slowly away from the President Hotel, watched by dozens of coloured hotel staff, all gawking at the splendid pageant played out before them. The procession continued slowly through the shopping area of Sea Point towards the city centre where the Gardens Synagogue dominates the Botanical Gardens. Built in 1905 in the baroque style, this synagogue, known as South Africa's Mother Synagogue, has classic twin towers and a dome, and was apparently inspired by Florentine architecture

In the distance the ever-present backdrop of Table Mountain was overlaid by its famous Tablecloth, a massive white cloud overhanging the flat-topped peak.

*

The limousines drew up smoothly in front of the Synagogue where we were met by more of Larry's university friends together with members of Serena's family. Putting on our Yamelkas, or skull caps, we entered the imposing building. An air of excited anticipation before a Jewish wedding is felt nowhere more so than in the crowded dark-wooden pews surrounding the chupah or canopy. This consists of a brilliantly patterned white velvet cloth supported by four poles all of which are festooned with flowers. Erected in front of the Bimah or elevated section from which the Chazan or Cantor conducts the Services, it is where the Marriage Ceremony takes place.

Beneath the semicircular dome is the Ark or the Aron Kodesh, the closet in which the precious Torah scrolls are stored. This is flanked by two beautiful mosaic panels, and light filters through an impressive stained-glass window.

Ordinarily in the Jewish Orthodox religion, women are seated separately in the gallery above. For weddings in England, they are allowed to occupy one side of the ground floor, but the South African tradition is for a complete mix, so couples and families all sit together. Africans, Coloureds and Malays, usually the families' servants, are able to watch from the gallery. The front rows are reserved for members of the bride and groom's families. Marty and I and two of Serena's cousins were to act as poleholders, standing and symbolically supporting the poles of the Chupah during the ceremony.

The shul was already crowded and an expectant buzz spread through the congregation as the Rabbi and Chazan took their places beneath the Chupah .We were instructed to assume our poleholder positions. Larry, looking nervous, was seated between Melvin Levy and our father in the box in front of the Bimah. At a signal, they escorted him to his place under the canopy, turned and walked the length of the shul to join the retinue outside.

The Male Choir and organist were assembled in a special balcony above the Ark and the sound of liturgical organ music echoed through the vastness of the Synagogue. All eyes were glued on the double doors at the far end when the choir and Chazan began the glorious "*Baruch Habah*", the welcoming incantation for the Bride and her retinue.

First to appear were a tiny three-year-old flowergirl and pageboy, children of Serena's cousins, followed by Serena and her father. She was flushed and smiling, in a glorious white satin wedding gown, her hair swept back from her face, with a floral arrangement holding an organza veil. She wore no glasses this day and her large brown eyes sparkled with excitement. In her hand she held an exquisite bouquet. Melvin held her arm, his face beaming with pride. They were followed by Aaron escorting Lucille, then my parents and finally, two bridesmaids all in turquoise.

The procession passed by the front row of pews, all the women oohing and aahing at the glamorous spectacle. Her father deposited Serena alongside Larry under the Chupah where he was shifting nervously from one foot to the other. The four parents took up positions on the periphery of the canopy and the Cantor began the Marriage service, combining in close harmony with the choir.

The service lasted about half an hour, with the ancient cantorial melodies ringing out, filling the shul to its magnificent vaulted ceiling with song. The rabbi addressed the young couple offering advice, explaining the significance of the canopy representing the openness and generosity of a Jewish home. The final act was the breaking of the glass, when Larry was called upon to stamp on a glass wrapped on the floor to represent the destruction of the second temple in biblical times.

"MAZELTOV"!!! the congregation as one erupted in joyous congratulation. From that moment all decorum was set aside as everyone hugged and kissed, the central area heaving with family and friends trying to get to the happy couple and the ecstatic parents. For my part, I was assailed by our close family, constantly being pummelled and asked leading questions like 'Nu when we gonna hear good news from you, Ray?' and 'Too much of a good time with the English girls in London, hey?' with many a nudge and a wink.

The Choir was now in full voice together with the organ, combining in a triumphant rendition of a Hebrew Wedding March as the congregation began pouring out into the tree-lined avenue bordering the Gardens. The Cape weather was in benevolent mood, blue skies, warm late summer sunshine filtering through the huge ancient oaks. The limos and Rolls drew up to transfer everyone to the Mount Nelson Hotel where the Reception and Dinner Dance was to follow.

Marty and I struggled through the crowd and eventually joined our parents and Melvin and Lucille as Larry and Serena entered the leading vehicle covered in confetti.

"Some wedding, hey boychick!," my father smiled, "Didn't Serena look beautiful?"

"Absolutely stunning," I agreed, turning to Melvin and Lucille and embracing them . "Your little girl looked really fantastic. Big Mazeltov to you both."

"And from me too," Marty chimed in. "She looked like a screen goddess!"

"Thank you, boys," Lucille grinned. "Please God by the two of you one day soon!"

"You got anyone in mind?" Melvin leered at me with a knowing look "A rich unattached and successful London dentist?"

I had another one of my mental flashes, this time of Crystal in a white wedding dress, but the surroundings were not, and I realised with a real pang of sadness, could never be the same. "No, no-one serious at the moment," I mumbled to no-one in particular.

"Come on," called Melvin. "This limo's ours. It'll take all six of us!" With that we bundled into the leather–lined interior of the air-conditioned vehicle and were driven the short distance to the massive stone arch which guards the entrance to the Mount Nelson, Cape Town's most luxurious and expensive hotel.

"Wow!" breathed Marty incredulously. "A bloody Hollywood film set!"

Set in twelve acres of manicured grounds, the Mount Nelson is an oasis of calm in the midst of the city, situated at the foot of Table Mountain. The reception was held on luscious lawns alongside one of the two massive swimming pools with occasional tables and large gaily coloured umbrellas for shade from the sun which even now in late afternoon was still beating down fiercely.

Marty and I, together with our parents, joined the crowd, sipping pink champagne and nibbling finger food from the liveried waiters and waitresses. In between bites and quaffing, I shook my head in awe. "This is the life, hey, Marty? Champagne and luxury and a view to die for...."

When he didn't respond I looked at him closely. "Are you OK? You're too quiet for my liking."

He shook his head. "No, I'm fine.Still just a bit of a headache though."

I gently moved him away from my parents. "Must be the aftermath of that crack you got last night. Take a couple of those tablets."

He nodded. "Yeah,OK. Will do. Maybe I'll also go a bit light on the alcohol."

I grabbed a glass from a nearby waitress. "Here, have some iced water."

Marty drained the glass swiftly with two capsules. I could see he was sweating profusely. "Come, mate, let's get you into the shade. I can see you're a bit hot."

Nothing escaped my mother's eagle eye. She was on to us in a flash. "What's the matter? Martin, are you not feeling well?"

He held up his hands. "Mom, I'm fine, really. Just feeling the heat and with the champagne on top of the tablets, I'll just cool down in the shade."

She pulled me to one side. "Ray, is that possible? Those tablets he's taking? Can it make him feel ill? He's sweating like mad."

"For sure, Mom," I said with more conviction than I felt. "I'll make sure he doesn't have any more champagne. Don't worry.....go on, go back to your new in-laws." I could see Melvin and Lucille calling to her from across the lawn. With a worried frown, she walked reluctantly across to them, with an occasional glance back in our direction.

The shade seemed to have done the trick and Marty was on his feet with his infectious grin back in place. "Ray, stop worrying, you look like you're seeing a ghost!"

Just then the Master of Ceremonies in brilliant red uniform was summoning everyone towards the banqueting hall. As we entered, our breath was taken away yet again. A huge room, hung with massive crystal chandeliers, contained what appeared to be at least fifty tables all decorated in silver and glass, each with floral displays and silver buckets with numerous bottles of wine. One wall, entirely glass from floor to elevated ceiling, looked out at Table Mountain. On a raised stage at the far end a seven- piece band, Hilton Ross and his Orchestra, was playing music from the shows, Fiddler, West Side Story and My Fair Lady. The main table ran along the interior wall, with magnificent flower arrangements and a colossal four-tiered wedding cake. Marty and I were at a table alongside, seated with the other poleholders, Aaron and the bridesmaids.

When everyone was seated, the MC ordered us all to stand up again to welcome the bride and groom to the tune of Cliff Richard's 'Congratulations'. Larry and Serena entered the ballroom, waving to everyone as they passed by and took their seats at the main table. The men were then asked to cover our heads, and the young Israeli Rabbi said the blessing before the meal.

Between mouthfuls of what was to be a sumptuous six course dinner, Marty turned to me mischievously. "Hey, Ray, I bet dad is happy he's not paying for all this. Must have cost a bloody fortune!"

I nodded. "You're too right, buddy. I've been to a couple of weddings in London and this is up there with the most splendiferous.!" I kept intercepting worried glances from our mother, watching Marty like a hawk, but I smiled back and waved nonchalantly.

After the main course came the speeches. Melvin Levy spoke first, welcoming everyone and gushing with pride as he described 'the most beautiful bride he'd ever seen, a completely unbiased opinion'. This drew loud applause and laughter. Then came the toasts, first to The President of the State of Israel, by Serena's best friend, Naomi, and second to The President of The Republic of South Africa, by Larry's close friend Kenny, accompanied by both national anthems. These were followed by the traditional Best Man's Speech, delivered by Aaron, describing in somewhat painful detail, all the escapades he and Larry had been involved in, including a reference to his recent involvement with the South African Police. This elicited hoots of amusement from just about everyone with the exception of Melvin, Lucille and our parents who shifted uncomfortably in their seats, fixed smiles plastered to tight faces.

The Ballroom then hushed as the MC stood up. "Silence please for the man of the moment, your Bridegroom, Larry.......!" I felt my hands clenching nervously as Larry took the microphone. "Rabbi Bender, Melvin, Lucille, Mom, Dad, relatives and friends, and of course my exquisite bride, Serena........." he paused for the wave of applause to die down, "and lastly and definitely least, my best man and closest friend Aaron...!" this brought another peal of laughter.......

I needn't have worried. Larry spoke impeccably, confidently, hardly looking at his notes. He thanked everyone for coming, paid tribute to his parents, spoke in glowing terms about his parents-in-law. "Melvin and Lucille, you welcomed me into your wonderful family, your sumptuous home and made me totally comfortable with your fabulous way of life," he gave a shy grin as laughter rang out around the room. "You have allowed me to capture your daughter's affections and I promise you both faithfully, that Serena will never want for anything."

"Not if her folks can help it!" came from one of the Driekoppen Residence boys, to yet another gale of hysterical mirth all round the hall.

Larry pursed his lips, gave a wry smile. He seemed a little taken aback, but continued bravely. "Finally, my gorgeous bride Serena..." he turned to face her directly. "You have made my life complete, we think alike, we love the same things, music, art, and what we have most in common is a love for our beloved South Africa." Big burst of applause. "I'm not going to get political here on this day of all days, but you all know our sympathies and how dedicated we are to secure a fair and just solution for all the races in our wonderful country. This we will continue with all our energy, but can I assure you, Melvin and Lucille, that I will devote my life to making your daughter happy and in doing that, I know it will make the two of you contented as well. Please everyone, enjoy yourselves, eat, drink and dance the night away. Thank you!"

He sat down to tumultuous applause and a hug and kiss from Serena and Lucille, followed by Melvin, Abie and Rosie.

Marty and I left our seats and took our turn. "Mazeltov, boet!" I hugged him close. "Not a bad speech for an Accountant. You did good, buddy!"

Larry smiled as Marty grabbed him round the neck. I could see tears in both their eyes. "I'm real proud of you, Larry," Marty said. "Hope you know what to do later tonight! Do you need any advice?" he whispered. They both burst into fits of giggles. Serena looked sharply, inquisitively at them both but let it go.

The band then struck up the first dance, "Always", a favourite of our father's and Larry and Serena took the floor. Unlike me, Larry had not been forced into the tender and sweaty embrace of Ted van Jaarsveld so his waltzing was less than strictly ballroom but they looked very comfortable together as the dance floor filled up with other couples.

For a few moments Marty and I remained at our table watching. As the two giggling bridesmaids were doing the same I nudged Marty and he nudged me back. As one we stood and courteously offered to take the two girls and join the throng. Mercifully for us the band then broke into *Hava Nagila* and a medley of Israeli songs when everyone joined in the Hora or Israeli dance so we were spared making idle chatter with the two fifteen year olds!

The evening flew by. The band was a resounding success and the dance floor was never less than crowded. Larry and Serena circulated graciously and eventually we were recalled to our tables for dessert and coffee.

Later, as the guests were leaving, I managed to corner Doctor Joe. Making sure that my parents were not around, I drew him aside into a sheltered part of the ballroom. "Doctor Joe, can I have a quick word?"

He smiled."Yes, of course, Raymond, my boy. What's the problem?"

"I'm worried about Marty. We didn't tell anyone before as we didn't want to upset anybody today but well, last night, he got punched on the side of his head and had a Grand Mal fit..."

I could see his normally jovial features changing to serious concern. "You're sure, Raymond? A Grand Mal?"

I nodded. "Yes, believe me, no doubt whatsoever. We got him to Groote Schuur and the Registrar saw him and did various checks but found all his signs and reflexes were normal. He still has a massive headache. We were given some tablets for him to take for the pain. Also I was given 2 milligram valium ampoules and some syringes in case it happened again."

Doctor Joe was frowning. "Hmm, you were right not to say anything last night or today but a Grand Mal is not good news."

"I know that," I said, looking nervously around for any sign of my parents. "But the Registrar said we should consult a Neurologist as soon as possible. We both felt that Marty should have a brain scan."

He nodded. "Yes, I'm sure that's the thing to do. Let me see, I do know a Neurologist here in Cape Town by the name of McGregor. I'll give him a ring first thing in the morning. In the meantime, how's the boy feeling?"

"Well, he was sweating quite a lot in the heat earlier on, but the painkillers seem to have worked. He's pretty worried though. He knows the difference between Petit and Grand Mal."

"OK, Ray. Don't let on to your folks tonight. Let them enjoy the nachus of this wonderful affair for another night and hopefully we'll get some action in the morning. Once I've contacted McGregor, then we can tell them. The honeymoon couple will be on their way early, won't they?"

"Yes. Eight o'clock their plane leaves."

"What's your room number at the President? I'll call you soon as I've made the call."

"4008. What do you think it can be? I'm just worried about all the possibilities."

He nodded. "I share your concern, Ray. I didn't like this sudden onset of epilepsy at his age. Didn't seem typical, and the headaches? Has he been having them frequently?"

"I don't really know. You know Marty, he doesn't complain... uh, I think I can see my folks coming over. I'll wait to hear from you tomorrow."

He patted me on the head affectionately and for the benefit of my approaching parents increased his volume. "Mazeltov, Raymond. Isn't it about time we were attending a wedding with you as the groom? Don't keep us waiting!"

Mercifully, I was saved from any difficult interrogation by the combined presence of Marty, our parents and Melvin and Lucille. Larry and Serena were saying their final goodbyes and were to stay overnight in the bridal suite at the Mount Nelson so this would be farewell from all of us as well.

We all wandered through to the sumptuous foyer where highly emotional loving embraces were taking place. I caught a meaningful glance from Larry and gave a reassuring nod in Marty's direction before clasping him and Serena in a three way bear hug,. "All the luck in the world, you two lovely people. Have a wonderful time, just relax, and if you get the chance, there's wonderful Scuba diving off Mauritius!!!"

This my mother overheard. "Oyvay! she yelled. "Are you crazy, Raymond? They're going on honeymoon! What do they want to be underwater for, for heaven's sake?"

Marty chimed in. "Mom, I believe it is wonderful to do it underwater. Raymond told me so."

The whole group collapsed with helpless laughter. Somehow, Marty always managed to get away with remarks like that when no-one else would dare. It helped defuse the highly charged emotions of the moment. After a prolonged typical Jewish farewell, we were ushered into our waiting limo, waving cheerio to the newly-weds who were standing on the marble steps arm in arm.

I could just make out the creased frown on my brother Larry's brow as he turned and went back into the hotel with his new bride. We sat back in the soft leather and felt the luxurious vehicle glide smoothly away. Marty quickly became engaged in animated conversation with our folks, raving about the wedding and a day and night none of us would ever forget. I closed my eyes, trying to shut out my anxieties about what the following morning would bring.

Chapter 26

Early the next morning I was disturbed by a crash from the small bathroom. Jumping hastily out of bed, clad only in shorts, I found Marty sitting on the side of the bath, holding his head with both hands. A glass tumbler had smashed in pieces on the tiled floor. He wore an expression of acute distress, his eyes were bloodshot and frightened. He was sweating profusely. The sour smell of vomit permeated the room.

"What's up, Marty?" I asked nervously, clumsily sweeping up the broken shards of glass.

"My head, Ray.....feels like it's exploding...."

"Those tablets, have you taken them?"

He nodded wearily. "Haven't helped a bit. Took two at three this morning and another two hours ago. Haven't touched sides".

I patted him on the shoulder. "Take it easy, I'll call Doctor Joe." I rushed back into the bedroom, picked up the phone and dialled our uncle's room.

"Yes, who is it?" came the familiar gruff voice. "What bloody time is this to call a person...it's six thirty for Christ sake!"

"It's me, Raymond. I think you'd better come and have a look at Marty. He's not too well, sweating, vomiting, a massive headache. Even those strong analgesics haven't touched it."

A short silence, then, "I'll be right down".

I put the hotel phone down and returned to the bathroom. "Marty, come lie down. Doctor Joe will be here in a minute. Watch where you walk." As I helped him over to the bed I felt acute alarm as he seemed unable to stand or walk unaided. His pyjamas were soaked and there was a wild, terrified look in his eyes. He lay down heavily on the bed, staring at me. "What's happening to me, Ray? Am I going to die?"

I tried my hardest to be reassuring, an emotion I honestly did not feel. "Don't be silly, Marty. Doctor Joe will get things moving. I'm sure this neurologist he knows will get to the bottom of it. Just take it easy now, relax, stop worrying."

I took a towel and mopped his damp forehead. His face was ashen-gray. He looked at me, the bewildered expression on his face alternating with a grimace as what must have been excruciating pain shot through his head. I stood there helpless, watching as he slowly closed his eyes. Something deep inside me was telling me that my poor brother was in the most serious trouble, although what it was I could not begin to imagine. The meagre knowledge I had absorbed from my years at medical school afforded me only a vague blur of possibilities. I began to feel cold sweat breaking out on my forehead as I noticed Marty's breathing slowing and his facial muscles relaxed. I could not help a feeling of rising panic. Was this a drug induced sleep or some kind of coma?

A knock on the door stirred me out of my confusion. I threw on a t-shirt and let our uncle in. He was dressed in a tracksuit, carrying his medical bag. He stepped over to Marty, opened the bag and took out an ophthalmoscope. After peering into each eye he straightened up and looked at me, a look of utmost concern on his face. Stepping back he gestured for me to follow him in to the bathroom. "We have to get Marty to hospital immediately. I think he has had or is having a brain haemorrhage." He turned and picked up the bathroom extension phone. "Hello, reception, listen this is Dr. Goldberg. I'm in room 4008. There's an acute emergency here. We need an ambulance to take a young man to Groote Schuur...... ....double quick. Can you get me through please, straightaway, NOW!" he barked.

He turned to me. "You told me he got a crack on the side of the head Saturday night, Ray?"

I nodded miserably "Yes, he was trying to help Larry against a few skollies, you know, crewcut Afrikaner Nazis." I said bitterly. "Why do you think he is having a haemorrhage?" I asked, swallowing nervously.

"His pupils are dilated and the optic blood vessels are congested, sign of possible papilledema which happens when there's increased intracranial pressure. Could have been caused by the blow he got but....." he hesitated, then leaned over and whispered softly. "What worries me is the so-called epilepsy he's had for a while now. At his age it's not typical, I said so at the time. Now we must urgently get the neurologist to do a brain scan."

I nodded. "Dr. Morris, the Neurologist in Port Elizabeth told mom she was a neurotic hysterical Jewish mother, didn't he?" I said bitterly.

Doctor Joe shook his head. "The man was an idiot, but to be fair, he didn't have much to go on at that time and the anti-spasmodic tablets seemed to do the trick for a while. But now, I just don't know"

We both jumped as the phone rang. Doctor Joe picked it up. "Yes? What? They want to talk to me? OK, put them on." He frowned impatiently. "They want to know who I am, and my qualifications. Can you believe it!"

He waited, his fingers drumming a tattoo on the receiver. "Yes, my name is Dr. Joseph Goldberg. I am a General Practitioner from Port Elizabeth. I am at the President Hotel and my nephew Martin Benjamin, aged nineteen, has what looks like a cerebral haemorrhage. He was attacked on Saturday night but is now in urgent need of hospitalization. Now will you PLEASE get a move on? I am deeply concerned about the lad's condition. You're what? It's on its way. OK thank you very much. We're in room 4008. They will need a trolley. I don't think he should be allowed to stand or walk. Yes. OK!"

He patted me on the shoulder. "Raymond, my boy, I think you had better wake your parents. I'll stay here with Marty. Try and break this gently to them although how that's going to be possible I don't know. But so far you've done all you can. It's such a tragedy after so much joy." He looked at Marty who was now in a deep sleep, snoring lightly. Then he smiled although a little tightly. "But maybe I'm a bit too pessimistic, hey? Maybe, hopefully, it's just a small problem but we gotta deal with it quickly, whatever it is. You understand a bit about what's happening?"

I nodded as I backed out of the room. "Trouble is, my limited medical knowledge makes me suspect all the very worst things. I'm just a lowly dentist after all!"

My uncle was now taking Marty's pulse and looking under his eyelids again. He looked up at me concernedly. "As soon as McGregor's office opens I'll be getting him involved. He'll be able to pull strings here in Cape Town better than I can. Go now, get your folks."

I stopped in front of my parents' room, gritting my teeth, then knocked. After a few moments came my father's sleepy voice through the closed door. "Yes, who is it?"

"It's me, dad. Ray. Let me in please."

The door opened and I felt a huge lump in the back of my throat at the effect my waking them with this bombshell was going to have, especially after the euphoria of the past days and weeks.

My mother's voice shrilled from the bedroom. "Ray, what's the matter? Is it Martin?"

Once again I was astounded at the accuracy of her maternal instincts. "Yes, Mom, I'm afraid that Marty, er, isn't at all well. I've called Doctor Joe and he's called an ambulance."

"Oh God, what's happened? Is it the epilepsy?" she quavered.

"I'll explain while you get dressed. I guess you'll want to go to the hospital with Dr. Joe and me." I hesitated then decided that they needed to know and understand the situation. I related the events of Saturday night playing down the severity of the Grand Mal attack but trying to explain why we had kept the knowledge from them during the wedding. "So there was nothing that could be done on the weekend anyway and Marty seemed to be OK."

"But he wasn't! I could see he wasn't himself at the wedding. You told me he'd had too much to drink." My mother broke down sitting on the bed, holding her head in her hands. "I knew, I just knew this wasn't just epilepsy. What does Joe think? Are you telling us EVERYTHING?" my mother screamed, waving her hands in anguish.

My father gripped her by the shoulders. "Rosie, Rosie, come on now, this isn't gonna help. Get yourself dressed and we'll go down to our boy. Ray, we'll be down in a few minutes. Go and see if Joe needs any help. Go now, son." He glanced at his watch. "Oh my God, the time, it's past seven. What about Larry, and Serena?"

I checked my watch. "Seven twenty-five. Their flight to Mauritius is at eight. They'll be at the airport, probably in departure by now. Really, dad, what could they do, what could we tell them at this stage?

I'm sure it's best to let them go off on their honeymoon without all this tsorris on their minds."

Abie looked at my mother, then at me and nodded. "You're right, Ray. Nothing to be gained, getting them all upset. Go down to your brother now. We'll come as fast as we can."

To be honest I felt relief at not having to break the news of Dr. Joe's diagnosis right at that moment and scuttled away to our room. Marty hadn't moved, was lying still, mouth open slightly. Just a slight movement of the bedclothes over his chest indicated he was breathing, that and a slight rasping snore.

"What's happening, Uncle?"

Joe shook his head slowly. "I'm not too sure, Ray, but I can't get any response from him now. His reflexes are still there but he seems to be in a coma. We need those bloody ambulance people, at least they'll put him on oxygen immediately."

As if on cue there was a knock on the door and two paramedics came in equipped with portable oxygen which they placed over Marty's mouth and nose. After preliminary examination they decided with Dr Joe that setting up a drip was not urgent and transferred Marty to their mobile trolley. As they were wheeling him down the corridor my parents came rushing towards them. My mother threw herself on Marty's chest sobbing.

She had to be dragged away by Dr Joe. "Rosie, let the paramedics take care of him. They know what they're doing. We'll follow them to the Hospital. I've left a message for Dr. McGregor and hopefully he'll be able to arrange everything at Groote Schuur, a scan and other tests."

Abie pulled Joe aside. "What's happened, Joe? Is this part of his epilepsy? Or was it that bloody skolly cracking him on Saturday night?"

Joe pursed his lips grimly. "Look, Abe, it does not look good at the moment. Marty seems to have raised pressure in his head which could be caused by a haemorrhage or a blood clot, but what happens is that the body goes into like a defence mode, unconsciousness, coma, call it what you will. What we need now is a scan to tell us what we're dealing with. Firstly, though, he has to be stabilized in hospital and that's what these guys will tell them when they get Marty to the Accident and

Emergency. Ray gave them the name of the registrar who saw Marty on Saturday night so they know what to expect. We'll go in Ray's car behind the ambulance. Just try and keep Rosie calm."

*

The ride through the Cape Town early morning traffic was a nightmare. The ambulance had its sirens and blue lights on. I did my best to keep close behind with my emergency lights flashing. Abie and Rosie sat pale-faced in the back. Dr. Joe gripped the handle above his head as we weaved between and around cars allowing us through.

We were directed to a seated waiting area in the familiar Casualty Department as the paramedics wheeled Marty into a curtained cubicle with Dr. Joe in close attendance. There was nothing we could do but sit apprehensively and watch the comings and goings of nurses, interns and auxiliaries as they coped with the inflow of injuries, acute illness and emergency that constitutes the drama of a modern Accident and Emergency Department. The overpowering disinfectant smell together with that of the slightly nauseating odour of sweaty alcohol-infused patients in various stages of collapse added to our discomfort. Two men sat near us, leaning against each other, their shirts covered in bloodstains They both wore blank looks on their faces, waiting resignedly, practically semi-conscious, to be called by the frenetic and obviously understaffed nurses.

After what seemed an eternity, Dr. Joe came out of the cubicle. The look on his face told us all was not well. He sat down next to us and composed himself. "I'm sorry to say that my first impression was right. Marty has suffered a brain haemorrhage and is in a coma. They don't know how serious it is until they have done a scan and x-rays but will be admitting him into the Intensive Care Ward until those procedures can be arranged, hopefully later this morning. I'm still waiting for Dr. McGregor to contact me but everyone here seems pretty competent".

"Can we see Marty?" my mother asked tremulously, wiping tears from her eyes. "Even just for a minute, you know."

Dr. Joe nodded. "Just peep through the curtain, Rosie, they're still busy doing various things but just poke your head in, I'm sure they'll understand."

I watched as my beloved parents, who had seemed to age years in the past hour, trudged over and peered through the curtain. Two people whose world had come crashing down from euphoric heights to plumb the deepest depths in the wink of an eye. My heart ached as I watched them turn and walk back to where Joe and I were sitting, my father with his arm around his wife's shoulders, her chest heaving with involuntary sobbing.

As we watched Marty being wheeled away to the lift, a young white-coated intern came over. He introduced himself as Dr. Malan, Senior Registrar. "I just want you to know that we are transferring your son to our Intensive Care Unit where we will do everythingwe can to stabilize his condition. The Radiology Department has been alerted and within a few hours we should know more about Martin's condition."

Dr. Joe stood up. "You should be hearing from Dr. McGregor, the Neurologist. I contacted his office this morning."

The Intern nodded. "Yes, we've already heard from Dr. McGregor. He will be coming round a little later but we have given him details and he has approved what we are doing for Martin. We've put him on a saline drip to counteract the dehydration. He must have lost a lot of fluid, sweating and vomiting etc. Unfortunately, until the blood test analysis comes through we can't use any medication."

Dr. Joe thanked the young doctor, turning to us with a shrug. "So nothing to do but sit and wait."

"Maybe you could go and have some breakfast in the Hospital Cafeteria," Dr. Malan suggested sympathetically.

"I couldn't eat a thing," Rosie said. "Not until I know that my boy's gonna be OK."

Dr. Joe went over to her, hands on her shoulders. "Rosie, dearest, it may be a long wait. We know Marty is in capable hands and everything possible will be done for him. You and Abe, and Ray and I as well, we need to keep our strength up. So come on, let's go to the cafeteria. That's an order from your doctor!"

"I'm sure that's sensible advice," said the intern. "We'll let you know as soon as we have any further information."

*

Hours passed waiting in a hospital for news of a loved one in trouble must rank as among the most depressing and emotionally draining experiences. We were now seated in a small waiting area along a corridor from the Intensive Care department. The Neurologist

Dr. McGregor had arrived and greeted Dr. Joe like a long lost friend. Apparently they had been in Medical School at the same time. He was a tall gaunt cadaver of a man, with sharp features, yet with a bright-eyed smile which lit up his otherwise serious expression.

"Mr. and Mrs. Benjamin, Raymond, pleased to meet you, although not in the happiest circumstances, I grant you. I'm sure you'll want to know how Martin is doing. You probably noticed them wheeling him along to the Radiology Department for x-rays and a scan a short while ago. I'm going in there now to see what the results are and will be in consultation with the radiologist and a Neurosurgeon."

My mother gave an involuntary gasp. "A surgeon, a brain surgeon, you mean? Oh, no!"

Dr. McGregor was quick to respond. "Mrs. Benjamin, we will have to deal with whatever the scan and x-rays show up. Martin sustained a heavy blow which, on top of whatever was causing his epilepsy, has left him with something in his head causing a shutdown, a protective shutdown, which is the body's response to a threat, an injury, or a blood vessel rupture. We must wait and see what the cause is. I have asked Mr. Neville Rosenberg, a highly rated and experienced Neurosurgeon, to join us as we view the scans. Rest assured that your son could not be in better, more capable hands if it comes to surgery."

He looked up and patted Rosie reassuringly on the shoulder. "I'm sorry, I see they are calling me. Hopefully we will have some information for you all very soon.

*

An hour passed. Countless paper cups of tea and coffee from the automatic dispenser were half drunk then discarded as we waited for some development, though fearful for what that development might mean for Marty. My parents sat huddled together, hands clasped, while Dr. Joe and I formed an assembly line between the coffee machine and our little enclave.

My father raised his head "What's the time, Ray?"

I looked at my watch although there was a huge wall clock directly opposite. Twelve thirty. Six hours had passed since this ordeal had started for us, although I couldn't help thinking of how long Marty's suffering had gone on without his making any complaint whatsoever.

Suddenly there was activity down the corridor. Orderlies were wheeling Marty on a trolley back to Intensive Care, still connected to a drip and various monitors. We all stood up nervously as Dr. McGregor and another white-coated man walked toward us. Their facial expressions could only be interpreted as grave.

Dr. McGregor held out his hand towards my parents. "Mr. and Mrs Benjamin, Martin's parents, Raymond, his brother and Dr. Joseph Goldberg, Martin's uncle and family GP, I'd like to introduce Mr. Neville Rosenberg, the Neurosurgeon I told you about."

Mr. Rosenberg was short, completely bald, and round-faced with rimless spectacles. After shaking hands with each of us in turn, he gestured to us to follow him into a consulting room. "We have the results of Martin's scans and x-rays and I think it best if we sit down and discuss the situation in private."

The room was sparsely furnished, a table and several chairs, a window overlooking a car park with the magnificent backdrop of the wooded slopes of Table Mountain. A gentle humming of an air conditioner unit was the only sound pervading the silence as we all took seats. Dr. McGregor placed several x-rays and scans on an x-ray viewing screen on the table in front of us. "I'm sorry to have to tell you that the news is not good. We can now see that Martin's Petit Mal epilepsy was almost certainly produced by a mass, a tumour probably, in the left temporal lobe of his brain." He pointed to a dark shadow on an illuminated film. "But now, this has been severely complicated by the trauma of the blow he received on that side of his head on Saturday. This has produced a haemorrhage and haematoma, leakage of blood into the brain tissues here and here at the base of the brain. This means that unless we act quickly, Martin's life is under serious threat."

My mother uttered a mournful wailing sound, holding her head in her hands. My father gripped the arms of his chair, his face contorted with anguish. Dr. Joe sat rigidly, clenching his jaw while I could only shake my head in disbelief.

For a few moments no-one said a word. Then Dr. Joe broke the deathly silence. "So what do you recommend, then?"

Dr. McGregor hesitated then turned to Mr. Rosenberg. "I reckon that the immediate problem has to be dealt with by surgery, the haematoma has to be drained, and the intracranial pressure reduced.

I think that Mr. Rosenberg is the person to describe what has to be done."

"Thank you, David," said the surgeon, tenting his fingers. "What we have already done is to insert a spinal tap to reduce the pressure. This is already having a beneficial effect in that the immediate threat to life has been avoided. However, I have to tell you that the location of the haematoma alongside the tumour is in an extremely awkward situation and is close to vital centres of the brain. An attempt to reach this area surgically carries with it a major risk, both of permanent impairment or even mortality."

"OH, NO! My poor child! What did he ever do to deserve this!" My mother rocked forward and back in her seat.

My father sat white-faced, eyes wide, tears trickling down his wizened cheeks. "So, Doctor what you are saying is that unless you operate, our son has little or no chance and yet if you do operate, his survival chances are slim. Is that what you are telling us?"

Mr. Rosenberg nodded, sympathetically. "Unfortunately I cannot do otherwise than describe the situation as honestly as I can. Martin's initial problem, the tumour, might have been removed successfully earlier on, although even then there would have been no guarantees, but now with the acute vascular problem over-riding everything else, the surgical challenge is infinitely more complicated. I'm so sorry but I think it is only fair to give you the total picture."

My mother raised her head, eyes red and swollen. "So you mean, if that bastard specialist Morris in Port Elizabeth, who told me I was being a neurotic Jewish mother, had done his job, we might not be facing losing our beloved son now?"

The neurosurgeon shook his head. "I'm sorry, I can't pass an opinion on that, except to say that the symptoms and signs he may have had to go on at that time were probably quite mild compared to what we have now."

Dr. Joe took hold of my mother's hand and patted it gently. "Rosie, my dear, we all wondered at the time why Marty had developed the Petit Mal. He was so fit and his reflexes and symptoms were absolutely normal. You can't keep blaming Dr. Morris although his comment was very hurtful. But now, for Marty's sake I think we have to think very carefully and swiftly because, correct me if I'm wrong," he turned to both specialists, "every hour that goes by makes the prognosis worse."

Rosenberg and McGregor nodded in unison. "Would you like to have some time to discuss it?" said McGregor.

My father turned to the three of us. "Do we have anything more to consider? To me it seems we have no choice but to go ahead. Rosie, my darling wife, we have to make this decision together. Please say something."

"How can you ask this of me? To ask a mother to put her son's life in jeopardy, to let people go digging inside his head? What will he be like after? Will he still be our son?"

Mr. Rosenberg pursed his lips. "Mrs. Benjamin, please understand. You all have our deepest sympathy. However your son's life is in jeopardy. What we are offering is an attempt to treat him in the only way possible in the circumstances." He turned to McGregor. "I think we should give the family some time in private, David."

Suddenly my father stood up. "No, that won't be necessary. Our son is in your hands. Please, I beg you, do everything you can to bring him safely through this so he can lead a normal life."

The two specialists stood up, looked at each other and nodded. They gathered up the x-rays and scans and walked towards the door. Mr. Rosenberg went to my father and shook his hand. "I assure you I will do everything I possibly can, believe me. We will wait until Martin's condition has stabilized before taking him to theatre. In the meantime I suggest you go back to your hotel and rest. We will contact you as soon as we are ready."

My mother stood, shaking her head. "I'm not going anywhere. I'm staying here where I can be near Marty. Abie, you Joe and Ray go back to the Hotel and maybe see if you can find a hotel nearby here to move to. I'm not budging, is that OK, Doctor?"

Rosenberg shrugged. "If that's what you want, that's fine. We'll send an Intern or a theatre sister to let you know what's happening."

The two specialists left the room, deep in discussion and after a brief argument, we decided that Dr. Joe and I would go back to the hotel leaving my parents huddled together in the bare confines of the consultation room.

We had barely reached the elevators at the far end of the corridor when a siren sounded followed by a voice over the PA system. "Mr. Rosenberg wanted in Intensive Care immediately." We turned abruptly to see frenetic activity, nurses, orderlies all rushing towards the doors leading to the Intensive Care department. My uncle and I looked at each other as if sparked by a single thought. Could this be anything to do with Marty? All thoughts of leaving the hospital were forgotten as we hurried back to the consulting room where my parents were already at the door, peering down the corridor.

"What's happening, Joe?" my mother cried. "Go find out if it's Marty. Please, I just know something's happening."

Dr. Joe was already striding briskly towards a nursing station opposite the I.C. department. We could see him standing at the desk, listening closely to the Ward Sister. My parents and I stayed where we were, afraid to get in the way, afraid to hear what Joe was being told. My mother was clutching my father with one hand, squeezing my hand with the other. We remained that way, leaning against the wall of the corridor, until we saw Joe nod and turn towards us, a grim expression on his face.

"Joe, Joe, what's happened? Is it Martin?" my father cried.

He nodded, miserably. "Yes, I'm very much afraid it is. Marty has had another Grand Mal attack and he went into cardiac arrest. They have managed to resuscitate him but he is now on a life support system. They are watching his EEG, his electro-encephalogram very carefully."

"W-w-what does that mean, Joe?" my father stammered. "Marty's life....is he in danger?"

My mother uttered a low moan and sank slowly to the floor. We managed to lift her and carry her back in to the consulting room. I ran to the nursing station to get assistance and very rapidly an intern came over and waved a bottle of smelling salts under her nose which had an immediate and dramatic effect. She opened her eyes and struggled to her feet. "What's happening, Joe, Abie, tell me what's going on?"

Uncle Joe gently lowered her back into a seat. "Rosie, Abie, they've told me as much as they can. At the moment they're battling to keep all Marty's functions going but there's only so much they can do. He's suffered a massive vascular insult, his heart stopped, they've managed to start it again but they don't know how much damage has been done. All we can do now is wait and pray."

*

An ominous silence had descended on the corridor outside our room. Every nurse or white-coated intern that passed by caused our already jangled emotions to escalate into overdrive. I had lost count of the number of visits to the coffee machine I'd made and the waste-bin was overflowing with used paper cups.

After what must have been an hour or more, Mr. Rosenberg and Dr. McGregor knocked on the open door of the consulting room. From their faces I knew it could only be the worst news imaginable. The neurosurgeon closed the door behind him and indicated to us all to take seats round the table. "Mr. and Mrs. Benjamin, Raymond, Joe, I'm so sorry to have to tell you that Martin passed away a short while ago."

"OH! NO! NO! NO!" my mother screamed, rocking back and forth on her chair. My father and uncle sat rigid, stony-faced. I felt my eyes welling with tears, my throat constricting as involuntary sobs racked through me.

Mr. Rosenberg waited momentarily, then felt he had to continue. "The Grand Mal episode that overcame Martin caused a further massive haemorrhage at the base of the brain and a cardiac arrest occurred. Although we were able to resuscitate temporarily the EEG indicated that brain function had ceased. We had no choice but to terminate the life support system. Once again, please understand that we were prepared to do everything possible for your son but the catastrophic attack made any surgery completely out of the question." He stood up and extended his hand to both my parents. "I'm so very sorry. Please accept my deepest condolences."

Dr. McGregor shook hands with us, his face lined with sympathy. My mother stood up, eyes streaming but ominously calm now. "Please gentlemen, can we see our son now?"

The two doctors looked at each other. Rosenberg nodded. "Give us a few moments. We'll arrange it immediately."

We were ushered into a small tiled room alongside the Intensive Care ward.

My dear brother was lying on a trolley, his face restful, eyes closed. I could even manage to imagine his slightly lopsided smile that he wore so often when playing a practical joke, but it became a blur as tears flooded my eyes. My mother bent over and kissed his forehead. Father and uncle did the same and stood aside for me. I could not contain the sobs as I touched my lips to his cheeks which were still warm.

I felt my uncle's hands on my shoulders. "Come on, Raymond. Be brave, my boy." I stood back then, taking a last look at the young man I'd spent so many fun years with, whose life had been so cruelly shortened. Clear memories of surfing the big waves together, listening to our favourite jazz records, him practically killing me on the squash court, but most of all his gentle humour, the way we both reacted with an almost telepathic sense of the ridiculous. It all came back to me with a rush, his merciless teasing of my parents to whom he could say anything, even tell the most obscene jokes and get away with it, also the way he took the mickey with Euphemia about her weight and her raucous laughter. All these memories were tumbling over each other in my mind as we were gently ushered back in to the hallway. We watched as orderlies wheeled Marty away. The four of us stood numbly looking at each other, seeming not to realise how the tragedy that had taken place would affect all our lives.

"Oh my God!" I murmured softly.

They looked at me questioningly. "What is it, Raymond?" my father asked, his face streaked with tears.

"Larry!......... How are we going to break this to Larry and Serena"?

CHAPTER 27

Serena's parents had insisted that we move in to their palatial home. We somehow made the journey, my parents, Dr. Joe and I, from the President Hotel in a kind of numb stupor. Everyone agreed that Larry and Serena had to be told immediately, and that funeral arrangements would be made for Marty to be buried in Port Elizabeth at my parents' insistence. The Jewish religion stipulates that burial must take place as soon as possible. Dealing with all the bureaucratic regulations, obtaining the Death certificate and permission to transfer Marty to Port Elizabeth would need a couple of days so the funeral was set for Friday morning. Funerals cannot be held on Shabbat or Sabbath which starts late Friday afternoon. We would all fly to Port Elizabeth with Marty on the Wednesday morning.

Tuesday afternoon we were sitting solemnly in the Levy's spacious lounge while Melvin made heroic efforts to telephone Larry and Serena's Hotel in Mauritius. After at least an hour's struggle he finally managed to get through and miraculously got the call transferred to their room. It had been agreed after some discussion, that Dr. Joe would be the one to break the horrendous news to the newlyweds.

"Hullo, is that you, Larry? Oh Serena, hullo, this is Dr. Joe Goldberg speaking. Are you having a good time?" Joe looked at us all, shrugged his shoulders, a helpless expression on his lined face.

Serena's cheery but incredulous tones came through the loudspeaker phone clearly enough for us all to hear. "Dr. Joe, this is such a surprise.

Yes, it's absolutely wonderful here. Is something wrong? No, wait you'd better speak to Larry."

"Yes, I know, sorry to alarm you but...." He turned to us. "She's calling Larry."

"Hi there, Dr.Joe. Larry here. What's up?"

Dr. Joe grimaced. "Larry, my boy, I'm afraid I have some very sad news. Your dear brother Martin passed away at Groote Schuur Hospital yesterday after a severe brain haemorrhage."

We could hear a choking noise from Larry and a short scream in the background from Serena. "WHAT? Oh my God, no, that's just not possible, what happened? How could it.......so fast......but...but.....he seemed fine....... when we said goodbye Sunday night......"

Joe pursed his lips. "Yes, well, it seems that the blow he got on Saturday night caused a brain haemorrhage. Only when they did a scan did it show a tumour as well, which was almost certainly the original cause of his epilepsy. The haemorrhage was close to the tumour and Monday morning Marty went into a coma. We got him to hospital but he then had another major epileptic seizure with a massive second haemorrhage which resulted in cardiac arrest. They did everything possible, but just couldn't save him." Tears were now pouring down Joe's cheeks and he gestured for someone to take the phone.

Wiping my eyes, I grasped the receiver. "Hi Larry. So sorry you had to hear this on your honeymoon. It all started early Monday morning... you would already have been in departure. We didn't want to call you straightaway, so many things to organise and the time difference as well. Also we all felt that an extra day for you two wouldn't make any difference here."

There was a long silence on the line. "What are the arrangements for the funeral?"

"Well, mom and dad want Marty to be buried in PE so it's going to be Friday morning. Think you can get back?"

"I'll see if we can get on a flight straightaway. Are mom and dad OK?"

I looked across the room at my grieving parents, offering them the phone but they shook their heads. "As well as can be expected, Larry. They can't talk right now. We're staying at Serena's parents' house."

"OK, Ray. Jesus Christ, I just don't believe this. Our poor, poor brother. Do they think it was purely the crack on the head from that bastard skollie? Damn, I remember he was trying to help me."

"They're not sure. The Neurosurgeon who was going to operate said that it might have been possible to remove the tumour earlier but even then it would have been very risky as it was close to vital areas of his brain. I guess we'll never know now."

"And all this time, those petit mal attacks....."

"Ja, they were responses to the tumour growing and causing pressure. And Marty just handled it all, the drugs, the headaches, so calmly, didn't ever complain or want to worry anyone." I stifled a choked sob. "He was one brave fella, our little brother."

"I'm just totally blown away, Ray. You can imagine. Serena is crying her eyes out. He was such a special guy." There was a momentary pause. "Did they do a post-mortem?"

"No. We discussed it with the doctors. Mom, dad, Joe and I all felt we didn't want Marty to be interfered with in any way Are you OK with that?"

"Yes. Definitely."

"Right, then. Anyway, see what you can do about getting back. The airlines are usually very helpful in cases of bereavement."

"OK Ray. I'll get busy right now. Give everyone our love. I'll call soon as I have details."

"That's fine, Larry. Be well, love to Serena." I walked across to Melvin's large mahogany desk and replaced the receiver.

Lucille stood up. "I'm sure everyone could do with a cup of tea right now. Angelina!!!"

*

Larry and Serena had managed to fly back into Port Elizabeth via Johannesburg on the Thursday afternoon. Serena's father and I met the newlyweds at the small but modern airport, and among the throng of happy holidaymakers arriving, it was difficult to hide our emotions. Larry and I simply clung to each other, unable to restrain our weeping, as did Serena and her father. We quickly retrieved their luggage and hurried the lightly tanned couple away from curious glances to the car park opposite.

As I drove through the suburb of Walmer, past our old school, it felt strangely like a normal homecoming but for this hardly believable catastrophe. In the end, I broke the silence. "I guess two things one can say is, firstly, Marty didn't suffer in those last few hours. He virtually didn't come out of the coma. Secondly, even if they could have operated and saved his life, there was a high likelihood he would have been left severely impaired. Who would want that for Marty?"

Larry shook his head. "I guess that's true. Was there absolutely nothing they could do to save him?"

I could see his face in the mirror. "No, not once the major grand mal occurred with a massive haemorrhage. Then his heart just stopped. You know how fit he was, squash and all, it made no difference. Apparently the second haemorrhage affected his vital centres. Everything just collapsed."

"You managed to get the funeral held over till tomorrow. That must have been difficult," Serena said.

I nodded. "Yes, the *Chevra Kadisha* (Burial Societies) in Cape Town and P.E. were amazing. There was a lot of red tape but thanks to your dad in Cape Town and the people here they managed to postpone till you guys got here."

Serena bit her lip. "Well, I suppose we'll go back to Mauritius one day. It was beautiful, wasn't it, Larry?"

Something deep inside me rankled at the tone of this remark but I kept silent, watching my brother's face in the mirror. He looked at his new wife with such complete adoration that any deeper reaction he might have had was not apparent.

We pulled in to the driveway of our parents' home, the scene of all those frenetic games of cricket in our youth. I had never seen Euphemia's normally smiling ebony face so desolate as she rushed out of the house to help carry the luggage. She wept as she embraced Larry and Serena but was too choked to say anything. Our parents were standing on the front verandah trying their best to be welcoming. We followed them indoors where all the family, cousins, uncles and aunts were waiting in the lounge.

Hours passed in sombre conversation, voices hushed and the room was already prepared for sitting *shivah*, the period of mourning which would start on Sunday. Low chairs, all reflective surfaces, mirrors, pictures covered with sheets. My father, Larry and I would now not shave until that period was over. Although my lack of belief was stronger than ever, for my parents' sake, especially my father, I had decided to conform to all the traditions. My adoration for my beloved kid brother was uppermost in my mind as I sat quietly watching my family endure the tragedy that had befallen us all.

*

The Jewish cemetery in North End, Port Elizabeth is a bleak place, a small section separated from the much larger general burial grounds by a low wall. There is almost always a strong wind blowing off the sea which is only a few hundred yards away, with motorway and railway lines in between. The Port Elizabeth Prison is situated just alongside and cries and profanities from the prisoners' barred windows which overlook the cemetery are often audible during funerals.This adds to the overwhelming atmosphere of sadness and loss. A small building contains the prayer hall with an adjacent room for the immediate family of the deceased.

We arrived at the cemetery late on Friday morning to find a huge mass of people, practically, or so it seemed, the entire Jewish Community of Port Elizabeth in attendance. The usual wind was blowing, clouds scudding across the horizon of Algoa Bay. I stared out at the dark grey ocean, remembering my sad departure aboard the 'SS Africa' which seemed like a lifetime ago. So many experiences I could recall, mostly highs, a few lows since then, but nothing like the desolation I felt at that moment.

We were ushered into the mourners room and waited silently until called to the crowded main hall. In the centre stood a trolley on which rested a coffin draped in black bearing an embossed Star of David.

For me the Funeral Service passed in a sort of haze. The prayers in Hebrew from the Rabbi seemed to exist in some distant place, the faces of the congregation, most of whom I knew from my growing up, all appeared like static blank ciphers in an abstract canvas. It was only when the Rabbi spoke in English about Martin that reality intruded .

"A fine young man has been so sadly taken from us, in the first bloom of his manhood. Multi-talented, a gifted sportsman, loved by all who knew him, Martin will be remembered for his sunny disposition, his kindness, his musical accomplishments, and above all his devotion to his parents and brothers to whom we all extend our deepest condolences and commiserations."

Loud sobbing rose from several of the women standing on one side of the room as the large doors opened. The trolley was slowly wheeled down the aisles between the gravestones, with some inscriptions dating back to the nineteenth century. We followed as a family with the congregation behind towards a freshly excavated burial plot. After further prayers in Hebrew my father recited the Kaddish, or Prayer for the Departed. "*Yitkadal ve yitkadash shemai rabah.......*"

I watched in disbelief as the coffin was slowly lowered into the ground. Spades were passed from hand to hand to shovel earth on to the wooden box from which the black cloth had been removed. Larry and I followed my father in this sad ritual, the clods of muddy earth making a dull thudding noise as gradually the coffin was covered.

After returning to the chapel, my parents, Larry, Serena and I sat on a low bench and the congregation filed past, wishing us all long life. The entire process for me was like a blur, a soft-focus film happening to other people in another place, not to me, not to us. It was only as we left the cemetery, pausing for the ritual washing of hands, that I fully realised that my wonderful brother was now lost to us for always, his presence marked by a numbered stake on which, in a year's time, a memorial stone would be erected to his memory.

*

The week's mourning became a pattern, early morning prayers which were well attended, then the day spent sitting in the lounge while friends and family came to pay their respects. The evening prayers were even more crowded, with people spilling into the large hall and dining room. My old friends Mark, Alec and Lalla came several times and even Rita turned up with them one afternoon. Their visits proved a welcome relief from the gloom and we all sat enjoying the sun in the back garden, exchanging news and recollections.

Rita touched me lightly on my arm. "Ray, I got a letter from Crystal in America. She says all is going well for her there and her legal job is fantastic. She sends her love and hopes to surprise you one of these days in London as she will be involved in some extensive travel to Europe."

In spite of the sadness of the situation, I felt my pulse rate quicken.

Alec could not help overhearing and smiled at my obvious reaction. "So Ray my old mate, the flame still burning, hey?" he laughed teasingly.

Mark and Lalla joined in."J-j-jeez, R-ray, you must have given her something to remember you b-b-y!" The stammer had nearly gone but not quite.

"I guess there's no love like the first love," Mark said wistfully "Do you think you'll ever get together again?"

I shook my head. "Nah, don't think so. Too much has happened and well, you guys know how I feel about religion but somehow," I hesitated, choosing my words carefully, "after this tragedy, I 'm pretty certain I couldn't do that to the folks. It would kill them if I married out."

"A Shiksa like me," Rita grinned broadly.

I patted her lightly on the shoulder. "No, no, for you, with all the money you've made from your salon, maybe they'd make an exception, might make you an honorary Yiddishe meidel!"

The explosion of laughter brought Larry and Serena out from the kitchen. Serena was frowning. "I don't think it's appropriate for all this merriment in the circumstances. We could hear you all in the lounge."

Larry was nodding in agreement. "Yeah, guys, maybe cool it down a bit. We don't want to upset mom and dad."

The five of us sat open-mouthed, silently digesting their disapproval. After a few moments, I decided to speak out. "Excuse me, Serena, Larry, but as I understand it the mourning period is for friends and family to rally round, to sympathise and cheer people up. I'm sure that if Marty were here he would have joined in the joke."

"Well he's not here, is he?" she retorted," and we're only repeating what your mother just said a few minutes ago in the kitchen." She whirled on her heel. "Come on Larry, let's go back inside."

Like a meek lapdog my brother followed her indoors leaving us wide-eyed in disbelief. "Whew!!!" breathed Rita, "That's one hell of a touchy lady. I guess Larry will have to keep on her good side if he wants happy ever after!"

Not for the first time I felt an unease, an instinctive feeling that my new sister-in-law had an acidic side to her nature which often seemed to be directed towards me in particular. My kneejerk reaction at first, though quickly stifled, was to follow the couple inside and have an all-out row. Logic prevailed however as the thought of what effect an argument and slanging match would have on my parents sank in. The levity had gone out of our conversation and Rita and the boys left soon after.

As she said her goodbye, Rita winked at me lasciviously. "I'll send Crys your regards, love or what?"

"Yes, all of those," I grinned, my mind doing cartwheels with the image of Crystal arriving in London after all this time.

*

After the episode in the back garden I made it my business not to provoke any further sarcasm from Serena. For Larry's sake, I decided the best way forward was to overdo the sweet and sugary big brother act.

By the end of the *shivah* on the following Thursday, the evening crowds for prayers had dwindled and the early mornings were down to a few dozen or so of the regulars who would normally constitute a 'minyan' or group of ten adult men which was the minimum for a service to take place.

The Friday night meal at our house still took place in an atmosphere of mourning although a sense of closure seemed to spread through the family. But not for my mother. Her expression of grief and disbelief was indelibly etched on her lined features. I realised that she especially had suffered a shock which would last the rest of her days. My father on the other hand seemed to endure in a sort of dreamy spiritual haze, taking part in all the prayers with the devotion and diligence of a rabbi. That night however, he spoke about going back to his business as if hardly anything in their lives had changed.

This brought about a swift reaction from my mother. "Abie, Marty's not even cold in his grave and all you can think about is business, business business!"

There was a hushed silence all round the table. Everyone stared at my mother in shock. My poor father was dumbstruck.

Dr. Joe was the first to respond. "Rosie, please, please, don't say things like that to Abie. He's suffering as much as you, as much as all of us."

My mother stood up, eyes blazing, "Don't tell me who's suffering more than me. A mother loses a child, there's nothing worse in the world. I knew Marty had serious problems right from the beginning and what did that no-good Neuro-whatever tell me? Not to be a hysterical Jewish mother! And you Joe, you and Abie, all more or less agreed with him. But, I was Marty's mother and I KNEW! Mothers know when their child is sick. SO PLEASE DON'T TELL ME ABOUT SUFFERING!" With that she threw her napkin on the table and ran out of the dining room sobbing.

No-one felt able to make any comment for several moments. Euphemia came in and solemnly began to clear the dinner dishes. Once more I sprang up to help her which caused surprised gasps all round the table. I guess my years spent abroad had diminished my familiarity with South African traditions. Nevertheless it enabled me to escape the bristling atmosphere and take refuge in the kitchen.

As she placed all the dishes in the sink, Euphemia looked up at me tearfully. "Massa Raymond, the madam, she is in very bad way. She cries alla time, just cries, cries, cries."

I nodded. "Phemia, I know, I can see, but there's no way to make her feel better. Marty was her baby."

"Ja, ja, an' he was mine too," she quavered. "I been here since before Marty was born, I carried him on my back till he was one year old! I know what your mother is feeling!" Her great body was shaking with emotion. Tears in rivulets flowed down her cheeks. I threw my arms around her and hugged her close.

"My, what a touching scene!" Serena suddenly appeared in the kitchen doorway.

I think the essence of her remark was sympathetic, but she just had this way of commenting that seemed sarcastic. In any case I stood back, a little embarrassed and walked over to her. "Where's my mom? Is she OK?" I spoke fairly abruptly.

"She's gone upstairs. Larry's trying to console your father. Maybe you should help." Again I felt the element of reprimand in her voice, but walked past her with no response. In the dining room everyone was crowded round Abie, offering sympathy. He sat glassy-eyed, unable to comprehend his wife's outburst..

The aftermath of Rosie's reaction left everyone with little alternative but to make preparations to leave. Larry and Serena were staying at the Elizabeth Hotel on the beachfront with Serena's parents. After gulping down coffee amidst valiant efforts to console my father, the guests left the house with assurances that we would all be together in shul (synagogue) the next morning. The house was terrifyingly silent when they had all gone. I followed my father slowly up the stairs to find my mother lying on her bed, fully dressed still but fast asleep.

"I'm sure she's taken her sleeping tablets," I whispered, "come in to my room if you want to chat."

Instead I followed him as he wandered into Marty's room and sat heavily on the bed. "She'll never get over this, will she, Ray?" He looked at me through swollen eyes, red with weeping.

"I guess probably not, dad. You're going to have to be very supportive for quite a while, I think."

"I just don't know if I can do enough for her. Her grief is so, so all-consuming. I can't get anywhere near her. Soon, when you and Larry are gone, it's just going to be the two of us. You know Marty was like a pal, always keeping us laughing and cheerful. We knew he'd go to University but that would have been different, he would come back on vacation. This......this is so permanent."

"I don't know what to say to you, dad. Maybe mom can help you more in the business, give her some extra stuff to do, maybe she can go to a group therapy session. They've got bereavement counsellors for these situations. But it'll have to come from her, I reckon. She will realise she's got to look after you as well."

"You've grown into a fine sensible man, Raymond. Thank you, you're right, we will have to help each other over this bad time. Maybe we'll even come and visit you in London." I caught a tiny twinkle in his eyes. "Maybe if it was for a wedding?"

I allowed myself a short laugh. "Dad, I promise you'll be the first to get an invite!"

"You mean, there might already be someone?"

"Nothing serious, we've dated once. I met her at a dinner party. She's Jewish, very lovely, very warm and friendly but....."

He winced. "But you're still pining for your little Crystal, hey?"

"I don't know, dad. Let's just wait and see. Right now I think you should get some rest. Why don't you take one of mom's tablets?"

He shook his head. "To get to sleep I don't have a problem. It's when I wake up realising what has happened, it comes back like a bad taste." He gazed sadly round the room, at Marty's school photographs, record player, his numerous squash trophies standing on the bookcase, and green and gold Springbok banners tacked to the wall. "I come in here and I can feel his presence, it's everywhere."

"I know, I can feel it too," I mumbled, feeling my eyes welling up. "Come on dad, its Shabbat and its late so let me lock up. We've got to be up early for shul tomorrow. You go to bed."

As he trundled along the corridor he turned suddenly. "Ray, I know you still don't believe in all our religious traditions and that you're only doing it for us. Please don't think we don't appreciate it. Thank you, my son." he whispered and leaned over to kiss me on my forehead.

Wiping my eyes on my sleeve I did the rounds, made sure all the windows were locked and set the burglar alarm. For me sleep did not come easy that night, concern for these two sad people uppermost in my mind. Worrying too was the thought of my Practice in London managing without me for far longer than I had anticipated.

I concentrated on thoughts of Jennifer, the new lady in my life in London, but somehow, as I closed my eyes, her image seemed to blur and merge, becoming a composite with the well-remembered face of my first love, who, now, was possibly, with her new profession and obviously well-remunerated status, considering flying in and out of London.

It was with these diaphanous spectral visions in mind that I finally fell into a restless sleep.

*

Another week went by. Serena and her parents had gone back to Cape Town and the time had come for both Larry and I to return to our respective jobs. Larry had moved in to our house and much discussion took place about South African politics and the perilous future that so many were predicting.

"You know how active Serena and I are in the anti-apartheid movement," Larry said over dinner, the night before both our departures. "Well, it looks as though the Black organizations, ANC here and ZANU-PF in Rhodesia are getting impatient with the white governments. They're beginning to threaten guerrilla war."

"I know," I replied. "And the Nationalists are not paying enough attention. With Mandela in jail and Vorster and Ian Smith having friendly talks, it's beginning to look like trouble ahead."

Larry nodded. "It will still take a long time but will begin with little isolated incidents, blowing up a pylon or something, maybe a few strikes. The United Nations sanctions will easily be sidestepped but eventually the economies of SA and Rhodesia will be affected."

"So what do you plan to do?" my father asked tremulously.

Larry pursed his lips. "Well, Serena and I have decided that this is not a country where we want to bring up our children. We've been saving every month and in about a year or so we are seriously planning to emigrate, Australia, England or Israel."

"Wow!" I said, wide-eyed. "This is a surprise. And Serena likes the idea?"

Larry clasped his hands together. "She does, but there's a problem. When we discuss our plan her dad Melvin goes bananas. He reckons South Africa is good the way it is for another fifty years. He simply cannot believe that the blacks will be able to mount a serious threat in the foreseeable future. The Afrikaners are much too tough, he says."

"So where does that leave you guys?"

Larry frowned. "You know what a generous man Melvin is, but he also likes to get his own way. Reading between the lines, I'd say that if Serena and I leave, he won't offer us any financial help at all whereas if we stay, the sky's the limit."

Abie interrupted. "I can't believe that of Melvin. He wouldn't let Serena struggle for a minute, no matter where in the world she is."

"I can't say for sure," Larry admitted, "but you wouldn't believe the fights that have erupted. So now we keep *shtum* and save each month. In a year we'll be ready."

I smiled. "Larry, you know I'd be overjoyed if you guys came to London. It would be great being there together. I could make starting out for you two much easier than say if you went to Australia or Israel where I think things are pretty tough at the moment."

Larry looked at me, eyes shining. "Yeah, Ray, we did think that London would be our best option especially with you being so well established there. Serena will be thrilled. She loves the theatre and the concerts. Her folks will just have to get used to the idea."

Abie held up his hands resignedly. "Yes and I suppose us two old folks here alone in PE will also just have to get used to it as well, hey boys?"

Larry and I looked at each other guiltily. "Well, dad," I said, "if we are all living in London, then wouldn't it be a good idea for you and mom to join us?"

Abie shook his head. "What, come to England and leave our beautiful beaches and weather? Not a chance, boychick. And as for your mother, well, how would she cope without Euphemia? Isn't that so, Rosie?"

There was no answer. My mother had taken little part in conversations for the past week since her Friday night outburst, merely sitting with a faraway look in her eyes, interspersed by bouts of silent sobbing. Attempts to cheer her up, or draw her into conversation had all failed.

"Much too early to talk about all this," Larry said. "We have to make the move first. In the meantime, mom and dad have got us in Cape Town, only an hour's flight away."

"Talking about flights," I interrupted, "my flight to Joburg leaves at eight tomorrow morning so I'm gonna finish packing and go to bed."

"Me too," Larry nodded.

We kissed each of our parents on the cheek and tramped up the stairs, feeling guilty about leaving them sitting at the dining table, staring at each other.

*

The airport was busy with departing holidaymakers as the season and school holidays were drawing to an end. My departure was first and the goodbye I was dreading actually passed quite swiftly. My flight was on time and was called almost immediately.

I grabbed Larry and hugged him close. "Listen, buddy, I meant what I said. I'll give you all the help I can in London. Try to make it sooner. I miss you guys. Love to Serena and her folks."

My father was busy consoling my mother so I embraced them both in a tight grip. "Listen, you two, look after each other now and start making plans for a visit to England soon. OK?"

Abie nodded sadly. "My boy, fly well, work hard and let's have some good news about, er what's her name, Jennifer, yes?"

I laughed. "Take it easy, dad, it's only been one date so far but I reckon you'll like her. I'll keep you posted."

My mother looked up at me, the almost blank forlorn look still in her eyes. "Ray, go well, and thank you, for all you've done, all the support." She looked up at the Departure board where my flight number was flashing. "I think you'd better get going. Go on, before you miss your flight!" This was the first attempt at levity from her since I had woken them that fateful morning just a few short weeks before. There was even the ghost of a smile playing round her lips.

I turned and waved. "You two look after each other now. That's an order. And Larry, write, let me know your plans." I was swallowed by the departure gates, taking a last glimpse at the three of them standing there, arms linked together. Blinking tears away I hurried through the departure lounge towards the South African Airways Boeing that would take me to Johannesburg then onward to London, a journey of close on 24 hours.

Chapter 28

1974 After Miners strike and the three day week, Edward Heath's Conservatives lose election to Harold Wilson and the Labour Party
Whites only Election in South Africa is won by the governing Nationalist Party led by BJ Vorster

Jennifer

She was, in many ways, like a refreshing gust of spring, uncomplicated, but enthusiastic, totally lacking in malice or envy in any way. Apart from being strikingly attractive, with jet black hair showing a few glistening strands of silver, she had that easy relaxed way about her that immediately infected those around causing them to loosen up and enjoy her company.

I guess that it could most probably have been these attributes that drew me to Jennifer when we were first introduced. It was at a time when I was becoming tired and bored with the endless dating game, a contest which seemed to revolve around targets of time-limited seduction.

We had met shortly before I flew to South Africa for Larry and Serena's wedding which had ended so tragically. I was invited to a dinner party at a fellow dentist's house in Elstree. His wife had instructed him to invite someone single and eligible for her friend Jennifer. After getting divorced some years previously, she was now involved in a hopeless tangle with a barrister who did not have marriage in his ambitions.

We were seated next to each other and although my hackles were sorely risen knowing I had been targeted as husband potential by our hosts, I found myself charmed and at ease from the very first moment. Jennifer had numerous London dentists and their wives among her acquaintances and friends and also exhibited a more than adequate knowledge of jazz, especially the modern variety which was also my preference.

"Do you play an instrument, Raymond?" Her voice was of a semi-cut glass variety which spoke of Home County private education. I only found out much later about her relatively humble origins. Her father had instilled in her the need to have a more cultured English accent than the East End Jewish Cockney that was their family background.

"A little," I admitted, "piano, but only by ear, I'm afraid."

"Hah, don't let him kid you," Harvey, our host laughed. "You should hear him, he's good. Pity we don't have a piano!"

I shook my head, embarrassed. "I amuse myself, like people who can't sing enjoy letting go in the shower."

"My father played the violin, I had lessons but never got very far," Jennifer smiled, my professional assessment highly responsive to a perfectly even and glistening white dentition.

"Mine too," I said, with more than a little poignancy. "We always play together when I'm at home. He knows all the standards of the forties and fifties."

By the end of the evening our hosts were congratulating themselves on a successful introduction. As I drove Jennifer home to her flat near Baker Street we voiced our amusement over their complete lack of subtlety.

Nevertheless, as I said goodnight at the entrance to her mansion block, I felt sufficiently encouraged to suggest that we go out again sometime soon.

"Thank you for the lift, Raymond, and for transforming what was one of those boring suburban dinner parties. Yes, I'd like to see you again. Call me." And she handed me a slip of paper with her telephone number.

We had only one opportunity to get together before I left for South Africa, meeting for a play in the West End and a somewhat hurried snack, after which we made our separate ways home. I was aware of her existing involvement from Harvey and his wife and so did not feel that anything more than occasional companionship was possible at that stage. Then came the trip to the wedding and on my return I found myself immersed in running and organising the Practice, catching up on treatments which had been delayed for the nearly five weeks I had been away. Truth to tell, Marty's untimely death had affected me in so many ways, some of which surfaced at odd times, leaving me drained and depressed. I found myself waking in the early hours, sweat-drenched after dreaming about him, vivid but convoluted scenes of the good times, the squash, the surfing and the music. Then too I would walk down the street and be certain I had seen him in a crowd only to pinch myself back to harsh reality.

Equally, thoughts of Crystal and her upheaval, struggling on her own in a new country, made me wonder if I could ever again feel any intense feeling for another woman. I realised that with passing time, she would almost certainly meet someone, and thoughts and memories of the tumultuous relationship we had known, might well be fading by now. After Rita promised to send my London address to Crystal in America, I had taken to rushing to the front door each morning for the post. I would rummage through the heap of pamphlets for Pizza delivery, Indian Takeaways and other local enterprises, searching for that envelope from the USA, hoping for the familiar perfume. The days then weeks went by and something inside of me began to lose faith. Cold reason too established itself in my mind. We had had a torrid roller-coaster relationship, forged in the face of white-hot opposition from both families. Now we were an ocean apart and perhaps the time had come to pick my shattered self up and in the words of the old song 'dust myself off and start all over again!'

After a month or so I picked up the phone.

"Hi, it's, ah, Ray..... Ray Benjamin."

"Who?"

"Ray Benjamin....we met at Harvey and Anna's dinner party a few months ago."

There was a momentary silence. "Oh, of course, Raymond. Yes, South African Dentist, right? Sorry, but you caught me on the hop. It's been quite a while."

"Yes, I'm sorry I didn't call but, er, I went off to South Africa for my brother's wedding and........."

"Anna told me about your younger brother," Jennifer cut in. "I'm really sorry. It must have been awful for you."

"Yeah, it was a horrendous aftermath to a wonderful wedding. We knew that he had mild epilepsy but it all happened so quickly."

"Were your folks all right afterwards?"

I twisted the telephone cord around my finger and swallowed deeply. "As well as could be expected, I guess. They coped, just about. Anyway, it took me a while when I got back here, to get straightened out......... but..... er.... things are sorted at the Practice now and if..... er.... maybe....."

"Yes, I'd love to see you .....is that what you were going to ask?"

I smiled into the receiver. "Great. How does Saturday night suit you?"

"Fine. Where are we going?"

"D'you fancy a meal? I know an excellent Chinese place up in Mill Hill. Kwan Yin, you eat in little cubicles. Quaint place. Do you know it?"

"No, but that sounds lovely. What time?"

"Will eight-ish do you?"

"Suits me. Remember my flat? I'm flat no 6, Cavendish Garden Mansions, Lissom Grove. Come up and we'll have a drink first."

*

Jennifer's apartment was a cosy one-bed flat, tastefully but simply decorated. The lounge had colourful abstracts on the walls, a large l-shaped couch, glass coffee table and a small dining alcove. Miles Davis' 'Milestones' was coming through loud and clear on a quality stereo set alongside a small TV in a wall cabinet. Jennifer was dressed casually but elegant in wine-coloured flared trousers and an open-neck pink blouse. No jewellery. Hardly any make-up.

I ventured a gentle peck on each cheek and looked around. "Great flat, Jennifer, really nice."

"Thank you, I do love it myself."

"Your taste in music couldn't be better also. And I must say, you look pretty good yourself. Do we have to go out?" I joked, eyes twinkling.

She laughed, showing that superb dentition. “What a line that is. I’m impressed.”

“Didn’t mean to be glib, but you do look lovely.”

She reddened slightly. “Well, thank you again, kind sir. Would you like a drink?”

I eyed the bottle of Macon Blanc with two glasses on the coffee table. “That’ll do me fine, thanks.”

We sat on the couch opposite each other sipping the ice-cold, fruity wine.

“That’s nice. Just what the doctor ordered,” I said, munching a crisp. “It’s funny, but seeing you again after all this time seems kind of strange, as though we’d been out more than just the once, like a familiarity.”

She nodded then grinned. “That’s not another line is it? Anna told me to be on my guard, you were not exactly a shrinking violet with the ladies.”

It was my turn to show embarrassment. “Oh God, what else did that chatterbox tell you about me?”

She waved her hand dismissively. “Not a lot, only that you’d been in London for quite a long time now, living and working in the Chelsea fleshpots. Also her hubby Harvey, is green with envy at the bachelor lifestyle you’re suffering.”

I shook my head. “You really mustn’t believe all you hear. I’m actually a workaholic. When I’m not bending over with my head in someone’s mouth, I’m probably on the squash court or in the gym.” I looked directly at her with slightly raised eyebrows. “And this is a two way thing, you know. I also got some information about you from our garrulous friends.”

She clasped and unclasped her hands nervously. “So, what did they tell you about me?”

I grinned and looked at my watch. “You’re gonna have to wait till later. The table’s booked for 8.30 and we’ve got twelve minutes to get to Mill Hill.”

*

The coffees came after a sumptuous meal. Jennifer excused herself to go to the ladies. I sat smiling inwardly at the warm feelings engulfing me. Yes, I said to myself, it’s only a second date but not for a long time had I felt so much at ease with a girl. Jennifer's relaxed way of chatting, her obvious warmth and sympathy when we talked of Marty had allayed any uncertainties that I might have had. All this apart, her physical attractiveness left me wondering how on earth anyone would have let her go. Yet, after marriage and divorce and now a relationship with someone who did not want permanent commitment, it seemed that Jennifer was not the kind of woman who would settle for anything less. But Oy! She was Jewish....and my folks would love her!

In the middle of my reverie, she returned with an audacious aroma of newly applied perfume. "Now, Mr. or is it Dr Benjamin, I have waited long enough. Just what did Harvey and Anna tell you about me?"

I looked at my watch. "Oh dear," I murmured, "I don't think we have enough time. They were most informative, you know."

My fragrant date leaned across the table and punched me playfully on the shoulder. "Come on, you promised!"

I laughed. "My God, I love violence in a woman. Do you want to do the other shoulder but harder, please!"

Now we were both giggling, and the couple sitting in a cubicle across the aisle were enjoying quite an interesting spectacle, watching to see what developed.

Jennifer put on a serious expression. "I told you what I knew about you. Fair's fair. Now it's your turn."

I told her that I knew she had been married and divorced with no children and had an ongoing relationship with a barrister. "And that's all I know, apart from the fact that you work as a highly paid legal secretary up in town."

She grew quiet "The ongoing relationship you mentioned is over. It wasn't going anywhere."

"I'm sorry."

"Don't be. I'm not."

Did I detect sparkling tearlets forming in the corner of those large brown eyes? I decided not. "So, where do you go from here?" I asked. "I mean ambitions? We're getting all maudlin. What do you want from life?"

She hesitated, smiling sadly. "Just the ordinary things, I suppose. Get married, have a family. Nothing spectacular."

What I said then came from somewhere deep within me. It just seemed like the right thing to say, what I wanted to say, so out it came. "Jennifer, this may sound crazy, it's only our second, or even our first real date but.......but....."

She peered curiously at me. "But what.....what did you want to say?"

I pursed my lips. ".........er.......your.....er.... ambitions, like you said, you know, I'd like you to consider me...... as a part of them..... your ambitions, that is ...."

Her eyes widened. "You are being very silly, or is this an extremely subtle line?"

I shook my head. "No, no, not at all. I know it's very early days but I just felt that that's what I wanted to say and so I said it. It's absolutely not a line. I haven't felt as comfortable with someone as I do right now, for a long time. So....." I gestured to the petite Chinese waitress for the bill, "let's just consider it said and filed away under work in progress, shall we?"

Jennifer smiled, a little relieved. "That's a lovely way to put it, Raymond. I'm very flattered."

"And I'm very relieved that all you said was for me not be silly. Maybe one day we'll tell our children........" I shrugged. "No, forget I said that. You didn't hear it, did you?"

A tiny grin flickered across her face "No, not a word."

The bill came, was paid and we made our way to my little white Mini parked in the service road outside. There was no conversation as we drove back through Swiss Cottage towards Baker Street until I parked outside her block. "I'll walk you to the entrance. My mother always told me that's what a gentleman should do."

Jennifer laughed out loud. "That's really funny. Anyway, Ray, thank you for a lovely evening. I had a great time."

I took her hand and then the kiss just happened. It started in a sort of formal, hesitant way then became more, two people beginning to react to each other. After a breathless eternity we stood apart and smiled.

"My, Dr. Benjamin, that wasn't in the script, was it?"

I shook my head. "No. Most certainly not. But my mother said not to kiss more than once on a first date so that'll have to do."

We were both laughing then, as if we both knew that something had started between us, something to be nurtured, not rushed. She turned and opened the large double doors.

"Goodnight, Raymond and thanks once again."

"I'll call you soon, OK?"

She nodded and was gone. I stood for a while in front of the building then made my way back to the Mini. Thoughts were whirling round in my head. What had I said? DID I REALLY SAY THAT? And did I mean it? The answer came back fast. Yes, with this girl, I think you did!

*

The next day, Sunday, dawned bright and clear, with sunny blue skies unusual for the normally grey London. After briefly leafing through my newspaper, the Sunday Telegraph, which I noticed was getting heavier each week, or so it seemed, I dialled Jennifer's number.

"Hello, who is it?" that flinty somewhat aristocratic voice came over loud and clear.

"Hi, it's me, you know, your date from last night?"

"Yes, Raymond, how could I not recognise that unmistakeable 'Serth Efrican' accent? How are you? You got home OK then?"

"Excuse me, I'll have you know that I was educated at Grey High School, in Port Elizabeth, an ivy-covered replica of a British Public School, and the home of the 1820 British Settlers. My English accent I've been told is pure Oxford!"

Her laughter echoed down the phone line. "Right, I'm so sorry if I offended your sensibilities. So what can I do for you this sunny May day?"

"As you said, it's a lovely day. If you aren't busy I thought you might like a drive and lunch out in the country?"

"My, you are a fast worker, aren't you?"

"Well, my mother always said.......oh, never mind what she said, it's 10.30 now, can you be ready at say 12 midday?"

"Sounds fine, Dr. Benjamin. Just buzz when you get here and I'll be down."

*

Thankfully my trusty white Mini behaved itself all the way out to Sonning-on-Thames where I'd booked at the French Horn, a picturesque restaurant with lawns sloping down to the river. Longboats and streamlined launches criss-crossed the wide expanse of serenely flowing water, overhung by willows and thick vegetation.

"What a gorgeous spot!" Jennifer exclaimed as we were shown to our table in the glass conservatory, looking out over the gardens. She was dressed in figure hugging white trousers and a revealing turquoise blouse. Again she wore no jewellery and her jet black hair was combed straight, framing her classic features. Male heads rotated at other tables, following her progress through the spacious dining area. I pretended not to notice.

The menu was classic English Sunday lunch, hot fresh vegetable soup, roast beef, Yorkshire pudding, the works, and apple crumble with custard to finish. The recommended house red wine was a Merlot and, knowledge of wines not being one of my strong points, I settled for that.

As we sipped coffee afterwards, Jennifer looked at me, frowning. "Raymond, this is our second real date. I don't think I'll be able to see you again after today."

Shocked rigid, I was unable to make a response until I saw the little twitch at the corners of her mouth, and went along with it. "W-w-w-whyever n-n-not?"

She laughed gaily. "Because after last night and today, I don't think I'll be able to fit into your cute little Mini. You've wined and dined me far too well!"

"Don't worry," I said, breathing a mock sigh of relief. "Soon as I've paid the bill we'll go for a long walk along the towpath and watch the swans and the boats. Work off both meals."

After an hour's stroll, the clouds began to gather and in the end we ran back to the car as, true to English tradition, the sun had vanished and it was beginning to spit with rain. We just got to the Mini in time and the journey back to London was slowed on account of the driving storm and not very efficient windscreen wipers.

It started the moment we entered her apartment. We simply melted into each other's arms. It seemed as though there was, for both of us, an urgent need, after a period of abstinence, for human warmth and closeness. Naturally I only knew about my recent past, but it was not difficult to gauge from Jennifer's response, that she too had not participated in much loving for some appreciable time.

However, after a lengthy session on the deep and welcoming couch, we came up for air. Looking at each other, hair all awry, we started to giggle. Jennifer spoke first. "Really Dr. Benjamin, what a way to behave on a second date. What would your mother say?"

I grinned mischievously. "She would say that nice girls don't do it on the first or second dates."

"And she would have been right. And I'm a nice girl!"

"I know that," I murmured, "and I want you to know that my intentions are strictly honourable............" I hesitated.... "for the time being anyway!"

Clear parameters having been set, we spent the evening watching TV, snacking on cheese, biscuits and coffee. Passionate clinches took place on the couch from time to time, but with mutual acceptance that any more complicated interactions would have to wait.

Much later, I rose and made my escape, but only after a breathless goodnight kiss and assurance that we would talk during the week. I skipped down the three flights of stairs, my heart singing. The briefest mental flashback to a not dissimilar encounter with Crystal all those years before, came and went. I determined to shut that part of my life away for good, and drove home with my head in the clouds.

My house just off the Kings Road was on four floors, consisting of ground and basement for the practice, with three surgeries, a waiting room and office. The top two floors comprised a two bedroom apartment with lounge, dinette/kitchen, bathroom, shower-room and WC. An unsatisfactory aspect of the arrangement, which in time I intended to remedy, was that the staircase was common to the practice so that the apartment was not completely self-contained.

Early the next morning I collected my paper and the post. A letter with a USA stamp leapt out at me. I recognised the handwriting immediately and, yes, sniffing, there was the perfume I remembered so well. I ran back up the stairs to my small kitchen and tore it open.

Mary Bennett House,
University of Pennsylvania,
Philadelphia PA
24th May, 1974

My dearest Raymond,

You have no idea what a thrill I got when I received Rita's letter with your address. I thought my heart would burst. It's been so very long, hasn't it? Eight long years! So much has happened to both of us. Rita told me you were now running a successful practice in Chelsea, and having a great time, skiing, jazz and all. I'm glad for you, you deserve it.

She probably told you all about the chaotic time that followed your leaving. After surviving that horrible scene at the harbour for which I can never apologise to you enough, I suppose, looking back, it was crazy to hope that we wouldn't bump each other's families before the boat left. Anyway, what happened, happened. I guess I went off the rails for quite a while after that. Lots of booze, dagga, the lot. Moved out of my folks' house, couldn't even look at my bastard of a father let alone talk to him. Then I got a job in Cape Town and in 1970 met Andre du Toit, a farmer in the Northern Cape. He was nice and gentle but very unsophisticated, not like my super smooth Raymond! (only teasing!) Anyway, I was sick of the big city and thought that peace and quiet on a farm miles from anywhere (nearest town Nababeep!) would give me the time to recover and lead a good life. We got married but I realised it was a mistake after only a few months. Andre was actually quite stupid and I was expected to be the quiet little *hausvrou*, domesticated with no mind of my own. Anyway I stuck it for a year then left, just walked out.

After that I went to Jo'burg, got a job teaching, but then heard about a Law Course here in Penn University. With my degree and only three years study, I would be a USA qualified lawyer. So with a bit of money I'd saved and a small settlement from Andre I made the decision and that's where I am now, in my last year.

I do like America. It's busy, it's free, with no bloody prejudices like my dad has and, well, I have to say, your folks too. Perhaps they weren't quite so bad. I'll be looking for jobs with some big companies when I finish and then I can live a good life here. There's no-one in my life right now, I'm too busy studying. How about you? I suppose you must be fighting them off!

Well I guess that's all for now. It would be nice to hear from you but I'll understand if you've drawn a line under that part of your life.

Love and kisses (as always)
Crystal xxxxx

I sat motionless at my little breakfast bar, unable to eat anything, heart pounding. I read her letter a second time, then a third. Ain't life a kick in the head, I thought to myself, like ol' blue eyes Sinatra would say. Here I was, after a weekend when a brand new love interest had entered my world, someone I had reacted to with an immediacy that had practically taken my breath away, only to have this echo from my past land on my doorstep the very morning after!

My day in the surgery passed in a blur. My chair-side assistant, receptionist and patients most probably, must have noticed but said nothing. Of course the latter would have been unable to with their mouths clamped open! I couldn't wait for the day to end, and as soon as my last patient left I dashed upstairs and poured myself a large scotch. Sitting in the lounge with the television on but sound turned off, I tried to take stock of exactly how I felt about Crystal's letter. Eight long years and still this incredible gut response!

After a second scotch, logic and reason started to assert themselves. Crystal was settled, making a life for herself. Here in London I had found Jennifer, a sensitive, delightful and unconventional woman who seemed to be on the same wavelength, and Jewish too, don't forget that, to whom I had practically proposed on the second date!

I stared groggily at my watch. Ten o'clock already. Where had the evening gone? Was it too late to call? I reached for the phone.

After several minutes listening to the ringing tone, I put the receiver down. Sleep was going to be difficult, I knew, so I swallowed a couple of Mogadon tablets which, on top of the scotch would assure me of a semi-inebriated slumber of a sort and a major headache the next morning. I took Crystal's letter to bed with me but the medication won the unequal battle.

*

The alarm clock rattled both my heads awake. Two paracetamol and three glasses of water took the edge off the hangover. Stumbling down the stairs as I heard the post being shoved through the letterbox, I tried to focus. This time a blue airmail lettercard from South Africa lay on top of the pile, Larry and Serena's name on the back. I managed to climb back up to the kitchen, put some coffee on and sat down heavily. With difficulty I sliced open the envelope.

Flat 3, Green Point Mansions,
Mouille Point, Cape Town.
25th May, 1974.

Hi Ray,

I guess you might be surprised to hear from us so soon. Hope you're settled back in UK and all going smoothly. Here things are not at all great. Since we got back from PE there have been ugly political developments, I won't go into details, you'll probably read about most of it in your papers. The Nats won another whites only election, big deal! And it looks like war with Angola. All things considered, Serena and I have decided to leave South Africa, to emigrate. You'll remember that we have been thinking about this for a long, long time but now we've finally made the decision. This has led to vicious arguments with Melvin and Lucille as you might have expected. Melvin, in particular, has been especially nasty, with a mixture of threats and inducements.

Anyway, to cut a long story short, I have been in touch with a big London firm of Accountants, Parker, Miller, Stevenson, and they have offered me a job, starting at the beginning of October. They will handle all the visas, working permits etc. So I have given notice to my firm here in Cape Town and also to our landlords. We've booked to come over by boat, the Athlone Castle, sort of a replacement honeymoon, and will arrive in Southampton on 15th September. That'll give us time (and you, HA HA!) to organise a place for us to live initially.

I have to tell you that financially we are going to be pretty tight. Melvin flatly refuses to help in any way, as he had threatened. Boy, the fights between my wife and her father you would have to have witnessed to believe. They are both pretty strong characters as you may have noticed.

Mom and dad are pretty upset as well as you can imagine but dad has been amazing. He has given us some money but as things are difficult here with boycotts and stuff, his business is not going all that well. He said that if you are able to help us with some of the funds he sent you that would be great.

Ray, I guess that's it for now. We are both very cut up to leave this beautiful city and the wonderful South African way of life but the way this nationalist government is going, it can only be a matter of time before the Africans rise up in revolt. So we're leaving, hopefully to a more civilised, if less luxurious life. We considered Israel, Canada and Australia but what with you being settled in the UK, it seemed the most logical choice.

So, boetie, prepare for family to land on your doorstep in a few months. Hope you can stand the strain but I suppose, with Marty gone and only two of us left, we need to stick close.

Your loving brother and sister,
Larry and Serena

After reading the letter a second time I sat back and pondered this new development which had not been totally unexpected. But the occasional remembered flashes of another and not very pleasant side to my new sister-in-law's nature filled me with apprehension. Also, Larry's complete subservience to Serena had me concerned. My mind seemed always to relate to old song lyrics. The current one swinging round in my head was 'There may be troubles ahead'.........

CHAPTER 29

I decided to let my fevered mind cool down for a couple of days, concentrating on working in the surgery and catching up with admin and overdue correspondence. It seemed to me that Crystal's letter needed answering first and Larry and Serena's requirements could be dealt with later. My thoughts and sympathies went out to my parents who, understandably, had expected that at least one son and his wife would be still only an hour's flight away. Now they faced the daunting prospect of travelling overseas, something they had never undertaken before.

Reinforced by the familiar, and quickly becoming regular, glass of scotch after work I collected my thoughts and seated myself at the typewriter.

4 Markham Street,
Chelsea.
London SW3.
1st June 1974.

My dearest Crystal,

Your letter had the old familiar effect on me even after all these years! I'm so impressed with the courage you've shown escaping from all your tangles in SA and being well on the way to achieving brilliant professional status. Never mind what they say about lawyers, I'm sure you'll be fantastic. See, I remember how you handled those policemen way back at Shelly Beach!! Funny, I thought even then that you had the talent and chutzpah to be a lawyer!

My recent time in South Africa, as I'm sure Rita must have told you, was a ghastly and terrible mixture, first the elation of Larry and Serena's wedding which was fabulous, then followed virtually immediately by Marty's sad passing. I still can't get my mind round that. He and I were so close, understood each other in so many ways. It hit my parents extremely hard, especially my mother. Not sure if she will ever get over this. Ah well, life can be very cruel, as we both know only too well.

Here in London though, things are pretty good. I have a nice house and practice in Chelsea, THE fashionable area (huge mortgage!), and at the moment, live in a flat above the surgery. I employ two Australian associate dentists so I have a pretty relaxed working day. Have paid many visits to Ronnie Scott's Jazz club, hearing most of my all-time idols, John Coltrane, Bill Evans, Ella Fitzgerald, Dizzy Gillespie, Art Blakey, the list is endless.

Socially, I'm kept pretty busy. My aunt and uncle keep finding eligible Jewish girls for me to link up with but, well, so far, I'm still footloose and playing the field, like your friend Rita!

Have been on a couple of ski trips to the French Alps, Courchevel and Lac de Tignes (sister village to the well-known Val d'Isere). My style I've been told is distinctive... don't know whether that's a compliment or the opposite but anyway, I get down most of the runs without any broken bones!

I reckon that's all I can tell you now. Stick with the studies and look after yourself. Maybe in years to come our fates will arrange a get-together, who knows?

In the meantime, keep in touch. I'll never forget you,

Love and kisses,
Ray XXX

I read the letter over several times. One thought kept running through my mind. I hadn't mentioned Jennifer. Should I have? Would it not be kinder to close any window permanently with Crystal, even though in any case her life now seemed to be more or less anchored in the New World? In the end I left it as it was, sealed it and added it to the pile of post for my receptionist to mail at lunchtime the next day.

I was just about to think about a snack for dinner and turn the TV on when the phone rang.

"Hi Raymond. Hope you haven't forgotten me already!"

"Jennifer......Hi!!! Hell, no, of course I haven't forgotten you. I tried phoning you Monday but there was no reply."

"Oh, sorry I wasn't in. Monday night I have French lessons."

"A letter from home arrived, bit of a jolt, really. My brother and his wife are emigrating here in September and they want me to sort out accommodation and so on. I'm not sure if I told you before, I've slightly uneasy feelings about her. She's got a very sharp tongue and can be quite nasty sometimes. Their letter's not an excuse for not calling you really, but.......hey, hang on it's only been three days!"

Her laughter pealed over the line. "No, don't worry. It's just that I'm still at the office in Regent Street and thought that, since you've treated me to two such great meals last weekend, I'd like to reciprocate..... if you're free, that is."

"Funny you should suggest that. I was just thinking...... what kind of bachelor mush I could rustle up for my supper......what do you fancy?"

"Well, we've had Chinese and French. There's a great place called Shezan, a quite snazzy Indian place just off Knightsbridge. How does that grab you? My treat, though."

"Sounds fine but we can discuss terms later. Where can we meet?"

"I'll get the tube to Knightsbridge station. Can you meet me there?"

"OK, I'll try and stop my trusty Mini outside the entrance or keep going round till I see you."

"Great. I'll book. See you in say, an hour?"

"Fine." I put down the receiver thoughtfully. Amazing how events collide, coincide and clash. There, facing me was my letter to Crystal, ready to go, alongside hers to me. And here I was trundling off to see Jennifer, with my euphoric senses alight, having semi-consciously omitted mentioning her to my American pen-pal. Just what my innermost awareness was making of my external behaviour and emotion I didn't dare consider. Only that, as I changed from my surgery whites into navy trousers and a crisp light-blue button-down-collar shirt, I was whistling, as a feeling of well-being and contentment arose within me.

Jennifer looked every bit the smart London professional working girl in a tailored dark grey trouser-suit, over an eye-catching low-cut turquoise blouse. I managed to pick her up on my second circuit around the frantically busy Sloane Street Knightsbridge intersection and we somehow found our way to the restaurant which was stuck away in a back street.

I tried in vain to persuade Jennifer in advance to share the Shezan bill which was going to be outrageously expensive, but got nowhere. The food was exquisite, spicy tandoori chicken pieces to start, followed by delicious barbecued lamb chops and yellow mushroom rice. All washed down with huge glasses of Indian lager.

"So, Raymond," she said, with the by now familiar licking of her lips after the kulfi ice cream dessert, "what are you going to do about your brother? I gather from what you've said that you're not so keen on his other half?"

I shook my head. "She's OK, but, well, has this sort of condescending attitude, you know, comes from a very wealthy background. Maybe I'm being a little over-sensitive, but it seems she's always trying to score points, especially at my expense, like bringing me down in Larry's eyes. It's as though she recognizes middle child symptoms in Larry and tries to build his ego up by making sarcastic comments about me. And he laps it up."

"And now they're coming here to settle?"

"Yup, sure looks like it."

Thoughtfully Jennifer cupped her chin with perfectly manicured fingers. "Looks to me like you'll have to play it very carefully from the beginning. Go out of your way to help them, but not with a big deal attitude. Have they any idea where they want to live?"

"Initially, somewhere in town, near me, I suppose, just to rent to begin with."

She smiled. "Well, maybe I can help a bit. The firm I work for, Lawson and Steele, handles a large account, Porchester Square Mansions on the embankment. There are always nice flats for rental there. It's a lovely series of blocks with squash courts and a swimming pool."

"Wow!" I exclaimed. "A squash court and a pool! Never mind Larry, I think I'd love that as well!"

"OK, then, I'll see what's available when I get to the office in the morning. September they're arriving, you said?"

"Yeah, Southampton, September 15th. Thank you, thank you..... and now please, can I help with the bill? I'm not used to all this female emancipation!"

Jennifer merely grabbed the bill and thrust several notes at the gracious, sari-clad waitress. "Not a chance, mate. I said my treat and I meant it."

I shrugged in surrender. "Well, can I offer you coffee at my place as a meagre compensation?"

She peeked at her watch then stared at me, searchingly. "Umm......, as long as it's not too late a night. I've got a heavy load of work in the morning."

I returned the look, trying desperately to retain an innocence I did not feel. "No problem, I'll drive you all the way home, I promise."

I drove one-handed back to Markham Street, Jennifer's head resting snugly on my shoulder. By the time we scaled the stairway to my second floor flat, matters were already out of control. Breathing heavily with curry and garlic overtones we landed on the couch, fingers and hands grappling in the darkness with buttons and zippers.

After several minutes, Jennifer sat up, peering at me in the half-light. I could just make out her smile as my eyes grew accustomed to the darkness. "Aren't you going to give me a conducted tour?"

"There's only the two bedrooms, and a bathroom on the top floor," I murmured, switching on a lamp on the coffee table.

"That could be interesting," she said throatily. "I certainly could use the bathroom."

I sat nervously on the edge of the large double bed. In my mind I could see which way this was heading, but felt uncertain about whether this was too early, whether it was right, with this special girl, after such a short time.

I heard the toilet flush then water running in the basin. The door opened and Jennifer walked toward me, urging me gently to my feet. As I rose, my hands seemed to attain a will of their own, and at the same time, I found the buttons on my shirt being undone. We stood there, silhouetted in the light from the bathroom, slowly undressing each other, our eyes locked in mutual understanding. Eventually, down to undergarments, I pulled back the covers and hand-in-hand, we slid between the cool sheets. I said a silent prayer of thanks to Katherine, the daily woman, who took an almost maternal pride in keeping my bachelor existence up to a reasonable standard of decency.

We slowly divested ourselves of the remaining shards of clothing, and, with almost slow-motion tentativeness, began to stroke, to touch, to explore. The hesitancy did not last long. It was replaced by burning urgency, rapid breathing and a gasping entanglement of mouths, lips and tongues. I threw off the sheets and blankets. Fully aroused, Jennifer's hand guided me towards her. My raised eyebrows were answered by a shake of her head. "It's OK," she gasped, and suddenly we were united, careful and gentle at first, then oblivious, wild abandon took over.

I looked down at her lovely face, eyes closed, mouth open, perspiration forming on her forehead. Suddenly she opened her eyes and smiled, and for me, it was as though all restraint was pointless. We panted and writhed, and the frantic explosion came suddenly, was mutual, lasting deliciously for what seemed like forever.

We lay collapsed, side by side, bodies damp with sweat. Outside we could hear the sounds of traffic on the Kings Road, together with shouts and yells of revellers, which routinely lasted till deep into the early hours.

After a while, Jennifer propped herself up and peered at her watch. "My God, Dr. Benjamin, have you any idea of the time?"

"Not a clue," I mumbled, pulling the mangled sheets up over us.

"Nearly one o'clock! And, like I said I've got a heavy day ahead!"

I sat up, reluctantly replacing my dozy contentment with awareness. "OK," I murmured, "seems to me we have two choices. One is, we get dressed and I drive you home as we planned, as I promised or....."

She smiled. "Yes, or what?"

"Well, you'd be more than welcome if you wanted just to put your head down and stay."

She pursed her lips, pondering. "I suppose...... I guess..... I could go straight to the office from here in the morning." She smiled. "Haven't got a toothbrush, though."

It was my turn to grin. "You are just one floor above a dental surgery. If I can't provide you with a brand-new toothbrush, what kind of host would I be?"

"Mmmmm...... promise me we'll get some sleep?"

"Trust me, I'm a dentist!" I said, leaning over and switching off the bedside lamp. Gently I held her face in my hands and kissed her softly. "I want to thank you most sincerely for treating me to dinner. I loved every minute!"

Jennifer suddenly sprang out of bed and headed for the bathroom. "Where did you say the new toothbrush was?" she laughed. "And whatever happened to the coffee you promised?"

*

We awoke early the next morning, enveloped, like spoons. There was no chance we could avoid a repeat performance and it was for me a revelation. We were now so familiar with each other, and, although fully aware of a work day ahead, this did not detract from the easy way we made love, considerately, yet passionately.

Eventually we untangled ourselves and Jennifer took her turn first in the bathroom. I lay still, arms behind my head, lost in heady amazement at how quickly this scenario had developed. Even with the letter to Crystal sealed but unposted on my desk, I had not for one moment imagined her lying in my arms instead of Jennifer. My entire being was becoming aware that this relationship was the one I had been waiting for, someone with whom I already felt totally at ease.

The bathroom door opened and Jennifer emerged glistening from the shower, damp ebony hair framing her face, ready to don her working clothes. "Your turn in the shower, Doctor!" She looked at her watch, "I've just got time for a coffee. You owe me one, I think, so do you mind if I get busy in the kitchen?"

"Make yourself right at home. I like mine strong, with a drop of milk, no sugar. I'll be with you in five minutes."

It was strange, saying good bye at my front door as she left to catch a bus. It seemed like we were an old established married couple, except that she was the one going off to work.

She hesitated at the entrance. "Ray, I hope you don't think any less of me.....er...."

I stopped her with a kiss. "Have a lovely day, think of me every so often. I'll call you this evening."

She smiled. "I had a wonderful time. You're a great host!"

I watched her walk along the pavement, her lithe figure swaying seductively, whether exaggerated purely for my benefit I couldn't be sure. Smiling contentedly, I closed the door, had a peep at my appointment book for the day, then went upstairs to finish my breakfast.

*

The weeks flew by. We started spending our nights together regularly, occasionally on weekends at Jennifer's apartment but mostly mine. It was extraordinary how quickly we adapted to each other's lifestyles and diaries. I introduced Jennifer to my aunt Estelle and uncle Harold, who had been like my London parents. They heartily approved, apart from my aunt's slightly critical view of the length of Jennifer's skirts which were, according to fashion, pretty mini-ish.

I was now becoming aware of Jennifer's history. She was two years older than me, but the youngest in her family by a long way, her two brothers eighteen and eleven years older respectively. They had lived in the East End of London during the war. Jennifer had been evacuated to Woking which accounted for her Home Counties accented English. Both parents were long deceased and the brothers and their families now lived in North London. Unlike Jennifer who, like me was a non-believer, they were all pretty strictly Orthodox and I had the pleasure of being introduced to the entire family at her nephew's Barmitzvah. Her older brother Alf greeted me effusively, with a strong Cockney accent. Turning to Jennifer, he commented in what was supposed to be for her ears only but was clearly audible to me and others. "Ere, Jen, why din't you bring 'ome a bloke like this years ago!"

I could not help grinning at Jennifer's discomfiture. She steered me away to a quiet corner. "Sorry about brother Alf. He takes some getting used to."

She had married young, aged nineteen to a boyfriend of long standing but they divorced after three years. She didn't volunteer any explanations and I didn't ask for any. They had sold their maisonette and with half the proceeds she bought her small apartment. Her barrister boyfriend, with whom she had dallied, off and on, for nearly two years, was now, as far as I could tell, out of the picture.

I was starting to feel like a kept man and to tell the truth, I didn't mind the feeling one bit. We saw eye to eye on most things, music, theatre, and sunny beach holidays. I hadn't yet convinced her about skiing but as it was summer, there didn't appear to be any hurry. She'd had an unfortunate experience at age five, nearly drowning in a river so had an absolute horror of going underwater when swimming. I found this out when Jennifer had arranged for us to view an apartment in Porchester Square Mansions for Larry and Serena. The apartment was simply but tastefully furnished, consisting of a large lounge/dining room, a fair-sized bed room with a neat little kitchenette and bathroom. The rent was very affordable and so I decided that with only six weeks to go before their arrival, it would be ideal in the short term. Being dealt with by Lawson and Steele, only a small, token holding deposit was required.

"I'm sure it'll be fine," I said as I made out the cheque. "Larry can get to work easily by bus or tube and with the river view and the squash court and pool, they can't have any objection."

"I hope that your sister-in-law will agree," Jennifer said, a little doubtfully. "From what you told me about their mansion in Cape Town, you don't think it might be a trifle claustrophobic?"

I shook my head. "No, I think they're prepared to be pretty frugal at first till they find their feet. Serena is a qualified Optician so she'll find a job easily as well. I'll write to them and describe it anyway but at least they'll have something to move into straightaway. In six months they can look for themselves."

We had been given permission to try out the large, ornately tiled indoor pool. She had this amusing style of breaststroke about which I teased her mercilessly.

"You remind me of the Queen Mary," I laughed. "Very elegant and graceful, kinda regal!"

"Get knotted!" she shouted as I dived beneath her and grabbed her legs. "Don't do that!" When I saw the real panic on her face I realised how deep-seated her fear was and guided her safely to the pool-edge.

*

Weekends we spent driving in the Mini, dodging the traffic jams by leaving absurdly early in the mornings, down to the coast, Eastbourne, Bournemouth, even grabbing a long weekend down to

Polperro in Cornwall. One of the best trips was to a small hotel in a tiny cove called Birling Gap, near Beachy Head on the South Coast. This brought back memories, echoes of a story I remembered from my childhood. Wandering hand-in hand over the pebbled beach I felt a strange sensation come over me. I stopped and turned, looked intensely into Jennifer's eyes.

"I suppose you remember telling me not to be so silly, what was it only a couple of months ago?"

She nodded, not saying anything, just an inquisitive raising of the eyebrows.

I pursed my lips. "I guess this is as romantic a place as any......do you.......er......do you....... fancy a long engagement?"

"Wh-wh-wh-what do you mean?"

"Well, everything in my mind, body etc. is telling me that this is as good as it gets. These past months with you have been the happiest of my life and.....and...... I want it to be permanent. There I've said it, owned up to my ambition, that is, to be...... er.... I'm putting this a little clumsily, but, it's to be part of your ambitions."

Jennifer looked at me, smiling but eyes glistening. "Is this a proposal, Dr. Benjamin?"

"Yes....I suppose you could call it that. I mean, you don't have to answer straightaway, I can wait. Maybe..........even till we get back to London tomorrow night."

Jennifer threw her head back, giggling delightedly. "I just love the way you've put this, as if we both didn't know already."

"You mean....you mean....you will......we can, ...er...... is that a yes?"

She flung her arms around me and we stood there amidst the gurgling of the wavelets on the stony sand, hugging, kissing, laughing, oblivious to the entire world around us.

*

That night we spent in a tiny hotel on the beach, with only a few other guests evident. A cosy, chintzy sitting room and dining room with a fire in spite of it being mid-summer. We registered as Mr. and Mrs. for the first time and the ancient receptionist did cast a suspicious look at us, which we returned with bland innocence.

The drive back to London was slow, a bumper to bumper crawl. Nothing could come close to dampening our euphoric mood, however, and in between dangerous fondling, there was plenty of opportunity for discussing future plans.

"Larry and Serena arrive in just over a month so what about planning to get my folks over next May or June, after the weather warms up?" I suggested.

"Fine by me," Jennifer nodded. "That'll give me time to get my GET, you know, a Jewish divorce.....that's if you want a shul(synagogue) wedding."

I shrugged. "I don't mind either way. I'm sure my parents would love an Orthodox wedding. Also it would be more than a year since Marty died so the period of mourning would be over."

"My brothers would prefer it too. But let's just make it a small do, none of the fancy Jewish London Hotel extravaganzas. I did all that before and frankly, couldn't face it again. Is that OK by you?"

"Absolutely fine by me."

We lapsed into silence then, each immersed in imaginings, smiling contentedly as the miles passed, dusk then darkness pierced by the stream of oncoming headlights and the ribbon of flashing red taillights of the procession of cars heading back to London.

*

On the day of Larry and Serena's arrival, I took the day off and hired a large station wagon for the journey to Southampton and back. Larry had warned me about the amount of luggage they were bringing so we decided that Jennifer would meet us at the Porchester Square flat that evening. We'd also decided to keep our delicious news to ourselves, feeling that there would be plenty of time once my brother and his wife had settled in. Jennifer had found out that her GET would take ninety days so our projected date of May or June seemed ideal.

I drove the unfamiliar and somewhat clumsy vehicle slowly down the A3 towards the coast, listening to swing music on the radio. My heart was singing as I contemplated my good fortune in meeting Jennifer, tempered only by the slight apprehension I felt at greeting my brother and his wife.

I somehow found my way through the maze of one way systems and eventually got to Southampton harbour where I could get a good view of the Athlone Castle as she sailed majestically into the docks. I parked the station wagon and walked to the quayside as the huge white liner was escorted by tugs to its allotted berth. I couldn't make out their faces amongst the crowds of passengers lining the railings high above me but contented myself with waiting patiently by the gang-plank.

"RAY! RAY! OVER HERE!"

I looked up and saw Larry waving frantically. Alongside him I could just make out Serena's auburn head. I waved back, then lost sight of them as they joined the queue to disembark.

After about half an hour, they emerged, hand-in-hand, followed by a porter with their cases on a trolley.

"Hey, Ray!" Larry grabbed me and kissed me soundly on both cheeks. We indulged then in a tight, three-way embrace.

"Welcome to Britain, you guys. Looks like you had a great trip!" They were both tanned and looked relaxed and happy. My heart leapt with genuine affection. "Come on, I've got an especially big vehicle in the car park. Should take all that lot easily," I gestured towards the trolley.

"That's nothing," said Serena, "our lift's due in about six weeks."

"What do you mean, you've brought all your stuff with you? Your furniture and everything?"

Larry nodded. "Sure have. Like we told you, this is a once and for all emigration. Instead of selling our belongings in Cape Town for next to nothing and then spending here, we decided to come, lock, stock and barrel."

My concern must have shown on my face. "Oh," I said, frowning.

"What's up, Ray?" Serena queried. "You look worried."

I shook my head. "No, nothing, really. It's only, you know, the flat I told you we've signed for, well, it's furnished and is a bit small so...."

Serena looked at Larry, perturbed. "You didn't tell us it was furnished, Ray."

"There aren't many flats in London let unfurnished," I said defensively, waving my hand nonchalantly. "Don't worry, I'm sure it'll be fine short term. When your stuff arrives, we'll do whatever's necessary."

"You mean put it in storage?" There was a slightly accusatory tinge to her voice.

"I really don't know until it arrives, but listen, you've just set foot on English soil, let's get to the car and get going. I'm sure you'll love the flat, its location and the squash court and pool are fabulous. Trust me, I'm a Dentist!" I laughed weakly at my standard throwaway line.

Larry and Serena looked at each other, then shrugged.

"Fine. Which way's the car?"

Chapter 30

It took some concentrated driving to emerge from Southampton city centre and reach the Hampshire countryside. Once the urban sprawl had been left behind I started to relax. "So guys, you had a super trip? You really look great, all tanned, and..relaxed....and....." I smiled at my brother in the rear-view mirror, "you look as though the food was good too!"

He patted his stomach and laughed. "Much too good, and much too much as well! We were lucky, had lovely weather virtually the whole trip and no rough seas. Serena gets seasick at the slightest swell."

"I do not!" she retorted. "You said you felt a bit queasy yourself in the Bay of Biscay yesterday."

I grinned. "Come on you newly-weds, stop arguing. What do you think of your new country, this is Hampshire, quite beautiful, isn't it?"

"Everything's so green, so lush," Serena, sitting alongside me in the front seat, agreed. "I must say I didn't like the houses as we came out of Southampton though, all the same, so gray and depressing."

"Yeah, well, it's very different here," I replied, "you don't see many individual architect-designed homes, except in very wealthy suburbs. Not like SA at all. But you get used to that after a while. How were all the parents when you left?"

Serena pulled a face. "Well, I know Larry's told you my folks didn't want us to go. They used every trick in the book to persuade us to stay, so their goodbye was pretty half-hearted, putting it mildly. Abie and

Rosie on the other hand, were wonderful, wishing us luck and even arguing with my dad that for young people now, especially like us, white and Jewish, South Africa's future doesn't look too good."

"How is mom now, Larry?" I asked hesitantly. "Is she getting herself together a bit better now? Is she still going to the cemetery every Sunday?"

"Yes, every Sunday. She just goes and sits by the mound of clay and cries. In fact dad had difficulty getting her to come to Cape Town to say goodbye as we sailed on a weekend. Anyway she came and put a brave face on it. Dad seems OK. He just immerses himself in the business. Things are very quiet, all these boycotts are having an effect but he still has that dreamy faith that all will be well. He goes to shul every morning and night."

"Now, Ray," Serena turned to face me smiling broadly, "let's hear all about Jennifer."

I hesitated before answering. "OK...... well........we started going out pretty regularly after I came back from SA. She's a lovely warm person, and we get along very well. I've met her family at a Barmitzvah and she's met uncle Harold and aunt Estelle."

"When are we going to meet her?" came Larry's voice from the back seat.

"She's gonna come over to the Porchester Square flat this evening. I told you that she managed to get the place through her legal firm. These flats are apparently very sought-after."

"More, more, we want more!" yelled Larry excitedly.

"I'm not giving you her vital statistics if that's what you're after," I grinned. "She's Jewish, not religious at all, very good looking. Blue-black hair, dark brown eyes. Has been divorced, no children. She's two years older than me. Works in a high-powered Legal firm in Central London."

"What are her family like?" Serena said, gazing out at the green countryside whizzing by us.

"Parents died long ago, two much older brothers with families. They all lived in the East End of London during the war. Jennifer remembers sheltering in Underground stations during the blitz when Hitler's v-bombers were landing all over the place. We had such a sheltered life compared to hers. They were evacuated to somewhere near here, Woking, a little village in Surrey." I looked in the mirror. Larry was fast asleep.

It was late afternoon when, after a struggle with rush hour traffic, we crossed over Battersea Bridge and pulled in to the car park of Porchester Square. I think that Serena was quite impressed when a uniformed porter emerged from the imposing entrance with a trolley for their luggage. I had a tiny inkling that Jennifer or her firm had pulled a few strings! Anxiously I led the way to their apartment.

I needn't have worried. My brother and his wife were delighted. They bounded around the flat, oohing and aahing. "Oh, God, colour television!" Larry yelped, "....and South Africa hasn't even got black and white yet!"

I gave the porter, a corblimey cockney named Norman, a generous tip and, with an exaggerated bow, he left us.

"Wow!" came Serena's voice from the kitchen. "Who did all this shopping?"

I poked my head round the door, feigning innocence. "Must be the traditional British welcome," I joked.

"Rubbish!" she retorted. "Only a woman knows what to stock up with like this. I think I'm gonna like your girlfriend, Ray."

I had a little guilty twinge about the slightly negative information I'd given Jennifer about Serena beforehand, but breathed an inward sigh of relief anyway. This was going pretty well. I looked at the pile of groceries in the well-stocked kitchenette. "Tell you what, guys, why don't you make a start unpacking and I'll make us all a nice English cup of tea."

"My, aren't we domesticated, Raymond," Serena said tartly. "You'll make someone an excellent husband one of these days."

Just then a buzzer sounded. I went over to the intercom by the front door. "Yes, who is it?"

"Room Service with your dinner menu," said a refined voice. Larry and Serena looked at each other incredulously.

"I'll press the button for the entrance," I said into the intercom, keeping a straight face. "Please come up straight away. Thank you."

Larry looked at me, eyes popping. "Ray, what on earth is going on here?"

"Didn't I tell you?" I frowned. "Sorry, I should have mentioned it. You can order meals in your flat from the restaurant downstairs."

They looked at each other, mouths agape. There was a knock on the door. Serena opened it gingerly.

Jennifer stood there with a huge smile on her face. "Hi, you must be Serena." She held out her hand. "I'm Jennifer. And you must be Larry. I've heard so much about you both!"

For a moment there was this incredulous hush. Then Larry gave a groan, and punched me on the shoulder. "Ray you bastard! Room service, like hell! Serena, we've been had!"

I laughed. "You know, it would have been the perfect April Fool except it's the wrong time of year!"

Serena just stood and stared at Jennifer, who shifted a little uncomfortably. "Ray's description didn't do you justice. It's lovely to meet you, even though, I must say, I was getting quite excited about being able to order meals from the room! But please, come on in!"

Her reaction broke the ice completely and the two girls chatted like old friends as they busied themselves in the kitchen making the tea. Larry and I sat on the large sofa. "Ray, she's gorgeous!" he whispered. "How the hell did you land her?"

I put a finger to my mouth. "Sh! Don't want her getting swollen-headed. But don't underestimate your old brother's charms either." I reached over and grabbed his shoulder. "It's really good to have you guys here. I think the flat's OK for now, what do you think?"

"It's just great. I know Serena was a bit iffy when we first got off the boat, with the furniture and all. But I'm sure this is going to be fantastic for us."

"Tell you what, we'll have tea, then we'll show you round, the pool, squash court and gym. Afterwards Jen and I will leave you for a bit. I need to go to the surgery. Maybe you'd like to unpack, shower and get organised. We'll come back later. There's a fab Italian restaurant across the road right on the river, Villa dei Caesari. We can have dinner there. How does that sound?"

My brother just sat there nodding, eyes watering. "Ray, I can't thank you enough. I can't believe all this is happening. We're here in London and it's all amazing!"

*

Villa dei Caesari was a great choice, good food, live music and even a small dance floor. I could tell that a rapport had developed between Serena and Jennifer. As for Larry, he could hardly take his eyes off Jennifer which did elicit, I noticed, a slight tightening round the corners of Serena's mouth from time to time. By ten o'clock they were beginning to yawn so I paid the bill, the size of which did draw a tiny gasp from both of them.

"Wow!" Larry shook his head incredulously. "What would that be in Rands?"

"You want to get out of that habit quickly," I said. "Once you start earning in pounds it will seem a bit more reasonable. But tonight I'm having no arguments," as they started to protest, "it's not every day I can treat my brother and his wife to a first meal in their new country."

We walked them to the entrance of Porchester Square and said goodnight.

"What are your plans tomorrow?" I asked.

"I think we're gonna be tourists tomorrow, Trafalgar Square, Piccadilly Circus, Buckingham Palace and all that." Serena smiled. "Might even take that open air bus tour."

"I want to go and see Parker, Miller Stevenson as well and find out about work permits and stuff," Larry said. "Maybe we can come to your surgery later after you finish work?"

"Fine by me. Perhaps we'll pop by Harold and Estelle. I know they'll want to see you. Give them a call anyway."

Larry nodded. "Will do." He turned to Jennifer. "Really lovely to meet you, Jennifer. Will you be around tomorrow night?"

She shook her head. "No, tomorrow I've got French classes but I'm sure we'll get together later in the week. So sorry about the poor room service, though!"

"Thanks for everything, brother in law, and Jennifer, a really big thank you for organising the flat, the groceries, everything." Serena smiled broadly, giving us each a hug. "It was a truly brilliant welcome!"

Laughing, we watched them go through the main entrance doors hand in hand. I felt a strong protective emotion towards them sweep over me as I turned and put my arm round Jennifer's slim waist. "Well, madam, I think that went off really very well, don't you?"

She nuzzled her head into my shoulder. "She's OK, and he's sweet. I see what you mean about her being stronger than him, though. I reckon that you'll always have to be a bit wary about getting on the wrong side of her."

"Yup," I agreed, giving her a squeeze. "You were just brilliant. Thank you."

"No problem, but frankly, I'm exhausted. Let's go."

I grinned. "Fine by me. My place or yours?"

She gave me that voracious look. "Yours. It's nearer!"

*

Days became weeks then months. Larry settled into his job and Serena landed a well-paid locum position in a nearby Opticians. We socialised with them on a fairly regular basis, eating out and going to films and theatre. They had discovered several ex-South African couples they had known back home so developed a circle of friends apart from us. Jennifer and I kept our intentions secret from everyone although it was pretty obvious in which direction we were headed.

Looking back, I think the first signs of friction appeared during discussions about the Christmas holiday. We had planned to go skiing to Tignes, a small new village in the French Alps. I had been there before and did all the preliminaries, a package deal for £120 per head, including flight transfers and half board at a small hotel right on the slopes. After much painstaking research, this seemed a pretty good deal to me.

"That's very expensive," Serena said over dinner at a small bistro near my surgery. "I don't know if we can afford that. We'd still have to pay for ski school, lift passes and hiring equipment."

"Well," I said, "I've looked at a lot of alternatives and it's pretty competitive. The French ski schools are much more advanced than say Austria where they still insist on spending days climbing up nursery slopes. Also, I feel uncomfortable going to Austria, just a prejudice I have, hearing that language. It sort of jars with me, you know."

Larry interjected. "Ray, it's just that we're coming towards the end of our six month tenancy and we're thinking about trying to buy a house out near where some of our friends live, out in the suburbs, near Radlett. Also, the shipment of our furniture has been delayed and won't arrive for another two months so that works out well too."

"But that's just great, guys. I'm sure it's a good idea and property is fairly cheap right now. So what's the problem?"

"Money, dear brother-in-law." said Serena icily. "We don't earn what you dentists earn, you know."

"Oh," I said, a little taken aback at the caustic edge to her voice. "Well, OK, would you rather leave the trip for this year, then?"

"No, no," Larry replied hastily. "But I've been meaning to talk to you about this anyway. You know the money dad loaned you to help you buy the Chelsea house?"

"Er....yes.....," I replied, cautiously.

"Well, dad said that you might be able to let me have some of that if we needed money for a deposit on a house."

I thought for a while before answering. "Ja, but it depends how much. I have a pretty big mortgage on the Chelsea house and the practice runs on a fairly hefty overdraft."

"Is that a refusal or what?" Serena asked bluntly.

I bridled at her aggressive tone. "No, it's most certainly not a refusal but, but, this is the first time you've mentioned this."

"No, it's not. Larry mentioned it in the letter he wrote you in May."

I felt a hot flush rising to my cheeks. She was editing his letters! "There's no need to be so bolshy."

Serena reddened but said nothing.

"I must say that I'm surprised," I continued, "and in fact I'm delighted that you guys are planning to buy a house so soon but I guess you can't really blame me. It's just a bit sudden, that's all."

"Is it not possible for you to help then?" Larry asked gently.

"Oh for God's sake, I absolutely didn't say that for one moment," I retorted, somewhat impatiently "Of course I'll do everything I can to help you, but what we have to do is to plan carefully. Have you found a house? If so what price are you looking at? Also have you found out what mortgage you can get?"

Somewhat mollified, Larry held up his hands. "Well, an agent in Radlett sent us details of a lovely house in a nice area. The price is £39,500. We need a 10 percent deposit. Parker, Miller, Stevenson can get us a 90 percent mortgage. So basically what we need is about £5000 to cover deposit, lawyers and bits and pieces."

Relieved, I smiled. "OK. That's fine. Have you made an offer?"

"No, not yet but the agent said they, the owners, wouldn't take much less than the asking price."

"Fine. When are you going to see the house?"

"Hopefully this weekend."

"Right. Here's what I suggest. Go see the house. If it's what you want make an offer of say £37,500, go up to £38,250 subject to survey. Tell them you have finance readily available and most importantly you don't have a house to sell. I'll need to approach my bank to extend my overdraft by say £6000. That will enable you to join us on the ski holiday and hopefully you'll be able to move in early next year." I looked straight at Serena. "Does that suit your requirements, madam?" I asked sarcastically but with a broad smile on my face.

They looked at each other, nodded, and smiled. "Thank you, big brother," Larry said softly. Just the slightest nod of acknowledgement from his wife.

We finished the meal in relative silence and went our separate ways. I drove Jennifer back to her apartment. "Well," I said, "a little show of her true colours coming through, would you say?"

Jennifer nodded. "Yes, I guess there's more than a little envy under the surface there. Never mind, you handled it pretty well."

*

"Dr. Benjamin, telephone for you. Your brother on the line".

"Larry, hi, how did it go?"

"You were right on target, we got it for £38,250!"

"And it's what you both want?"

"Absolutely. Near schools, near the shul, a lovely Jewish area and our friends just a few blocks away."

"Mazeltov! Lots and lots of luck. Is Serena pleased?"

"She's delighted. I owe you big time."

"Not me, mate. It's dad's money."

"Anyway, my bosses are being great, they've started the mortgage application. Have you a name of a solicitor?"

"Sure. Use Jennifer's firm. Lawson and Steele. Tel 9352071. Ask for Jennifer Harris. They're pretty good and I'll get on to the bank straight away. Also you'll need a survey, I'm sure the mortgage company will want that. Any idea when the sellers want to move?"

"Yeah, there's good news there too. They want to move in February/ March so our furniture will only go into storage for a couple of months. And we'll fit in our ski trip as well".

"Right. I'll transfer the deposit money to your account. That's brilliant. See you later."

"Come over to the flat. We can have a game of squash and a celebratory drink afterwards."

"Deal."

That evening there was no sign of the ascerbic Serena. She was as pleasant and cheerful as she could be. After Larry had thrashed me on the squash court and we'd had a refreshing swim in the pool, we were treated to Serena's delicious home cooking, typically South African chicken *sosatis* and rice.

Afterwards I brought out all the brochures and pamphlets for Tignes and the girls planned a shopping expedition to Alpine Sports in Kensington to tog themselves out with anoraks, salopettes, gloves and thick socks.

While Jennifer and Serena busied themselves washing up after the meal, Larry gave me a knowing look. "She's the one, right? Have you made any plans?"

I shook my head. "We're very contented as we are at the moment, Larry. But take it easy, you'll be the first to know, I promise."

"Come on, buddy, I've seen the way you two look at each other. It's just a case of when, isn't it?"

"Don't push me, brother. We're doing just fine. You think mom and dad will approve?"

"Approve? They'll adore her. I've written to them and they're waiting impatiently for news."

"They'll have to wait a bit longer. Let's see how the holiday goes."

*

The trip to Tignes was marred by delays at Gatwick airport because of fog. On the train from Lyon to Bourg St. Maurice, the spectacular Alpine scenery simply took our breath away.

The Hotel Aiguille Percee was a stone-built traditional *Pension.* The name was taken from a rock arch above the village resembling a needle's eye. The original village of Tignes had been flooded to make way for a hydro-electric scheme, the foundations now submerged beneath a huge lake.

"Well, what did I tell you, folks?" I shouted as we clambered out of the taxi. "Isn't this something?"

"I think I've died and gone to heaven!" Larry shouted.

Serena and Jennifer trod gingerly over the icy road, pink-cheeked with the freezing temperature, gazing open-mouthed at the grandeur of the peaks surrounding the village. All Jennifer could do was to exclaim "Wow!" exhaling clouds of steam.

Serena hugged Larry close, her eyes alight. "Ray, I take my hat off to you, this is truly beautiful!"

We lugged our cases into the warmth of the hotel foyer. Our rooms were small, with tiny bathrooms but the views were extraordinary. I felt rather than saw Serena's disdainful expression as she looked at the cramped accommodation.

Larry and I left the girls to unpack and trudged around the village centre. I showed him the ski lifts, ski school and the runs which all ended on the central plaza.

"I just hope the girls take to it," I said. "Jennifer has done her pre-ski exercises quite religiously. Has Serena?"

Larry nodded. "Yes, she's spent hours in the gym. She's pretty fit. She was a pretty good water-skier back home."

That night we ate early, French cooking at its best. After coffee we went to bed exhausted, filled with anticipation and in the girls' case, some trepidation for what the following day might bring.

In dazzling sunshine Larry, Serena and Jennifer registered with the beginners class. I landed in the advanced group. After helping Jennifer with her equipment I watched them go off towards the nursery slope with some apprehension.

My class went straight to the ski lifts and once out on the mountain, the magic took over. The morning passed in a flash. We flew around the resort, hurtling down easy blue runs then somewhat more carefully down the steeper, bumpier reds.

We met at a pizza place in the village for lunch. My relief must have been apparent when I saw the three intrepid new skiers come smiling toward me. "So, guys, how did it go?"

"Brilliant!" Larry bubbled. "These two ladies were sensational. They managed the button lifts and learned to turn and stop in no time. The instructor was very impressed."

"I have to admit, Ray," Jennifer said, "I was a bundle of nerves to begin with but the instructor was fantastic. I also practised my French as he couldn't speak English at all."

"Very handsome, he was, though," Serena chuckled through a mouthful of pepperoni. "Ray, I think you'd better join our group, he had big eyes for your lady friend."

"Oh rubbish!" protested Jennifer, blushing in spite of the cold. "I saw him holding you pretty tightly when you battled with the ski-lift. I reckon he makes a play for all the women!"

The ensuing days passed happily without any injury or argument. The three beginners graduated and were thrilled going up on chairlifts to easy blue runs. Gatherings in the bar after the day's exertions became animated descriptions of 'close-to-death' experiences.

"I was going so fast I would have killed someone if they got in my way," Serena giggled after several glasses of mulled wine.

"I watched you go," laughed Larry. "I thought you'd learned to turn by then. I would've disowned you if you'd mown anyone down. You're a real speed merchant."

"Oh, I just love the wind in my face" she countered. "And where were you? You couldn't keep up, admit it!"

"I loved skiing behind you," I said to Jennifer. "You've really got a nice style but....."

"Yes, I know, I'm too cautious, but I'm still petrified. I like to be in control."

"I guess all my waterskiing experience helped me a lot," Serena glanced at Jennifer. "I suppose you didn't have that advantage when you were young, did you?"

I noticed the sudden blush of colour in Jennifer's cheeks. She put down her tall sugar-encrusted glass firmly. "No, Serena, I certainly didn't come from a privileged background like you did."

"Serena," I said angrily, "That remark was uncalled for. You owe Jen an apology."

It was clear how furious I was. Serena, embarrassed and contrite, put her hand on Jennifer's arm. "Jennifer, I'm terribly sorry. I really didn't mean to upset you," she turned to me, "or you, Ray. It was thoughtless and stupid. I actually meant the South African climate was more suitable......." she stopped in mid-sentence,"oh blast, just ignore it, won't you?"

After a moment's silence Jennifer looked up and smiled. "Don't worry about it. We all say things without thinking sometimes. Forget it." She picked up her drink and drained the remnants in one gulp.

During this entire conversation, my stunned brother had not said a word, head swivelling, unable to intervene. I shrugged and let the atmosphere calm down. We went to our rooms that night on fairly cool terms. It was as if something had occurred which began to define the tension between us.

We lay side by side in the fairly narrow bed, frosty moonlight peering through a gap in the curtains.

"I thought my brother would say something, didn't you"? I reached over and stroked Jennifer's cheek.

"Well, it shows we were correct assessing how their relationship works, weren't we?" she murmured. "Mmmm. I like that, more please."

Any further discussion regarding our family relationships was put on hold. The next day was 31st December, our last day's skiing so we relegated Larry, Serena and her forked tongue to the back of our minds. Sleep came easily, in our by now well-established spoon position. Not until bright sunlight penetrated our windows did we re-enter the world of the living.

*

New Year's Eve was celebrated by a magnificent five-course dinner with plentiful champagne. Everyone then congregated on the large terrace to watch the instructors' torch-lit descent of the black run down Toviere, the peak directly above our hotel. The spectacle was unforgettable, flickering reflections of the flames coming off the frozen lake below.

Later we all assembled in the bar, well lubricated by alcohol and excitement. We waited for the countdown to midnight with mounting euphoria.

I looked at Jennifer, raising my eyebrows and received an encouraging nod in return. I gestured to Larry and Serena to come out on the terrace to watch the firework display celebrating the beginning of 1975.

In French, the countdown came over the PA system loud and clear. CINC, QUATRE ,TROIS, DEUX, UN... BONNE ANNEE!! HAPPY NEW YEAR!!!!!!!!

The four of us grabbed each other in a tight hug. Jennifer and I had decided to ignore the animosity of the previous night. She melted into my arms. The kiss was long and passionate. I turned to my brother and sister-in-law with a huge grin. "Hey guys, I said you'd be the first to know........Jennifer has agreed to become MRS. BENJAMIN!!!!!"

There in the icy cold midnight, fireworks bursting overhead, we danced and hugged, kissing and screaming. There was no point in questions like when or where. It was just a moment of undiluted joy and when Jennifer and I finally retired to the privacy of our room, the alcohol-fuelled passion was still as fresh, inventive and rapturous as it had ever been. Through our window, the sky was still lit by the cosmic flashes and flares which suited our mood to perfection.

"Well, now, my love," I murmured, "I guess it's no longer a secret. How do you feel?" I could just make out her smiling face, eyes shining, lit periodically by the intermittent lightning outside.

"I love you, Dr Benjamin........."

*

The following day was Saturday, our last day. The taxi came to fetch us at ten o'clock for the first stage in our trip home. Things began to go wrong after the first stage of our train journey. A loudspeaker announced that we would have to change trains at Chambery. As our carriage pulled out of the station, Serena gave a scream. "OH SHIT! LOOK! THERE'S MY BLOODY SUITCASE ON THE PLATFORM!!! LARRY!!"

Sure enough, there stood her expensive pink leather case all by itself as our train moved down the line. We stood helplessly as platform and case receded into the distance.

"LARRY YOU IDIOT, DIDN'T YOU MAKE SURE ALL OUR CASES WERE TRANSFERRED?"

My brother stood shamefacedly looking forlornly out the window. "Course I did, I tipped the porter and showed him our luggage. He must have just forgotten or got it mixed up."

"HOW COULD HE GET IT MIXED UP? FOR CHRIST' SAKE MY STUFF IS ALL MATCHING!"

I felt really sorry for Larry. "Don't worry. It'll come on the next train. We'll check when we arrive in Lyon Station."

Serena sat glowering by herself. "All my best stuff was in that case. I bet we'll never see it again. Larry, why didn't you check?"

"Calm down, Serena," Jennifer said quietly. "Even if we don't collect it at Lyon it has your name and address on it so if the worst comes to the worst French Rail will send it on."

Serena started to reply angrily then thought better of it, spending the remaining hours to Lyon in a sulk.

*

There was further mayhem to come. Our flight to Gatwick was cancelled due to fog. We were sent back to spend the night at a seedy hotel in downtown Lyon. Serena's mood improved only after Larry and I returned from the railway station late that night with her precious suitcase. It had arrived on a later train.

Nevertheless, we had been made aware yet again of our sister-in-law's temper, and the absolute disdain with which she had treated Larry.

Chapter 31

Sunday 2nd July 1975

The Wembley Synagogue was packed. The notorious British summer weather had been kind to us.It was a bright warm, even quite humid, day. I stood beneath the Chupah (wedding canopy) with my proud parents beaming from ear to ear. Alongside stood Alec, my best man who, to my delight, had decided to make the trip from South Africa with them. I had been saddened to see my parents' decline in the past year, Marty's tragic death taking its inevitable toll. I consoled myself that their spirits would be uplifted by the ceremony which was about to begin.

Jennifer and I had met them at Heathrow. My mother had looked her up and down, taking in her short skirt and her dazzling smile. "So this is Jennifer," she said. "I have to say, Abie and I had all but given up on Raymond but," she smiled, "I can see already he's made a wise choice."

Since New Years Eve in Tignes, letters and phone calls between London and SA had been too numerous to count. Larry and Serena had moved into their house, a comfortable detached cottage house in a quiet residential road, and their jobs were keeping them busy. Our parents were staying with them, overwhelmed with excitement at seeing all of the sights of London as well as contentment at seeing both their sons settled and reasonably prosperous. Jennifer had let her apartment and moved in with me in the flat above the surgery. We were beginning to think of moving to a house but with all the arrangements for the wedding, our searches had been put on hold.

The organ and choir began The Wedding March. I stood nervously facing the rabbi and cantor. I could see out of the corner of my vision all heads craning to get a view of my bride as she entered, arm in arm with brother Alf, followed by a retinue consisting of her friend Anna, Matron of Honour and four bridesmaids. Suddenly I was aware of her fragrant presence beside me. I turned my head and was as stunned as ever by her beauty. We shared a nervous smile. She was wearing a sky-blue crocheted dress with matching flowers adorning her blue-black hair.

The ceremony passed by in a blur. I remember repeating ancient blessings and resonating music. I sensed Jennifer circling me seven times and Alf's wife lifting her sky-blue veil so she could sip the wine. I vaguely remember the rabbi's exhortations to maintain an observant Jewish home and then, after being allowed to kiss my bride, I stamped on the glass. The shul echoed to shouts of MAZELTOV! and all was bedlam. Crowds of people approaching, kissing, crying and hugging. My parents, tears running down their faces, could hardly contain their emotions. I had to practically tear them away from Jennifer as we were escorted to the synagogue's inner sanctum to sign the various documents, the Ketubah, or marriage certificate.

The reception was held, after the generous insistence of Harvey and Anna, at their gracious home in Elstree where Jennifer and I had first been introduced. Jennifer had been adamant in wanting a small affair, firstly because she had already been through one large London wedding, and secondly, because of the small number of guests from the South African side, she preferred to keep invitations strictly to close friends and immediate family, which in her case was pretty sizeable. The reception took the form of a lavish garden party, with a jazz pianist and continual finger food served by smartly attired waitresses.

Under our strict instructions, the speeches were brief. Alec was allowed some latitude but kept references to our youth on a purely innocent level. I responded, thanking our hosts for their generosity, and my parents and Alec and others who had made the long journey.

Finally I turned to Jennifer with a smile. "Jen, just over a year ago, you turned my life inside out. Since we met, I have found enjoyment and fulfilment in the most extraordinarily ordinary things, as long as we were doing them together. I'm not a religious person but I bless the good fortune that shone on me the day we were introduced in this very house. I remember virtually proposing on our second date." I paused. "You told me not to be so silly." Gales of laughter spread throughout, creasing the faces of everyone present. "What made me feel that way, even then? I cannot answer, but something deep inside me knew for certain, that you were the person I wanted to share the rest of my life with. And may I say Amen!!!"

That evening Larry and Serena made a farewell supper for Jennifer and me, my parents, Alec and his wife. They were returning to South Africa the following day and Jennifer and I were flying to Malta for our honeymoon. It was a fairly sombre evening after the euphoria of the wedding and garden party.

Jennifer and I said our goodbyes, especially poignant when it came to my parents. I hugged them both close. "Mom, dad, I promise we'll be coming to visit you soon, if not this year then next. We'll go to Plettenberg Bay and just have a relaxing time. So it's not gonna be too long, OK?"

My mother who was nearly too choked to speak, held me tightly. "Thank you, Ray," she whispered. "I'm so glad you've found Jennifer. She's a wonderful girl. Look after her properly, you hear?" She hesitated, then wiped her eyes. "It's so sad that your little brother Marty couldn't be here, he...........he would have ......" she could not finish her sentence, just shook her head and turned away.

"Ray, Jennifer," my father said haltingly, eyes brimming, "Have a wonderful honeymoon, be well, and write soon, you promise?"

We gathered at the front door. Larry gave us each a bear hug and wished us luck. Then Serena did the same. She held Jennifer closely and whispered what was obviously intended only for her to hear but I was right close by. "Have a lovely honeymoon. Hope it doesn't get cut short like ours did."

At this point we were already out on the front porch so our reaction of astonishment and hurt was not visible to anyone else. We staggered to the Mini, turning to wave to everyone who had streamed out to witness our departure.

As we drove off I was shaking with anger. I turned to Jennifer, who was white-faced. "So, now, my blushing bride, you've again seen the other side of our dear sister-in-law. How could she say a thing like that? On our wedding day?"

Jennifer frowned. "That's not all, Ray. I overheard her in the garden, saying to one of her buddies 'humph, not much of a wedding is it? Should have seen OURS in Cape Town!' She turned to face me, jaw clenched rigid then her expression softened "Didn't you enjoy today, Ray?" she asked uncertainly. "We agreed it should be a low-key affair, not a glitzy show-off do, didn't we?" Her eyes were filling with tears.

I patted her hand. "Jen, my sweetheart, I loved every minute of today........ with the exception of the last few minutes. What I said in my speech I meant, every single word. And I'm not going to let that cow spoil our wedding, our honeymoon or our lives."

"Yes, but she's Larry's wife. He's your brother."

I changed gear with a violent jerk, producing a shrill grating noise. "Dammit! I know, but that's his problem. I don't think he has any idea of what she can be like, he's too bemused by her, and she is careful not to let that side of her show when he's around. She's much too clever for him."

Jennifer ran her hand through her hair, pursing her lips in puzzlement. "She's been so sugary sweet these past six months, I really began to feel that I could confide in her as a friend, you know, in spite of what happened in Tignes and all."

"Well, now again you've seen her other face. We will have to bite our tongues for the time being. I can't just go and have it out with Larry."

"No, what could you say to him? Better just put it to one side. In future, if she says something nasty, we should be prepared to respond straight away."

"I agree, but listen, we are a newly married couple, on what's supposed to be the happiest day of our lives. We're off for two weeks in the sun and I'm gonna make love to you day and night. No more thoughts about our dear sister-in-law. OK?"

"OK! You're the boss!"

I leaned over and kissed her on the cheek with a loud smack. "Yes, and that's the way I like it, MRS BENJAMIN!" I looked at my watch. "Hey, its late, hope they'll keep our Bridal suite at the Hilton!"

*

Two weeks of sun and sea were just what the doctor ordered. One week on the solitary isle of Comino, a blob in the ocean between Malta and Gozo, just a hotel, a lagoon and the clearest water I'd ever seen. We sunbathed, hiked the entire island and swam nude in the lagoon. The hotel boasted an open-air dance floor cut into the rocks just above the lapping ocean. The DJ seemed to have a propensity for Procol Harem, for he played their huge hit of the late sixties, 'A Whiter Shade of Pale' several times every evening. We were frequently the only couple on the dance floor and so the haunting song with its incomprehensible lyrics played on our subconscious to such an extent that it became our song from that week onwards.

The second week we moved to Ramla Bay, across a channel on the main island. We hired a motorbike and did some local touring but my questionable skill with the machine left Jennifer a nervous wreck. At the hotel there was a scuba diving school and after intensive persuasion, the good-looking instructor and I were able to allay Jennifer's lifelong fear of being underwater. We did some introductory dives, marvelling at the underwater life as well as getting hooked on the sensation of weightlessness.

"Ray," Jennifer shouted as we surfaced after a particularly spectacular dive," I think I'd like to do a proper diving course so we can get our licences and go out on our own."

"Fine by me," I said untangling myself from the equipment. "I think the Red Sea's the place to go. Apparently since the '67 War, Israel has made the Sinai peninsula a nature reserve. There are safaris we can go on, living rough in the desert and diving all along the coast. Sound good to you?"

"What, and sleep in sleeping bags on the sand? Aren't there scorpions and stuff?"

"I'll protect you, my love. Haven't I always? "

"Er...... see if you can find a trip where we can sleep in comfort." Jennifer smiled, "I don't mind the diving now, in fact I love it, but you may have noticed, Dr. Benjamin, I like my creature comforts, a hot bath, good shower, nice clean cool sheets.....”

I laughed, winking at her suggestively. “You’d better stop talking like that. You know what’ll happen and then ....for sure....... we’ll miss lunch.....”

*

Flying home, the topic of Serena came up.

“How are we going to handle this, Ray?” Jennifer asked as the seat-belt signs came on.

I shrugged, staring out at the approaching land. “I’ve no idea. What you said before made sense, be on our guard for the next catty remark and pull her up on it straightaway. Preferably with Larry around.”

This time there was no meet-and-greet at Heathrow airport. In a way, it was nice to be on our own, no crowds, just a taxi ride back to Chelsea and peace and quiet of our little nest above the surgery. Jennifer had wrought extensive changes in my bachelor abode, matching curtains, sheets and duvet covers, and colourful cushions for the L-shaped couch. For the bathroom, a multitude of bottles, shampoos and perfumes occupied large tracts of my formerly Spartan existence. His and hers towels, naturally! Our combined collection of records and tapes gave us a huge choice of music. Her Bang and Olefsen stereo was a welcome replacement for my outdated set-up.

Jennifer was busying herself in the freshly-equipped kitchen making supper when the phone rang.

“Hi, Benjamin residence,” I answered cheerfully.

“Hi Ray. Larry here. Have you just got back? I wasn’t sure but your receptionist said she thought you’d be back this evening.”

“Yeah, we got in about an hour ago.”

“So, how was Malta? Did you have a good time?” I could detect a nervous edge to his voice. “How’s the blushing bride?”

“Fine, thanks. We had a marvellous time, lots of sun and sea, food was good and very relaxing. We’re gonna do a scuba course in the Red sea later this year, we decided.” I paused, mouthing ‘Larry’ to Jennifer who had poked her head round the kitchen door inquisitively. “How’re things with you guys? Serena OK?”

“All’s well this side.” There was a momentary pause. “Er..... Ray, is it OK to talk right now, I’ve got something to discuss with you.”

"Sure." I took the phone over to the settee and sat down. "What's on your mind?"

"Well, it's like this, I've been at Parkers now for just over nine months and have become friendly with two of the other junior accountants here. To cut a long story short, we are thinking of setting up our own partnership practice."

"Hey, that sounds good," I said approvingly. "What does it involve?"

"You see, these guys have been here for three and four years respectively so they've managed to build up some capital. Of course I haven't, seeing as I've only been here less than a year, but we get along well, and have similar ideas."

I didn't need much insight to see where this was going. "So what's the deal, Larry?"

"Ah, well, they reckon if we each put in an equal amount we should be able to make a move by the end of the year."

"That soon?" I said. "That's pretty bold. What money are they talking?"

There was a pregnant pause. "They suggest £20,000 each to cover most things, leasing premises, hiring staff, office furniture and electronic equipment etc., including tiding us over the first year till fees start coming in regularly. They've both got quite a large number of clients who will come with them whereas I haven't, but rather than me putting in extra cash initially, we agreed to review the structure after a year, when we can see who is bringing in the most fees." Larry was speaking hurriedly, as if embarrassed. I could almost visualize Serena sitting there, egging him on.

I was determined to let him make the running. "So what are you asking of me, Larry? Have you spoken to your bank?" At this point Jennifer came and sat beside me, a reproving look told me all I needed to know about her feelings.

"Yes, I saw him this week. He said that because of our large mortgage, he couldn't allow me more than £5,000 on a second charge on the house, payable over three years. I've only got about two grand in my account so with the balance of dad's money, £4,000, I'm still about £9,000 short."

'Serena must be hating this,' I thought to myself. 'Never had to think about money her entire life and now finds herself in this humble position.' "Larry," I replied slowly, "I've got to think carefully about our own situation at the moment. You see, we want to move to a house pretty soon. Jennifer really wants a garden and we're pretty cramped in my little flat. You know that I extended my overdraft to get the £6,000 for you guys last November. Now I'm sure I can let you have the other £4,000 of dad's with a bit of a stretch, but the other £9,000, I really don't know. Like you, I have a huge mortgage on the Chelsea house. I'd need to tie myself up pretty steeply if we want to put down a deposit on a house as well."

I could hear Serena's raised voice, muffled in the background, just catching a few words like "I told you......let you down........knew it!" Then Larry came back. "So is that it, then? You can't or won't help?" This was a different tone, an echo from the distant past, of a small boy throwing a tantrum when he didn't get his way.

"Larry," I said as calmly as I could, "Let's not get heated about this. You've sprung this surprise on me when we've just come home from honeymoon. I haven't even unpacked or sorted through a mountain of mail. I'm running a busy practice here and have no idea what my current money situation is at the moment until I've had a chance to sort through what's happened the past fortnight. So cool down, let me sleep on it tonight and we'll talk again tomorrow. Right now Jen has just put dinner on the table so you'll have to excuse me. Is that OK?"

The background was silent now. "Yes, I suppose so," Larry said grudgingly. "Welcome back, anyway."

The line went dead.

"Wow!" my irate wife said as we sat down to eat. "What a welcome home! I don't know how you kept your temper."

"Nor do I," I replied, still shaken by the tone of my brother's demands. "One thing is sure, she's pushing him and he's letting himself be pushed."

"What do you think of this proposition of his?"

"Well, I don't know the other guys and I also don't know too much about accountancy as a business. It depends on Larry's judgement. Clearly it would be better for him to be a principal rather than an employee but he's putting himself in hock on the expectation that fees will come rolling in. That's the key gamble and I don't feel that I want to have him owing me a large sum of money when we're going to need every penny."

"So what are you going to do?"

"I think....." I mumbled, chewing on a delicious piece of Jennifer's Coronation chicken salad, ".......I'm going to suggest that he writes to dad for a loan. Either the £9,000 he needs or £13,000 excluding the money I still hold for dad. I'll see how the practice is doing anyway but I can't see my way clear to jeopardising our finances right now."

"Mmmm," Jennifer frowned, "I can see problems coming."

"Yeah, I know. The way Larry spoke just then reminded me of when he was a little boy, getting all up tight like that. Well, I've made my decision. I'll speak to him tomorrow. Right now we better unpack and get to bed. I noticed I've got a very heavy appointment book tomorrow."

Jennifer smiled. "All your little Chelsea dollybird patients can't wait for their handsome dentist to look down their mouths, hey?"

I picked up one her embroidered cushions from the couch and hurled it across the room at her. Fortunately it caused no damage and missed her by a mile. Before she had a chance to retaliate I scooted off down the stairs to the surgery to have a peek at the books and the earnings for the past fortnight. "You unpack first, see you later!" I yelled up the stairs.

Her response was unrepeatable.

*

I hardly had time to think during the day, having to cope with several complicated oral surgery cases under general anaesthesia as well as a number of emergencies. My associates had been busy while we had been away but my patients had preferred to wait until my return. When the last patient left, I trudged up the stairs and flung myself, exhausted, on the couch. Jennifer had not returned from the office so I poured myself a stiff whiskey and turned on the TV. Lord Lucan guilty of murdering the family nanny but nowhere to be found, the referendum on Britain staying in the EEC carried by two thirds, Prime Minister Harold Wilson on holiday in the Scilly Isles after being mercilessly savaged by new Tory leader Margaret Thatcher. The usual chaos surrounding the UK economy was boring me to tears. My eyes were just closing when the telephone rang.

"Hi, Ray. Larry here."

"Hi," I replied sleepily.

"You OK? Sounds like I woke you."

"Nah, just dozing. Where are you?"

"Finishing at the office. Can you talk?"

"I'm half asleep."

Larry was insistent. "Listen, I really need to talk this through with you."

I sat up, gathering my senses. "Right. Do you want to come over, maybe have a bite with us?"

There was a pause. "Er...I'll need to call Serena. She's expecting me home."

"Fine, do that. I'll know what I'm talking about by then."

"Right. If I don't call you back straightaway I'll be there in an hour."

*

Jennifer came home exhausted about forty minutes later. When I told her to set an extra place for dinner she pursed her lips irritably.

"Don't think I've got enough for three. I bought some nice lamb chops, but there's not enough to go round. "

"All right," I said. "You don't look high on energy. Let's go across the road to that little Italian place and have a pasta. Put the chops in the freezer. We'll have them tomorrow night."

"Sure that's all right?"

I nodded. "Fine. We'll clear the air with Larry first, then hopefully have a bottle of Frascati with him."

Just then the doorbell rang. I took the stairs two at a time and opened the door. My brother stood there, a worried frown on his face.

"What's the matter, Larry? You look like you've had a fight or something? Come in."

"Ja," he nodded as we sat down in the lounge. "I did have a big argument with one of the partners at Parkers. He's a real bastard, always picking on me. Just as I was leaving he started demanding accounts that I was supposed to have finished.....oh what the hell, don't let's discuss it, it's just the sooner I'm out of there the better."

Jennifer came in from the kitchen. "Hi Larry, fancy a drink? You look like you could do with one." She turned to me with a reproving look. "What kind of a host are you, Ray? Give your brother a drink. He looks parched."

I poured Scotches for the two of us and a medium sherry for Jennifer. "So, how are discussions going for your venture, Larry?"

"Well, it's like I told you last night. I'm £13,000 short of what I need to go into this partnership."

"And if you can't raise that money?" I asked gently.

"Well, they'll either go on their own, just the two of them, or look for someone else. It's an opportunity I just can't afford to miss."

"And how confident are they, and you, that within a year the fees will be coming in?" I clasped my hands in front of me, 'a moneylender's gesture if ever I saw one', I thought to myself.

Larry sat up, sipping his drink. "Naturally we can't be certain, but these guys tell me they've had assurances from a large number of their clients. They've done their sums so I guess I have to take that chance."

"Larry, look, I was dumbfounded last night when you sprung this on us just after we walked in the door, but, even though I've been up to my ears in patients today, I have given it a lot of thought." I unclasped my fingers and placed my hands on my knees. "The truth is, although I could stretch to get the £4,000 balance of Dad's money for you, there is just no possibility of my getting any more right now. As I told you, we want to move to a house within the year, and we're going to have to build up capital for a deposit. I'm right up to my limit with the bank and to even get the £4,000 I'm gonna have to go to the bank with a begging bowl."

Larry looked at me with those forlorn eyes. "I just don't believe what you're telling me, Ray. You promised you'd help us in our early years here and now you're saying that all you can do is to give me back the money that dad loaned to you. That doesn't sound like the brother I've always known and loved."

I could see the tears welling up. "Larry, listen, be reasonable. You can't expect to come with a request like this with no warning and expect me to lay my hands on £13,000 just like that. In any case, you said that it is a big chance you're taking."

Larry stood up, shaking with anger. "You know what I see when I look at you and Jennifer? I see you living like kings in fashionable Chelsea, planning expensive holidays, running a thriving dental practice, yes, don't worry, I know what you dentists earn, we have several on our books. So don't give me crap about not being able to lay your hands on a measly thirteen grand. You could if you wanted to." He stood shaking, sweat pouring down his face.

I tried to remonstrate with him. "Larry, listen, take it easy, sit down. When I needed a loan desperately to buy this place, I asked dad. Have you thought of asking him?"

Larry sat down, wiping his forehead with his sleeve. "I've already asked him. Spoke to him on the phone yesterday. Firstly the boycott has hit PE really badly. Secondly he's been so generous to those Afrikaans partners of his that he is now battling financially himself. I've even thought of asking Serena's dad but she won't let me, although he could do it without blinking an eye. You're the only one I can turn to, Ray."

I breathed deeply. "Larry, I simply can't do it, not right now, maybe .....maybe next year......."

He was on his feet once again. "I didn't believe her when she said it. I didn't want to believe her but....... but...." He was waving his arms about in rage, an uncontrollable fury.

I stood up then. "What do you mean.....who..... who are you talking about, Larry? Your wife Serena? She told you what.......what did she say?"

Jennifer had been sitting on the edge of the settee, saying nothing. "Ray, Ray, please, just calm down, take it easy, don't, please don't say anything you'll regret"

Larry and I were now standing facing each other, bristling. Part of me could not believe what was happening yet an interior voice insisted this was inevitable, having seen the malign influence Larry was acting under. I tried to settle things down again. "Larry, listen to me, please try and see things from our point of view....."

He shook his head. "NO!" he bellowed, "I don't have to listen to you anymore. I'm not interested in your bloody point of view! I asked for help and you refused. Serena said that when push came to shove you would let us down. She sees right through you, both of you!"

That was, for me, the last straw. Disregarding Jennifer's anguished shaking of her head, I grabbed Larry firmly by his shoulders. "Let me just say a word about your lovely wife, my brother. She can be a two-faced, nasty piece of work. We've taken quite a few of her snide remarks over the past year, and said nothing, especially when she wished Jen a happy honeymoon, hoping it wouldn't be cut off like hers was. What a shame our poor brother had to die and spoil her precious honeymoon! And remarks she made about our meagre wedding........not like her shpraunzy affair in Cape Town, oh no! Just let me tell you, Larry, you don't see what she's like, you're blinded by her ....."

I hardly saw the slap coming but it caught me high on the side of my head knocking me backwards across the couch. An image of Gerry Webber flashed through my mind.

Jennifer was screaming. "STOP IT! STOP IT! STOP IT! THE TWO OF YOU! PLEASE, PLEASE ,STOP!"

I regained my balance, struggling to stand up, holding my head. I looked at Larry, seeing the pure hatred in his eyes. "I think you'd better leave our home now. I don't think there's anything more to say."

"Don't worry, I'm going. My Serena's worth a dozen of you. You can both get stuffed!" With that he turned and ran down the stairs.

Jennifer looked at me aghast. "Oh my god, Ray, how did this happen? How on earth did it come to this?"

I felt the side of my head where the blow had landed. My hand came away bloody. "I think you'd better find a tissue, a plaster or something....."

I sat down, holding my head in my hands, but no tears came.

Chapter 32

The letter arrived a week later. It made good breakfast reading!

27 Albury Crescent,
Radlett, Hertfordshire.
24th July, 1975.

Raymond,

I am writing to you to express the disgust and disappointment both Serena and I feel at the way you have treated us. We moved to the UK because you had settled here, and had promised to help us, when I probably could have done better in Australia. The heartless way you behaved in response to my perfectly reasonable request we both feel was totally unacceptable. Also the horrible and insulting things you said about Serena were unforgiveable.

In addition, we were both aghast at the greedy way you grabbed all of our late brother's belongings before we had a chance to choose anything as a keepsake to remember him by. Up till now we have refrained from mentioning this in order to preserve our warm family relations but feel quite justified now in airing this grievance.

My future partners have agreed to allow me to pay off the money I would be putting into the venture over a period of two years so I will not be requiring any charity from you!

Serena and I are agreed that in the circumstances, we do not wish to have any further contact with you.

Larry.

"My God!" breathed Jennifer, after reading the letter a second time." So much hatred, and after all you've done for him too!"

I nodded, still numb from the tone of the letter. "I wonder what this business about Marty's belongings is all about. All I've got are a few of his LP records and his Wits University Tracksuit. I know mom gave Marty's watch to Euphemia, she did love him so much! Oh, and I've got this Star of David pendant I'm wearing, which I gave him on his Barmitzvah!"

Jennifer shook her head. "You know, I think your brother may be a bit paranoid. The way he ranted on the other evening and now this crazy accusation. It seems as though he feels persecuted, and if his wife wants to pull him away from us she's certainly succeeding."

"You think she's behind all this?"

"From what I've seen of her, and watching her recent behaviour, I'd say she was the main instigator, together with quite a dose of envy on his part. What you told him was the truth, it was too sudden, it was beyond your ability to help just now and he went off pop! She probably told him to expect a refusal and when it came it lit his fuse. He just wasn't prepared to accept your situation for what it is."

"I guess you're right," I agreed. "She is bitter that he's battling financially and can't help making comparisons with us, but she's forgetting that we've been at it for a lot longer. Anyway, I'll reply to this epistle and I might just enclose a cheque for £4,000 - which would absolve me of any accusation of hanging on to dad's money. What do you think?"

"If you can afford it, sure, that's the way to go. Kill with kindness, I always say." Jennifer shook her head doubtfully. "But I don't hold out much hope that it'll change their attitude one little bit."

"Fine, we're agreed. I'll draft a reply tonight." I shook my head in sad resignation. "You know, it's extraordinary. Here Larry and I are, having just lost our youngest brother in tragic circumstances, and now it seems that we're about to lose each other. I find that unbelievable. I pity my parents when they find out."

Jennifer nodded. "Yes, I'm not sure how much more tragedy your mother especially, can take." She looked at her watch. "Do you know its 9 o'clock? Your first patient's probably here. Go on, off you go."

3 Markham Terrace,
Chelsea,
London SW3
28th July 1975.

Dear Larry,

I enclose my cheque for £4000 thus providing you with the balance of the money loaned to me by dad all those years ago. I offered dad interest several times but he always refused.

I am not prepared to respond to the antagonistic and hurtful sentiments in your letter, however I will take issue on the most upsetting item of all, one that can and must surely lead to a permanent breakdown of relations between us.

You (and Serena) accused me of 'greedily grabbing Marty's belongings'. This was probably the worst and most injurious accusation you could have made and I must assume that you intended it to be so. Before making such a wild and unfounded statement, you should have checked your facts. Mom gave most of Marty's clothes and his watch to Euphemia who adored him. The extent of my 'collection' of Marty's things consists of a Wits University Tracksuit which I wear with pride and sorrow, five Sergio Mendez LP records and a Star of David pendant which I gave him on his Barmitzvah! So before putting your accusation down on paper, you should have checked with our parents. As it is, what you have done is, both Jennifer and I feel, unforgiveable and most probably irremediable.

We wish you luck with your new partnership but do not intend to have any further correspondence or relationship with you.

Sadly,
Raymond and Jennifer.

*

Four months later
November 1975

"Hey Jen, they've accepted our last offer!" I burst into the kitchen waving a letter from the Estate Agents in St. Johns Wood.

Jennifer dropped the tray with our breakfast she was carrying into the small dinette off the lounge. "OHMIGOD! REALLY? YOU'RE NOT KIDDING? OH SHIT LOOK WHAT I'VE DONE!"

"No, really. They're prepared to exchange contracts as soon as we like!" I bent down to help her clear the mess on the carpeted floor.

We had been in protracted negotiations for a delightful Regency house in a tiny private street called The Lane off Abbey Road. Offers and counter-responses had been flying between us and the vendors for weeks. Now that the deal was definite, we would be renting out the flat above the surgery and with the income from that and Jennifer's apartment I had calculated we could just about afford the new purchase.

"Ray, that's brilliant! I can't wait! I'd break open some champagne but your patients wouldn't appreciate alcohol on their dentist's breath this early in the morning, would they?" Jennifer was on her knees beside me picking up the remnants of fried eggs and bacon off the carpet. Her almond eyes were shining with delight. "St Johns Wood! Bloody hell, we won't know ourselves! Are you sure we can afford it financially?"

I nodded. "Yes. I've discussed it with the accountants. With the combined rents we can do it fairly comfortably."

Jennifer placed the salvaged food on the table. "Do you think you can eat that now ....you know, it's really funny......." she stopped, with a shy grin on her face.

I took a forkful of egg and bacon. "Course I can eat it, the carpet's clean isn't it? What's so funny?"

My wife looked at me bashfully, a faraway look in her eyes. "You remember that old saying....... 'New House...... New Baby'.....?."

This time it was my turn to drop things. The fork clattered on to the floor with a splat, soft fried egg creating a yellow abstract on the plain carpet. “You don’t mean, you’re ....we’re gonna have ..... shit!..... why didn’t you tell me before?”

It could have been a hackneyed scene from a corny Hollywood movie. We ignored the mess and danced around the room, hugging each other, laughing and crying hysterically.

Jennifer pulled away and collapsed breathlessly on the couch. “I didn’t say anything for weeks when I was late because I’d been irregular before, but now two months have gone by and then this morning I did the test in the bathroom. About half an hour before you came in with that letter. I was bursting to tell you! A big beautiful brown ring! I’m.....,no.... we’re pregnant! If that’s not an amazing coincidence what is?”

I patted her flat tummy tenderly and looked deep into her eyes. “You know, you are without a doubt the best thing that’s ever happened in my life, Mrs. Benjamin. Thank you, from the bottom of my heart,” I hesitated a moment... “and from the baby’s bottom too!”

The ensuing months were occupied with visits to a gynaecologist, prenatal clinics and the whole production of being expectant parents. Jennifer had been granted a generous maternity leave from Lawson and Steele who insisted that her job would be waiting for her when she was ready to come back.

Naturally, the double-header good news for my parents heralded the start of regular phone calls to check on the condition of the baby via the gynaecologist, and how Jennifer was feeling and to hear details of the new house.

“So, Ray, all’s well with Jennifer and the baby?” my father’s voice quivered with joy.

“Yes, dad, Jennifer’s gynaecologist is very pleased. All’s well.”

“And, the new house, when will you move in? Won’t it be too much of a strain for Jennifer?”

“No, dad, she’s fit and strong. We hope to move in early in the new year.”

There was a pause. “Have you heard anything from Larry and Serena?”

“No, dad. Not a word.” I let the silence hang for a few seconds. “Dad, you and mom mustn’t go on torturing yourselves about this. Things that Larry said and wrote just aren’t easily forgivable and right now, we are quite happy as things are. So please, don't keep asking. It upsets us too."

"Well, I told them about the baby and they were very happy for you both."

"That's nice, thank you. Dad, I gotta go, next patient's here. Love to you both and to everyone in PE especially Dr Joe." I put the phone down gently, cursing my brother and his wife under my breath for casting gloom on what should have been, and I was determined to make it be, the happiest occasion for Jennifer, me and my parents.

*

Jennifer gave birth to our daughter Gabriella by Caesarian section after a prolonged labour of more than 20 hours had dictated that safety of both baby and mother would be threatened by waiting longer. The date was June 6th 1976. Gaby weighed 7 pounds 4 ounces and was blessed with a head of auburn hair and blue-green eyes.

We had moved to The Lane in January 1976 and, after some months living in makeshift conditions, had finally managed to furnish the lounge, dining room, main bedroom and baby's room to Jennifer's satisfaction. My Natwest Bank Manager must have grown tired of my frequent requests for leniency but with both flats let and the Practice buoyant, he had been more than generous.

Apart from occasional bits of information from mutual friends, we had had no contact with Larry and Serena. Several letters from my father begging us to make up had served merely to underline the rift, especially as it appeared that he and my mother blamed us for the breakdown of the relationship. We had decided that to criticise Serena or Larry to my parents would serve no useful purpose except to upset them further so we maintained a dignified silence. I had never received an acknowledgement of receipt of the £4,000 which nevertheless had been deposited! As far as I was aware, Larry's partnership was growing and functioning well, for which I was genuinely pleased. Any temptation to make contact, however, was soon set aside. The thought of hiding our dislike for Serena and ignoring our still raw reaction to their final letter, made any effort at reconciliation on our part unthinkable.

Chapter 33

1979 Bomb outrage in Soweto. Bishop Abel Muzorewa elected Prime Minister in Rhodesia
After the winter of discontent Margaret Thatcher becomes
Britain's first Woman Prime Minister

Three years later..... December 1979/ January 1980

Our excitement mounted as the South African Airways Boeing circled Port Elizabeth. Gaby had her nose glued to the window as I tried to point out familiar landmarks.

"See, Gaby, that's where daddy went to school, see those big green fields and those funny buildings. And look over there, you can see the sea and the beach, look at all the big waves, all white and foamy!"

The plane landed with a bump. Traditional Port Elizabeth wind nearly blew us off our feet as we struggled across the tarmac with pram and assorted infant paraphernalia. Despite the wind, the sun bore down on us relentlessly. In the distance we caught a glimpse of my parents standing by the arrivals gate. I picked Gaby up and ran towards them.

"Look, Gaby, that's your grandpa and grandma!" Jennifer shoved her towards their open arms.

I was shocked seeing the deterioration in my parents. Although we had begged them countless times to make the trip to London, health problems and their financial situation had made it impossible. Apart from photographs, this was the first time they were to meet their one and only grandchild. My father had been diagnosed with early colon cancer which was one pressing reason for us to make this journey now, apart from escaping part of the London winter.

"Hi, mom, hi dad," I embraced them both as they bent over to hug Gabriella. "Thanks for the traditional windy city greeting!" I looked carefully at my father to see if I could detect any of the signs of advanced malignancy but apart from his lined face and thinned gray hair, there were none. The eyes still twinkled behind thick coke-bottle lenses.

We all hurried inside to the relative calm of the Arrivals hall to await our luggage. Jennifer and I might as well have been on another planet for all the attention we got. To her credit, Gaby lavished kisses on my parents' withered faces even though this was the first time she had seen them.

"Ray, Jennifer, your baby is exquisite!" my father stammered, tears of joy cascading down his cheeks. "She's gonna be a movie star, for sure!"

My mother said nothing, just held our daughter's face in her hands, shaking her head in disbelief. Then she looked at me, sadness in her eyes mixed with a happy smile, a graphic portrait of all the suffering she had endured these last traumatic years. "I never thought we'd live to see this day, Raymond, Jennifer. Thank you, thank you so much for bringing us this little angel!"

'Little angel' was an apt description of our curly-haired, green-blue-eyed three and a half year old. Her auburn locks danced as she jumped up and down, tightly holding on to her grandparents' hands, revelling in the attention she was receiving, not only from my parents but from amused people all around. She was jabbering away in her very English accent to everyone's amusement and dragging the two old people up and down, fascinated by the luggage carousels.

"I've got the luggage," I yelled.

Instantly an African porter leapt forward with two trolleys. He tipped his cap extravagantly. "Here I am baas....... I take cases!"

Although our suitcases were fitted with wheels I relaxed, letting the smiling African man load the luggage and set off behind my parents. We followed them across the main thoroughfare to the car park where my father's Vauxhall and, to my delight and astonishment, my mother's venerable old Morris Minor were parked.

"I just don't believe it, you've still got the old Morris Minor, mom!"

She nodded, smiling slightly.

"I've tried for fifteen years to get her to trade it in. Might as well try and move the Rock of Gibraltar," my father said ruefully. "Come on, we'll take Gaby with us," he insisted.

"I'll go with them, then," Jennifer said firmly, "Come on, Gaby, into the back seat with me!"

I was left on my own to drive the Morris with most of the luggage. As I followed them through the suburbs, past the old school and Cape Road, memories flooded back. A glimpse of the old Greek cafe, modernised but still there on the familiar corner, images of the Swimmers but mostly of Crystal swam through my mind. It was as though a lifetime had passed, so many vivid recollections of our youth which had receded now came hurtling back. Emotions even more poignant surfaced when we arrived at the old house, with the 'cricket-pitch' garage.

Euphemia came waddling down the garden path. She gave me a short but violent bearhug. "Hullo, Massah Raymond!!! Welcome back! But you very naughty.... you'se been away too long! An' you'se mus' be Miss Jennifer.!" Then she spied Gabriella and after that even my parents had to take a back seat. "Oh, Lawd!" she cried, gathering Gaby up in her massive arms and cuddling her to her copious bosom.

Gaby took it all in her stride, although the sight of this huge, smiling ebony face above her must have ranked as the most striking experience in her young life.

"My name, its EUPHEMIA," our loyal old maid pronounced slowly, with her ear-to-ear ivory smile. "Can you say that, baby?"

"U-FEE-ME-AH," Gabriella obliged.

"HEH HEH HEH!" came that old familiar cackle. "See, Massah Ray, she knows me already!" She then disappeared with our little daughter on a conducted tour of the house and the garden while I showed Jennifer around. After a good old English cup of tea and my favourite, Euphemia's baked biscuits, my parents were exhausted by the excitement of our arrival so were content to rest for an hour until dinner.

Jennifer and I climbed the stairs to my room with its view of the sea and Algoa Bay. I could almost smell Crystal's scent as we unpacked, guilt and even tiny stabs of longing for those old, yet still passionate, memories bubbling up uncontrollably.

Jennifer was staring at me concernedly. "Are you OK, Ray? You look like you've seen a ghost."

I shook my head. "Nah, it's just, there's a lot of history for me in this house."

She smiled. "All those old girlfriends, hey?"

I gulped guiltily. I had never disclosed to my wife the full intensity and trauma of my relationship with Crystal, preferring for it to remain in the dim and distant past. So I was relieved when the call came for supper. Euphemia had cooked up all my favourites, ox tongue with crispy roast potatoes and fresh newly- shelled green peas, with ice cream and her special chocolate sauce to follow.

Gabriella was to sleep in Larry's old room, which had been converted into a little girl's nursery for our visit. There was a miniature bed with side supports, colourful curtains and bedspreads to match, as well as a large basket of our old toys, which although they were entirely for boys, would certainly keep her amused. We put her to bed after supper and read her a favourite bedtime story. She was sound asleep after just three pages.

I peeked into Marty's room and not surprisingly, it had been kept exactly as it was when he was alive. I shut the door quietly after spending a few quiet moments gazing round at all his pictures, sports teams, school class photos and trophies.

Later we sat with my folks in the lounge. Jennifer and I were pleased that the subject of Larry and Serena did not come up. More important was my father's health.

"Your father has to have an operation, Ray," my mother said softly. "The abdominal pain has been getting worse. They say it's better to remove the growth soon before it can spread."

"So when is the op scheduled?" I asked. "Why didn't you write and tell me?"

My father lifted his head slowly. "I telephoned Larry and told him last week. I hoped he would let you know, but in any case I knew you were coming now."

I felt a spurt of anger race through me. "Dad, you know we haven't spoken in over three years. I know you and mom find it hard to accept, and it never fails to fill me with sadness as well. I'm afraid that things were said in a letter, which we've kept, by the way, that we just cannot forgive. I don't want to give you any more sadness but you know brothers do fall out, families do have feuds."

"I never thought it would happen in our family, though," he murmured quietly.

"Nor did I, dad, nor did I, especially after losing Marty." I went over and sat on the arm of his chair. "But look, we're here now. I want to know when your op is due so I can make arrangements to stay and help you through your recovery."

He looked at me misty-eyed. "It's after you folks leave, a week later. I've booked us at the Beacon Island Hotel in Plettenberg Bay for ten days, starting tomorrow. I know how you love the place and Gaby will have a ball on the sand and in the waves."

Jennifer stared at him concernedly. "But dad, are you feeling up to going away? We really don't need to go anywhere special. The PE beaches look every bit as good. Perhaps you shouldn't leave the op any longer. Have it sooner, while we're here."

My father smiled gently. "Jennifer, it's so kind of you to suggest that but look, I asked the doctors whether another three weeks would make a difference. They said no, they think its slow growing and I should go and enjoy being with my children and my gorgeous granddaughter. Also, I know Plett is Ray's favourite place. You should have seen him and Martin years ago, surfing a huge wave with dolphins. People on the beach stood up and cheered." He blinked and smiled proudly at the memory.

"Maybe I should speak to the doctors?" I asked. "I can talk their language. Would you mind, dad?"

He nodded. "Ja, that's OK but Dr. Joe has explained it all to me. Talk to him if you want."

"Fine," I said. "I'll phone him in the morning, but in the meantime give me the exact date of your operation so that I can change my return flight. And I'm not having any arguments. Jen, would you mind if I stayed on for a couple of weeks?"

She shook her head. "Course not. I'll need to get back to work at Lawson and Steele though. The au pair can take Gaby to nursery easily enough. We'll manage just fine."

Late that night I lay awake, staring at the ceiling. Alongside me in a separate single bed, Jennifer raised herself up on one elbow. "Can't sleep Ray? What's bothering you?"

"Nothing much," I muttered. " I was just a bit upset that my folks told Larry about dad's operation not us."

In the darkness I saw the silhouette of Jennifer's head nodding. "I thought that too at the time but I think I understand. Your dad wants more than anything for you and Larry to get together so by letting Larry know he must have hoped he would tell us."

"Hmmm," I whispered back, "In which case it has made it even worse for him knowing the split is so wide that Larry wouldn't even pick up a phone to me. It's backfired badly, if that's what he intended."

"I guess so," Jennifer answered. "Anyway, having Gaby here is a real uplift for them. Hopefully two weeks in the sun in Plett will do us all a world of good. Walking on the beach will build up your dad's fitness and help prepare him for the op. I'm gonna miss you for two weeks, though." She stretched out her arm. "Feel like coming over to my bed?" I saw her smile glinting in the moonlight "We can be very very quiet....."

*

The two weeks at the Beacon Island hotel were over in a flash. Gaby was now a confirmed sea-lover. She screamed with delight as I held her above incoming waves and ran breathlessly in the shallows as the rippled surf chased after her. My parents sat under umbrellas most of the time but I was able to persuade them to walk along Lookout Beach to the lagoon and back and even got dad to go in the water with Gaby and me. Jennifer was alarmed at the size of the waves and kept her bathing strictly to waist depth. For old times' sake I went out with rubber fins and caught a few 'big uns' as Marty and I used to call the huge twelve-footers!.

We came back to PE tanned and invigorated. My old friend and co-perpetrator of the Froodella disaster, Alec, and his wife Barbara came over to the house to see us the day before Jennifer and Gaby were due to fly home. What I found strange was how far apart we had become in our attitudes. Alec was now firmly convinced that apartheid was the only answer to South Africa's problems. "Look what's happening north of us. Rhodesia was a breadbasket for Central Africa but now it's rapidly descending into chaos. It's only because of our large white population and its expertise that we can go forward. The blacks will have to be educated, but at a much slower pace than these ANC guys want."

I tried to argue gently. "But Alec, there's no way five million people can control and subjugate twenty-five million people permanently. You should be talking to their leaders, Mandela for example, instead of letting him rot on Robben Island."

"Never!" he cried. "He's a convicted terrorist. Try dealing with him and it'll be goodbye to South Africa. It'll be black rule and a banana republic like all the other African dictatorships."

In the end we agreed to disagree. It was entirely understandable. They had an extremely comfortable life with all the trappings, large architect designed house with pool, two cars, three servants, and Alec ran a thriving medical practice. Who would want to walk away from a life like this?

I asked him if he knew the surgeon who was to operate on my father.

"Ja, Dirk van Rooyen, very good man. Top class surgeon and very meticulous. Your old man's in good hands."

I felt comforted by Alec's opinion and so, when they left, we made plans to meet at the hospital after dad's surgery. Lalla and Mark had moved with their families to Cape Town so our little Swimmers group was now spread far and wide.

He shook me by the hand. "Really good to see you guys again, Ray." He looked at my abdomen with an envious smile. "The squash is keeping you fit, hey?" He patted his bulging stomach resignedly. "Sadly I just don't get enough time. I keep meaning to start jogging or something. Too much lazy living!"

"Ja, and too many *braai's* (barbecues)!" his slim, dark-eyed wife interrupted. "Come on fatso, time to go. Let's let Jennifer get on with her packing!"

The scene at the airport was heart-breaking for all of us. I felt guilty at letting Jennifer make the long trip on her own with Gaby but watching my parents cling on to their beloved grand-daughter was just too much for me. I turned away and wiped tears from my eyes. When it came time to say goodbye to Gabriella I steeled myself, battling to keep voice and face cheerful.

"Daddy, why aren't you coming with me an' mummy?" she quavered, her enormous blue-green eyes portraying her consternation.

Jennifer patted her reassuringly. "Don't worry, Gaby, darling. It's only for a few days. Daddy's gonna stay with granma while grandpa gets better in hospital."

I lifted my daughter high above my head and nuzzled her tummy, which elicited the usual delighted giggle. "Give daddy one of your biggest kisses so it'll last till I come home!"

Gaby obliged with resonating lip-smacking kisses on both cheeks and then, overwhelmed with the excitement of going on the big aeroplane, she waved wildly. Grabbing hold of Jennifer's hand, they both disappeared through the departure gate.

*

The surgeon, Mr. van Rooyen said he was pleased with the outcome of the operation. In his consulting room at St. Joseph's Hospital, my mother, Dr. Joe and I sat quietly while he described what he had found. "The tumour was well encapsulated and I'm sure that we removed it all together with a piece of bowel on each side just to be sure. We also took samples of lymph glands in the abdomen to check on any possible spread but they looked normal to me. We'll just have to wait until the microscopic examination results are through in a couple of days but," he gave a thin smile, "I don't think there's much to worry about, and he doesn't even need a colostomy bag."

"How did dad take the whole procedure?" I asked. "Was the anaesthetist happy with his general condition?"

Van Rooyen looked at me over his half-lensed spectacles. "You're the dentist son, aren't you?" he smiled and I nodded. "No, for a man of his age, he came through very well. We'll keep him in Intensive Care for a couple of days observation and I think after a two weeks he'll be OK to go home."

"What about any treatment, radiotherapy? Will that be necessary?" Dr. Joe queried.

The surgeon frowned slightly. "As I said, I'm pretty sure we got the whole tumour, in which case no further treatment is required. Unless the tests on the lymph glands show anything, I think we can safely avoid all that nasty stuff."

We were permitted a few minutes with my father, who was still pretty dozy, tubes and wires emanating from everywhere, but he opened his eyes and gave us a weak smile.

Arriving home later, Dr. Joe and I insisted that my mother take the sedative he had prescribed and we escorted her up to her bedroom to rest. The telephone was ringing as I came down the stairs. Somehow, I knew who it would be and steeled myself before answering.

"Hi, Raymond here..."

"It's Larry," came the familiar voice, but with a cool edge audible even across six thousand miles. "How's dad? How did the surgery go?"

"Fine," I replied, equally coolly. "He's awake, out of theatre. The surgeon's pleased, and is pretty sure he got it all. No radiotherapy needed unless the lymph nodes show anything. They'll know in a few days."

" How's mom? Can I speak with her?"

"We've put her to bed with a sedative, Dr. Joe's orders. She's OK though."

"How long will dad be in hospital?"

"The surgeon reckons a couple of weeks, depending ...."

"On what?"

"How quickly dad's healing, his general condition, heart, circulation, stuff like that."

"And if the lymph nodes are involved?"

"Well, then they'll have to reassess. At the moment, Mr Van Rooyen, the surgeon, is pretty confident. So we just have to wait and hold thumbs."

There was a silence on the line. I waited a few seconds then, when there was no response, just framed what I thought was an appropriate question. "Do you want me to wake mom? Or shall I get her to phone you back later when she's up?"

"We'll call her tonight. Tell dad I called and wish him a speedy recovery."

"Will do." The call was terminated abruptly from my brother's side.

Dr. Joe had been standing by, with a sad expression on his face. "No thaw yet between you two?"

I shrugged. "Dr. Joe, that's the first time we've spoken in over three years."

"Raymond!" My mother stood on the landing, in her nightgown. "Was that Larry on the phone? Why didn't you call me?" Her voice was slurred, the drug beginning to have its effect.

"Mom, I thought you'd be sleeping with that sedative Dr. Joe gave you."

"Why, oh why must you two boys be enemies? What did we do to deserve this? Raymond, you're the eldest, couldn't you have helped him? He said you treated them like dirt! We lost one son, now our remaining boys are strangers, I just don't know why God is punishing us this way....." her voice faded to a whisper and she sank slowly to the floor of the landing.

I took the stairs two at a time and cradled my mother's head in my arms. Her eyes were open and she was breathing regularly.The anguish in her eyes made me curse my brother and his wife for being the prime cause of this pain. What on earth motivated Serena to alienate my brother from me, shattering our parents' last few years knowing that even after Marty's death, their remaining sons were poles apart, enemies, more or less? Was it jealousy, bitterness, or dissatisfaction with Larry as a provider? These thoughts ran through my head as they had done repeatedly during the past few years. I became aware of Dr. Joe kneeling next to my mother and between us we gently lifted her to a standing position.

"Come on, Rosie, back to bed. That tablet will give you some rest," my dear uncle mumbled as we slowly helped her back into her bedroom. As we walked towards the landing he looked at me inquisitively. "You were in another world there, Ray, weren't you? What were you thinking about?"

It all came pouring out in a torrent. I described the continual acidic remarks that had emanated from Serena, about our wedding, and other occasions, and how Larry had reacted to my unwillingness to finance him to his complete satisfaction.

Dr. Joe listened silently, fingering his moustache. "You know my boy, we all did think, when Larry came back to PE originally with

Serena, that is, your mom and dad and I, that he was getting involved with a very strong-willed young lady from a powerful wealthy family. We wondered how easily he would cope with her. What you are now saying bears out our concerns but please, please don't let your parents know I said this. They'd never forgive me."

By now we were back down in the sitting room. I raised my voice from a whisper. "You mean, you aren't all that surprised, the three of you, at what's happened?"

The old man shook his head. "Not really. What you've told me about the nasty side of Serena's character I must admit surprises me but thinking about it, I can see the logic. You've made a great success of your profession in London and live life to the full with your lovely wife and gorgeous daughter while they are battling on several fronts. Her natural competitive nature, which she gets from her father, would generate envy and resentment so she takes it out on you, trying to bring you down in Larry's eyes and he, being a middle child, laps it up."

I grinned ruefully. "That's it in a nutshell! Well, at least it's good to hear that there's some support here for us. Jen and I felt that mom and dad were blaming us entirely for the rift."

Dr. Joe shook his head. "No, they're most certainly not but they do expect you as the eldest, to make some concessions, to try and understand. That's the way with parents, they only want peace between their children. You'll find that one day when you have more kids."

It was my turn to disagree. "I guess that's where the impasse lies. After what Larry wrote about my grabbing Marty's belongings, I don't see any room for reconciliation. I think he was even quite jealous at how close Marty and I were with our interests in music and a sort of rapport that we had. So I don't think the animosity is completely on Serena's side. As for making concessions, until both Larry and Serena make a complete and genuine apology, which I'm sure is unlikely, matters will just have to continue as they are."

The determination on my face and the firm tone with which I spoke left my uncle in no doubt about our position. With a shrug he put on his jacket and walked to the door. "I suppose you know there are many parables in the bible about brothers hating each other?" he said, compressing his lips resignedly. "Cain and Abel, Jacob, Esau, Isaac and Ishmael?"

I nodded glumly.

"But did you also know", he went on, "that your father's father, Woolf, and his brother Louis, never spoke to each other for forty years? They made up only on your grandfather's deathbed, crying bitter tears at all the years wasted in animosity."

With his words ringing in my ears, I watched him walk slowly down the path to his car. I went up to my bedroom and lay flat on the bed, plunging my head into my pillow. I didn't want to know about family feuds or history. All I wanted was for my father to get better and to go back to my loved ones in London.

CHAPTER 34

My father made an amazing recovery. He was out of bed walking around the ward after a week and was allowed home ten days after the surgery. Mr. Van Rooyen was very optimistic in his prognosis. "Abie has many years ahead of him," he told us as we helped pack my father's things into a small suitcase. "All the tests were clear so I don't want to see his face around here for a long time, if ever," he joked.

"Thanks very very much, Doctor," my father mumbled. "And thanks to all the staff here at St. Josephs. They were first class."

"And so say all of us," beamed Dr. Joe. My mother and I nodded our heartfelt agreement, each shaking the surgeon's large hand firmly.

After she had collapsed on the stairs the evening after my father's operation, Dr. Joe and I had managed to calm my mother down and help her back to bed. The sedative did its work after a short while and she slept like a baby. When she woke many hours later she had no recollection of what had happened. Now, nearly two weeks later, she had cheered up considerably and the feud between Larry and I had not been mentioned again. Larry had telephoned several times, although I had not spoken to him, with the good news that Serena was finally pregnant. As my mother sat and listened to my father playing his violin with me accompanying him on the piano it seemed as though both my parents' spirits were now at last on the mend.

Completing a medley of their favourite songs, 'Always', 'Nature Boy', 'It Happened in Monterey' and others, I swivelled round on the old, velvet-cushioned piano stool. "Mom, dad, I guess that it's time for me to get back to Jennifer and Gabriella."

"So soon, Ray?" my mother quavered.

"No, Rosie, he's right," my father said, putting down his fiddle. "He's got a practice to run and a family to support. He looked at me smiling. "You've been a wonderful support to us over all this *tsorris* (trouble) my boy, and your mother and I can't thank you enough. But now it's time for you to get back to London. Have you booked yet?"

I pursed my lips. "Yes, dad, as a matter of fact, I've got a flight day after tomorrow."

He grinned wryly. "So, nu, you'd better make the most of these last few days, you're going back to London winter. Go, take the car down to the beach and do some surfing, at least then you can show off a South African tan to all those pale Limeys!"

I did just that. I drove down to the Pollok beach, spending hours walking on the sand on my own, deep in thought. Past the flat behind the Summerstrand Hotel where Crystal and I had spent those last few idyllic days, then plunging into the heaving surf as if to cleanse and wash away, once and for all, that part of my youth and past. I passed by Rita's Hair Salon which had now grown into a substantial establishment, but resisted the temptation to stop and say hello. Although the New Year was already months old, I had made the resolution to count my blessings for what I had, a gorgeous wife and child, a prosperous way of life, and to erase forever the memory of what I now realised, had been an impossible dream.

At the departure gate, I embraced my parents, still trying to persuade them to make a trip to London. "You haven't seen our home, and I know you love the Theatre. See if you can organise it." I directed my words to my father. "It's time you sold the business to your partners, dad. You've definitely served your time. I spoke to them while you were in hospital. They're keen and you could do with getting rid of the responsibility and the long hours."

He nodded. "Yes, you're right, Ray my boy. I'll speak to the accountants."

But deep down I knew he wouldn't. His work was the lifeblood that kept him going. I shrugged. "Mom, give him a talking to. You both could do with a well-earned retirement."

She nodded patiently. "Yes, all right, Raymond. And you, what you can do for us is try and make *sholem* (peace) with your brother. You know how happy that would make us."

I kissed her lined face on both cheeks. "I love you, mom, but .... well, who knows, maybe time will heal the rift." I said without much conviction. "Don't let's make that the last discussion before I go. Just look after yourself and dad, and start planning to come visit us."

My father interjected firmly. "Ray, my son, that won't happen while my boys are not talking to each other. Make up and I promise we'll be on the next plane."

I shook my head, eyes brimming. "I really love you guys. Write soon, and now that long distance phone calls are cheaper, we can start talking more often."

Shouldering my grab-bag, I turned and with one last wave, strode through the archway towards the enclosed nether world of air travel.

*

My reception at Heathrow Terminal One could not have been sweeter. Jennifer stood holding Gabriella at the railings as I came through and the second she set eyes on me she wriggled free of her mother's grip and hurtled towards me, running straight into my arms. "DADDY!!!!" she squealed and covered me with wet kisses. "We missed you sooooo much!"

My old mini had been replaced on Gabriella's arrival by a Peugeot Estate car. Jennifer did battle with the early morning traffic while I indulged in a long and complex conversation with my daughter, touching on subjects as diverse as her Barbie collection, the horrible boys at the nursery school she went to, and how she just loved Bill and Ben and the Wombles of Wimbledon.

My wife had difficulty getting a word in. "How were your folks when you left, Ray?" she asked, keeping her eyes riveted on the slow-moving traffic ahead of us.

"Not too bad. My dad has done really well, going for long walks and even swimming in the sea. But mom is still a very sad lady, I'm afraid. I guess nothing will ever get her out of the depths of her depression. She goes to the cemetery every Sunday, rain or shine, and just sits there. Having Gaby in the house cheered her up considerably but there was always that faraway haunted look in her eyes."

"Daddy," Gaby snuggled her head into my chest, "did you come on the same aeroplane we did?"

"Well, I'm not sure, baby. It was probably the same kind of aeroplane but maybe not the VERY SAME ONE."

"Ours had a movie and I had earphones on me with music," she said proudly.

"Your mommy said you were as good as gold, and slept for a long time too."

"Yes I did so, and the lady gave me crayons and paper and I did drawings."

"That's very good, honey." I turned and patted her on the head. "Now I want to ask your mommy something, OK?"

"Yes, that's OK by me daddy and I really, really love you."

It took a few moments for the spurt of pure joy to subside, my cheeks aching with the broadest grin plastered all over my face. I turned to Jennifer who was also beaming. "I've been thinking, Jen, that if all is going well at the Practice, we might try and go back to Tignes over Easter. We haven't skied since before Gaby arrived. I'm sure she'd have a ball in the snow. What do you think?"

Jennifer laughed. "My God, you're not bad! Just back from nearly five weeks in the sunshine and you're thinking more holidays! I don't believe it!"

"Didn't I tell you, m'lady, that I gave up religion a long time ago and replaced it with my new philosophy of Hedonism, pursuit of pure pleasure?"

Jennifer shrugged. "Well, I've spoken to the surgery a few times and everything seems to be going well there. The Aussies are frantically busy. It seems there's an influx of wealthy Iranians fleeing from the new regime in Persia after the Islamic revolution and the Shah's removal. They all want their gold crowns replaced with porcelain so the private earnings are really buoyant!"

"Right," I said, with a laugh, "that's settled. I really fancied that place and I remember they had a great nursery ski school for little ones." I turned to Gabriella. "Gaby, how would you like to play with Mickey Mouse in the snow?"

There was no answer. Our little angel was fast asleep.

*

Easter 1980

The same thrill engulfed me as we rounded the last bend in the winding icy mountain road.The majestic snowfields and sadly ultra-modern architecture of Lac de Tignes were a visual contradiction. Concrete apartment blocks were interspersed with wooden Alpine chalets, a haphazard mish-mash. The valley itself, though, surrounded by rugged blindingly white peaks, laced with rocky outcrops like giant canine teeth,was simply unforgettable.

Two months of really hard slog at the chairside just faded into insignificance. A feeling of well-being flooded through me as I watched Gabriella's face light up in childish wonderment as she couldn't make up her mind which way to look.

This time there was no Larry or Serena to dampen our spirits. There had still been no contact, although we had heard that Serena had given birth to a son, Monty, named after our late brother Martin. We'd sent a card but had received no acknowledgement which suited us fine. I did have pangs of regret and guilt at the vacuum existing in the family but the thought of renewing a relationship with Serena stopped us dead in our tracks.

"Daddy, look at all the snow! And look, people skiing!"

"I know, sweetheart, and tomorrow we're gonna get you some little skis to try on, OK?"

We'd booked at the same hotel but had simplified the travel arrangements by flying to Geneva and a bus ride straight to the resort. The manager and his wife were delighted to see us again and we were treated like royalty.

Gaby found her balance on mini-skis almost immediately and, after some initial shyness, especially as most of the nursery instructors spoke only French, was managing nursery slopes easily. Watching her progress with immense pride, Jennifer and I felt confident to leave her with the *Flocons des Enfants* and go off each morning, meeting her for lunch. She was almost reluctant to come away even for the short hour break and rushed back for the afternoon session with hardly a backwards glance.

Jennifer looked at me grinning. "Looks like you got your wish, Dr. Benjamin. You've got a blooming ski-buddy on your hands."

"What do you mean, on my hands?" I retorted testily. "Do you mean to tell me you're not enjoying the skiing same as me?"

"Er..... well..... yes," Jennifer replied guardedly, "But I get nervous when we go too fast. I've told you before, I like being in control."

"But that's just it," I protested, "The key to getting better is to use what I call controlled panic.....when you're going too fast you get out of control. Battle to regain it and you develop the reaction you need. You stop and turn in fear! Gradually it becomes automatic, sort of."

All I got from my beloved wife was a rueful grin!

By the end of the two weeks, Jennifer and I were easily coping with steep red runs and Gabriella had skied with us down a blue run. I had become friendly with a local estate agent introduced to me by the owner of the hotel and was seriously considering buying an apartment.

My wife thought I needed my head examined. "With the mortgages on our house and the Chelsea property, where on earth is the money coming from?" she stared at me incredulously.

"I'm making no decisions now," I said firmly. "But the flat is right by a ski lift, and right at the end of a run so one need hardly carry skis anywhere. Ski in, Ski out. I've got all the details. We'll think about it when we get back to London. OK?"

The idea grew as we made our way back to London. In spite of Jennifer's concerns, I had made up my mind. The brand-new apartment had two bedrooms, two bathrooms, and two magnificent balconies with fantastic views of the frozen lake and a 270 degree view of the mountains. The pound was strong so in franc terms the cost was not prohibitive. The prospect of owning a small part of such an exquisite place gave me a warm feeling. Oh well, I thought as the plane touched down at Heathrow, see if you can make this dream a reality!

The dream was short-lived, however. No sooner had we brought our cases into the house and let Gaby loose up to her room to make re-acqaintance with all her toys, than I turned on the answering machine which was blinking furiously. The first message was a shock. It was from Larry. "Ray, you need to phone Mom urgently. Dad's had a stroke."

I got through almost immediately. My mother's voice was a barely recognisable croak. "Ray, your poor father is back in hospital. He's had a bad stroke and is completely paralysed down one side".

I was just about speechless. Jennifer stood nearby, pale-faced

"When did this happen, mom?"

"Yesterday, after breakfast. He was just out of the house on his way to work when he collapsed. Thank God for Euphemia, she's done a St. John's Ambulance course in Care of the Aged so she knew what to do straight away."

"What does Dr. Joe say?"

"He's right here. You'd better talk to him."

"Hello, Ray," came my uncle's solemn yet comforting voice. "Sorry we always seem to be talking in emergencies these days."

"So, what's the situation? Is dad in Intensive Care?" I stammered.

"Yes, I'm afraid the outlook is not good. They think he had some kind of blood clot or haemorrhage, they're doing tests but his whole right side is paralysed."

"Is he conscious?"

"Barely. He slips in and out of coma. Ray, my boy, I think, if you can manage, you should think about coming out here pretty quickly. Your mother's had just about all she can take. The neurologist doesn't know how much time there is."

I hesitated before answering. "Right.......er....we've just got back but I'll see what I can do." I looked over at Jennifer who nodded her agreement, mouthing the words 'you must go'. Instantly I made the decision. "Tell mom I'll be getting a flight as soon as I can."

"Good boy, Ray. I'll tell her. I've given her some sedatives so she can rest. She's been at the hospital for nearly thirty six hours."

*

It took me just a day to organise the situation at the surgery, just saying a few silent thank-you's to which ever power was behind my good fortune in having two totally reliable dentists to carry the workload yet again.

After some hesitation that evening I made a telephone call to my brother. When Serena answered I resisted the urge to put the phone down.

"Hi, Serena. It's Raymond. May I speak with Larry, please?"

Her voice, full of sympathy, invoked in me a wariness which I managed to suppress as I listened to her. "Ray, I'm really sorry about your father. You're going out there ?"

"Yes," I replied curtly. "Thanks for that. I'm flying early tomorrow."

"Please give your mother our love and tell dad we're thinking of him. Here's Larry."

My brother's voice was sombre. "Hi Ray. Shame we only talk when there's tragedy, isn't it?"

"From what I can gather, they don't think dad has much time left," I said, not wanting to enter into any sort of recrimination or argument. "I'll be there tomorrow evening. I'll keep you posted on what's happening."

There was a brief silence. "I just can't afford to get away right now, Ray. Please tell mom that we're thinking of her and dad every minute."

"Ja, I'll do that. By the way, mazeltov on your son, Monty. We did send a card."

"Oh, did you? I don't remember ever getting anything from you."

'I'm not surprised,' I thought to myself. 'Why don't you ask your beloved wife?' Instead I just said, "Well, we certainly sent one. Anyway, I believe he's a bonny lad. We hear things on the grapevine, you know."

"Thanks. Yes, he's a great little guy."

Another awkward silence. "Anyway, Larry, I have to get going now. Keep in touch."

"Travel well, Ray."

*

The doctors managed to stabilise my father over the first seventy-two hours which are critical in terms of vascular damage to the brain. When I arrived he was able to sit up and speak in a faltering voice from the left side of his mouth. His complexion had a dull grey pallor and the right side of his face hung down helplessly. Yet the blue eyes still held that familiar twinkle in spite of everything and the lop-sided smile he gave when he saw me for the first time made the trip worthwhile.

"Raymond, boychick, so sorry to have to drag you back again so soon," he quavered, a dribble of saliva trickling down the right side of his chin. My mother was amazingly quick with a muslin cloth to wipe it away. She had rallied once she was assured that my father was out of immediate danger and was hovering over him like a mother hen.

In the opinion of the doctors who treated him, the trauma of the anaesthetic for his abdominal surgery could have been a contributory factor for a man of his age but his generally good physical condition had probably prevented the stroke being fatal.

I leaned over and kissed him on his left cheek. "Not a problem, dad. It was an easy decision to make. Who's more important, my patients or my father? No contest."

He shook his nearly bald head sadly. "Wasn't thinking about your patients, Ray. I was worried more about you leaving your two beautiful girls on account of me once again in the space of what, only four months?"

"It's OK, Dad, really," I said reassuringly. "Jen is amazingly efficient at handling things at the surgery and I'm lucky to have two great Aussie guys working there. I'll have to be careful that my patients don't all want to change to them seeing as I'm becoming an absentee dentist. We just came back from a great ski trip. You should see Gaby coming down the mountain on her little skis. Here I've got some pictures."

My father held the photos in his left hand which was shaking so badly that my mother took them from him and held them up for him to see. "What a darling she is, Ray. And she looks so confident on her skis, too."

"Yes, I said proudly. "She came down a blue run with us, only fell once and didn't even cry!"

*

My father came home from hospital two weeks later but was now a dependent invalid. We hired a day nurse for him and between her and Euphemia they managed to do all the necessary things, such as helping him bathe, dressing him and nagging and supervising him to do what the physiotherapist recommended. Larry telephoned every day to keep informed of dad's progress. The main topic of my discussions with Larry, after the medical issue, was how to help manage the transfer of the business to dad's Afrikaans partners.

"Dad showed me the partnership agreement where they had formulated a fixed price for the business, but Piet, the senior partner, said to me that because of the African boycott of white-owned shops, the profits weren't anything like those when they made this agreement so I think there's trouble ahead there," I said bluntly to my brother.

"Does dad know?" Larry asked.

"No," I replied. "We felt he should believe that all was going ahead as planned. Mom's very upset about it though."

"I'm sure she is," came the reply. "So what should we do?"

"I've talked to our lawyers and accountants and they've not been very encouraging. The whole of North End is being bought up by Indian businessmen and as dad owns the property, they feel we should offer the business together with the freehold on the open market."

"Won't his partners be upset? Aren't you breaking the agreement?"

"Well, in a sense yes, but by not being prepared to pay dad his agreed full share as per the document, they broke it first so it's null and void. Dad had always expected that the property rental from the business and the flats above would give them an income after he retired together with the lump sum from his share. That's not going to happen now. They're being obstructive every inch of the way."

After a moment's pause, Larry came back hesitatingly. "Do you think I should fly out?"

I thought for a few seconds. "No, it's not strictly necessary. Dad's condition has stabilised now. Also his advisers can handle whatever we decide with mom. She's being incredibly strong and agrees with me that we should try and sell the whole property, business and all."

"Then that's what we should do," Larry agreed. "But what if Piet and Johan come to visit dad? Won't they want to discuss it with him?"

"They've already been and agreed not to discuss it with him at all, just to pretend that all is OK which they did. The doctors were specific that dad has to be kept absolutely free of stress or hassle."

"How long can you stay on, Ray?"

"Not much more than a week. I'm afraid, but don't worry, he's being well taken care of. Dr Joe comes every day and the day nurse is here with Euphemia. Dad even flirts with the nurse, much to Mom's annoyance but she hides it well."

"Ray....." Larry's voice seemed to fade into a whisper, "Listen, I'm sorry you've had to do all this without me but I'm sure you appreciate my situation. I'm working flat out night and day to bring in fees to pay off my partners..." his voice tailed off inaudibly.

I felt a stab of guilt. "I understand fully, Larry. I'm sure you would have come if you could. Hopefully the situation here will improve and the sale will go through. The main thing is that dad remains uninvolved.

Given his inquisitive nature that's not going to be easy, but mom will just have to tell a whole string of white lies as I've been doing."

"I'd better go, Ray, I'm phoning from the office. Just ......well, thanks....... thanks for what you're doing."

"Don't mention it. I'll be home by the end of the week probably." With that, I replaced the receiver gently.

*

The May chill tainted the familiar Port Elizabeth winds as I said yet another tearful goodbye to my mother and Dr. Joe at the departure gate.

"Thank you, Raymond, so much for coming and helping us over this ordeal," my mother wept. "Your poor father should only know what is happening now with those partners he treated like they were his own sons. But given the way they have behaved, I'm sure we're doing the right thing selling the whole property. Hopefully we'll get a buyer soon. I know that the Indians are the only ones with money to buy these days but they drive hard bargains."

"Don't worry too much, mom," I said, wiping away her tears with my fingers. "The lawyers and accountants will deal with things from here on and we're just a phone call away."

Dr. Joe patted me on the shoulder. "Fly well, Ray, my boy, give love to your lovely wife and daughter from us. Don't worry, we'll look after old Abie like he was royalty!"

I embraced them both then turned and fought my way across the gale-swept tarmac to the aircraft to begin the lonely trip back to London.

Chapter 35

1981-1983 War of Liberation in South Africa. Bomb explosions throughout the country Port Elizabeth Law Courts attacked. Separate parliament for blacks Asians and Coloured races. Boycott of white-owned businesses has major effect on SA economy 1983 After victory in the Falklands, Margaret Thatcher defeats Michael Foot's Labour party.

June 1983 three years later

The telephone rang late on a Monday evening.

"Hi, who's calling so bloody late?" I asked in a tone somewhere between semi-serious and nervous.

"Raymond," came my mother's anguished voice, "it's your father. He's been taken to hospital. He's had another stroke. They don't think he's .... they think he's only got days, it's serious."

I felt cold shivers plunging down my back. "What's happened, mom? He was fine last week when we spoke."

"Yes, I know, Ray. We went to bed early, just lying there, half asleep. Dad sat up, complained of a splitting headache then suddenly fell back unconscious. I got the ambulance straightaway and they've taken him to the Provincial Hospital. The paramedics told me it looks very serious. I'm just waiting for your uncle to come and take me to the hospital. Raymond, I think you'd better come quickly."

Jennifer walked in from the kitchen, alarmed at the expression on my face. "What's happened, Ray? Is it your dad?"

I nodded then resumed talking on the phone. "Mom, I'll try to get on a plane tomorrow. Just be brave, I'll be there as soon as I can." I thought for a moment. "Has anyone told Larry?"

"No, I hoped you'd phone him but if you'd rather not....."

I frowned. "No, don't worry. I'll call him right now. I'll phone you in the morning to find out what's happening and let you know my flight number."

"Thank you, my boy. I know you don't believe but maybe say a little prayer for your poor father, he's been so brave these last few years. Wait a second, I think Dr. Joe's here. I'm going now. I'll speak to you in the morning. "

"Night, mom." I replaced the receiver gently and looked over at Jennifer who was sitting silently now, watching me, apprehension all over her face. "The paramedics said it was a bad one, another stroke."

She nodded. "You knew it was going to happen sooner or later, didn't you?"

"Yes," I mumbled, my voice too strangled to go into detail. "I'll phone Larry now then the airline. It's late, perhaps you should go to bed, its going to be frantic tomorrow."

"No, it's OK, I'll wait for you."

I dialled the number and Serena answered. "Hello, who is this?"

"It's Raymond, your brother in law," I said curtly. "Can I speak with Larry, please?"

There was a short silence. "What's happened? Is it your father?"

"Yes, he's had another stroke, worse this time."

"Oh, I'm so sorry. Hang on, I'll get Larry. Wait a minute, he's just come in from squash."

The minute Larry spoke I could tell that he'd been drinking. "Raymond, wh....wh....what's up?"

"Mom just phoned." I said shortly. "Dad's been taken to the Provincial Hospital after another stroke, a bad one. The paramedics don't think he's got much time left."

"Oh, shit!" came the response. "Is he conscious?"

"No, seems like he's in a coma."

"What're you gonna do?"

"Well, I said to mom that I'd let you know and now I'm going to phone South African Airlines to see if I can get on a flight tomorrow. She needs all the support she can get."

In the background I could hear a brief discussion, with Serena's shrill voice saying 'course you must go'. Larry came back on the phone. "OK, Ray. Will you see if they can get a ticket for me as well? If you pay by credit card I'll sort out the money with you at Heathrow."

"Are you sure, Larry?"

Again came the slurred voice. "Sure I'm sure. Sorry, just came back from the club, had a few too many."

"I can hear that," I said somewhat reproachfully. "Phone me in the morning and I'll let you know what I've managed with SAA."

"Thanks." The phone went dead.

I looked at Jennifer helplessly. "What could I do? He was clearly pissed. More to the point, what on earth are we going to say to each other on a long flight when we've said hardly two words to each other for years?"

South African Airways were very sympathetic and booked us the following evening to Johannesburg, with a connection to Port Elizabeth first thing the next morning. I lay awake deep in to the night unable to sleep.

The past three years had been good ones for us. Jennifer had given birth to twin daughters, Rachel and Leah, on the 12th December 1981 and we had happily decided that that was to be our family. Gabriella was now a flouncing seven year old, with an answer for everything and never-ending questions about anything. The twins were dark-haired and had dark eyes, quite different from their older sister. Gaby took great delight in assisting Jennifer with the new arrivals and now that they were toddling everywhere, had assumed the all-important role of mother hen, supervising and reprimanding at every opportunity.

We knew that Larry and Serena had also had another child, a girl named Miriam but there had been no contact between us until this very evening. I also knew that Larry's partnership had thrived. They were now in smart new offices in Watford so my conscience was pretty clear. My brother had managed to make his way on his own and I was sure it had been the best thing for his self-respect.

In the early hours Jennifer sat up in bed. "Are you still awake, Ray?"

"Afraid so," I replied. "Too many things flying round in my head, I guess."

She cuddled up to me, her warm body a great comfort. "You know, in some ways this may be a blessing in disguise for you and Larry."

"How do you mean?"

"Well, it'll be just the two of you together without his cow of a wife. Maybe you can have a sensible discussion in the next few days. You mustn't try and bad mouth Serena, though, because, whatever we may think of her, that'll put his back up like before. But look Ray, he is your brother, and you've now probably got a bereavement on your hands. Surely this would be the right time to try and patch things up between you?"

I yawned involuntarily. "Yes, you may be right," I smiled in the darkness in spite of the anguish I was feeling, "but I wouldn't bet on any great reconciliation."

Jennifer entwined her fingers in mine. "Are you feeling sad, Ray?"

"Yes, very, but more so for my mom, really. She has dreaded being left on her own since dad had that tumour. Now it looks imminent. For my dad, well, I know he has hated being an invalid, having people help him with everything for the past few years. He's always been so self-sufficient and dignified. I expect he's probably had enough. You know, I can't believe I'm actually saying that."

"It's such a shame, he's such a sweet man." I could see Jennifer's tears reflecting in the half-light from our bedside clock. "I think you should try and get some sleep now."

"OK sweetheart, I'll try." My usual remedy for sleeplessness was to close my eyes and imagine I was skiing down the Grande Motte glacier in Lac de Tignes. I knew every bend and bump in the run and could imagine in my mind's eye the changing vista of the rugged mountains I loved so much. I still cherished dreams of one day having a cosy little chalet or apartment of our own there.

As usual, the technique worked and I woke with the alarm buzzing in my ear. At first, the events of the previous night seemed like a dream then reality crowded in with my beloved wife holding out a large mug of steaming tea.

"Here you are, my love." she smiled. "This is a special consideration as you've got quite a day ahead of you. Gaby and the twins have been awake for an hour already and they want to say good morning." She turned to the open door of the bedroom. "Come on kids, your dad's awake but carefully, he's got hot tea in his hand."

With that all hell broke loose. I drank the hot liquid down in a couple of gulps, burning my tongue in the process, but just in time to prevent a scalding catastrophe as a boisterous little girl and two identical toddlers landed on our bed with a flurry of duvet, pillows and cute nightdresses.

I spent the next half-hour with my children, storing up images to take with me on the long journey I was facing. I kept thinking that my parents had not had enough time with these glorious little creatures, with only pictures to console them and show off to their friends and the rest of the Port Elizabeth family.

Then it was time to face the day. I had patients to see and somehow to explain to my long-suffering receptionist/secretary, Pauline, that I was going to be away again for I didn't know how long. She would have to peruse the appointment book and make a huge number of apologetic calls. As always she responded magnificently and somehow, the hours passed.

The call to my mother had been short and sad. "How are things at the hospital, mom?" I asked, knowing the answer would not be encouraging.

"Not good, Ray. He's holding his own but is still in a coma. They say his heart is strong but he's had a massive haemorrhage. God only knows, first with my son, now my husband. Does he have no mercy?" The sobs came over loud and clear.

"We're on our way this evening, mom, Larry and I. We'll be with you tomorrow late morning, all being well."

"I'm so pleased, my boy. Thank you. You're travelling together?"

"Yes, mom. Jennifer and I are meeting Larry at the airport."

"OK, that's good, maybe you can be brothers again, who knows? And how are your lovely children? Shame, Abie didn't get to see the twins, he carries the pictures of the three of them with him everywhere."

A deep sense of guilt overwhelmed me. Selfishly we had spent idyllic holidays over Christmas and New Year the past few years scuba diving, our newest craze, in the Red Sea and the Maldive Islands, instead of in South Africa, much to the disappointment of my parents. Now, it seemed, it was too late for my father to enjoy his grandchildren in person.

"Never mind, mom. Just tell dad to hang in there. We'll be there in twenty four hours."

"I'm off to the hospital now, Ray. Travel well and give our love to all your girls."

*

We met Larry and Serena at the check-in counter of Terminal One, Heathrow. The tension between us was palpable although, in such sad circumstances each one of us did our best to behave amicably. Larry was now sporting a full beard and Pancho Gonzales moustache, with his hair grown long and bushy, while Serena's face was thinner with her hair clipped short, framing her already severe features. Handshakes and sideways-on cheek-kisses were duly completed with total lack of warmth.

Larry reached into his coat pocket and pulled out his chequebook. "How much was it, Ray?"

"Five hundred and forty pounds, returning two weeks from today but I explained that we may need to change the return date. They were very understanding and said they make allowances for reasons of compassion, bereavement etc."

Larry wrote out a cheque on the flat-topped check-in desk and handed it to me. "Here you are. Thanks." he mumbled, not looking at me directly.

I gave the cheque to Jennifer. "Thanks. Let's get checked in, then I guess we'd better go through. There isn't much time."

Jennifer and Serena stood silently by while we went through the formalities. It was as though four complete strangers had been flung together in a crisis with nothing to say, all wishing the same things, that this was a situation none of us wanted, and that the sooner it was over, the better.

On the other hand, my goodbye to Gabriella and the twins at home had been heart-rending. Gaby had given me a note to her grandpa in her neat joined-up writing, wishing him better soon and their combined hugs and kisses had left me with a deep yawning gulf in my solar plexus. As we walked towards the check-in desk Jennifer clasped my hand tighter than I could ever remember. I realised that the stress of coming face to face with Serena was getting to her.

I returned the pressure. "Don't worry, sweetheart," I reassured her. "Just remember my wise words.... 'this too will pass'!"

She smiled grimly. "I'll try, Ray. But it's OK for you, at least he's your brother. She's like a creature from another world to me. But don't worry, I'll manage. You just help your poor mother all you can."

But now as we said our final goodbyes at the departure gate and Larry and I walked through, waving our respective wives farewell, I found myself hoping fervently that the two women would go their separate ways without actually tearing each other's eyes out.

*

By some ironic twist of fate, Larry and I were upgraded to Business Class so, as the South African Airways Boeing took off, we were seated in some luxury with glasses of champagne to take the edge off our departure.

As we sank deep into the cushioned seats with the acceleration, my brother turned to me inquisitively. "Any idea why we got the special treatment, Ray?"

I shook my head. "No, not a clue, except maybe the late booking and the reason I gave for the trip got registered somewhere in the computer. You know I spoke to mom this morning?"

"No, what did she say?"

"Well, it's not good. The doctors say dad's had a massive haemorrhage, is in a coma and they don't expect him to last more than a day or two at the most."

"How about mom? Was she OK?"

"Pretty tearful, but thankfully, Dr. Joe hasn't left her for a moment. I guess she's been preparing for this ever since he had his first stroke."

We lapsed into silence, there being little to talk about after the prolonged alienation. Business Class treatment meant that we were given superb attention by the stewardesses, our glasses continually refilled with champagne, together with having menus for the sumptuous dinner thrust under our noses.

Larry eventually broke the impasse. "I suppose that you've been under the same pressure as I have, from mom and uncle Joe to patch things up between us?"

I nodded, not saying anything, waiting to see where this conversation was going to lead.

"Well," he prompted, "what do you think?"

I thought for a few moments. "I guess, naturally, they all feel it's very sad that two brothers should be at loggerheads, especially after losing Marty. They find it difficult to understand."

Larry stared out the window at the blackness beyond. "Well, you've always been the one with the answers. What do you suggest?"

I tried to ignore the implication of his remark but in the end felt it better to react straightaway. "What do you mean, I've always had the answers? I've always tried to be fair and brotherly towards you but....."

"Not helping me when I needed help most of all? Is that what you mean by being brotherly?" There was an edge to his voice now, his hands clenching the armrests.

"Larry" I said, trying to keep calm, "I explained to you as clearly as I could what our situation was at the time but, from what I've heard, you've done pretty well on your own. I have to say that hearing about the success of your partnership filled me with great pleasure."

Larry sat back in his seat, a look of confusion on his face. "It appeared to us, Serena and me, that all your promises of help were just empty ones, that you just left us high and dry, to fend for ourselves."

"Larry, that's just not true. We welcomed you here with open arms, organised your flat in Porchester Square, and helped you with the deposit on your house at a time when we ourselves were heavily committed financially. When you demanded that large sum, we just could not stretch ourselves that far. And as time has proved, you've managed brilliantly. Surely you must feel proud that you got to where you are by your own efforts. I would have liked to congratulate you but, well, the letter you wrote with that awful accusation about Marty's belongings was so full of hate and acrimony that we had no option but to say that, if that's how you really felt, then there was no point in having any kind of relationship."

Larry had listened in silence, chewing his lower lip. "Yes, I realised afterwards that that accusation was wrong and groundless but, well, we were having other problems like Serena's not falling pregnant and so I guess, with you guys on top of the world and us getting nowhere......" his voice drifted off into a whisper.

"You know," I said softly, "that I had a long discussion with Dr. Joe when I was in PE after dad had his first stroke. He asked me what it would take on our part to get us back together."

"So what did you say to him?" Larry stared at me directly.

I smiled. "In a way, what you've just said about that accusation, that it was wrong and groundless, was precisely what I told Joe was needed. Just an apology for the remark in the letter, the actual writing of which meant you had time to think about it and the effect it would have, that really hurt me deeply, especially as it was so unfair."

Larry folded his cupped hands under his chin. "You know, Ray, when we came haring back from our cut-short honeymoon, Serena was inconsolable. I mean, I know the circumstances were tragic, but this was our honeymoon, something we had planned and looked forward to for months. Then, on arriving back for the funeral to be told that there was nothing of Marty's that we could have to remember him by just threw both of us into a rage. We didn't say anything at the time because the family was in such grief but....."

I interrupted him. "You must realise that your letter was the first time we'd known about how you felt. Perhaps if you'd said something at the time..." I hesitated, "But even so, Marty was only nineteen years old. What treasures did he have? Maybe mom should have given you his watch, perhaps it was thoughtless of her to give that to Euphemia, but......"

"I guess you're right." Larry said glumly. "Maybe it's best to come right out with things at the time. So where do we go from here?"

"OK, Larry," I placed my hand on his arm, "let me say something to you now as we're levelling with each other. Please take this in the spirit intended." I hesitated nervously then plunged in headfirst. "It has seemed to Jen and I that Serena has a dislike and distrust of us, me particularly. Remarks she makes appear to be aimed at bringing me down a peg or two. I don't say I don't need that from time to time but it accumulated and almost became a vendetta."

Larry shook his head agitatedly, his face visibly reddening beneath the heavy beard. "Now just wait a minute, Ray. Serena's my wife and I won't listen to you badmouthing her under any circumstances."

I held up my hands. "But that's just it, Larry, I'm not badmouthing her, just saying that over the first few months when we were all getting to know each other, she tended to make some quite hurtful and sarcastic remarks. If it had been only once or twice, we might have overlooked it, but she did it quite a lot and it always seemed to be at my expense."

"OK, Ray," Larry admitted reluctantly, "I know Serena's got a bit of a sharp tongue, she's used it on me often enough," he grinned ruefully, "but she means nothing by it, I'm sure. She was very grateful for the way you guys helped organise us at the beginning, but when you refused that loan, together with the problems we were having conceiving, I guess we both just blew our tops."

"Since we're having a frank discussion, what about her parting shot to Jennifer and I, hoping our honeymoon wasn't cut short like hers was, and saying that our wedding was nothing compared to hers in Cape Town?"

My brother looked shocked. "She didn't say that. I don't believe it!"

I held up my hands, deciding it was time to soft-pedal the discussion. "Look Larry, we both heard her remark about the honeymoon and Jennifer overheard her making a nasty comparison about our wedding to one of her friends. But, in any case, if we're all going to try and start again, I think maybe we should draw a line under the past. We can get together, the four of us, when you and I get back from SA, and talk it through. Meantime, we've got a very sad situation on our hands and I've had a lot of champagne so what do you say we try and get some sleep?"

He smiled, one of the old Larry smiles I remembered affectionately from our youth. "Hang on a minute, Ray." He put his hand into his small travelling briefcase and it came out with a photo folder. He held them out to me. "You haven't had the pleasure of meeting our kids, Monty and Miriam."

They were cute children. Monty looked the image of his father, round-faced, curly-haired and a wide grin. Miriam was thinner-faced, but pretty with straight brown hair and large eyes. She looked more like Serena.

"They're lovely kids, Larry. I'm really pleased for you." I pulled out my wallet. "I've got a picture of our three here somewhere. Here we go. Meet Gabriella and the twins, Rachel and Leah."

Larry held the picture for quite a long time. "How on earth did you manage twins? There haven't been any twins in our families that I know of. They're all gorgeous."

"Thanks. Jennifer's grandmother was one of twins," I said, putting the photo back in my wallet. "Hopefully, we can get all of them together soon."

"Yeah, that'll be good." He yawned. "Right, I'm looking forward to a good sleep now. Especially with these comfy seats." Smiling, he pressed the button and his seat went back nearly horizontal. "Goodnight. See you later."

I did the same, and as the seat gently reclined I blew out a long relieved breath. At least Larry and I would be saying farewell to our father on reasonably amicable terms, not as deadly enemies. But my feelings about Serena did not dissolve as easily.

I closed my eyes, took the imagined skilift up to the top of the glacier, and with the gentle vibration of the aircraft adding to the sense of comfort, drifted off into a champagne-fuelled slumber.

*

Wednesday

The view of Port Elizabeth from the air as we made our approach was becoming very familiar. The stopover in Johannesburg had been reasonably short and several relatives had come to spend a few minutes with us in the cafeteria. But I was filled with dread as Larry and I walked across to the arrivals gate. This time there was no joyous welcome for us as previously. We looked in vain for a familiar face and the only one around was my old friend Alec. But it was not the jovial smiling version. The look on his face and the absence of anyone else to greet us told us all we needed to know.

"I'm so sorry, Ray," he said softly as he embraced me in a ferocious bear hug. "Your dad died in the early hours of this morning." He turned to Larry. "Hi Larry. My condolences and I wish you both long life."

As we looked at each other, Larry and I both seemed unable to shed tears. It was as though we had already confronted the loss of our dear dad and anticipated that, even should he still be alive when we arrived, it would be in a comatose state that we would be saying our goodbyes to him.

"Thanks for coming to meet us," I managed to say, choking on my words. "Where's mom? Is she at home?"

"Ja. Dr. Goldberg's with her. They phoned me to ask if I'd pick you guys up."

"How is she?" Larry asked, rubbing his eyes.

Alec gesticulated to a porter to take our luggage to his car. "Tell you the truth, I haven't seen her. Dr. Goldberg gave her a sedative once she'd been to the hospital and seen your dad after he passed away. I think he's looking after her well, you don't have to worry."

"Thanks once again, Alec." I said, clapping a hand on his shoulder.

"From me too," Larry added.

"Ag, man, that's what friends are for, hey, isn't that so? Come on, get in the car. I'll drive you to your folks' house."

*

Our mother was sitting up in bed but fully clothed when we arrived. She managed a faint smile when Larry and I entered the room together. Dr. Joe was sitting by her bedside. Euphemia was everywhere, providing continual cups of tea and biscuits, even though her ebony features were streaked with tears and for once the cheerful giggle was absent.

"So, here you are, my two boys," my mother murmured softly. "It's a shame your poor father couldn't wait for you to say goodbye, but really he wasn't there anymore since this thing hit him Monday evening." She kissed both of us tenderly. "Anyway, he would have been pleased for one thing only, that this stroke brought the two of you out together."

"So what time did they call you?" I asked gently.

"It was about two o'clock in the morning. The hospital staff were very kind. They telephoned Dr. Joe first so he was already on his way here to pick me up and that gave me time to get dressed."

Larry took her hand. "So was the end peaceful?" he asked.

She nodded. "Very. Your father died as he lived, a gentle peaceful man." She smiled sadly. "He looked much better without all the tubes and things that were attached to him before."

"So can we see him?" I looked across at Dr. Joe.

"Well", he responded slowly, "the *Chevra Kadisha*, the Jewish Burial Society take over from the hospital and do the necessary preparations. You'll be able to see your dad in the special room at the cemetery just before the funeral, which they are planning for tomorrow."

*

Thursday

The scene brought back painful memories of Martin's funeral just a few short years before. The Port Elizabeth wind as usual gusted strongly and cold off the sea. The large crowd were dressed in warm coats and gloves and as before, we, the close family were ushered into the Mourners Room and then through to the main hall where our father lay in his coffin, open for us to pay our last respects.

He looked at peace, his face a little artificial, but none of the stresses and strains of living were evident any longer. Larry and I both touched his cold forehead with our fingers then brought them to our lips as a farewell kiss. A nod from the Rabbi and the coffin was closed and draped with the black cloth.. The congregation was allowed in. The silence was pierced by the howling wind outside. Mercifully, the shouts from the convicts in the penitentiary nearby could not be heard inside.

My mother stood dressed in black supported by various cousins and aunts. Larry and I were placed on the opposite side of the coffin. The rabbi conducted the Burial Service in Hebrew. Then, in English, he extolled our father's contribution to the Port Elizabeth community, his charitable efforts and his devout attendance at synagogue throughout his life. "A true *Mensch* (gentleman) in every sense of the word, who was always available to make up a *Minyan* (ten males required to proceed with a service). He leaves behind his adoring wife, Rosie, and his two sons, Raymond and Larry, who have flown here from London."

Then it was time for Larry and I to recite the Mourners Kaddish, "*Yiskadal v yiskadash.......*" after which the double doors opened to the concrete pathway for my father's last journey to the burial site. Poignantly this was located alongside Martin's grave with the top of the tombstone fractured off as was the custom for premature death of the young. According to my father's wishes, and even sadder still, a space had been reserved on the other side for my mother. We stood around the open pit as the Rabbi said further intonations, then once more Larry and I said Kaddish as the coffin was slowly lowered. Shovels were handed to us and we spaded muddy earth on to the coffin. My mother stood beside the gaping hole in the earth, just staring, hands clasped together. Tears came easily now as we turned and made our way back to the main hall for the closing service. The Rabbi announced that prayers would take place at our home each morning and evening excluding the Sabbath.

After our final *Kaddish*, Larry and I sat on low benches with my mother as the congregation filed past wishing us long life in the traditional manner. I was astounded to see so many friends from years past, even Rita had turned up, looking very much the wealthy and glamorous business woman. She bent over and whispered in my ear, "It's good to see you again, Ray. Come down to the salon, we'll have a coffee while you're here."

I nodded, ignoring the suspicious look from my mother. All of a sudden we were on our own in the hall and it was time to make the sad journey back to the house where family and friends were gathering for drinks and snacks as the seven day *shivah* began.

The week passed slowly. Prayers every morning and evening, with Larry and I making *Kaddish* so many times we knew the words by heart. The main topic of conversation concerned my mother's future. Here Larry and I had differences. He maintained that she should come and live in London as soon as possible. Serena had already insisted that she come and live with them. I was concerned that mom would find being torn away from her life in Port Elizabeth too traumatic although I was stung by the subtle unsaid implication that Jennifer and I had not made a similar offer.

My mother, however, was adamant. "This is my home, boys. I visit Marty's grave every Sunday, now I'll visit both him and Abie. It's very kind of you, Larry, and Serena, to make the very generous offer, (I found myself restraining a grimace) but thank you, no. Here is where I'll stay. Hopefully, you'll come and visit with all your lovely children, maybe a little more often than the past few years."

But Larry was persistent. "Mom, your place is in London with your children and grandchildren. Now's the time to start planning to come. What do you say, Ray?" He looked at me pointedly.

I hesitated. "Mom, I want you to know that our house is open to you whenever you want to come. Jen and I have talked this through many times after dad's first stroke. At the same time I know how well-organised your life is here with Dr. Joe at your beck and call, your lifelong friends, the card school ladies and Euphemia to help you. We both feel that making a new life in London at your age might be too much for you, and as you say, you want to be able to visit the cemetery as you do now. But....."

Larry flared up. "Why don't you just come out and say it, Ray, you and Jennifer don't want the additional responsibility! Your lives are too full of luxury holidays and expensive restaurants to be bothered. Isn't that so?"

"No, that certainly isn't so," I retorted, raising my voice. "Don't allow your petty obsessions with our lifestyle to cloud your commonsense. We would do everything in our power to make mom's life in London as easy and pleasant as possible if she chose to come. She knows that. But think about National Health Service, how it fails senior citizens in the UK. I know a lot more about that than you. Can you see mom sitting in an NHS hospital waiting hours for a junior doctor? Even privately she would not have the same access to immediate treatment she has here. She wouldn't drive so how would she get around London? What would she do?"

My brother stood up, eyes blazing. "Petty obsessions! Rubbish!! We don't give a damn about what you do!! Serena would make sure mom was well cared for and I somehow don't see your posh wife taking time to do anything for her." He kneaded his fists together angrily. "Mom, look, I've said my piece. I'm sorry that at this bad time we are fighting but you know we've not spoken for nearly three years. I thought that on the plane Ray and I had made some kind of peace but you can see we're still pretty far apart." He raised his voice several decibels. "I'm going to my room. I've had enough of this!" He looked at me feverishly. "AND MORE THAN ENOUGH OF YOU, RAY!" With that he stormed out of the room.

My mother had been sitting on her low stool, listening to all this with a growing sadness. She shook her head mournfully. "Even as a little boy he used to have tantrums like this. Now the two of you are arguing about me. I already told you both my decision. Ray, I know you and Jennifer would be kind to me if I came. It was very unfair of Larry to say those things. But for the present, your father has left me very quite well off and you were right, my life here is very comfortable. Maybe in a few years things will change but right now I'm staying put. Please go up and make *sholem* with your brother. That would give me more satisfaction."

I shook my head. "Mom, for your sake I would do just about anything but what I won't accept are words against my lovely wife. You know Jennifer pretty well by now and a kinder, sweeter person was never born. Whereas Serena......" I hesitated, "no I'm not going to descend to Larry's level. I think the best thing for me is to go out for a drive. I'll see you later. Get some rest."

I tore down the garden path in a blind rage. A thought now filled my mind with blazing clarity. No matter how much everyone wanted us to mend the rift and resume closer ties as brothers, I could see no possibility now of that ever being possible. Not while Larry flew into his uncontrollable tantrums and was perpetually dominated by his shrew of a wife.

I slammed the door of my mother's Morris so hard I was surprised the aged hinges didn't snap under the impact. My only thought was to get away from the house and smell the cleansing aroma of the sea. The engine of the little car groaned under my violent treatment but made it safely down to Pollok Beach and there I sat, pondering the future.

Chapter 36

After the *shivah* ended, the weekend passed by in an extremely tense atmosphere with Larry and I barely acknowledging each other. Instead of being a comfort to our grieving mother, the obvious schism between us exacerbated her anguish.

Monday morning our family lawyer came to the house to give us the details of my father's will. Larry was leaving the same afternoon while I had decided to stay on for a few days, mainly to be around for my mother but also to avoid travelling back with my brother at all costs.

Lawyer Samuel Leibowitz was a red-cheeked, rotund ball of a man who had advised my parents for decades. We all sat around the dining room table and Euphemia, as usual, provided a sumptuous morning tea. He unpacked documents from a well-worn briefcase and then, adjusting his gold-framed spectacles, placed one sheet in front of him.

"Of course, Abie's Estate will take months to be finalised and accepted by the Master of the Supreme Court as is usual. But as you boys," he glanced first at Larry then at me, "are only here for a short time, your mother asked me to read you the aspects of your father's will as it applies to the two of you." He cleared his throat, fiddled with a ballpoint pen to be used as a marker then ploughed on. "The will leaves the bulk of his estate to Rosie, with amounts to Dr Goldberg and other cousins and a special bequest to Euphemia but I'm not going into all those details now."

Larry and I were sitting on either side of my mother, not for one moment looking at each other. Dr Joe's presence, as always, was reassuring and with the animosity that now existed, something of a guarantee that the situation would not become too heated.

The lawyer shifted position on his seat, took a sip of tea then continued. "As you know, the proceeds of the sale of the property and business in North End did not reach your father's expectations, with the result that he had to revise the amounts he was leaving to you boys in order to make sure that Rosie has enough to support her for the rest of her life. Naturally it will be up to her as to how she bequeaths her estate," he smiled momentarily, "many years from now, we hope, which will be the subject of her will in due course."

By now we were all growing impatient, especially Larry. "Mr. Leibowitz, I don't mean to rush you," he interjected, "but as you know I'm flying back to the UK this afternoon and I still need to complete my packing so if you could perhaps....." My mother shot Larry a reproving look but he appeared not to notice or care too much.

"Yes, yes, of course," the flustered man mumbled. "Sorry, I do tend to ramble on at my own pace sometimes. Well, the amount your father set aside for you two boys amounts to a sum of three hundred thousand rands. This is to be divided as follows: on the basis of the number of your children, Raymond will receive three fifths, that is, one hundred and eighty thousand rands, and Larry will receive two fifths, that is one hundred and twenty thousand rands."

My brother was instantly on his feet. "THAT'S BLOODY UNFAIR! I CAN'T BELIEVE DAD WOULD DO THAT! MOM, YOU SURELY DIDN'T AGREE TO THAT, DID YOU?" he screamed, waving his hands wildly.

Our mother retained an icy calm. "Larry, please, please, sit down and try to behave with some dignity. I know your father believed that the money he left to your two families should reflect the costs of rearing and educating the children and so that is what he felt was right."

Lawyer Leibowitz intervened as Larry sat down smouldering. "There is one other aspect of the will which applies to your sons, Rosie and I think I should read out what Abie instructed me to do."

My mother nodded her assent, giving Larry a withering shake of the head. "Please go ahead, Sam."

With a concerned look towards Larry, Mr Leibowitz looked down and read from the paper in front of him. "Thirteen years ago, I loaned my son Raymond ten thousand pounds which, although the South African Reserve Bank stipulated it should be repaid, we agreed between us would be a gift. Raymond then gave this money in two tranches to Larry, first to help with the purchase of his house and later to assist when Larry bought in to an accountancy partnership which I was pleased to hear had turned out to be very successful." He cleared his throat yet again, blinking nervously. "At Larry's request I then also contributed to his partnership purchase to the tune of a further nine thousand pounds."

My gasp was audible to everyone but I managed to refrain from interrupting. My brother, however, would not look in my direction.

The lawyer read on undeterred. "So that, in order to be fair to Raymond who has transferred my gift to his brother, I hereby instruct you to pay direct to Raymond the rand equivalent of nineteen thousand pounds so that, apart from the bequests to them for their children, I have treated my two sons fairly and equitably." Mr Leibowitz lifted his spectacles on to his bald head which, in spite of the chilly temperature was sweating profusely. "Ahem, that concludes the relevant section of the will."

There was an ominous silence around the table. My brother got to his feet, a look of shock and fury combined on his face. Deliberately and slowly, he pushed his chair back and, ignoring everyone except my mother, shook his head. "Mom, whether you knew about all this or not, is unimportant now. I'm sorry to have to say this when you've just lost dad, but what he's done is grossly unfair. He knew how well set up Raymond is, the luxurious life he and Jennifer live, and how Serena and I have struggled. Yet he leaves Raymond far better off than us to the tune of well over one hundred thousand rands. And he calls that fair. Well, I know what I call it, blatant bloody favouritism!" He paused as if to wait for a reaction which didn't come. "I'm sorry I shouted earlier on but I'm very calm now. I'm going upstairs to finish packing and I'll catch my plane this afternoon."

"Larry!" I interrupted, "I think your behaviour stinks. Mom doesn't need your temper or your hot-headed remarks right now and....... "

"I DON'T CARE WHAT YOU BLOODY WELL THINK! I HOPE YOU CHOKE ON THAT MONEY!" Larry yelled as he flounced out of the room.

"Larry, Larry," my mother called after him, "Come back, let's discuss this, lets......."

He turned at the door of the dining room. "Mom, you know exactly what dad has done. If you want to you can put it right, you have the legal right to do so. I'm going back to London this afternoon to my wonderful wife and family but as far as Raymond is concerned, if I never see or hear from him again it will be too soon!"

He clumped noisily up the stairs to his bedroom. We sat stunned, my mother weeping silently. Dr. Joe and I came to her side trying to comfort her but it was no use. She just held her head in her hands and sobbed.

Mr. Leibowitz gathered his papers and stuffed them in his briefcase. "I guess I'll be going now, Rosie. Joe, Ray, I'm really sorry this all blew up in your faces but then," he smiled apologetically, "I'm just the messenger. I'm sure Abie felt he was doing what was fair. Obviously Larry doesn't think so. Rosie, give me a call in a few days. Finalising Abie's estate will take a long while yet and so if you want to make any adjustments just let me know. Don't worry, I'll see myself out." With that he shuffled towards the front door with Euphemia helping him on with his coat.

"Mom," I said quietly, "You must do whatever you think best. If you want to make up the financial difference I'm happy for you to do so. But please don't ask me to try and make *sholem* with Larry and Serena. In addition to his jealousy and temper, she constantly poisons his mind against me. I'm afraid that our lives will always be separate."

She looked up at me with bloodshot eyes. "And that's the main reason I won't ever consider coming to live in London with either of you. As far as the will is concerned, your father felt he was being just and fair and I must respect that. I'll make no changes. That's how it will stay."

I felt just a bit ashamed at the kneejerk gratification, whirling deep down inside me at that moment. My brother had never mentioned the additional funds he had received from our father to pay off his partners, leaving me to presume he had paid it off by his own efforts. By contrast, I had always been open with him.

Dr. Joe was helping my mother to her feet. "I think Rosie needs some rest. She's had a lot for one morning. Who's taking Larry to the airport?"

"He can get a taxi for all I care," I said, then immediately regretted it. "No, I'll take him, that's if he'll agree. Won't be much of a pleasant drive," I said with a rueful grin.

I desperately needed a break from the house. Once my mother was upstairs resting I climbed into the Morris, fully intending to make my way to the bleak wintry solitude of the beach but somehow found myself sitting outside Rita Coetzee's hairdressing salon. From her main reception position she saw me, and waved for me to come in. Rather than go into the salon packed with women in various stages of beautification, I gestured for her to pop out to the car. After a few moments she emerged. I smothered a gasp of admiration but it must have shown in my eyes. Gone was the fluffy buxom teenager of tight sweaters and cut off jeans. Even when I had seen her at the funeral and *shivah* she had been dressed sombrely whereas the woman who now appeared was an exotic creature, provocatively attired with nothing, so far as her cleavage was concerned, left to the imagination. Rita opened the passenger door and I was assailed by a torrential wave of perfume. She climbed in beside me and planted a full-blown kiss right on my surprised lips.

"Ray, it's so good to see you like this, rather than at funerals or during, what do you guys call it, a *shivah*?" She smiled broadly showing a perfect and, I was professionally pleased to notice, totally natural dentition. "How's it going, buddy?" Looking round the aging interior of the Morris she burst out laughing. "I just don't believe it, Ray, this can't be the same old Morris we went to the drive-in all those years ago? It is, isn't it?"

I nodded with a broad grin. "Sure is. D'you remember that fiasco with you and Crystal sitting in the back seat and Lalla and me getting very frustrated in the front, then........oh, hell..... I remember it so well. That afternoon Alec had instructed Lalla to yawn so that he could put his arm around you and in the middle of the film he asks when is it time to yawn.... I nearly wet myself!"

Rita laughed out loud. "We had planned to show you Jewboys... I don't mean that derogatorily," she added hastily, "that you couldn't just phone up us Afrikaner *meisies* and be sure of a good time, but boy, look what developed between you an' Crystal. That was a turn-up, wasn't it?"

After the hilarious reminiscences we grew quiet, just re-appraising each other. Then Rita's expression became serious. "How are things at the house now? We heard that you and Larry aren't getting on so well. You seemed OK at the shivah though."

Obviously, the rift between Larry and I was common knowledge in Port Elizabeth, but given the essentially small-town nature of the place, it wasn't surprising. "I'm OK," I said, still taking in this new Rita Coetzee image. "I'm mostly sorry for my mom, though. My brother and I sort of made up on the flight over but on hearing my dad's will, Larry behaved pretty badly and she's right on the edge." Then, looking her straight in her bright blue but heavily made-up eyes, I smiled. "But you're looking great, Miss Coetzee. Looks like life is treating you well."

She returned the look, unabashed. "No, can't complain. Salon's going great guns, got five stylists working for me now and a staff of fifteen altogether. Thinking about doing an overseas trip one of these days soon."

"That'd be just great., Rita. I..., er.... we'd insist you stayed with us in London, no arguments, you hear?"

Rita grinned mischievously. "Would that invitation include a certain lady of your past acquaintance with whom I'm planning to tour Europe, a Mrs. Crystal du Toit?"

I was momentarily speechless. "Oh, ...mmm...... well that might create some complications........!"

Rita placed her hand on my knee. "And with me on my own, there'd be no complications?" she laughed flirtatiously, then looked at her watch. "Oh, god, I'd better get back, someone's waiting for my opinion on what colour her latest streaks should be. Listen, Ray, I'm free later this afternoon. Why don't you drop in for a drink? I'd love to show you my super duper pad overlooking the beach." She opened the door and looked back with an innocent expression. "We're old friends, right? No harm in us having a drink together, is there? Looks like you could do with a bit of cheering up. Besides, we've got a lot of years to cover. Say about four-thirty, I'm Flat number 907, Marine View, just past the Summerstrand Hotel. OK?"

I was so taken aback by her directness, all I could do was nod and she was gone, with a wave and a further whiff of intoxicating scent. Licking my lips I could still taste the fruity flavour of her lipstick.

*

"I'll drive you to the airport, Larry," I said over lunch.

"There's no need. I'll get a taxi."

My mother intervened. "That's silly, Larry. Whatever you two feel about each other, at least when I'm around try and behave like brothers, for my sake."

"Sorry mom. You're right, of course." Larry wiped his mouth with his napkin and stood up. "Ray, the flight's at five o'clock," he said icily, "so I need to be there at about four fifteen."

"That's fine by me," I replied, as he left the room. Fifteen minutes was more than enough time to get to Rita's flat. The tiniest speck of guilt was creeping insidiously into my mind. A tete-a-tete with Rita in her apartment, just the two of us? What on earth was I getting into? Then another voice surfaced, from a more rationalising source. ('Why imagine anything more than an innocent drink?') First voice answered instantly. ('Because ol' buddy, we saw that look in her eye, and we know a predatory female when we see one.... don't we?')

With this debate raging in my head, I noticed my mother staring at me with a concerned look. "Are you all right, Ray? You look a million miles away."

I flushed guiltily. "Well, actually," I lied, "I was six thousand miles away, thinking about Jen and the girls," ('you bloody liar',) said first voice, ('you should be ashamed of yourself!') "and what they'd be doing around now," I finished weakly.

"Yes, I'm sure they must be missing you as much as you're missing them. Never mind, you're going back when, in four days time?"

"Ja," I said sadly. "I'm really torn between wanting to help you over this difficult time and getting back to all my girls. Still, I think that although the estate settlement is a long way off, dad left you pretty comfortable, didn't he? And with Dr Joe around, and Euphemia, you're doing OK, aren't you?"

She smiled sadly. "I suppose so. Somehow I wish I wasn't as strong as I am. In spite of Dr. Joe fussing round me, I know I'm like an ox. I think it would have been better if your dad and I could have gone together."

"Mom, that's rubbish. Don't forget you have five grandchildren whom you adore and who love you to bits. I know that we could and should have come more often. Somehow scuba diving and skiing just tempted us away. I'm really sorry but I promise you that we'll come out more often and let you spoil your grand-daughters rotten. So no more talk like that, OK?" I leaned over and kissed her lined forehead.

She gave a smile. "Thanks, Ray. I guess it's quite common that the men folk die before their wives but your dad was pretty fit, you know. The doctors said that he could go on for years. He may have had a bad reaction to the previous general anaesthetic but there's no point in thinking that way now. I've just got to join all the blue-rinsed widows at the bridge club and the rummy school and make the best of it."

"That's more like it, ma, you've got to think positive," I said smiling gently. "I'm just going up to see if Larry's ready. It's nearly three thirty." I left her sitting at the dining room table staring blankly out the window.

Rubbing my chin I decided I needed a bit of a shave so got out my electric razor. Watching myself in the mirror I kept thinking about this visit to Rita's with growing anxiety, at the same time stifling the earlier voices. I was merely an old friend having a drink in mid-afternoon with someone who had been very supportive in my young days, that was all. Wasn't it????

With that thought uppermost, I splashed on some aftershave and made my way downstairs where Larry was waiting, suitcase packed, ready to go.

The journey to the airport was made in silence as there really was nothing more either of us wished to say to each other. I had considered taking him to task about his evasion regarding the money, but decided there was no point at all, it would just degenerate into another slanging match, I dropped my brother at the Departure entrance. We nodded the briefest of goodbyes and I was on my way to Summerstrand.

Rita lived in the top flat of a luxurious modern block overlooking the Bird Rock Drive, scene of many clandestine meetings with Crystal.

I took the lift up to the ninth floor and pressed the bell. "Coming!" I heard from inside. The door opened and there was another surprise in store for me. Rita was now loosely clad in a sky-blue Japanese-type kimono, barefoot, with her blonde hair hanging loose, shoulder-length. "Hey, Ray, welcome to my little private paradise! Come in, get your jacket off." She grabbed me by the elbow and guided me through a spacious hallway into what could only be described as a majestic combination living-dining room. The entire front consisted of glass sliding doors onto a large terrace. As she slid one panel open, the blast of wintry wind nearly blew us back indoors. "You've just got to take in the view then we'll go straight back inside. It is our winter, you know," she said cheerily.

The view was truly magnificent. From St. Croix Island across Algoa Bay round the coast line to Port Elizabeth City skyline and harbour, past oil tanks in Southend with its picturesque minarets, on to golden-white sandy beaches, Kings Beach, Humewood and Pollok Beach right in front of Rita's building. To the right one could see the end of Cape Receife with it's forlorn lighthouse .

"Woweee!!" I exclaimed. "Just unbeatable!! No wonder you call it your little paradise. A gorgeous pad for a gorgeous young lady!"

Rita smiled. "Why thank you, Dr Benjamin. I love the 'young lady' bit especially. Come over here, have a glass of wine with me. She led me across the lounge to a deep L-shaped leather couch in front of which was a large glass coffee table. A bottle of Boschendal, a well known South African white wine stood cooling in an ice bucket with two glasses. Rita poured the wine and handed me one, the glass properly cold to the touch. "Cheers, Raymond! It's lovely being able to spend some time with you away from all the hassle you've been through."

I raised my glass. "I'll drink to that, Rita. I'm grateful, not only for your coming to the funeral and the *shivah*, that was really appreciated, but also for a long time ago, all the risks you took helping Crystal and I. Seems like ages past, doesn't it?" I took a deep gulp of the cool fruity liquid. I looked across at Rita as she bent over refilling my glass. The front of her robe opened to disclose her sumptuous breasts. I tried unsuccessfully to avert my gaze, managing merely to lock eyes with my hostess, who, not self-conscious in the least, left the garment as it was.

She laughed. "Am I making you nervous, Ray?"

"Not at all, just totally appreciative," I replied with a grin.

"Would you mind if I came and sat next to you?"

"I'd be delighted to share the view with you, my dear," I drawled, reviving the old Ray Milland act.

. Rita started to giggle uncontrollably. "Oh, my god, that voice, that American movie star accent, that brings back memories, big time." She placed her hand on my arm. "You may not have any idea, Ray, how much that act of yours creased us in the old days. You were so unlike all the other local boys. I could see what Crystal found so irresistible in you."

"I just used it when I was tongue-tied, it sort of helped being another person, I could behave differently," I said modestly, wondering what to do about her hand which was slowly caressing my arm.

"She was so mad for you, you know, I don't think she ever got over your time together."

"What's her situation in America like now? I replied to a letter I got from her but since I got married I didn't hear again."

"Crystal's a very successful lawyer now in Philadelphia. She flies all over the country and has a lovely apartment. No special men in her life at the moment. She says she's too busy."

"I'm pleased to hear she's done well. Took a lot of guts to do what she did. Give her my regards when you write." I paused for a moment. "And what about you? Any men in your life?"

She shook her head "Nah, nobody special. Like I told you before I like my freedom. I 'spose if a really knockout guy comes along then maybe I'd think about getting hitched. Right now I'm happy just playing the field like all you guys did in your bachelor days." She took a sip of wine. "You know, I'm sorry you didn't bring your wife in to meet me in the salon when you were here last time. She sounds nice, what's her name, Jennifer, is that right?" Slender fingers were now slowly unbuttoning my cuff.

"Ja, Jennifer," I said, reaching forward with my other hand to take another gulp of the delicious wine.

Rita did the same, clinking glasses with me. "Here's to old friends, here's to the good old days." She sipped her drink slowly, her eyes never leaving mine. "You know, Ray, I always wondered what it was like between you two, the sex, I mean. I mean, Crys never gave any details, just said it was just about the only time she ever really enjoyed being with someone. Do you mind my asking?" She hesitated momentarily, fingers exerting pressure on my arm. "I suppose, I was such a pivotal factor in your affair that I felt cheated somehow, that I never had the delicious low-down!" She laughed languorously, flicking her long blonde hair away from her face.

I watched as her hand crept up my sleeve, caressing my forearm. "I guess it was because it was the first big love affair of our lives, for me at any rate. We were so young, everything was so exciting. The risks we took made it seem like nothing like that had ever happened to anyone else. I don't know for sure about Crystal, she certainly seemed more experienced than I was at the time but…" I took another deep slug of wine, "she did tell me I was a fast learner!"

"You bet she was more experienced," Rita giggled. "She had a little fling with a French guy the year before you who knew a thing or two. But there was no real love itself with him, not like with you. She told me all the graphic details about him, never a thing about you and her."

"And Jimmy McEwan? Alec said Jimmy had gone all the way with her."

Rita shrieked with laughter. "That imbecile! He was the number one fumbler. No, Crystal and he went steady for a while but nothing much happened, then this French guy came along. That was very hush-after hush, and after him, you, Mr. Ray Milland. You were, for her, a big first, except for her ox of a father spoiling it all."

She had now moved close to me on the couch. Her perfume, mixed with the wine aroma on her breath, made a heady mixture. Suddenly her lips found mine, her hand left my elbow and was inside my thigh, perilously high up. There was contact everywhere, her tongue pressing deep inside my mouth, her breasts against my chest, and her legs began to swing over mine, a knee gently at first, then insistently pushing my legs apart.

I was uncertain whether I wanted this or not. What I did know was that my body was reacting involuntarily, my hands were inside her kimono, rubbing her large already erect nipples, my tongue was as busy as hers, and my nether regions were hardening as her exploring hand found me.

"Ray," she whispered in my ear, tongue flicking it like a serpent, "Ray, I know what you're thinking, you're thinking wife, Jennifer, you may even be thinking Crystal, but listen, let this just be us, just for now, just the two of us, just this once." She stood up, her gown wide open now, revealing her pendulous breasts in all their glory, plus a tiny bikini covering just enough. She held out her hand. "Come, Mr Movie star, I haven't shown you my bedroom yet."

I stood up somewhat bent over, aware of my state of excitement, also that my fly was already undone. I looked up at Rita, whose mouth was open, panting. I half-walked half-staggered after her into the bedroom, which was already darkened, shades pulled down. (My Jiminy Cricket conscience muttered in my subconscious ear.... 'god, this doll was sure of herself wasn't she?') Rita pulled me towards her as she sat on the edge of the bed and began to undo my trousers. I stood there allowing this all to happen as if I were a dichotomous personality, my mind and morality being somewhere distant while my body was........ suddenly she took my erect penis in her mouth. That was the moment when mind and body became one again. I pulled away and kneeled on the floor in front of her.

I clasped her face between my hands. "Rita, I don't think I can do this. I........I'm just feeling, I don't know what I'm feeling. I know I want you, my body wants you, you can tell that without my saying so but.......but......."

"Feeling guilty?" she smiled gently. "It's OK. It's fine. Please don't worry. I half expected that but listen, I'm a person who understands, heaven knows I've been around. And one thing I know is that a one-off experience with someone one genuinely likes and trusts can be wonderful." She moved onto the bed, pulling me with her. "Come lie with me and just talk. I promise we won't do anything you may regret but whatever we do, it will remain our secret, that I promise you faithfully." She patted the bed next to her. "Come and lie next to me, take those trousers off, they look funny round your ankles." She began to giggle. Against my better judgement I did as I was told, removing shoes and socks as well.

That was the moment when I should have run. But as I lay there with this beautiful woman caressing me, whispering about old times, wanting nothing from me but a few stolen hours I began to think, 'what the hell, what's the harm, after the last few hellish weeks, perhaps an uncomplicated experience was a sensible antidote.' Once more, my reverie was interrupted as I felt Rita's hands on me, gently caressing me to hardness.

There was now no resistance left in me. Nor any inhibition whatsoever. Two lonely beings became totally enmeshed, in as many original and acrobatic ways imaginable.

She cried and moaned, stimulating me to greater effort. Eventually we lay drenched, side by side, breathless and exhausted.

Rita rolled herself right on top of me and crushed my mouth with hers, her tongue penetrating deep. She looked into my eyes as she took a deep breath. "No regrets, Raymond?" she murmured with a small almost embarrassed smile.

I actually meant what I said but only for a moment. "No, not at all." This despite the gnawing feeling deep down that I was kidding myself.

"I'm pleased. Now at last I know what Crystal was raving about!" She gave a raucous giggle then we were both laughing, friends and now secret lovers even if only for one night, or rather afternoon.

As we said our goodbyes at the door of her apartment, she looked up at me wistfully. "How long are you still here for, Ray?"

"Three more days. I leave Thursday," I replied.

"If..,if you want to do this again, I'm free Wednesday afternoon."

I hesitated."Do you?"

"Yes, very much," she whispered.

I hesitated again. "Can I call you?" I said, feeling a mixture of guilt and amazingly a tingle in my loins.

Disappointment flashed across her face, disappearing quickly. "No probs, lover boy. Drive safely." She stood on tip toe and gave me a long open-mouthed kiss, then slowly, reluctantly opened the door and let me out.

The drive back to the house of my parents passed in a state of total turmoil, exhaustion and remorse in equal measures. It was fortunate my brother had left because he would certainly have suspected something when I returned home quite late, with dinner ready to be served.

"Sorry, mom, Euphemia, I met some old friends and we had a few drinks. Time just flew. Everything OK here?"

"Yes", my mother said. "Thanks for taking Larry. Got off OK, did he?"

"Yes, mom. He just asked to be dropped at Departures. We didn't have much to say to each other."

"No, I'm sure you didn't. What an absolute tragedy. Euphemia!" she yelled, "You can serve the dinner now!"

I was pleased to hear the familiar dictatorial tone returning to my mother's voice. It surely meant she would somehow manage her life competently.

After dinner I went to bed early which suited my mother very well. I lay reading and thinking late into the night, conjuring up images of my darling wife, Jennifer and our three little girls but the vision kept kaleidoscoping with blurred pictures of large rose-red nipples, long blonde hair and even Crystal's disapproving features appearing from time to time. Eventually I fell into a sort of contorted, punctuated sleep, forcing myself to think snow and mountains, banishing guilt to the furthest extremities.

Chapter 37

Tuesday morning

"Massa Raymond, telephone for you," Euphemia yelled up the stairs. I picked up the extension on the landing.

"Hullo, daddy," came Gabriella's delicious little girl voice. My heart melted instantly.

"Good morning my sweetheart, how are you? I'm missing you sooooo much! Are you looking after your mummy and your little sisters?"

"Yeth daddy. Howth grandma?"

"Grandma's fine, honey. I'm looking after her very well."

"When you coming home, daddy?"

"Well, today's Tuesday, tomorrow's Wednesday and on Thursday I'm going in the big aeroplane so I'll be home Friday morning and I'm gonna bring you all lovely presents. OK?"

"OK daddy. Hereth mummy....."

Jennifer's voice filled me with longing. "Hi, Ray, how's it going? How's your mom?"

"Not too bad, Jen. She's beginning to argue with Euphemia and that's always a good sign." I could hear her laughter 6000 miles away. "How are the kids? Gaby sounds wonderful. I just can't wait to hug all three of them."

"They're fine, the twins tend to wake each other up quite early and then Gaby hears them so that's the end of my night's sleep but the au pair is good and plays with them for a while. So......you're coming back Thursday night?"

"Yes. I'm arriving Heathrow Terminal One, Friday morning at eight thirty. Can you book me a cab?"

"Will do. Have you had any more discussions with your mom about the will?"

"No, she's decided to let it stand as it is. Really I've no sympathy for Larry. He behaved like an idiot and his evasion about dad's money was just infuriating." I paused for a moment. "Jen, how are things at the surgery? And our tenants?"

"No real problems, slight leak in the kitchen in Chelsea but Pauline got a plumber pretty quickly. Surgery's going well. Basically you've hardly been missed!" She gave a chuckle. "Except for us, of course and we're managing pretty well!"

I frowned into the phone. "Oh, is that so? Well, you know I can always extend my stay, the South African summer's not so far off."

"You're kidding, its months away yet. The weather here is just beautiful right now. Blue skies, and hot. But, seriously, hon, I miss you, and the kids ask every day 'when's daddy coming home' so you'll be receiving a pretty rapturous welcome from all of us, and well, you know what you'll get from me."

I swallowed hard, a sour taste in the back of my throat. "I'll remember that, my darling. Say goodbye to the girls for me."

"No, they want to say good bye themselves, now come on you three, here's the phone, say 'see you soon, daddy'."

"SEE YOU SOON DADDY! BYE BYE!"

I put the phone down and returned to my room, filled with self-loathing. What had possessed me to expose myself to Rita's obvious intentions? Was it vanity, the male priapism that convinces a man that he is irresistible? Or was it a hankering after the lost love of my youth, that by allowing myself to be bedded by Crystal's closest friend, I was somehow drawing closer to the unforgettable experience of my juvenile sensuality?

Whatever the diagnosis, I determined there and then to cancel the arrangement with Rita for the following afternoon. After speaking with my beautiful, sexy and loving wife, what on earth was I looking for? And what about the sweet voices of my daughters, longing for my return?

Was it an act of insanity to soar nine floors for a further adventure in sexual gymnastics which had no basis in affection, merely animalistic pleasure–seeking, a genital eruption which one would regret almost as soon as it had occurred?

('Yes, but don't bluff yourself, you loved every minute you spent with her, didn't you?') came that persuasive voice. ('What harm did it do anyone? Who would ever find out?')

"That's not what this is all about," I said to myself in the bathroom mirror. "It's me who would know, and me who would feel that I had transgressed, been unfaithful. I'm just not prepared to do that so just get lost and don't start on me again. I'm cancelling, first thing after breakfast."

"Massa Raymond," from Euphemia downstairs. "Your breakfast's ready! The madam's called you twice already. Who youse talking to anyways up there? Yourself, oh my god, madam, your Raymond he talking to hisself up there, heh, heh, heh!" she confided to my mother with an accompanying cackle.

I went down the stairs smiling. "Don't you worry yawself 'bout me none, Euphemia," I said, mocking her accent, "I'se often be talkin' to mahself in de mirror, gotta have someone clevah to be talkin' to once in a while, does you unnerstan? I ain't plumb off mah rocker jes yet!"

It was refreshing to see both our ancient cook and my mother burst out laughing at my awful Bantu accent. I sat down at the table to be confronted by Euphemia's gargantuan breakfast, French toast, Matabela porridge, fresh orange and guava juice.

*

Later that morning I dialled the number of the salon. "Hair Today, Gown Tomorrow, Rita's Beauty Salon, can I help you?" came the broad Afrikaans accent.

"Is Miss Coetzee there please? It's a personal call," I whispered into the mouthpiece.

"Nah, sorry. Rita's not in till twelve o'clock today. Can I say who's calling?"

"No. I'll call back after twelve," I said hurriedly and put the phone down.

Twelve o'clock came and went. Dr. Joe came round to see my mother , and we became involved in a discussion about the possible sale of the house which was now far too big for her on her own. A residential complex with frail care for the elderly on Park Drive near St. Georges Park Cricket Stadium was my mother's preference and we decided, as soon as a unit became available for rental, she would move and put the house on the market. Then lunch was served and when Dr. Joe finally left it was well past three o'clock.

All through lunch I had engaged in a silent mental tussle with myself. Cancelling Rita would look like the act of a coward, yet going would certainly lead to a repetition of the titanic sexual congress we had been embroiled in the day before. For an hour I busied myself reading through the papers our lawyer had left with me relating to my father's will.

Then just after four, I picked up the phone. This time Rita's familiar voice answered. "Hair today, Gown tomorrow, Rita's Hair Salon. Can I help you?"

"I think you helped me more than enough yesterday afternoon"!

After a stunned silence she recovered. "Raymond you bugger! How did you know it was me? You took a chance, didn't you? "

As in times gone by, Ray Milland came to my rescue. "Throughout my life, my dearest Rita, I always was a chancer, a gambler relying on instinct, and something deep inside told me it was your sensual voice I was hearing."

That throaty giggle came over loud and clear. "You are such a bullshitter, Dr. Benjamin, but God that voice does bring back memories! How's things? Am I gonna see you tomorrow?"

I paused for a moment, swallowed, then in full vocal disguise, took the plunge. "I'm terribly sorry, dearheart, but the entire family are coming round tomorrow to say their farewells and it's likely to go on all afternoon. So, very sadly, I must decline. However, what occurred between us yesterday will always remain in my fondest......."

"Oh, enough already, Ray!" Rita was shrieking with laughter into the phone. "I didn't think it was gonna work out anyway. But not to worry. Yesterday was a real unforgettable experience!"

I breathed a sigh of relief. "For me too, Rita. You have no idea what a state I was in after all the hassle here with my brother and the will, etc. Our little party, shall we call it that? was the ideal antidote.

Please let me know when you plan to come to London and send love to Crystal when you write. Stay as sweet as you are!"

"It was truly lovely, Ray. I shall treasure our little secret deep in my memory chest. Travel well. *Totsiens, ou maat.*"

As I replaced the receiver I felt an unburdening, as if what had transpired between Rita and I had been a salve on the wounds of the past weeks, a warm emotional exchange between two people with a long history of friendship and connivance which had flared for those brief moments into a raging furnace of desire and now would subside into glowing embers of our shared memory.

*

Dr. Joe and my mother drove me to the airport. During the past week I had begun to feel that she had regained her confidence to deal with living on her own. I cursed my brother time and again for initiating the horrendous scenes so adding to her anguish. In a way, though, I was pleased that he had shown his true colours which in turn absolved me of much of the blame for the breakup.

Now the time had come for me to go through to departure and I hugged her close. "Mom, I think you've been immensely brave and I hope that my being here has helped. We'll be planning to come out at Christmas with the girlies as I promised so it's only a few months away. I've asked an estate agent here in PE to let me know the minute anything comes up at Carriageway Estate and then we'll help you move. Just keep up all your activities, don't hide away at home. I know your friends won't let you."

"Thank you, Raymond, I don't know what I would have done without you and Joe here." She kissed me hard on both cheeks then dabbed her face with a tissue.

I turned to my dear uncle who had seen us all through so much torment in the years that had passed. "Dr Joe, we owe you big time. You've been at mom and dad's side every important moment. I can't thank you enough. You are truly a wonderful friend." I embraced him and patted him on the back.

Dr. Joe for once was without many words. He kissed me on the cheek and I felt the rasping bristle of his beard. "Go well, Raymond. You've been a fantastic son to your folks. Fly well and give love to your girls, all four of them."

"And from me too," my mother said as she waved sadly, watching me heading for the departure lounge.

*

Whether my title of Dr. on the flight booking had anything to do with it was not my concern. I meekly accepted the upgrade to Business Class yet again and settled back in comfort for the long twelve hour flight from Johannesburg to Heathrow, London. Once again I was plied with champagne and constant attention, served a meal with real china and stainless steel cutlery.

My mind was fraught with guilt and indecision. In all the years we had been married, nothing like this aberration, for that is what it now seemed to me, had ever occurred. Temptations there certainly had been. A Dental Surgeon in one of London's most glamorous locations was bound to experience those, but to have pursued any of them when I was totally besotted with Jennifer was beyond logic.

Fully wined and dined, I pressed the recline button, lay back with earphones eliminating the roar of the engines, and a black mask to shut out the dim lights left on as the Boeing nosed it's way northward over the dark continent of Africa.

In spite of attempts to block out extraneous invasion of my mindset, I kept coming back to my major element of concern. Jennifer and I had always been strictly honest with each other from the beginning but neither of us had pried much into our earlier life. I knew she placed great store in fidelity, the lack of which had been a factor in her divorce. I also knew that she was very much a realist, with friends who had not kept their vows, yet still stayed together with their spouses. So my dilemma was this........ mention Rita and own up to the single afternoon delight, or completely consign the episode to the furthest recesses of my conscience?

With these thoughts whizzing round in my head, I must have slept at some point because I was suddenly awakened by a hand gently nudging me on the shoulder. I shook my head, then realised why everything was black and feeling like an idiot, pulled the blackout mask off my face.

The smiling face of the stewardess hovered above me. "Sorry to wake you, sir, but we are serving breakfast."

I could hardly hear her then felt the wires connecting to the earphones under my chin which I hastily pulled off. "Sorry," I said sheepishly. "What's on offer?"

"Ham and Cheese omelette or bacon sausage, tomato and mushroom."

I chose the bacon, having been starved of anything non-kosher for some three weeks. After consuming the meal hungrily I set about getting myself in some sort of order for the impending arrival at the ungodly hour of six-fifty on a Friday morning.

The grey skies of London were a stark contrast to the winter sun of South Africa but somehow, after the sadness and friction of the past weeks, I was more than happy to be back in my adopted country.

The taxi-driver with my name on a placard was easily located and within an hour we pulled up outside No 5 The Lane. Three tiny faces were glued to the window by the front door and as the door opened I was greeted rapturously by a hurricane of little girls. "DADDY! DADDY! DADDY!!!!"

It is no mean feat lifting three children in your arms while carrying a suitcase in from outside but I managed somehow.

Jennifer stood patiently in the background awaiting her turn. "Welcome home, my husband. I've missed you." With three giggling infants hugging our legs we managed a semi-passionate kiss and embrace and then the door was closed behind me and I was home amongst my loved ones.

*

Once I was back in my comfortable life with wife and children any thought of a confession of any description simply vanished. What had transpired, I told myself, was part of another world, another place, a throwback to my youth and had no place in my life now. Any idea of giving Jennifer cause to mistrust me in our future together simply disappeared. I was sure that the small voices of my conscience agreed with the pragmatic decision.

*

Several weeks later, I was asked to play team squash for my club against a team from Watford, Hertfordshire. On arrival in the changing room, the first person I bumped into was none other than my brother,

Larry. Stunned and amazed, my first reaction was one of greeting. "Hi, Larry, what a surprise! Are you playing for Watford this evening?" I asked.

To my astonishment he looked me straight in the eye, turned on his heel and walked out of the room. I was left standing open-mouthed.

Moments later, the captain of our team, Roger Terrell, walked in. "What's up, Ray, you look positively gobsmacked?"

I hesitated momentarily, considering what to say. "Rog, have you got the playlist for the match tonight?"

"Yes, why?" he asked, puzzled.

"Who am I down to play?"

He looked at a team sheet, shaking his head in confusion. "Oh, that's funny, you're due to play Larry Benjamin, number four. Isn't he your brother?"

I scratched my head, then came to a decision. "Rog, we have a bit of a situation, we're not on the best of terms right now. I think it would be better if you played me at number five or three."

"Oh," he replied with raised eyebrows, then smiled. "A brotherly tiff, hey? That might make for a great match!"

"No." I said firmly. "I don't think so. He just turned his back on me. Playing him would not be a good idea."

"OK, sorry to hear that," Roger said. "I'll move you to play at five. I'll let the other skipper know." He walked towards the door.

"Thanks, Rog. Much obliged."

Five minutes later he was back, grinning. "Funny thing, your brother just asked his captain to play him against someone else as well."

I laughed bitterly. "Well, there you have it in spades. What's been decided?"

"Larry will stay at four, you'll play five. OK?"

"Perfect by me," I said, getting into my togs, then making my way to the glass-backed competition court with its four tiers of seats for spectators.

The five matches went on for just over two hours. I was first on and won easily as my opponent was a late and somewhat inadequate replacement for their regular player. Then Larry came on and made short thrift of our number four who should have been playing at five.

Throughout the matches, my brother studiously avoided eye contact with me and this continued through to the shower room afterwards. The icy atmosphere between us became even more obvious during the supper following the match which our club managed to win three games to two. Larry made certain he was sitting furthest away from me on the long table.

This suited me fine. By the end of the meal, when the serious drinkers got into their stride, I made my excuses and was preparing to leave when Roger gestured for me to come over to the bar where my brother was standing drinking.

"Hey, you two," Roger said, swaying slightly, "We can't allow this nonsense to go on, not between two squash-playing brothers. What do you say, shake hands and make up?"

I stood embarrassed as Larry, who had clearly drunk several pints of beer by then, looked blearily at me, a cold expression on his face. "I've got fuck-all to say to him, why don't you mind your own fucking business?"

Roger, a large man and never one to tolerate obscenity, grabbed Larry by his shirt. "You are totally out of order, mate. Whatever your gripe is with Ray, we don't accept language like that in this club. I want an apology right now." He was tightening his grip on my brother's collar, nearly choking him.

"Roger," I interceded, pulling him away, "Let it be. Larry's had quite a bit to drink. Let him go, I don't need any apology, I was on my way out anyway. It was a nice idea but really, there was no point."

"OK, Ray, if you say so," Roger said, relinquishing his grip on Larry's shirt. My brother glared first at me, then at Roger, then, straightening his collar, slowly turned his back. We watched as he lurched back to the bar where he picked up the pint he had been drinking and drained it in one gulp.

"Thanks, Roger," I said. I nodded to the remaining players and made my way out with a heavy heart. There was now no doubt in my mind at all that Larry's public display added to his flare-up in Port Elizabeth had put a final seal on the total breakdown between us.

On reaching home I tip-toed into our bedroom trying not to disturb Jennifer but she turned on the bedside lamp just as I was undressing.

"How did the match go, Ray? Did you win?"

"Sorry if I woke you, darling. Yes we won, three two."

"Well done. No you didn't, wake me. I'd just stopped reading and put out the light a few minutes ago. How did your game go?"

"I won easily, but you'll never guess what happened? My brother was there!"

Now she was wide awake. "What?"

I related the events leading up to the ugly scene at the bar. "Honestly, it was wrong for Roger to interfere like that, but he's well-intentioned and meant no harm. Larry's reaction was way out of line. He'd had quite a few and his language was horrendous."

"A huge embarrassment for you, though." Jennifer sat up in bed. "What do you think will happen now?"

"Well, he may be disciplined by his club and our Captain may write a report. Probably nothing will come of it, but as far as I'm concerned, that was the final straw. I want nothing whatsoever to do with him or his family ever again."

Jennifer held out her arms, smiling sadly. "It's been on the cards for a long time now, hasn't it? I feel really sorry for you, Ray, you don't deserve this. Come to bed and get a good night's sleep."

I undressed and got under the covers. Sleep didn't come easily in spite of Jennifer's warmth and consolation. I lay awake deep into the night, wondering what my poor father, wherever he now was, would say if he was aware of the complete disassociation of his two surviving sons, let alone what he thought about my adulterous dalliance with Rita Coetzee, just a few short weeks after he had passed away.

Chapter 38

11th February 1990 Nelson Mandela freed from prison after 27 years
18th March 1992 South Africa votes to end Apartheid
1993 Mandela and de Klerk awarded joint Nobel Peace Prize
1994 FirstSouth African non-racial election won by ANC
10th May 1994 Nelson Mandela becomes South Africa's first black President
2004 Israel: Violence continues as Prime Minister Sharon plans evacuation of Gaza Strp and orders more settlements to be built in the West Bank
United Kingdom: Tony Blair promises a referendum on the EU Constitution

21 Years later   November 2004

"RAY! RAY!" Jennifer yelled from her small office. "E-mail from Gaby! She and Ariad are engaged! They're in Dahab, the Red Sea village where we went scuba diving! She couldn't get to a phone. She's so excited!"

I rushed into the TV room, squeezing on to her chair.

Hi Mom and Dad,

You won't believe this, I'm e-mailing from an internet cafe in Dahab. Ariad and I were diving the Canyon this morning, an amazing site, 40 metres down then up a chimney, out through the glass fish cave at 15 metres. In the cave Ariad calmly puts this beautiful diamond ring on my finger! I nearly drained my tank!!!! Almost impossible to seal with a kiss but we managed!!! My romantic guy had the ring attached by a piece of string! No phone here so will talk from Eilat. Thought I'd email to make your day. June wedding here in Israel? Pick yourselves up from the floor my lovely parents!!! Will phone soon as poss......!.

Lotsa luv,
Gabriella (your engaged daughter!)

We danced round the tiny office until breathless. Ever since our beloved eldest daughter made Aliyah (emigration) to Israel having fallen in love with Ariad, a handsome sabra (Israel-born) she'd met some years before, we had struggled to contain our anxiety. Would he or wouldn't he? In spite of our subtle warnings, our headstrong radiographer daughter had followed her man, an IT expert. Now at age 28, after three years of living together, he had finally popped the question.

"You were right about him, Ray," Jennifer beamed. "I'm sorry I had my concerns but three years was a long time. I certainly wouldn't have let you go on that long!"

I gave her a hug. "No, you had your claws well and truly embedded pretty quickly, didn't you?" I teased.

"Oooh! you sod!" She slapped me playfully on the cheek. "You couldn't wait to get me into bed!"

"You didn't put up much resistance, as I recall!!"

"Never mind, Raymond, darling, what does it feel like to be the father of the bride-to-be?"

"Well, like I said, Ariad is a great guy, got a good job and besides, he likes squash, skiing and scuba diving, all my passions. How could I not like him?"

"So........June 2005. Doesn't give them much time but most of it will be arranged in Israel. We won't be able to help much. Still, Israeli weddings are much more casual anyway, aren't they?" Jennifer's face was a picture of happiness. "How's about I get us a celebratory drink, Dr Benjamin?" She skipped her way across the lounge to the kitchen.

"Do you think my mother will be able to make the trip?" I called after her. "I know she'll want to be there." I knew the answer before Jennifer replied.

My wife stopped halfway. "Ray, she's nearly ninety, in constant need of frail care. It'll be impossible to get travel insurance at any price. I know how forceful she can still be but it would be crazy, in my opinion."

"I guess you're right." I shrugged then smiled. "The twins are going to be frantic when they hear. They'll certainly be bridesmaids, won't they?"

"I'm sure," Jennifer yelled from the kitchen. "It's too late to wake Leah now. We'll tell them tomorrow evening over dinner. Come down, drink up then I'll reply to the email."

After two large sherries each, we went our separate ways, Jennifer back to her office with her beloved laptop computer, while I, with a list of implant cases the following day, retired exhausted but elated to our large comfortable bedroom.

*

As the years had flown by, my wife and I could look at our situation with some satisfaction. The family had blossomed, Gabriella qualifying as a radiographer, Rachel and Leah earning their own living as optician and pharmacist respectively. They both had fairly stable relationships but as per the general trend were in no hurry to commit to marriage.

"You guys are so old-fashioned," Rachel laughed one evening some weeks before. "Keith and I are happy as we are. We each have our own place and value our independence but like being together. Having our own space is more important at the moment."

Before Jennifer or I could respond, Leah, who still lived with us, put her two cents worth in. "I agree. I'm still at home with you guys but I value the freedom you give me. When John and I are earning enough for our own place we'll move in together, then we'll worry about putting anything on a piece of paper. That's all marriage is anyway, isn't it?" she laughed, eyebrows raised in a direct challenge.

"No, marriage is a lot more than a piece of paper," I said firmly. "A lot more. These days young people walk away at the first disagreement or dissatisfaction. I'm sounding like a fuddy-duddy but look around, mega divorce statistics, single mothers, child abuse, etc. It all stems from lack of commitment, in and out of relationships, God how I hate that word! without a backward glance. There now, I've said my piece.

What does your mother think?" I grinned at Jennifer who was hunched over her laptop.

"What was that, Ray?" she said absentmindedly. "Sorry, I was just reading about the violence in South African townships. You mentioned commitment, and girls, I totally agree with your father."

The two girls laughed out loud. "You always agree with him, mom," Leah chortled. "Nowadays women don't always agree with everything men say. It's a much fairer society."

"Fair?" I couldn't avoid raising the temperature of the discussion. "What's fair about men walking off leaving umpteen kids behind them, or boyfriends of single mums beating the shit out of the poor unwanted offspring?"

My beloved twins as usual disagreed, but allowed me to have the last word. They had grown into attractive women, accentuating their minute physical differences by dressing differently, sporting outlandish hairdo's and trying to convince everyone of their individuality. Yet, in spite of all their efforts they remained alike as two peas, intellectually and emotionally.

The Practice had developed into a specialist organisation with various specialties, an Endodontist, a Prosthodontist and an Orthodontist, whilst I concentrated on Oral Surgery. Advances in Implantology had ensured that hopeless oral situations had been transformed, provided the spiralling costs could be borne. Now in my sixties, I was looking forward to retirement, although the complexity of the cases I was treating continued to fire my enthusiasm.

Contact with Larry and Serena had been practically non-existent, apart from cool but civil meeting at mutual friends' celebrations, weddings or barmitzvahs. Years had passed without any reconciliation. They were leading conventionally comfortable lives and I knew that Larry was also a keen skier, often going with clubmates to Tignes.

The Rita episode was consigned to history. Neither she nor Crystal had to my knowledge ever made their joint trip to Europe. I supposed that their lives were settled in their respective countries and my transgression had mercifully remained unexposed.

I sometimes found myself wondering how I would react if Crystal or Rita ever suddenly arrived in London. Little did I know that that possibility was closer than I could have imagined.

*

Gabriella's romantic engagement to Ariad met with a totally predictable response from the twins that evening.

"WOWEE!" yelled, Rachel. "Absolutely outta sight!!!"

"Oh boy, that's cool!" Leah jumped up and down. "Wait till I tell John. He's gonna have to be real original when we decide to get hitched."

"Now wait a minute," I interposed, highly amused. "Let me play back what you've just said. 'JOHN's gonna have to be original when WE decide'. If you can't see the contradiction there then...."

"OH, DAAAAD!" the girls chorused in exasperation, "You know what we mean, you're just being pedantic!"

*

"Dr. Benjamin, there's someone in the waiting room to see you," my ageing but reliable and loyal receptionist, Pauline, came through loud and clear on the intercom. From her tone I knew something unusual was afoot.

"Who is it, Pauline?"

"Won't give her name, says she's an old friend. Wants to surprise you," came the somewhat disapproving reply.

Mystified, I excused myself to my patient on whom I had just completed an examination, removed my rubber gloves and walked into the waiting room.

She was standing at the window with her back to me, looking out at tree-lined Markham Square. As she turned, I swallowed deeply, my legs turning to jelly. Dressed in a severely-tailored business suit, I saw that the young girl I had known all those years before had matured into an elegant woman, retaining her svelte figure. The smile and sparkling eyes were the same, auburn curls replaced by sophisticated yet becoming style, framing her oval face with its still flawless complexion. A few, hardly visible smile lines round the corners of her mouth and eyes were the only traces that the passing years had left.

"Hello, Dr Benjamin. Long time no see." Crystal's voice, deeper now, with a trace of an American accent, but huskier than I remembered, left me speechless. I stood rooted to the floor. She held out her hand and I grasped it weakly. I was acutely aware of curious stares from Pauline and other patients sitting in the none-too-spacious waiting room.

Finally, I found my voice. "Wow! Crystal!!!! Mrs. Du Toit, rather. What a surprise!!!!" I shook my head in disbelief trying to clear my frazzled thoughts. "Pauline, meet Crystal, a very old friend from South Africa."

Shaking Pauline's hand and ignoring her suspicious look, Crystal turned to me with an impish grin. "Not so much of the old, if you don't mind!" She looked round at the other patients. "Sorry if I came at a busy time, I just thought it would be a hoot to pop in unannounced."

I shook my head. "No, not at all. Actually it's quite convenient. I was just finishing my last patient before lunch." I turned to Pauline. "Paul, the last time Crystal and I saw each other was in 1966, just about forty years ago! I think you'll allow me to take her out for a quick bite of lunch, won't you?"

Pauline cast a concerned gaze from me to Crystal, taking in the vibrations. Crystal was an unknown part of my history which I had no intention of divulging to her. Pursing her lips, she looked at the appointment screen on her computer. "That's fine, Dr. Benjamin. Your next appointment is not until two-thirty."

I turned to Crystal, who was smiling amusedly at the little interaction. "Give me a minute, Crys, I'll just get out of my surgery clothes."

"Fine," said that low-keyed transatlantic voice. "I'll be here." With that she sat down, crossing her legs provocatively solely for Pauline's benefit and grabbed a magazine.

It took me more than a minute to settle my scattered equilibrium. When I returned, the waiting room was empty save for Crystal. Pauline had made an excuse to see the other patients in person to their respective surgeries, something she hardly ever did.

"Your receptionist is a suspicious old bat," Crystal grinned. "What did she think, I was gonna attack you right here in your waiting room?"

I laughed, shaking my head. "No, but she's been with me almost as long as I've been in London and is much more than an employee. She's mad about Jennifer and the girls and views you as someone she'd never heard about from my distant past. She behaves like Jennifer's guardian angel." I motioned her to the door. "Come on, let's get outta here while the coast is clear!"

*

We ate at Meridiana, a fancy Italian restaurant along the Kings Road. Seeing Crystal again had completely unnerved me. She had retained her bubbly, youthful appearance and cheeky persona in spite of what must have been a pretty difficult time making her way in America. To say that old memories had not been awakened with explosive force would be to deny Mother Nature herself.

I listened spellbound as Crystal related the saga of her struggles in America, battling to survive financially as she completed her legal qualifications, then succeeding despite vicious competition for employment in a high-flying Law firm. She glossed briefly over a relationship that had ended after several years. I watched fascinated as she demolished her lasagne, eating with fork in her right hand as Americans do. Her plate empty, she looked at me with that intense focus that I had never forgotten.

"So Ray, it looks like you've got it all here in London. I'm really pleased for you, I mean that absolutely sincerely. I heard about your marriage from Rita and so decided that there was no point in continuing to write. I've been through London on several occasions but I guess I just felt unable to make contact. This time, though, well, I just had an insane desire to see you again, just to say hi. Apart from anything else, I realised it was the 40th anniversary of our aborted departure on the 'SS Africa'." Biting her lower lip as she spoke told me that her mind was flying backwards to our youth, our grand passion, just as mine had been since I saw her framed against the waiting room window.

"How long are you in London for, Crys?" I mumbled through a mouthful of canneloni.

"Two days," she replied quickly. "I leave Thursday morning." Again that look that said many things, some of which I wanted with all my heart to respond to, others I feared had best be ignored. "I have meetings this afternoon, this evening and all of tomorrow, but ...." she hesitated, "I could be free tomorrow evening if...." she left the sentence unfinished.

My mind was racing, that old friend conscience making rude noises in the distance. "Wednesday.......mmmm..... I'm not sure, but let me see, have you a cell number I can call? Let me see if I can re-arrange something."

With a smile she handed me a business card. It read 'Crystal du Toit, Attorney at Law', with an address in Philadelphia, telephone numbers, fax number, email addresses and a London cell number.

"Very impressive," I said. "When's the best time to call?"

"Anytime. If I'm in the middle of a meeting it'll go on to voicemail. I'm at the Hilton. If you can make it, it'll be great, sort of like time travel. Forty years, whoosh!" She looked at her watch. "Hey, you've got five minutes to get back to what's-her-name, Pauline and I've got an appointment at three. You go, this is my treat, its all on expenses, courtesy my huge American firm!"

Ignoring my protests, she signalled for the bill and as I stood, she rose, threw her arms round me and kissed me ardently, her tongue being no respecter of the Meridiana's other customers. "Call me whenever, Ray, it would be wonderful just to have a little more time."

I was acutely aware of the attention we were receiving but as Crystal sat down, I held her face in my hands and kissed her again. "I'll call you for sure. Thanks for lunch and nearly giving me heart failure." This last was with the full Ray Milland treatment bringing a wistful smile to her lovely face. I was certain the sudden sparkling in her almond eyes were tears for all the years we'd lost.

*

Over dinner that evening Jennifer was aware of my preoccupation. "What's up, Ray? You seem uptight. Everything OK at the surgery?"

Looking at her still attractive face, creased slightly now by concern, I felt turmoil and a sense of disquiet. In all our years, I had never been dishonest with my wife, indeed had never had any need to. That I had not divulged the Rita encounter more than twenty years before did not count as deception in my mind as I had never been asked to account for each and every minute I had spent in Port Elizabeth. So easy to rationalise a sin of omission rather than to commit a barefaced lie to the woman whose life I shared, who had borne my family, with whom I had enjoyed years of contented marital bliss. Yet, here I was, on the horns of a dilemma, tempted beyond reason and conscience to spend an evening with the love of my early life, whilst to do so would entail making up a fictitious and potentially catastrophic excuse for the following night.

"No, nothing serious, hon, just a small argument between one of the nurses and the new dentist." This at least was truth. I shook my head reassuringly. "Always the same with the young dentists, they need a bit of coddling."

"OK," Jennifer said, the frown disappearing. "You looked really concerned. Now, by the way, are you busy tomorrow evening?"

I nearly choked on a piece of roast chicken and grabbed a glass of water. "Ah....no not specially....why, what's up?" I gasped.

Again she gave me a look of utter concern. "Are you sure you're OK, Ray?"

Somehow I regained my composure. "Yes, just a bit of chicken went down the wrong way. I'm fine, really. What's up?"

"Nothing much. It's just that the girls asked me to make a fourth at bridge tomorrow night and I said I'd see if you'd made any arrangements. You often play squash on a Wednesday evening."

I couldn't help breathing a relieved sigh. "Well, no, I hadn't got a game arranged but I can phone round tomorrow and see if I can get an opponent. Shouldn't be difficult. You go ahead and tell the ladies it's OK."

Jennifer smiled gratefully. "Thanks. I'll go and confirm now. Will you eat at the club, then?"

"Don't worry," I called as she headed for the office. "I'll get a snack or something."

*

How easy it is in life when faced by a difficult decision to simply delay, procrastinate, or put off. Somehow matters have a habit of solving themselves with the passage of even a short space of time. And so, as I headed for the Hilton Hotel the next evening, my pulse rate racing, I managed to rationalise my way around the little white lie I had told Jennifer on the phone. Far easier to be dishonest into a plastic electronic instrument, and told myself that, after all, a romance that had been torn away from two young people very much in love, after a gap of forty years, deserved an evening of reminiscence, a few hours of private recollections before once again being separated, probably for ever.

*

"Mrs. Du Toit is in room 1305.You can reach her on the lobby phone. I'll put you through," said the effeminate reception clerk.

"Ray, hi, come on up," Crystal answered. "I'm on the thirteenth floor."

As the elevator zoomed up I could not help a flashback vision to a similar ride to a fabulous marine view and garishly coloured wide open kimono, Rita in all her seductive glory. I was reasonably certain that Crystal had not been told, for with that knowledge, the likelihood of her ever contacting me would certainly have disappeared.

The door to 1305 opened. Crystal stood there smiling, wearing a white tracksuit, her straight auburn hair hanging loose. She ushered me into the spacious suite. A bottle of champagne and two glasses stood on a table by the window, which afforded a sensational view of the glittering lights and dark shadows of Hyde Park and Kensington.

She helped me off with my jacket. "So glad you could make it tonight, Dr. Benjamin." She pointed to the champagne. "I think this reunion calls for something special, a celebration after nearly forty years, don't you think?"

I nodded, unable to say anything in any way suitable. Crystal was standing very close, and my arms slid around her still slim waist. The tips of our noses met first as eyes locked, almost squinting, and the gentlest of feathery lip contact was followed by a deeply searching kiss. Unlike the kiss in the restaurant the day before, this kiss spanned the years of separation, adolescent love lost, the promise of a life together wrenched away in a violent spasm, not only by a brutish father, but by the prejudice and hatred endemic in the South Africa of our youth.

She drew away slightly, smiling that unforgettable, wistful smile. "I didn't think we'd go anywhere tonight, Ray, so let's make a toast to old friends reunited, shall we?"

The sweet scent of her breath and the taste of her mouth banished any remaining guilt or conscience. We stood side by side, drinking the effervescent champagne, gazing down at the jewel box of London by night. "Are you hungry, Ray? We can order room service if you like?"

I shook my head. "Not in the conventional food sense, my dear."

Crystal burst out laughing, a deep throaty sound. "My unforgettable movie star, hang on a minute, I've got a surprise for you too!" She walked across to her bedside table and fiddled with what looked like a little black box. Suddenly the room was filled with Frank Sinatra's 'Come fly with me' from her amplified Ipod. Smiling, she held out her arms. "Dance with me, Ray. Pretend that the years never disappeared."

Slowly we gyrated, pressed against each other, the old magical never-to-be-forgotten sensations racing through our bodies. As Sinatra finished, a sensual discarding of clothing began until, standing entirely naked before all of London by night, Crystal took me by the hand and led me to the king-size bed. Pulling the covers back, she whispered softly. "Let's pretend some more, my dearest Raymond, that this was our first night on board the 'SS Africa', shall we?"

We made love as if the world outside no longer existed. The music played on. We laughed, we cried, we uttered words of endearment, and with it all, the futility of the lifetime of alienation did not invade our little nest, high above the crowded streets. After what seemed like hours later, finally, we lay in each other's arms wondering at how fate had played such devilish games, which had led us to this moment.

"I didn't think this would ever happen again," I murmured, stroking her cheeks, moist with tears.

"No, nor me," she said. "All through the years, I wondered if .... if you'd have forgotten me, forgotten how we were then."

"Where do we go from here?" I closed my eyes, not really wanting a response.

Crystal didn't reply immediately. Her hand gripped mine deep under the covers. "Our lives are so far apart now, Ray, I guess, we both know that.There's no chance that we can change things but...."

"But what?"

In the darkness her voice became soothing, reassuring. "Well, you have a wonderful life here, a wife, family, I have my life in America. I'm in a marvellous position with my firm. I don't suppose that there's anything to stop us seeing each other like this when I come over to London, even if it's only for a short time, is there?"

I thought hard before answering. The prospect of a continued and perpetual deception, the look on Jennifer's face if she ever found out, set against the irresistible desire to share blissful moments with the first true love of my life, tore through me like a knife. "We'll manage, somehow," I whispered and felt the intense pressure of her hand in mine.

"Yes, my love, somehow we'll manage," came her tremulous voice in the darkness.

*

I opened the front door as quietly as I could. I looked at my watch. Eleven thirty. Taking my squash bag to the laundry room I placed my gear straight into the washing machine and tip-toed up to our bedroom. Thankfully Jennifer was fast asleep. Silently I undressed and climbed into bed without disturbing her. I must have lain wide awake for over an hour, a maelstrom of emotions tumbling around in my mind. Guilt, elation, consternation amongst a myriad of conflicting sensations. My glacier descent didn't work so I concentrated on the forthcoming wedding in Israel and somehow or other, that did the trick.

I slept the restless sleep of the accused.

Chapter 39

June 2005
Ronit Farm near Herzliyah Israel

The lake glistened in the moonlight. Rising like a green colossus from the calm water, the island, lit by hundreds of fairy lights, was alive with the large congregation eagerly awaiting the wedding procession. The Chupah, spotlit on the apex of the hillock, was a vision, white flowing drapes laced with lilies and greenery willowing in the gentle evening breeze.

For us, at water's edge, preparing to lead the procession over the footbridge, it was breath-taking. Music began. Rachel, Leah and Ariad's sister, in violet and pink, Gabriella's favourite colours, took the first hesitant steps on to the bridge. Ariad's parents then escorted the groom, tall and smart, uncomfortable wearing a tie, alien to Israelis.

The moment I saw Gaby in her bridal gown earlier, lumps constricted my throat. My lower lip was chewed raw, choking back tears about to cascade down my cheeks. Jennifer was clearly similarly affected.

Gabriella's usually curly hair was straight, glowing darkly, resting on her bare shoulders, brown from Israeli sun. Her eyes sparkled with love and happiness. I felt prouder as a father, than at any time in her life. Her dress, after months of debate, was magnificent, accentuating her tiny waist then flaring like a summer parasol. With Jennifer and I at her side we crossed the bridge and, nearing the Chupah, we were surrounded by friends and family, many of whom had come from South Africa, America and naturally from Britain.

Our daughter's smile broadened with each recognition. Taking her place next to Ariad, they gazed at each other with such devotion that, even before the service began, women were hastily reaching for the Kleenex.

The ceremony was conducted by a kindly-faced Rabbi in both English and Hebrew. At the climax, Ariad looked down and with a mighty stamp, broke the glass after which all was chaos. The entire congregation came charging up the slope, much hugging and kissing followed, tears of joy ruining carefully applied makeup.

Dinner and dancing took place back on the mainland, food of every variety, steaks, seafood, pasta, even a vegetarian table. Wine and champagne flowed freely and a violinist made a virtuoso performance. After the meal, on Gaby's orders, the speeches were short, Ariad's father in Hebrew and me in English followed by Ariad's witty and brief response. A ten-piece band took over stirring the huge crowd, over five hundred, into whirling Israeli folk dances followed by Jazz, Rock and Latin. Gradually older dancers vacated the floor and withdrew some distance as the volume increased. Walking round the lake, they enjoyed the spectacle from a lower-decibel vantage.

We never left the dance floor, keeping pace with the youngsters until later, as if by magic, thick fog descended over the lake. It was so misty that one could not see the Chupah. By this time, three a.m., only a few guests were left. The video cameraman insisted my daughter and her new husband walk across the bridge to be enveloped by the impenetrable cloud, a closing shot to a wedding if ever there was one.

*

The "honeymoon" consisted of some thirty of us flying to Sharem-el-Sheikh on the Red Sea for a week's scuba diving aboard the VIP One, a luxury live-aboard dive vessel with honeymoon suite on the top deck. We snorkelled and dived, Jennifer included, amongst the glorious shallow corals. The more adventurous dived with sharks at Ras Muhammad, explored the wreck of the Dunraven, circa 1890 and the Thistlegorm, an arms carrier sunk in 1941, with jeeps, motorbikes and machineguns still visible in the hold.

The newlyweds left us after a week for a few days in a luxurious hotel near Dahab where Ariad had proposed. Jennifer and I and the twins returned to Tel Aviv, staying in Ariad and Gabriella's new apartment near Netanya, an 11th floor flat with stunning beach views until the honeymooners returned.

Amid tearful farewells at Ben Gurion airport, we boarded our El Al flight for London. At take-off, I sat back, closing my eyes. Jennifer placed her hand on my arm. I noted the red eyes and running mascara and gently took her hand. "Honey," I said softly, "I hope those tears are happy ones. Gaby has never looked so contented."

She nodded, wiping her face with a tissue. "I know, Ray, it's.....we both love Israel, Ariad's adorable and is mad about Gaby, but......"

"But what, sweetheart? Most mothers would be delighted to see their daughter so blissful with such a great guy."

"You're right, but Israel's such a long way away, he's got to go in the army, saying nothing about the dangers for the country from its neighbours."

I cradled her face in my hands. "Don't worry, darling, I'm sure Ariad will take great care of her. Anyway she's pretty strong. She learned Hebrew in a few months, with managing position in the Neuroradiology department."

"I know, Ray, but you're not a mother, men don't understand."

I tilted my seat back as far as it would go. "OK, you win, Jen, be a Jewish mother, worrying yourself sick over nothing." I sighed. "Me, I'm going to snooze and dream about diving with sharks!"

Sharks played no part in my airborne dreams. Images of Crystal and Rita interposed themselves on an abstract canvas depicting a wedding scene disrupted by angry female voices coming from dark periphery. I found myself sweating profusely, hovering between consciousness and slumber when the stewardess with a meal tray tapped me on the shoulder.

"You want meat or fish?" was the brusque demand.

"Meat!" I said, equally tersely," and a bottle of Carmel white wine, please."

We arrived back in St Johns Wood grateful to slip between clean sheets and switch off, knowing that our daughter was now a happily married lady.

*

Reports from the Holy Land spoke of marital bliss via Gabriella whilst never-ending Palestinian terrorism occupied minimal space in the British media. I was convinced that Middle East unrest was a festering sore that would never be solved in spite of well-intentioned diplomatic efforts. Mounting aggression from Iran and its bearded President with his threats to 'wipe Israel off the map' did not calm our fears. In Israel, however, the locals seemed to live their lives in calm acceptance of threats surrounding them, Hezbollah in the north, Hamas in Gaza and a potentially nuclear-armed Iran.

Emails and phone calls with Gaby reflected her joyous marriage and contentment with her work in a hospital where war-wounded paraplegics were being helped to walk and stroke victims to regain their lost facilities.

Jennifer and I drove down to revisit Beachy Head, scene of our early courtship. The twins were living in fairly comfortable accommodation with their boyfriends. Friday night dinners were a regular family get-together at our home. We were becoming resigned to the new 'partner' morality, being in 'relationships'. To object was futile, so we treated the boyfriends hopefully as potential sons-in law.

Crystal had flown into London three times since her first surprise visit and the initial pattern repeated itself. We reminisced about our youthful escapades and although Rita's name was mentioned, Crystal never indicated any knowledge of our brief encounter, for which I was supremely grateful.

Occupied during the days with business appointments she and I would spend the evening in her hotel suite. There were times when guilt rose acidically in my throat, especially on each journey home but the thrill and anticipation of those stolen hours partly allayed my conscience. It was as though we could shut the door and beam ourselves back to that little apartment on Pollok Beach, where our plans took shape all those years ago. Those imaginings would be rudely torn asunder late each night when we both knew I had to leave.

The most recent occasion, late in November, with frosty evenings drawing in, developed into soul-searching. Crystal stood by the picture window, smoking. "This is becoming difficult for you, Ray, isn't it?" she asked softly.

I was slowly getting dressed, watching the plumes of smoke rising from her lips. "What do you mean, Crys?" knowing exactly what she meant.

She stubbed the half-smoked cigarette out in a large ashtray. She knew I hated cigarette smoke and the taste it left in her mouth so she walked across to the sumptuous bathroom. I could hear sounds of toothbrushing. "I guess, for me," she called out, her voice blurred from foamy rinsing, "it's easy. I have no excuses to make, no lies or alibis to worry about, whereas for you, I can tell when you start to feel anxious about getting home, about how you worry about Jennifer finding out." She came back into the bedroom and sat beside me.

"It's that obvious, is it?" I murmured.

She nodded, helping me button my shirt. "We've said 'if only' a million times, haven't we? We both know what we've been attempting to do here in these moments, to relive what we had and ....."

I placed my finger on her lips, swollen from hours of passion. "That will have to remain my problem, Crys. We've talked this through over and over. I know how you feel when I leave, I feel the same, but it's the way things are. You know I'm not unhappy at home, but when I get your email at the surgery I still feel all the old excitement bubbling up inside."

Crystal smiled sadly. "For how long can we keep it going like this, Ray? You're the one running the risks."

I stretched, shaking my head. "I know. Also, with just a few hours together every couple of months, it's so bloody empty when we part."

She gave a wicked smile. "You know, I've often thought, if we could manage a few days together somewhere, away from London, just us, wouldn't that partly make up for all the years?"

I returned the smile. "This feels just like it did when we were planning our crazy scheme to get on the boat together, but.....listen.... I've had an idea."

She drew closer to me and in spite of the late hour I felt the old excitement building, and with it a recklessness which I immediately suppressed. "No, don't start, you know what will happen.......but here's my idea."

Crystal sat back, pouting. "So, tell me, my movie star....what's the plan?"

"Well, first week of January I go skiing to Tignes in France with a few friends. It's a regular annual thing, Boysweek we call it......and....."

She laughed. "You want me to come skiing with a bunch of guys?"

I shook my head. "No, no, well, we could spend a few days getting to the ski resort before I meet them. You're a business-woman, couldn't you arrange appointments in Switzerland?"

Crystal thought for a moment then a smile warmed her lovely face. "Maybe, just maybe it could work. I've skied quite a bit in the States, Vail, and Vermont. First week in January hey? I'll see what I can arrange. Wow, a few days in the mountains, sounds brilliant." She looked at her watch. "Hey Mr Milland, it's late. You'd better get outta here, go on, get your skates on."

She gave me a long lingering kiss at the door and suddenly I was alone in the heartless hotel corridor. Driving home, my mind was awash with possibilities, risks and the thrilling prospect of being alone for days and nights, not just hours, in my beloved Alps with this glorious creature of my adolescence.

All the lights were off when I reached home. Thankfully I performed the usual routine with my gear and as silently as I could, crawled in beside the warm body of my beloved wife.

*

Monday 2nd January 2006 5.00 am

Jennifer followed me to the front door where my taxi was waiting. Bleary-eyed, she flung her arms round me and kissed me tenderly. "Have a good time, darling and don't take any chances, there's been a lot of snow recently. Promise?"

I hugged her close, feeling her shivering as the wintry blast rushed in. "I promise. Go back inside now, it's freezing out here. Say bye to the girls when you see them. I'll call when I arrive in Tignes. Love you."

She blew a kiss then stepped back, closing the door against the cold. I picked up my holdall and climbed into the taxi. "Heathrow, Terminal 2 please," I called to the swarthy driver. With the heater on full, drowning any further conversation for which I was grateful, we left The Lane and headed west.

As we sped along the M4 I began to feel childlike excitement, like embarking on an enterprise one knows is sinful or forbidden. A wicked elation allied to casting off moral shackles took over as I reviewed the plan.

Our flights to Geneva would arrive within an hour of each other, hers from New York. We would hire a car and meander through the mountains spending three days getting to Tignes where I would be meeting my ski-buddies, two of whom, Bruce and Rodney, Australian dentists, had worked for me in the Chelsea practice years before. Having returned to Australia, they now spent six weeks every year skiing all over the Alps, one week of which was our Boysweek. The other friend was Thierry, a crazy Frenchman from Marseilles who ran a seaside restaurant in the summer and spent the winter skiing. He owned a chalet in Lac de Tignes which had become our regular accommodation. With the superb lift system, reliable snow levels and the wealth of off-piste opportunities Tignes remained our choice year after year. I had decided to introduce Crystal semi-truthfully, namely as an old friend from South Africa, leaving the rest to their imagination. I felt secure enough in their comradeship that they would regard our liaison with good-natured tolerance, probably some envy, but would keep the issue to themselves.

*

She came through the arrivals exit looking ready for the slopes in a fur-collared white anorak and tight-fitting jeans to match. Dark glasses hid her eyes and a fur hat covered the auburn hair. Even so her appearance had many males swivelling their heads. I was keenly aware of envious glances as we embraced tightly.

"I can't believe this is actually happening," I whispered in her ear.

"Nor can I, Ray, but from the feel of you, I would say, it's real enough," she giggled.

I felt my face reddening, then concentrated on getting her baggage trolley out of the way of the crowds of passengers. "How was your flight?" I mumbled as, arm-in- arm, I led her to where I had parked the hire car.

"Tiring, bloody tiring, hence the dark glasses. You don't wanna see my bloodshot eyes right now."

"Right, madam." I smiled as I eased the VW Polo out into the airport traffic. "First stop, the glorious alpine village of Megeve, a lovely quaint little hotel called 'A Fer a Cheval' that's French for horseshoe, for good luck. About an hour's drive so sit back and relax."

It was as if our brief meetings in London had never happened. As I drove, I did my best to keep my self-control as her hands invaded my space. Far from supposedly suffering from jet-lag, Crystal seemed energised, rampant. The winding mountain road through the stunning Mont Blanc area took all my concentration and I found myself having to curb her wandering fingers. A nice volte-face to the adolescent fumblings and the advice of Jimmy Macdonald!

By the time we arrived at the timber-clad hotel, it was all we could do to restrain ourselves until we were shown to our room where we spent the remaining hours of the day in the huge double bed.

"Mmmmmmm," she murmured as we watched the sun go down over the distant white peaks. "This is divine. How much time can we spend here, lover?"

"Today's Monday, we're due to meet the guys at Thierry's chalet on Thursday. I thought we could ski here for two days, then drive up to Tignes Thursday. How does that grab you, Madame du Toit?"

"And where are you supposed to be at this moment, or shouldn't I ask?" Crystal raised her eyebrows, a mischievous glint in her eye.

Somewhere deep inside me a small annoyance flared. "That's a sensitive nerve you're closing in on, Crys. Enough said on that subject, OK? "

Her face flushed immediately. "Sorry, Ray, I didn't mean to tease. Forget I said that, will you? It was uncalled for." She blew a kiss. "Please?"

I fumbled with my cell-phone. "Fine. Forgotten. But don't do it again," I said with a grin. "We both have our boundaries, don't we?" I walked over to the window. "In fact I must send a text home 'arrived safely'. That OK with you?"

Crystal nodded and disappeared into the bathroom without a word.

*

The dinner in the wood-panelled dining room was spectacular .After two bottles of wine we had recovered from the minor tiff and hurried back to the room. Crystal turned to me, an arch come-hither look on her face that I knew well. "This, my movie star, was what I was longing for. The two of us, no time restrictions, just you and me, as if forty years had not passed by. Let's be those two juvenile lovers again, shall we?"

There were no words after that. Clothes discarded haphazardly, lights dimmed but not in total darkness, two sixty-something-year-olds made slow, sensual love, unhurried, rejoicing in reunion and realisation of promises made over a generation before. 'What could possibly be wrong or immoral' I asked myself, 'for two human travellers, whose lives had been so blighted by bigotry, to at last achieve, although of necessity temporarily, ecstatic joining of minds and bodies'?

I felt no guilt that night or indeed the rest of our stay in Megeve. We woke early, ate delicious breakfasts and skied the picturesque but undemanding slopes of this fashionable resort. Crystal proved to be a totally competent and even adventurous skier which I felt augured well for the latter part of the vacation with my fellow 'boys'!

Late afternoon we wandered the old town centre with its ancient church and square. Crystal registered astonishment at the prices of the clothes in all the chic boutiques. We behaved like a long-married couple, walking arm-in-arm through the arcades and narrow pebbled streets, stopping every so often to look at each other and smile in delight at circumstances that had allowed us, through subterfuge, it was true, to spend precious days and nights together.

I kept up a constant flow of texts to Jennifer with rave reports about the skiing, the snow, the weather. My conscience prevented me from making a phone call for fear that my intuitive wife might sense something in my voice, my conversation, that might give her reason to suspect. All in all, my self-respect was at a pretty low ebb, but when the electricity between Crystal manifested itself, it was as though I was no longer in control and morals, ethics and fidelity just disappeared.

Then suddenly it was Thursday morning. Having settled the bill, we set out via the stunning Val d'Arly, the road twisting through narrow ravines eventually heading out to Albertville, the centre of the Winter Olympics in 1992. Here motorways built for the Olympics made driving a delight, especially with magnificent green foliage and forests covering the snow-capped mountains on either side of the valley.

"I think I'm dreaming and have gone to heaven," Crystal whispered in awe, craning her head in every direction to absorb the scenery. This did not deter her hand from its usual position high up on my thigh. Recklessly, I was able to make reciprocal moves.

"I think, that along with the South African coastline and beaches, these mountains make me feel life is just wonderful, and," I moved my hand a fraction higher, "sharing all this with you is like the cream on top....Corny hey?"

Crystal smiled that wistful smile, eyes shining. "I realised long ago that one must grab opportunities when they arise, '*carpe diem*', if I remember my Latin. I never dreamed we'd manage time together like this, though. I'm savouring every single moment."

I nodded. "Me too. Its just too good to be true and this is only the third day." I pointed up to a castle high up on the side of the mountainside. "There's a restaurant up there. Fancy lunch? We've only got another couple of hours driving to Tignes."

Crystal nodded enthusiastically. "You bet, Dr. Benjamin. Take me to your castle!"

My 'Castle', actually called Chateau de Feissons, is situated high up a winding road overlooking Albertville valley. Suits of armour guard corridors and the dining hall boasts a minstrel's gallery bedecked with flags of many nations. Food is served on long wooden refectory tables by waitresses in traditional costumes. The walls are hung with oil paintings of ancient battles.

As we finished our dessert, we were each given a juicy pear and I couldn't help remembering Albert Finney as Tom Jones with his wench, juice running down their chins, eyes filled with unadorned lust.

I reminded Crystal of the scene and she burst out laughing. "Are you going to pick me up and carry me down to some dingy cellar here, then?" she asked.

I patted my stomach. "I would have liked to but after all that food I think we'd collapse in a heap. Never mind, we'll be at the chalet in a few hours and you can put your feet up."

The journey became more tortuous as we passed Moutiers then Bourg St Maurice with the snow level seemingly advancing down the hillsides to meet us. A large man-made lake which covered the original village of Tignes, so familiar to me, was restrained by a massive concrete dam and hydro-electric scheme. Here the road split with one leading to Val d'Isere and the other still ascending further. The last few kilometres were completely snow-covered. I had some difficulty keeping the car from skidding. Rounding the final bend, the first view of the glistening lights of Lac de Tignes and its icy slopes gave me the same thrill it always had.

"Wow, that is just plain exquisite!" breathed Crystal. "I just can't believe we're here, and together. It's all too incredible."

"Just wait till you see the view from the chalet," I grinned , enjoying her reaction. "Like mountains wall to wall."

*

Thierry was at the door to greet us, all Gallic charm and showing no surprise whatsoever at my bringing a companion even though this was a first and decidedly radical departure from tradition. In true French fashion, he paid substantially more attention to Crystal. A great roaring fire in the large lounge overlooking the frozen lake gave the chalet a warm welcoming feel and we were soon sitting in the low-slung leather settee drinking kir royales.

"Soooo, my friend Raymondo, you always manage to surprise me," Thierry said with a wave towards Crystal. "Your lady improves the aesthetics of the chalet one hundred percent! This will be a Boysweek with a difference, n'est ce pas?" This was said without any trace of a leer.

Crystal blushed slightly. "Thierry, I think you have a piece of paradise right here. The view, the lake and the mountains, absolutely wonderful! I just adore the way the chalet is done, such style, it's just fantastic!"

"Thank you, madame," he said, modestly, with a mock bow. "I hope you will enjoy my humble hospitality."

I laughed. "I knew you wouldn't mind, Thierry, especially as Crystal is so much more attractive to have around than us boys, especially the wild men from Australia. When are they due, by the way?"

"Any time now." He looked out the window at approaching lights of a vehicle through the thick snow falling. "In fact that looks like them now."

Moments later there was a heavy banging on the front door. Amidst shouts of welcome and broad Australian accents, Thierry ushered Bruce and Rodney into the lounge. As I went over to greet my old mates, I could see their eyes widening as they caught sight of Crystal lounging demurely on the settee.

"Allow me to introduce Crystal du Toit, an old friend from SA, now a celebrated corporate attorney operating out of Philadelphia, US of A."

It did not take long for the boys to adjust to Crystal. The ease of her acceptance into our little group gave me immense pleasure. I knew questions would come when they had me alone but I determined to play the situation as cool as possible.

As the weather had closed in, for dinner we settled on Thierry's cassoulet which he had prepared earlier, a stew of local spicy sausage, potatoes plus other secret ingredients. It went down well with three bottles of Fleury, a full-bodied red wine.

"So, *mes ami*," Thierry expounded after a dessert of bananes flambee, "the next few days is going to be much new snow so we can ski all round Tignes, show Crystal all the off-piste runs between here and Val d'Isere. You are happy in deep snow, cherie?"

Crystal nodded. "Sure, I've skied the back bowls in Vail a few times. Hope I'll be able to keep up with you hotshots, though."

Thierry gave a typical Gallic shrug. "I am sure you will be excellent. Monday, my instructor friend Michel has a group organised for a wonderful full day's itineraire, from Tignes through the back valleys to the villages of La Plagne, Les Arcs and Villaroger. We are meeting with him and his group on Sunday evening at Harry's Bar in Lavachet, the village below us."

"Wow!!" I enthused," I've always wanted to do that trip. Any avalanche danger with the heavy snowfall?"

"No problem, Raymondo. Michel knows the mountains...... as you say.....like the hand of his back, no?"

We all collapsed at his desecration of the cliché, even more hysterical as he had not understood our hilarity. Crystal took pity on him. "It's the back of his hand, Thierry," she said with a disarming smile.

"Ah, merci, mon petite. You are kind, unlike these monsters Anglais. They are uncouth, yes?"

Thierry insisted on us drinking a *digestif*, a liqueur containing a dead adder. Crystal sipped hers with undisguised disgust.

Thereafter we retired to the bedrooms, Crystal and I generously given the master bedroom with en-suite shower. Dizzy from alcoholic intake, we collapsed in each other's arms under the huge duvet. Lovemaking in that state of inebriation can be disastrous. In this case it ended in hysterical laughter, possibly with some physical satisfaction, it was hard to remember.

*

Three days passed in a flash although sadly the weather and visibility made skiing the massive Tignes/Val d'Isere complex in its entirety impossible. Crystal's ability impressed my buddies and we still managed to get in several hours each day. Sunday night we took Bruce's 4x4 down the road to Harry's Bar in Lavachet, to meet Michel. The bar is hung with ancient ski gear and old rusty farm implements, smelling of beer and stale cigarettes, resounding to English accents and football hysteria. Michel came to greet us, a slim man with a mass of grey-black hair and chiselled pointed features, a typical Frenchman. He gave Crystal an appreciative appraisal then led us to an enclave where several men were watching football on a television lodged on a ledge above.

"Gentlemen," Michel loudly interrupted their viewing, "please meet the other members of the group for tomorrow's expedition. Here is Thierry, Bruce, Rodney Raymond and the exquisite mademoiselle, Crystal!"

A figure at the back suddenly stood up open-mouthed, staring wildly at Crystal and me. Through the cigarette smoke fug it took us a few seconds but then sudden and wholly shocking mutual recognition occurred. A bolt of lightning could be an apt description. The man looking at us now with an astonished and accusatory glare, was none other than Larry, my brother to whom I had not spoken nor had anything to do with for umpteen years!!!!!

Chapter 40

Finale

Crystal gripped my hand fiercely as together we watched Larry clamber over the bench behind the other men. He landed in front of us, close enough so that we could smell his beery breath. He looked in astonishment from Crystal to me then a light dawned. He smiled leeringly. "Good God! My big brother, pillar of morality, here with a lady who is NOT, repeat NOT his wife. Well, well, well. Crystal Webber, or is it du Toit??? Long, long time no see, hey?"

The entire group now watched the confrontation with wide-eyed curiosity. The TV football commentary faded into insignificance. Here was real-live drama being played out in front of them.

My first instinct was to turn my back on Larry and usher Crystal out of the bar. She must have read my mind as I detected a tiny shake of her head. What she then did to my utter amazement was to step forward, grab Larry in a bear hug and kiss him on both cheeks. "Larry," she breathed in her sexiest voice, "fancy meeting you here of all places. My God, it must be nearly forty years! Apart from the beard, you haven't changed much!"

Her action had a dramatic effect on my brother. His gaze swivelled uncertainly between us. "Uh," he stammered," Crystal..... uh....what on earth are you doing here? I heard you were a big-time lawyer in America?"

She shook her head. "Not so much big-time," she said modestly, "but yes, I live in America, in Philadelphia, actually. I do a lot of business in Europe."

Recovering his equilibrium Larry pointed a quivering finger at me. "So what the hell are you doing here with him? Looks a bit too cosy to me. Does his wife.....does stuck-up Jennifer know about this?" He thrust his chin out accusingly, staring into my face.

My fists clenched as I saw Crystal flinch. I was about to speak out angrily but Michel intervened. He placed his hands on Larry's shoulders. "Now, listen, Larry, *mes ami*, why don't we cool things a little. Sit down and have a drink. Whatever's going on here can be resolved over a beer or two."

Furious but holding back I pulled Thierry to one side. "Are we going on this trip tomorrow with this group?" I whispered. "I don't see how that can work. You can see what an impossible situation this is. My brother and I haven't had anything to do with each other for years!"

Thierry shook his head. "Ray, come off it, just take it easy. Here in the mountains we are all friends. Michel is right, let's sit down and have a drink. You can have a discussion with your brother later. We are here to discuss tomorrow's trip. I think your lady had the right idea. Calm down and behave. OK?" He gestured to Michel to take over.

Michel reached up and switched off the TV. We all squeezed into the small alcove. A buxom waitress appeared with large tankards of draught beer for everyone. With Larry and I glaring at each other from opposite sides of the table, Michel smiled. "OK, so we have a little family drama here......" laughter all round the table, "but ," he looked at Larry then at me, "I am sure that what we are going to experience tomorrow will make all these little problems seem unimportant. We are to ski most beautiful unspoiled valleys and snowfields in perfect powder snow and I know you will all come back ecstatic." He raised his tankard to a chorus of 'cheers' all round the table. "So.....we meet at 0700 at the bottom of Secteur Palet lift. They are opening it 'specially for us. Please nobody should be late, OK? No alcohol either in backpack or in stomach. We ski through avalanche territory so everyone must be 100% sober. You will each have an avalanche transceiver for safety. There will be time to drink tomorrow evening. We leave Tignes controlled area and ski maybe ten kilometres through the Val de Champigny, part of the beautiful Vanoise National Park. We hope to see much wildlife, chamois, buffalo maybe even mountain lion. Also eagles, vultures and hawks. But when we ski a steep traverse along the big Champigny ravine, it is *tres important* we ski in line, but not on top of each other. You must follow my line because there has been much snow and I know where the best route is to avoid danger. Everything OK so far?"

"It's snowing lightly now. What's the avalanche danger reading?" Thierry asked.

We peered out the window at gently falling flakes.

"It was level 4 today," Michel replied, "but provided we get through the ravine in early morning it will be fine. Tomorrow's forecast is sunny so we will have good visibility. Now I continue. At the end of the ravine we have a 2 kilometer hike on skis, gently downhill to Champigny-des-eau where a minibus takes us to cable car on outskirts of La Plagne. We ski fast through three Plagne villages to Montchavin and to Les Arcs for lunch. From the fantastic Arc glacier we descend to Villaroger where taxis bring us back to Tignes. Cost is 150 euros per person. I collect now, *s'il vous plait.* Any questions?"

"Yeah," piped up a shaven–haired chap named Kevin, "can we have the football on again?"

This brought a gale of laughter and Crystal took the opportunity to lean across and whisper in my ear. "Leave Larry to me, Ray. Whatever you do, don't start having a slanging match with him."

"OK, my friends," Michel said to the group after collecting the payments, "see you early tomorrow and please no more alcohol the rest of this evening." He turned to Larry and me with a smile. "We all ski tomorrow as friends and depend on each other in emergency. So please talk to each other, you are brothers, don't forget. Try forget differences, even if only for tomorrow, *compris*?"

Crystal stood and tapped Larry on the shoulder. "I think Michel's advice is good. How's about you me and Ray going to have a coffee in a quiet corner?"

Larry looked at her bleary-eyed but nodded nevertheless. I was reminded of how cool Crystal could be in a difficult situation all those years before when she had charmed the pants (very nearly) off the two policemen who caught us at Shelly Beach. Now she was using her considerable legal skills on my slightly inebriated brother. We found a quieter alcove and ordered coffee.

"Look, Larry," Crystal began quietly, "whatever battle there is between you and Ray has nothing to do with me. You knew how close Ray and I were years ago and what happened when my bully of a father broke us up. Am I right?"

Larry once again nodded vaguely. I stayed silent, staring at the man my brother had become. His hair was wild and long, with plentiful streaks of grey. The beard was multicoloured, ginger and grey amongst dark brown. He was wearing large thick-lensed glasses, giving him an owlish appearance.

"Now," Crystal went on, "understandably, Ray and I have kept contact over the years. We see each other in London when I come over on business. I became a keen skier years ago and persuaded Ray to bring me along. So whatever your beef is with him, just forget about causing him trouble with Jennifer. We're just old friends, and I'd like to think that you and I could also be on good terms."

Larry smiled, a little humbly. "I can understand you being a hotshot lawyer, Crystal. You certainly know how to present a case." He looked straight at me. "How long has it been, Ray, when was our last fight?"

I pondered a moment before answering. "That squash match, a few weeks after dad died. We nearly came to blows at the bar of our club."

He shrugged. "Yeah, 1983, twenty three years ago. Lot of water under the bridge since then, hey?"

"I guess so. I often wonder how things are with you, you know. So many people ask why we don't talk, why there's still this feud between us."

Larry rubbed his hairy chin. "Well, there was always this animosity between you and Serena. That made things awkward. And then there was dad's will...... " He hesitated, noticing Crystal shifting uncomfortably. "I hear Gaby got married in Israel." He said it without reproach, almost wistfully.

"Ja, it was a great wedding, Ariad's a nice bloke, they're very happy."

"That's good. I'm pleased. And the twins?"

"They're fine, both living with boyfriends, doing OK." I wanted to reciprocate, to ask about his family but having a senior moment found I could not remember his children's names.

Just then, mercifully, Thierry and the two Aussies, Bruce and Rodney joined us. Thierry smiled. "Well now, I'm pleased to see brothers talking. Could it be the lady lawyer's done some mediating?"

Larry and I looked at each other and we managed a grudging smile. "Maybe twenty-three years is too long to keep one's distance from one's brother," I said, holding my breath.

Larry held out his hand. "You could be right, Ray. And Crystal, sorry I was a bit aggressive earlier. It was quite a shock seeing you both suddenly, just like that after all these years. I guess my imagination sort of ran away with me."

I shook his hand firmly. "Well, at least now we won't be tempted to push each other over a crevasse on the trip tomorrow, will we?"

Crystal laughed. "I think I'd better ski between you two just in case." She turned to me, stifling a yawn. "Listen, Dr. Benjamin, it's ten o'clock. We're up bloody early tomorrow. D'you mind if we go back to the chalet?"

As one we all rose, thanked Michel, said our goodnights to the rest of the group and paid for our drinks. Larry and I parted with mystified looks on our faces, wondering how nearly a quarter of a century of animosity seemed to have ended over a few drinks.

We were relieved as we climbed into Thierry's 4x4 Range Rover, to see that the sky had cleared. The snow had stopped, leaving a clear starlit sky, delicious fresh atmosphere and crunchy sensation under our moonboots. Crystal and I sat in the back, careful now not to show any affection in case Larry was watching. I turned to her with a broad grin. "You, my dear Crystal, are the most elegant and persuasive liar I have ever met. I was on the point of dragging you out of the bar that first moment when Larry saw us. On reflection, though, that would have been the worst thing to do. How on earth did you manage to keep a straight face?"

Crystal giggled. "First I had to break the ice with the hug and kisses. Then get his sympathy with the old friends routine. He was a bit drunk anyway but it was easy, you learn how to do that in my profession!"

"I'm lost in admiration but I shouldn't have been surprised, I remember those two policemen on the Marine Drive."

Her hand sneaked along under my anorak. "I remember it like yesterday," she murmured. "Anyway it looks like you guys will be OK for the time being but how will you feel back in London? Will you ask him to keep *shtum*?"

I was constantly amused at Crystal's usage of Yiddish words absorbed from Jewish members of the American legal profession. "Yes, that could be a bit of a problem. Let's see how the trip goes tomorrow and the remaining few days. I'm also not sure if I will ever get to associate happily with his wife again, nor will Jennifer."

Mentioning Jennifer's name sparked an awkward silence between us for the rest of the short drive back to the chalet. Thierry reversed in to the snow-covered parking space and we hurried inside. Turning down the offer of a nightcap we made straight for our room where to my relief 'old friends' transmuted into 'reunited lovers'.

*

Monday 9th January 2006 0700 hours

The day dawned to perfection, a cloudless Tignes-Blue-day, as Thierry described it. The sun was just creeping over the distant mountain horizon attempting to warm our well-insulated yet shivering interiors. The group assembled with fevered excitement. Even Larry managed a friendly greeting, more for Crystal than me however. As the only female in the group, she was the subject of much attention.

We were each given an Ortovox Avalanche transceiver and shown how it operated. Michel demonstrated on Crystal, naturally. "This is the switch which remains on from now and sends out a bleep," he said. "In avalanche when we are searching we change the dial to receive to help us locate the skier. Everyone familiar with these? You have all used one of these before, yes?" Everyone nodded. "So, let's go!" and we trooped behind him to the four-seater lift.

The lift operator, surly-faced at being dragged out of bed early, nevertheless gave Crystal an admiring glance. Two lifts took us to the Col de Palet ridge, end of the Tignes controlled region. In turn we ducked under a rope which emanated from a large red sign with skull and crossbones, reading 'Attention! Danger! Hors Piste! Risque d'Avalanche!' From here on we were into unprepared snowfields. With a whoop, Michel set off, soft new snow up to his knees, showing off with some dazzling perfectly symmetrical tracks. Crystal and I followed hard on his heels, screaming with delight as we felt the powder bounce, as it is called, making our turns seemingly effortless.

We breathed steamy exhalations as the first descent left us speechless. Exhilaration was etched on everyone's faces as we sped down a second incline, trying to keep pace with Michel.

"Fuckinell! Bloody marvellous!" came an Aussie yell from Bruce or Rodney, we couldn't distinguish which, the fan-shaped snowspray blurring our vision.

Crystal wore a smile as wide as Niagara, her cheeks glowing. "Ohmigod, this is the best!" she yelled, swerving in front of me, nearly colliding with Thierry. "Oh sorry, Thierry! Couldn't resist showing Ray what an Afrikaans girl can do on skis!"

Reaching an upslope, Michel came to a halt, waiting for the group to arrive. "Well, my friends, is this not the best powder ever?" he smiled ecstatically.

We were too breathless to speak, just nodded, eyes shining behind goggles.

"Unbelievable! Amazing!" gasped Crystal.

"And this is only the beginning, *cherie*," Michel laughed. "So now we have a steep, narrow gulley where you must make some jump turns, O K? Then more fast open snowfields."

The group were all competent with no stragglers. Reassuringly Michel had appointed Thierry as back marker in case of any fallers but so far there had been none. The sun was higher now and we were all warming up considerably. Approaching an outcropping, Michel waved us to a stop. "So now we come to the ravine. Round this next bend you will see we are high on the steep ravine wall with the frozen river hundreds of metres below. Here is our most dangerous time. Please follow strictly in my path, but leave at least five metres between each of us. It is better not to look down, just remember weight on lower ski always. OK?"

I could see from Crystal's expression that his instructions had alarmed her. I reached out and patted her comfortingly. "Don't worry, just look ahead, you'll be fine."

Larry, who was just in front of her turned. "Us Port Elizabethans got to stick together, hey? Listen Crystal, just keep your eyes on my behind. You'll have no problem!"

I caught myself thinking....'years of silent animosity and now he's joking with us? How strange life can be!'

"Thanks, guys. Look ahead or on Larry's behind, which?" Crystal grinned nervously.

"One more thing," Michel held a gloved finger to his lips, "it's important we make little noise as possible, so no shouting or screaming. Understood? OK, here we go...!" He disappeared from view.

As we rounded the bend we saw what he meant. Our pathway was a narrow track Michel was making in the fresh snow, cutting into a steep almost vertical wall of ice. The view was sensational, a deep ravine hundreds of metres across with a frozen river strewn with snow, rocks and uprooted trees far below. The valley stretched into the distance where it curved away to our right and disappeared. We watched, our stomachs churning, as Michel and the front members of the group made steady progress along the path, all in that strange traverse stance, upper body leaning outwards away from the mountain wall. Larry moved off followed by Crystal with me the prescribed distance behind her. I saw the look of intense concentration on her face as she let her skis slide along the now-well-flattened but narrow track. Just before I moved I broke the rule by looking down and had a vague feeling of vertigo which I managed to suppress. Thierry was behind us, bringing up the rear.

The silence was deafening. All we could hear was the swish of skis on ice. Apart that is, from the sound of our own hyperventilating.

The traverse seemed to go on forever. We rounded bend after bend, and each time ravine and valley stretched out to yet another breathtaking vista. There was no stopping on this wall. I began to feel cramp in my lower back from persistent leaning to one side. I watched Crystal navigating the track superbly, her girlish figure and graceful movement filling me with desire and gratitude that had afforded us this adventure together. Mental images of Jennifer and my daughters kept popping into my mind as the repetitive balancing rhythm lulled me into a dreamlike state, no guilt, just euphoria, an adrenalin rush eclipsing most or all previous thrills.

We rounded the next bend and thankfully saw that Michel and the group had stopped. Thierry skied past us to join them. Then we saw the reason. Ahead of our guide was a huge mound of rocks, tree remnants and large ice fragments, aftermath of a recent avalanche some 40 metres wide stretching below and above us. From Michel's concerned expression it was obvious this constituted quite a problem, namely how to get safely across the debris. We watched in trepidation as he started to tramp down hard with his skis to try and create a pathway through the rubble but soon he retreated, shaking his head in frustration.

"It is impossible to ski across. Please take off your skis and we will all have to climb across."

A sharp cracking noise, then a rumbling above us made Michel look up, eyes wide with alarm. We followed his gaze to see an enormous puff of white, high above, reminiscent of explosions when pisteurs were dynamiting overhanging snow cornices. But this was no controlled explosion. We all realised simultaneously what this was, a major avalanche right above where we were perched! There was no time to turn and ski back out of the way.

"GET YOUR SKIS OFF!! TAKE COVER!!! TRY TO CURL INTO A BALL!!!!" Michel screamed.

Crystal and Larry looked at me in horror, dumbstruck, unable to move. I tried to get closer to them but it was too late. We were engulfed by a choking white snowy blast, accompanied by a roar unlike anything I had ever heard in my life. I heard screams and shouts and suddenly I was tumbling, over and over. I knew enough to hold my breath, the inhalation of snow vapour kills more people in avalanches than anything else. I felt a sharp searing pain in my right leg as a ski sliced through my skipants. I was aware of being hurled down the steep slope then a violent impact on the side of my head. My world went black.

*

Slowly, painfully, the veil of unconsciousness enveloping me began to dissipate. I was aware of two areas of agony in my body, my right leg and the left side of my head. Opening my eyes slowly made little difference. Nothing could be seen save an all-embracing whiteness.

A deafening silence. Trying to move my hands I was able to create a small space around my face in order to breathe. I could not work out if I was upside down. I remembered reading that skiers trapped in avalanches established their bodily position watching their urine obey the force of gravity. I was unable to reach my lower body but used saliva instead, discovering fortunately that I was right way up. Moving my arms I encountered a ski pole which helped me increase my small clear space.

Then reality struck. Crystal! Larry! The rest of the group! Where were they? Had anyone survived? I was battling to breathe in the confined space. By thrusting the pole upwards repeatedly a chink of light appeared above me. Struggling madly to lift myself to the surface I enlarged the opening and gasped massive lungfuls of air.

"HELP! ANYBODY!" I yelled at the top of my voice but got no response. I managed to look at my watch. The digital readout was 08:55. The last time I remembered looking it was 07:45 just before the traverse. Unconscious for close on an hour! Panic rising I thrashed about wildly so that my head and upper body were above the snow surface. Now I could see around me, the same debris we had seen Michel climbing over. Ironically, bright sunshine was now flooding the valley. Although my body was numb with cold, I felt rivulets of sweat running down my face from exertion.

"HELP! CAN ANYBODY HEAR ME!!!!" I screamed in frustration then listened intently. I was sure I could hear groaning, quite close to me.

"I CAN HEAR YOU!" I shouted towards the sound, "IT'S RAY!!!! WHO IS THAT?"

A feeble voice echoed faintly through the snow. "Ray, oh thank God, it's me, Larry."

"Where are you? Are you OK?"

"I think just a few feet from you. But I can't move......my lower body is numb. I can't see anything .What's happened? Where's the rest of the group? Where's Crystal?"

"It was an avalanche," I yelled. "Whole side of the bloody mountain came down on top of us. Can you breathe OK? "

"Yeah, just about. Dunno how I managed but I think my face is clear. Must still have skis on. I'm stuck fast. I think there's someone right next to me. Yes, oh Jesus, it's Crystal. I can feel her fur anorak. But, shit, Ray, she's not breathing!!!"

I started to struggle with superhuman urgency in Larry's direction. "Larry, see if you can clear the snow from her face. I'm trying to get my second ski off. I'll get to you somehow."

"MICHEL! ROB! TONY! ANYBODY! HELP US!" Larry began to scream.

I managed to reach my remaining ski release and pressed down hard, groaning as I felt the limb moving, a certain sign that the bone was fractured. But my leg was free. I dragged myself across the snow towards my brother. His head was visible just a few feet from me. As I drew near, I could see that he had cleared a space alongside him and exposed Crystal's face which was devoid of expression, a dull colour, with no sign of life.

With a frantic effort I pulled myself toward her. Ripping my gloves off, with one hand I held her nose and placed my lips over hers and blew desperately.

"Larry, see if you can get your hands on her chest. Push hard on her sternum. We've got to get her breathing. I'm not going to lose her!"

My brother did as I asked, looking at me strangely as he realised the 'old friends' routine had been nothing but a facade. I didn't care, all I was focussed on was bringing Crystal back to life. So we pumped and blew and all the while my mind was racing. Where was the rest of the group? Were we the only survivors? What chance of rescue? Who knew where we were?

Suddenly Crystal's chest gave a heave and she spluttered, coughing violently. A stream of white sputum flew out of her mouth, spraying our faces. Her eyes fluttered open behind her goggles. She coughed again, a deep hollow sound. I leaned back exhausted and started to clear the snow around the three of us.

"We've done it, Larry. We got her back. She's breathing!!!!!!"

"That's good, Ray, but I still can't see anything. My goggles were ripped off as the avalanche hit. I got the blast full in my eyes. Also, I can't feel my legs. I'm all twisted around and I'm so cold."

I scrabbled snow away from his lower body. "Take it easy, buddy. I'll get your skis off first then try get us closer together. Let me look at your eyes." It was as though I was looking at a blind man. Larry's eyes were not focussing, just swivelling side to side. Crystal moaned gently as I cradled her head in my lap. I was able to create a hollow in the snow around her and my brother, and in spite of painful jolts from my leg, managed to slither down between them so that we generated warmth for each other.

Looking around there were no signs of the rest of the group. Just snowy rubble. "Did you see what happened to any of the others, Larry? I know Michel had a radio. He was right out front, wasn't he?"

"The guys in front took the full force. I just glimpsed bodies hurled about then my lights went out. D'you think any of them survived?" he whispered.

"Doubtful" I replied. "We were lucky."

"Lucky! You call this lucky?"

"We're alive, that's lucky! Larry, I'm waving my hand in front of your face. Can't you see anything at all?"

"No, everything's dark. Think my back's broken? It's all so quiet. My head's throbbing like crazy. How's Crystal?"

I was holding her close, feeling her regular breathing. "She's OK, I think. Breathing's regular but semi-conscious."

"Lucky, you say. I think just plain stupid," Larry moaned. "We should never have been on this goddamned trip. Even our taxi-driver said we were crazy after all the snow that fell the last few days."

"Yeah, well, Thierry said that Michel's a very experienced guide. He knows these mountains. He was sure it was fine."

"Well, it bloody wasn't, was it?" Larry flared up. "The three of us may be the only ones alive. I'm blinded and dead from the waist down. One of my mates said that Michel was strapped for cash so he needed to take a big group this week whatever the conditions."

Just then Crystal gave a moan and coughed again. She opened her eyes. "Ray, Ray, what happened? Are you guys OK?" She gave a weak smile of relief.

"Yes, sweetheart, we're OK. It was a massive avalanche. Just you and me and Larry here, don't know about the others." I looked at my watch. "It's 10.40. Just over two hours since it hit us. No sign of Michel and he had the bloody radio. Nothing we can do except keep warm and hope a rescue party come for us."

Larry shook his head. "We're in serious trouble, big brother. We're way outside the patrolled area. Our taxi driver said no-one else would make this trip for days because of heavy snowfall. What the hell are we gonna do?"

"Maybe Michel logged the trip with the ski-school?"

"He didn't. He just laughed and said they were pussies and would never have sanctioned it. He never even told his wife!"

*

After what seemed like an eternity I looked again at my watch which read 12:00. There had been no sign of or sound from any of the rest of the group so we had to assume they had perished. The three of us huddled together in our makeshift igloo. I established that Crystal was the least injured. Larry had no sensation in his lower body and was totally snow-blind. I was sure my right leg was broken so trying to move anywhere was out of the question.

"Ray," Larry mumbled, coming awake suddenly, "we may die here if no-one comes by tonight. Do you realise that?"

I nodded. My watch read 15:45. "Ja, I know, only too well. I'm trying to be positive. Crystal's stronger now, she's trying to find Michel, maybe get hold of his radio. The snowslide was massive, could have taken them right down into the bottom of the ravine."

"It's ironic, isn't it, we've been strangers for more than twenty years and land up like this........ sort of patching up our squabble and now who knows?"

I nodded. "I know, little brother. Our whole fight seems pitiful now, doesn't it? We lost Marty then lost each other? I've often wanted to try and make overtures but......."

"You mean, trying to get together?"

"Yes, but, well, Serena and I never seemed to be able to hit it off so ...."

"Well, if we ever get out of this, maybe it'll be worth a try, hey?" He shivered violently. "Christ, I'm so cold." His complexion was becoming greyer as the wintry sun started its descent.

"Larry, I just want to say this to you, that if I ever did anything to cause you to dislike or distrust me, then I'm really terribly sorry. I know we gave you a hard time when we were kids but I was really proud of you and what you achieved. Please believe this." I could feel hot tears running down my ice-cold face.

Crystal appeared from below us, shaking her head. "No sign of anyone, only a ski here and a pole there. I tried my avalanche thing but got nothing. They could be anywhere. I'm afraid we're stuck here till a rescue party comes. Maybe the minibus called in an alarm when we didn't show."

I nodded. "That looks like our only hope. Got to keep each other warm."

Larry stared blankly in our direction, smiling weakly. "Ray, I want to say something to you now in case, well, just in case. I always admired you when we were young, perhaps envied you. You were always first with everything. I had to try and live up to you and your achievements."

"Larry," I shook my head, "there's no need for any of this right now. Save your strength."

"No! I want to clear the air between us right this minute. I was jealous, and I guess my behaviour and tantrums made that obvious. I want to apologise and say that you always were great and ....oh Jesus, I can't stop shivering..........just want to say sorry.....and ......I love you Ray..............OK?"

I put my arms round him and held him close. "I love you too. Just forget it. We'll get out of this somehow and get to be a big family again, you'll see." Tears were welling again in my eyes as I watched Larry's breathing become slower and his face a grey mask of pain.

With some effort he smiled weakly at Crystal and me in our little icy cave. "You guys must have thought I was born yesterday. I saw the way you look at each other. Don't argue, I'm glad, I remember the early days, what you two had in spite of everyone being dead against it. I'm pleased you've got together even for a short time. You were so mad for each other......all those years ago......but.........."

Crystal waved him to silence. "Shhh ! Can you hear anything.......?"

In the distance we could hear a faint rumbling.

"OH GOD! NOT AGAIN !" Larry screamed.

"GET DOWN, CRYS!!!!!," I yelled. "BOTH OF YOU!!!!!GET YOUR HEADS DOWN!!!!!"

And then it was upon us. And all was darkness.

*

1800 hours

The helicopter hovered high above the avalanche, directing the search party with floodlights and dogs below. The voice of one rescuer came over the intercom. "There's two more over here, both gone, frozen. One looks like a broken neck. Oh, here's another, looks like a female. Hang on! Quick! Over here, she's still breathing!!!!"

***

Epilogue

As Jennifer walks slowly out through the arched wooden doors of the chapel, she sees the woman in black in the distance and, ignoring her family, she hastens to catch her.

"Excuse me, do we know each other?"

"I know who you are, but no, you do not know who I am."

"Why were you at my husband's funeral?"

"I knew your husband when we were very young, in Port Elizabeth, South Africa."

"Is.......is your name .....Crystal?"

"It is."

"Raymond told me about you. He said he loved you very much. When you were young, that is."

Crystal fiddles with her veil. "I'm glad he told you that."

"How did you know that he was killed? How did you know to come to the funeral?"

"I......I was the only survivor of the avalanche." She looks away, her face a mask of pain.

"You.....you were ....there?"Jennifer stares at Crystal open-mouthed.

"Yes." Crystal hesitates then, summoning up her resolve, places a gloved hand on Jennifer's arm. "Raymond's last words were to tell you that he loved you."

Jennifer's swollen bloodshot eyes spill over with tears.

"Please, won't you come to the house. It seems we have much to talk about."

"Thank you, Jennifer, but sadly, I have a plane to catch in just over a few hours." She leans over and touches her lips to Jennifer's cheek. "We both have our memories of a wonderful man."

She turns and walks away. Jennifer holds her hands to her mouth as if to call, then changes her mind as she is surrounded by her loved ones.

In the distance, Crystal turns one last time, pausing momentarily to observe the family gathering round. She lowers her veil and walks away.

THE END

Brothers and Lovers Michael J. Davidson

Printed in Great Britain
by Amazon.co.uk, Ltd.,
Marston Gate.